DARK PUPILS

(COWARDICE)

Éanna Cullen

BauPuu | ™

Baxter Hunt Publishing Limited

London ○ Dublin ○ New York

BAXTER HUNT PUBLISHING LIMITED
London

First published in Great Britain
In 2008 by BhuPub™
Baxter Hunt Publishing Limited

A CIP catalogue record of this book is available from
the British Library and Trinity Library Dublin.

ISBN: 978-0-9558537-2-2

Addresses for Baxter Hunt Publishing can be found at
www.baxterhuntpublishing.co.uk
Baxter Hunt Publishing Limited Reg. No. 6572403

Baxter Hunt Publishing Ltd makes every effort to ensure
that all paper used in its publications as sourced
legally from renewable credibly certified forests.

ACKNOWLEDGEMENTS:

Special thanks to DBG & Babsy for their tiresome... sorry, tireless constructive criticism without which this book would probably include a supernatural showdown of some sort. An Garda Síochána – Who is Inspector Doyle anyway? Áras an Uachtaran – A beautiful scene of the crime. Psych Central - DSM-IV Mental Disorders Index. Coffee – between two and six. The City of Dublin – Above and Below Ground level, St Michan's church and the Duvlinia Exhibition. The American Journal of Psychiatry. London Borough of Ealing Fire Brigade. Emedicine –Encyclopaedia information gleaned about Psychotic disorders. www.Montenet.org. Also thanks to: Cornelius Scipio (Roman Consul 16BC), Marcus Aurelius Casey, Batemanius Edivis, The clan of the Julii in Grevstonium and the entire Legion (whomever they are). Angela & Mark, my editors, for making sense from the original Gibberish and wondering where the extra people came from. BhuPub™. May this novel help them grow into the type of publisher that supports lunatics like me. Rafael Reina – www.reinaphotographer.com

Dedicated to Eithne:

For taking a young boy below the city of Dublin, and for teaching to look for everything else besides. Ar dheis Dé go raibh ana - may she rest at his right hand.

THE PROLOGUE

*U*sed...

The terrible truth is that we use and are used without exception.

The old use the young to prove what they have learnt, and the young, to fight against their future, use the old in defence of their actions.

Use each other. Take, take and be taken. Society welcomes you.

I am responsible, not in part, for this new state, built on manipulation. I thought because I believed in the outcome, that I could do as I wished to whomever I desired; all being for the greater good, and all sacrifices being worth their standing as pieces of the ultimate and overwhelming plan.

I used those poor children, and even myself, in that final rigid strategy. For them, it began with their meeting each other, and the months of preparation they unknowingly endured for my ends. But for me, it started at a different point. A point in the future where fruition lived and all else was mere background and rehearsal. In corpus congregatio, where success was a mathematical surety and Society, my Society, would be born into the world.

Corpus Congregatio...

For me, it began with flashing lights. There was rain too, and it made the lights take over and surround everyone and everything. All around the cordoned off area, people were mumbling and making summations about what it was that had occurred inside the mansion, their numbers growing, drawn in by the obvious nature of police secrecy.

The lights that flashed were red and blue. It was because of them that the crowd were drawn. The lights made a statement of their own: "Come and see," they said, "Something has happened." And so the people gathered round and hoped that something terrible had befallen someone, as is the nature of people in such situations. It wasn't wrong of them. People are animals.

All of this was exterior and being such, superfluous to the greater reality. Inside the mansion lay the cold and unambiguous truth. There was no supposition required for the people on the inside of those thick wooden double doors.

In there, they could see the blood, the witnesses, the weapon of choice, and the PR men ranting ineffectually about the presence of blue and red flashing lights. They could see each other's pale faces as they skirted around the cold blue meat, as it soaked into the expensive carpet.

Yes, to give credit, there were a few of them who could possibly have understood where this event could lead, and how it could ever have been planned. Yet beyond the obvious fleshy evidence, no one could have guessed who had really been wronged, or by whom.

I know now the flaws in my design. By letting this be the beginning for me, I was avoiding the real beginning, and thus manufacturing a greater tragedy.

I should have begun with the students; looked more carefully at the elements used to build my machine; felt something more than piety. Yet I didn't. But this is not the voice of regret speaking, or remorse in the face of what I have done. This is a cold analysis of events, starting at the correct point in time, with them.

This is the least of what I owe them.

CONTENTS:

PART TWO:

THE PLOT

CHAPTER ONE:
RETURN TO FLASHING LIGHTS

The consequences of my murder went far beyond the horrible demands it made upon the souls of Peter, Rachel, and Terry. These results I was expecting, but beyond their product of the desired political atmosphere, I had not spared enough thought for the people who surrounded me, and enriched my life, and the strain, distress and desolation it would cause.

How can a man know what effects his life can have upon the emotions of others? Politically and economically, I had a very clear idea of its consequence, I'd even drawn a graph. There was a pie chart too, now that I am admitting and remembering, the red slice being the amount of percentage population resistance to the new practices and ethos of the Progressive Party, and the green slice stood for those with a favourable inclination towards it. According to my calculations, with direct correlation to the studies I'd carried out on the psychology of public opinion, the red had been reduced to the stature of a mere line in the aftermath of my gruesome destruction, leaving the green of the project's success.

As I sat in my study, contemplating my equations and enjoying my green circle, I did but once give a moment for those around me.

My sister: she did not suffer overly, yet when I picture her face, sadness takes from me any warmth or comfort that I have self installed, with false and unfounded pleasantries.

My father was a broken shell, his mind strained and weak. His ideal had been challenged, and they were found wanting. When the time came for the world to say goodbye to Walter Thisgo, I expect my dad, a word I allow myself to use only as punishment, felt nothing but relief.

My family were not the only ones that suffered. Ireland, the entire country, endured great trials as a result of my death; it was an outrage against them, against each and every single person. How could this have happened, just when good old Walter had been leading them towards the Celtic Tiger once more? Their leader was murdered, and who was to blame? The Regressives! This was my plan from...

Rubbish!

There I go again with the same idiocy. Even now, I cannot rid myself of the obtuse fantasies that drove the events you are now experiencing. I was supposed to be talking about the people I hurt when I chose to die in such a manner. People like Siobhán, a true believer in the Party, or Cullen, my chief protector. These were everyday companions of mine who believed in Walter Thisgo, would do anything for him, and I let them believe that they had failed me. That is my shame.

As it was at the beginning, their story begins with the flashing lights that marked the end of Walter Thisgo.

Siobhán Sloane arrived at Áras an Uachtaran and fought her way through the crowd by the gates. The Gardaí were calling all of the Treoraí's staff in, and even though she had no idea what was happening, Siobhán paled as she was allowed to enter the reception hall through the back entrance, crossing as she did through the footsteps of the three students who had been there only a half hour before. She was ushered into the state reception room where the night staff were gathered, waiting nervously for some leadership.

Something was very wrong in the Áras, there was an ambulance out front, and people were gathering at the gates. Walter would never have let the image of the situation become so negative. She shook aside the foreboding that this thought conjured in her, and took to doing what she was good at. She looked around at the assembled staff, good; Sarah and Dan were there, she could see him wringing his hand, attempting not to light a cigarette, while Sarah was eating the end of her pen, looking pale and confused.

"Sarah," said Siobhán, "Get that ambulance out of here."

"But..." Sarah began,

"Unless we need it?"

"I don't know," said Sarah.

Dan piped in. "They wont tell us what's going on."

"How long have you been here?" said Siobhán,

"About thirty minutes," they both agreed.

"Then we don't need an ambulance." She paused before finishing the sentence, "Get rid of the ambulance and get in touch with the pathologist before they bring anything too conspicuous. Go on!" These last words were directed at Sarah, who went to work. Dan looked around the room at the assembled staff: A cook, two maids, the head gardener, and three security guards. Siobhán noticed that Cullen wasn't there. It must have been his night off, which would explain a lot. If Cullen were here already, they still wouldn't be in the dark.

There was an officer at the door to the state reception room and according to Dan, he had refused to enlighten them in any way since they had arrived, probably because he didn't know anything. Siobhán took charge of the situation and approached the Garda.

"Excuse me," said Siobhán.

"Please, miss, if you would just wait for a few more minutes, someone will be along to…"

"Now, listen to me…?"

"Garda Slant."

"Mr Slant. I know that you are doing your job, and quite well too, but there is something you should know about me."

"Yes?" asked the Garda, unsettled by the confidence of the young woman standing in front of him, wagging a finger.

"Something very bad has happened here tonight, yes?" asked Siobhán, continuing without waiting for a reply, "Yes, something very bad, and important. Now, you may think that you are handling the situation by keeping us all cooped up in here and out of the detectives' way, or whomever is in the President's study right now, but you're forgetting something even more important than that. This is Áras an Uachtaran, the Treoraí's home, and people know that something happened here tonight. Already, there are hundreds of them outside, and TV is on its way. They all want, no, deserve to know what is happening, whether terrorists have attacked and if they should be concerned with their own safety too." Siobhán leaned forward until she was eye to chin with Garda Sloane. "And who is handling that? Is this detective…what's his name?"

"Doyle," said Garda Sloane automatically.

"Is Detective Doyle handling that?" Sloane didn't know.

"Of course you don't know, no one does. But people need to know. This is a modern country and..."

"Ok, ok," said a voice from behind Siobhán, "there's no need for that, Ms Sloane, I've been waiting for you to arrive." The man who had come through the partition door had a grim smile, and wore a short brown leather jacket with a T-shirt hanging over his blue jeans. He was easily in his sixties, but the outfit, though modern and fashionable still suited his white hair and wrinkled expression. *This must be Doyle,* Siobhán thought.

"Detective Doyle?" she tried.

"Inspector Doyle (SDU)," he corrected, "now, if you'll follow me?" Doyle gestured towards the through door, and Siobhán exited ahead of him into the State Drawing Room. Now she was one step closer to the President's Study, and the scene of the crime she'd already realised. This was a much different room. In here there were at least a dozen people, all with purpose, working towards a common goal.

"Why are there so many people?" Siobhán asked.

"There is a lot of... work to be done in the Treoraí's room." Doyle seemed reticent to continue and Siobhán took control.

"I need to see him," said Siobhán, dreading what she would see, but knowing that she had to witness it for herself. She needed to ensure that all of this was a reality, and not some wicked dream brought on by the Jamaican bombastic Pizza she'd eaten earlier, and a restless snooze on her living room couch.

Doyle wasn't convinced, "I don't think you really do," he said, "at least not yet. Let me ask you a few questions and fill you in on a couple of things first, ok?"

"But!"

"Then you can make a statement. And then, you can come in and see him."

"Are you not going to move the..." Siobhán started.

"No," said Doyle, "it will be a while before we move the, em... body." There was something in his voice that heightened Siobhán's dread. Doyle didn't seem the sort that let "ems" and "ers" into his conversation very often. He looked like he had the experience of many years behind him, yet Siobhán was sure that the man was deeply shocked by what was happening. How bad could it be?

"Ok," she agreed, "we need to make a statement."

"Good then. As far as we can guess so far, it happened about forty," Doyle checked his watch, "fifty minutes ago. At least that was when the security guards broke down the door and discovered the Treoraí." There was commotion from the hallway.

"Let me in! I wanna see what's happened!" demanded the thick accent that Siobhán was quick to identify as Cullen's. The Chief of Security sounded furious, and she worried that there would be a few sore heads out in the hallway when he got through.

"It's Cullen," Siobhán told Doyle.

"Ah, the security man, on his night off. Williams!" Doyle called, but there was no answer. "Williams!" A red face peered around the door, hatless and out of breath.

"Sir," said Williams, "we're a bit busy out here."

"Bring him in here, Williams," Doyle instructed the Garda, who looked first relieved and then confused.

"Are you sure, sir? He's a bit… pissed, drunk." Doyle turned to Siobhán.

"Will he do anything stupid?" he asked her.

"No," Siobhán didn't hesitate, and Doyle took this as the good sign it was meant to be, and told Williams to continue with his orders.

When Cullen was shown in, he was already looking embarrassed as a result of his outburst. He was a professional, he should know better than to react in such a way. Doyle rose and greeted him at the door, shaking the huge man's hand and walking him across him into the room, gesturing to the large oak table.

"Please sit, Mr Cullen, my name is Doyle, I'm in charge."

"Thanks."

"Hi Cullen."

"Hi Siobhán."

"Now," continued Doyle, "I was just telling Ms Sloane here the facts, as we have observed them so far." He looked at his watch, "About fifty five minutes ago, the body of the Treoraí was discovered in there," he pointed to the President's Room. "It has become obvious that two, maybe three persons gained access through the back window, opening the clasp through a pane that had been covered up by a wooden board, for some reason..."

"A bird flew in," Cullen interrupted.

"Excuse me?"

"A bird smashed the glass the other day and was flying around the room, we ordered the new pane but it was a long time coming. The beams should have set off the alarm though!" Cullen was speaking desperately.

"Absolutely, Mr Cullen, the alarm did sound, and your men came straight to the room and broke down the door, which proved to be difficult, by the way."

"It's not supposed to be locked."

"Indeed, well, it was. They both were." Doyle looked up and to his left, adjusting something in his mind before continuing. "All that we can surmise at the moment is that there was a fault in the alarm system that allowed the... intruders to spend at least ten minutes in the room."

"Ten minutes!" Siobhán exclaimed, "How could they have been in there ten minutes? Did they torture him?" Cullen growled at this.

"It is impossible to say," said Doyle, "all we know is that it must have taken at least ten minutes to do what they did."

"And what did they do?" It was Siobhán who asked, just beating Cullen to the question. Doyle stood and walked to the adjoining door.

"Mr Cullen, if you would like to have a look?" Doyle addressed the officer at the door and walked back to silence Siobhán's protests. Cullen needed no further prompting and moved from his chair to the door in three quick bounding strides.

"But I have to see him, I need to see him!" Siobhán beseeched of Doyle, who put his hands on her shoulder and spoke softly.-

"I understand that, but the Treoraí is dead. And someone needs to go out there and tell the world, don't they?" Doyle was making sense.

"Yes," said Siobhán, "but..."

"If you go in there," Doyle gestured to the door of the

President's Study, "you will not be able to do your task in the," he paused, "professional manner that is required."

Then, on cue, there was a scream from the room beyond as Cullen beheld the carnage of Walter Thisgo's assassination. The sound proved to Siobhán that Doyle was correct. She nodded at him and walked to the door. She stepped into the hall and approached the front door, added in recently by Walter Thisgo himself. It was just another thing that bore the mark of his influence.

She did not stop to take a deep breath and steel herself for the task, nor did she rehearse her lines, as she would normally have done. It was not bravery that helped her step across the threshold to face the cameras that had gathered there in the presence of the flashing lights and craning necks, it was faith in the automatic, and fear that any large exhale may set off in her a fit of wailing that might never stop.

"The office of the Treoraí would like to make the following statement." The crowd became silent; this was what they had been waiting for, confirmation, and explanation, perhaps even revelation. The people of Ireland, having heard second-hand that something was happening, had all switched on, logged on, or were listening to what Siobhán Sloane was about to say.

"Exactly one hour ago at eight o'clock, the Treoraí of Ireland, Walter Arthur Thisgo, was murdered here in the President's Room of Áras an Uachtaran. It is not yet clear who is responsible for this terrible crime, but all of the country's resources are at this moment being mobilised to discover those responsible. This is a terrible moment in our country's history, and one that we will remember forever. All we can do now is hope that the perpetrators are brought to justice quickly, and that all of the great work that Walter Thisgo has done for this country will not end here along with his life. Thank you."

Siobhán turned to the door and was accepted inside. She was shaking and only managed to keep control of herself long enough to make it to the bathroom, where she broke down, her back to the door and her tears slipping silently down between her fingers. The words that she had just spoken were lost immediately from her memory. Only by watching the statement being played over the weeks and months, and even years to follow, would she again discern its contents. She had spoken straight from the heart, and in doing so, said exactly what she was supposed to, her compassion being a factor of the overall plan.

CHAPTER TWO

UNDER THE RIVER, BESIDE THE STREAM

The scarecrow bounded across the open field, his ragged old coat fluttering behind him, and his appearance alien to the wet dark greenness of the mountain slope. After a failed furtive attempt or two to conceal his presence alongside a piled stone wall, and then a solitary tree that was alone in the landscape but not as remarkable as the figure, the scarecrow decided on a more direct and speedy route towards his goal.

The stream lay straight ahead of him at the foot of the slope that he was now descending, and it was obvious that he needed to get there sooner and with much less running across open ground. Back up the hill in the opposite direction from the flapping of the long black coat lay the road that wound its way through this part of the Wicklow Mountains, but there was no car there that would explain the presence of such an out of place individual. So where did he come from? And, what was it that he was in such a hurry to return to?

On the other side of the road from the field and stream lay a line that someone who evidently preferred camouflage to the open nature of the field, would certainly value highly: The tree line.

It was back behind this line that the missing car was parked, and there, amongst the rubble of an old church, lay the objects of the scarecrow's apprehension. Here was where the bodies lay, as they were little more than that at this juncture, sweating and moaning as they were. They were showing signs of disease, or heavy withdrawal, the most recent symptom of which being the burning fever that was the cause of the vital and risky search for water that the scarecrow was now undertaking.

Amongst the bodies, the girl's condition seemed to be worsening, if her jerking movements and occasional cries could be taken as any indication. However, these outward signs were in fact an indication that the fever was breaking. And that the girl was dreaming vivid physical dreams, the strongest of which being memories of trauma, and a recent period of great personal peril.

***

The escape...

Rachel was back in the Phoenix Park, amidst the confusion and her red hands. Were there pieces of bone on her hands? She'd been too frantic to clearly discern the truth.

Rachel, Peter, and Terry were at the gates of the Phoenix Park where the road came out beside a pub, called the something Tavern, watching as the gates admitted a string of Gardaí cars as well as an ambulance. They were panting and freaking out, unsure of what to do, or where to go, or what to do, or what the fuck to do.

Then there was Oscar, outside the something Tavern, gesturing wildly at them, for how long, Rachel didn't know, but when they noticed him, he seemed to be extremely agitated.

"Look," said Rachel, "there's Oscar." It was the first time that any of them had spoken, so it was more of a cough-squeal than anything else. Peter looked at her with eyes completely coloured in black. His pupils were huge, and when Terry turned to face her, it was clear to Rachel that the excitement was having the same effect on all of them.

"Your eyes," said Rachel. Peter looked at her in question, but then he noticed.

"You too," he said, and turned back towards Oscar. "Terry." Peter asked, "Can we trust him?" Terry looked at them both, his teeth were clenched and his nostrils were flared.

"Who cares," he gasped, "who fuckin cares?" And he left the cover of the wall and dashed through the gate, with Rachel and Peter taking his lead, and following closely behind.

As she reached his position in front of the bar, Oscar turned and ran away from the three in the direction of the welcoming city, where soon they were able to find a corner to disappear around, and alleyways to hide in. For the next twenty minutes, it seemed that they were going to get away easily, but the imagined safety was brushed aside by their repeated encounters with Gardaí blocked streets, preventing the four of them from getting east of Greek Street or Chancery Place. They were trying to get to Christchurch, and hopefully to the car they had abandoned there that morning, but both the Mellows and the Fr. Mathews bridges had been closed. The group were running strongly on their luck, and they had managed to turn away, mid-flight from each new Gardaí barrier they reached, without being noticed. It was only a matter of time before they were picked up and asked to explain the blood and gore that covered their clothes, and was spattered on their guilty faces.

Rachel was breathing hard as she fell into the churchyard of St Michan's, but immediately she knew that they had come to a dead end. This was the place where they would be caught, fitting really, maybe they had enough time to ask God for forgiveness before they were made to pay by a corporal jury.

"What the hell is this place," she heard Terry ask, as he too panted through into the darkened surroundings of the churchyard. Peter looked around him, and then to Rachel.

"It's a dead end," Peter said, with no volume or surprise, "a dead end."

"Where the hell is… There you are! What are we doing here?" Terry approached Oscar with no more menace intended than his gory slouched and shaky exterior could transmit. Oscar looked him over once, did the same for Peter, and then turned to Rachel.

"And you, girl," said Oscar. "Are you ok?" He looked concerned and she believed that he was. A part of Rachel that was lost and bewildered reached out for Oscar's fatherly comfort, but her stronger side fought against this preferential feminine treatment. In pattern with the night and its events, confusion won out and Rachel didn't care whether Oscar was being chauvinistic, she only cared about escaping, and he looked like the only one who had any idea how they could grant such a fanciful hope.

"I'm fine," said Rachel, "what are we going to do?"

"Yeah," Terry demanded, "what are we going to do?"

Oscar smiled, "Do you know what we're going to do?" He turned then to Peter, "Do ya?" Peter only shrugged and shook his head. Rachel felt concerned that he would display such hopelessness, and wanted to take his hand and smile, to give him hope, but Oscar bounded to the wall of the church and began banging on a large metal door.

It looked like a coalbunker door, and not quite the saviour that Oscar's smile suggested.

"Here we are," he said, "this is our way out!"

"You want us to hide in a cellar?" said Terry, "Is that it?"

"I don't want to go down into some dark cellar," Peter added, "if we're going to get caught, then I'd rather we just walked up to the next copper we meet and not sit down there waiting, not knowing where they are. Especially with all those... you know." Peter shied away from the metal door.

"Ah," said Oscar, "then you know what's in there?"

"What's in there?" Terry asked Peter, and Rachel also waited for his answer.

Peter shuffled his feet and whispered, "Bodies."

"Bodies?"

"That's right," Oscar told them, patting down his Cromby pockets as he spoke. "This is St. Michan's church. And there *are* bodies down there, mummified some of them. But, there is something else too. Do you know?" Oscar asked Peter, who shook his head.

"What?" said Terry. "A helicopter powered by maggots?"

"Oh, very funny. Let me just get us in there and I'll show you. Now do you know what this is?" Oscar located something in his pocket and whipped it out as though it were a sparkling gem stone. It looked like a bent piece of metal.

"It looks like a bent piece of metal," Terry told him.

"This, young man, is a shim." Oscar moved over to the large padlock that sealed the crypt, and began to fiddle and curse over it for a few long and fretful seconds. "And," Oscar said with relief, "with a bit of dexterity and luck..." There was a clank as the lock opened, "you can open any padlock with it."

Rachel failed to see the triumph that Oscar held for the opening of the heavy metal door. All she saw was a dark hole leading to mostly unknown contents, and those she knew about, the corpses, hardly had had her skipping up and down with joyous anticipation. But the door was open and Oscar was already moving down the unseen stairs.

"Come on," said Oscar's disembodied head after the dark had swallowed his body whole, "let's go."

Neither Rachel, Peter, nor Terry made any move to follow.

"I'm not going down there," said Terry, rummaging in his own pocket and taking out a little jar. He twisted the lid and filled his palm.

"I'm getting distressed again," he stated as he raised his hand to his mouth, "really fuckin distressed."

"Don't!" shouted Oscar. "Throw those away!"

Terry laughed, "What these?" He gestured to the blue pills, "They're just to help calm me down, that's all." In an atomic second, Oscar moved out of the cellar and slapped the pills from Terry's hand.

"Get in there," the old tramp growled, and pointed into the crypt. Terry's automated response was to comply immediately, and Peter in his apathetic state, just sort of wandered after his friend, looking bored. Oscar turned to Rachel.

"You're going to have to trust me," he said to her.

Rachel looked into the opening and considered her situation with as clear a perspective as could have been expected. She was covered in blood, as were her friends, and this man was going to try and help them escape regardless. Options were few and singular.

"Alright," she said to Oscar, taking his hand and letting him lead her into the darkness, "let's go."

Below the Liffey…

In the tunnel, it was dark. Forgetting the fact that this was not an unusual condition in respect to tunnels and places of general undergroundness, the dark that lay in the chambers beneath St Michan's church was far more oppressive than its name described. Bleak is far to grey a word, and gloomy conjured thoughts of squinting through, and dim outlines of murky shadows. Extra-dark was a closer description of the blackness that Rachel experienced beneath the 16th century church. Threatening-dark, described it flawlessly.

The black around the group didn't thin or clarify as they

made their way down behind Oscar, and though there were lights above them, no one had even suggested that they be lit, such was their fear of the tightening of the laws' vice from above. The Gardaí were squeezing the north quays of the Liffey, and the three guilty students were painfully aware that even here, so deep in the ground, they may still be manipulated into captivity like a shallow black-head, easily eradicated and discarded from the earth's skin.

Oscar was the only one who knew where they were headed, and Rachel hoped he knew also how to get there safely. She felt the closeness of the walls and then strange open spaces that made her shiver as she realised what they were. These were the crypt rooms, the un-singed byres of history's remaining dead, a face mask of one notorious now-heroic rebel, the body a man once acclaimed and now confused by tourists for a much less worthy counterpart. To Rachel, it seemed as though the coffins were leaning towards her through the blackness, and she shivered whilst hastening on behind their unlikely saviour.

"How much further?" she heard Peter ask from behind her.

"Dear boy, we haven't even started under the river."

Under the river; dear God, Rachel thought, *could they just walk under the Liffey? Could it be so easy?* They walked on into the darkness until a hand on her shoulder informed Rachel that Oscar was reaching back to halt her progress.

"Hold on there," the old man told them, "while I get me bearings."

"Your bearings?" Terry exclaimed. "Do you not know where we're going?"

"Shh! Quiet, I need to find the spot on the wall where the tunnel opens, that's all. He said it was just around here."

"Who said?" Terry asked, "You mean you've never been here before?"

Rachel heard a rustling and some heavy breathing.

"Listen, Terry." Oscar was behind her now and to the left. "Stop your yapping and help me check the walls at the end of this corridor. We're looking for two circular holes side by side, cut at an angle into the rock. Now start looking."

Rachel could feel panic rising in her as Terry squealed in

response to Oscar's harsh treatment.

"All of you," Oscar said, "find a wall and start to feel for two circular holes side by side."

Rachel stepped forward to the right as she heard the others rustle into action, and raised her hands out in front of her, expecting to meet the wall at any moment. She encountered a chain; over which she stepped carefully and then she felt softness beneath her fingertips. She pushed and her fingers sunk into the wall; no, it was not the wall. It was the rotten wood of a coffin. Rachel's arms recoiled into her chest and she held them close to her breast, shuddering at the thought of where her finger had nearly been. Uck! Inside with the corpse, could even have touched it had she pushed a centimetre further through the elderly timber.

"I found them!" Rachel heard Terry gasp from behind her. *Thank God,* she thought, the air was creepy and she only wanted to get out, get away, get lost. Crippling, heart-dropping depressive despair was dragging its wormy corpse through her soul. There wasn't much more of her left to push on, though it was her only option. They were irretrievably guilty. She was guilty.

Rachel took a careful step over the chain and witnessed the blossoming light of a matchstick a couple of yards away, she could see the huddled figures of her companions illuminated by it and as well as that, two dark holes, ketchup bottle thick and an inch apart, the focus of the spluttering twin ending flame.

"That's it all right," Oscar's voice said.

"So, what do we do now?" said Terry. There was a pause.

"I'm not sure," said Oscar.

"What! You don't know how to open it?" Terry scoffed, "What sort of escape is this?"

"Listen, boy. I'm not the one who just-"

"Pull them apart!" Peter interjected and Rachel felt the joy of his renewed presence. He was a smart boy and he'd figured it out.

"What do you mean?" Oscar asked.

"It's logical," said Peter, "two holes half way up the wall. The stone would be too heavy to lift and you could never pull it toward you without some sort of tool to operate it. So, if there isn't one, then two people could pull it apart- it's the only logical explanation."

There was no need for further discussion. Rachel could hear heavy breathing and groaning from Terry and Oscar, as well as the straining unseen workings of the entrance. Then there was a gust of air twinned with the sounds of sighing from the men, and though there was still only blackness all around her, Rachel was sure that she now stood in front of an opening, so obvious was the space in front of her.

"So," said Oscar, "Are ye ready?"

This was it. The four of them were about to trust their lives to the masonry skills of seventeenth century workmen, and walk beneath the River Liffey to freedom on the other side. Would the tunnel hold? Would they be able to find a way out once they reached the south bank? Rachel didn't care either way, and it was obvious that the others shared this sentiment as they turned without hesitation towards the space beyond the darkness, to the tunnel that had been sealed for centuries.

After the events of that night, they feared little.

"Yeah," they said, either aloud or inwardly, "we're ready."

~*~

In the abandoned church, Rachel's fever had begun to calm. She still moaned and twisted in her sleep, and Oscar was sure that the water he'd managed to trickle down her throat had actually caused her to cry out in pain. Could it be that the water was polluted? No, five minutes ago, he'd been crouched by the mountain stream gulping down the cold water with a rare thirst. The water was clean and fresh. It must have been something else that made the girl cry out.

~*~

In the beginning, the tunnel, in comparison to the rest of that night was an uneventful experience.

At one point, though, Peter stopped ahead of her and she heard a rattling sound.

"What was that?" she asked.

"Nothing," said Peter, "just getting rid of something." He moved on and Rachel followed, but as she stepped forward, her foot struck against a small bottle or something, and she heard the rattling sound again. It sounded like tablets being shaken, or even a homemade tambourine full of beans.

The thought amused her for a second, but the blackness of both the tunnel and their circumstances soon burdened her heart.

The fear of doom was there throughout, but it seemed unfounded as they made swift progress through the tunnel. After all, it wasn't difficult to believe that a tunnel that had survived this long would choose that night to collapse? Rachel relaxed. They were going to make it, she felt, there was some hope after all.

But what was that; a drop of water on her cheek? Rachel wiped her brow, covered in sweat and streaked red with the- Aw! She couldn't complete the thought. A drop of sweat was all it had been. There was nothing to be worried about. This tunnel was not going to suddenly collapse; it was solid. Unless opening the crypt entrance had somehow weakened the structure, upset the delicate balance of time, or even set off some sort of...

Another drop! She was sure of it.

"Peter?" Rachel reached out ahead of her and touched his shoulder.

"Yes?" said Peter.

"Did you feel?" She stopped, not sure how to ask.

"Drops?" Peter whispered back to her.

Then it began to rain.

~*~

With a gasp, Rachel woke to the bright sunlight that broke through the forest canopy. Oscar was beside her in a moment, and she gripped him in fear, smelling that street smell of long unwashed fabric, foetid but reassuringly arresting to her senses.

"The tunnel," she wept into Oscar's old Cromby coat, "it collapsed."

"Shh," said Oscar, trying to summon the fatherly tones of the long forgotten past, "no, girl. It didn't collapse. You're safe."

Rachel sighed and opened her eyes to the brash afternoon while the sun shone directly overhead. She remembered now her fear that the tunnel was going to collapse, and the mad dash for its south entrance. She recalled how they had heaved, strained, and screamed in panic at the unresponsive door, until Oscar located a groove near the ceiling to one side that allowed them to pull the door open, and collapse into the main chamber of the Duvlinia exhibition, in a shower of broken plaster and chipboard.

But that was all she could recollect. She didn't remember coming here to- what was this beautiful place? The air was so lively that even Oscar's musty odours were borne from her nostrils and replaced by the smells of pine and sun-dried earth. Above her, a lonely wisp of cloud released a shower down upon them, and the drops refreshed the fevered skin of her face, and she smiled once, because of its soothing properties and continued; Rachel opened her mouth and allowed the cloud to wet her lips.

"It's raining," she said, and fell backwards, asleep once more in the autumn spray.

CHAPTER THREE
THE OPPOSITION

"Show it to me again," Doyle requested, as he scanned the large plasma screen, "no, not that bit, yeah, back, back, there!" Inspector Doyle was sitting in the main computer lab in the Gardaí Headquarters of the Phoenix Park, scanning through the surprisingly sparse surveillance footage from the cameras at Áras an Uachtaran. It was unbelievable how sparse the coverage was. The murderers had managed to walk right through a blind alley and right up to the Treoraí's window, without being seen.

"Unbelievable," said Doyle. This was the only piece of usable footage that was of any use, and from the first second he'd viewed it, Doyle knew that there was something amiss. The footage clearly showed the suspects as they crouched behind a large tree in the garden at the rear of Áras an Uachtaran, facing the general direction of the window they would soon enter and commit the goriest murder that Doyle had ever seen. The view was from high up in the eaves of the building, and it was hard to make out all of the suspects' movements but just before they moved off...

"There! Exactly there," he said to Jane, who had been rolling the CCTV media file forward manually using an orb shaped device, set into the control panel. Usually, Doyle would order one of his men to,-"Get a face for me from the surveillance cameras and give me a shout." But this was different. The recently retired NBCI Inspector had been put in charge of this investigation and reinstated as an SDU inspector. This was the most important investigation in the country's recent history, and Doyle wanted to personally view every piece of evidence as it arose, to ensure that he missed nothing in bringing a conviction. This wasn't just a crime, it was political, which meant that things would always be as they seemed. Reasons behind reasons.

Doyle had clear picture of the murderers, and their fingerprints all over the crime scene, some even inside the corpse, but that wasn't good enough for him.

For starters, the criminals were young, very young, early

twenties tops. Then there was the ferocity of the crime; a destruction rather than an elimination. No, this was not a normal assassination, if one existed, and though the politiks had already begun to push for these three kids to be captured and tried, Doyle had been holding out for another avenue of investigation to open up. And now, he felt he had it.

Moments before breaking from the cover of the tree, whatever sort of tree it was, the three assassins had embraced each other and- yes, they had been smiling.

"Blow that up for me, will ya?" he asked Jane. "Get one of each face in turn." Jane nodded. "I want to see those smiles," Doyle said and turned for the door.

***

Conspiracy...

Siobhán was sure of it, and Cullen was too. They were so convinced that they hadn't even bothered to ask each other's opinion.

"Those bloody Regressive bastards!" Cullen raged, as he paced the waiting room, dwarfed by his massive bulk. Siobhán, though feeling the same outrage and shock, spared a moment to think about Cullen. Normally, his size did not dictate his appearance. Sure, if you saw him from afar, you would notice that the man was massive, a seven footer as wide as two people, but with no sign of flab. But Cullen's manner was gentle and kind, a man serious about his job, but confident enough in his abilities to meet his charge and those he encountered on duty with a pleasantness that softened him, and helped him to blend in with the surroundings. Siobhán was sure that it was this quality that had endeared Walter Thisgo to his bulky protector, important as it was in the great man's ethos to minimise the distance between him and the public.

Cullen was raging now though, and as he fussed and clenched his fist, Siobhán could see his power and his tremendous menacing potential.

"Bastards," Cullen cried as he fell into a chair, with a sigh of impotence and a hateful expression. Then he fell quiet and began to look at Siobhán in a manner that she found disturbing. His eyes squinted with the thoughts behind them, and his brow furrowed with the same. Cullen was looking at her and thinking, and Siobhán wasn't sure if she liked being the new focus of his attention.

"What?" she asked, deciding to be bold and hide her apprehension. The huge man paused and locked eyes with her.

"Did you know?" said Cullen, fixing her with unblinking scrutiny. Siobhán gulped, probably not a great reaction under the circumstances, and Cullen came at her, rising smoothly from his chair and crossing the room in an easy graceful movement. Siobhán let out a yelp as he loomed above her and put his hand on her shoulder.

"What did you know about it?" he asked, "How did they get past the cameras and the night men? Come on-" and now Cullen's voice grew soft and sinister, "you can tell me. I just need to know what happened. I HAVE TO KNOW!" Cullen screamed these last words into Siobhán's face, and she felt saliva on her cheek as she cowered from the threatening brawn of him.

"Please," she whispered, gasping through her muscle clenching shock, "Please, Daniel. You know that I would never do such a thing, never."

There was a brief moment when she was on the verge of becoming a casualty of Cullen's rage and impotence. He had failed his charge. The most important one he had ever had. And though anyone would tell him that he was not at fault; that he could not have saved Walter Thisgo whilst on a night off with the boys, Cullen would never let such an excuse stop him from taking the blame, hijacking the guilt, and claiming full responsibility. Cullen was a foolish captain, rubbing himself down with liniment oil, and diving into the sea, miles away from the necessity of his sinking ship.

Cullen relaxed and stepped away from Siobhán, as she knew he would once she beseeched him from her position of supplication, and played to their friendship.

"I'm sorry," said Cullen, "I'm- I'm such a waste of space." Cullen sat into his chair and leaned back against the wall, where he stared out of the window, blinking through the tears that were now falling freely down his face. He did not hide his eyes in shame; he did not wipe them away. They were his to bear with shameful pride.

"Walter," he said, "why did this happen to you?" Cullen's voice carried baleful tones that struck the saddest note on all octaves in Siobhán's heart. The work that she'd had to do in the last twenty-four hours had prevented any long reflection. The subsequent practical shock; a state she'd witnessed before in the behaviour of the bereaved; in her own mother. One she could never have understood until now. The aunt that organised the sandwiches and made sure everyone was taken care of, the grieving widower that drives to the airport to pick up distant relatives and comforts them upon arrival. This confusing display of working and getting things done, that leaves others shaking their heads and wondering. "How can she...he... be holding up so well?"

It was denial and Siobhán knew it. So it was only then, with nothing to do but wait there in a room in Gardaí headquarters for Inspector Doyle. Waiting with the crumbling remnants of Cullen, the strongest man she'd ever known, apart from Walter, of course, wondering and thinking. There was nothing to occupy her here, and the grief began to fall around her in a fallout of memories and *ifs* that never made it to the floor, and so could never be swept away for good.

Siobhán felt herself begin to cry.

Moving down the corridor fast, Inspector Doyle was feeling the pressure and trying to decide on a new strategy for the investigation. He'd expected to get backing from his superiors to bring in a specialist to take a look at the strange behaviour of the three suspects in the CCTV footage, but he'd been shocked by the negative response he received. It seemed that he was on a mission only to pick these kids up and dump them in the courthouse and nothing else.

It stank of a cover-up and Doyle hated cover-ups. As a high-ranking detective, he'd been involved in too many of them for comfort. Nothing as big as this mind, the assassination off the Treoraí was huge, but still, he'd turned a blind eye enough times to know that ignorance was definitely not innocence. Damn!

Doyle reached the door to the room where the Treoraí's bodyguard and assistant were waiting. He still wasn't sure how to approach them. If this was a cover up, then one of them, or both may be involved. *Ok,* he thought, *let them do the talking.* As always, Doyle was going to have to calm himself and initiate his other self, the honest instinct that he may or may not have abused throughout his career.

So, the people in charge wanted him to play figurehead in a quick fix trial and sentencing? Well then, that was what he would look like he was doing. Over the years, he had rationalised all sorts of compromises to his self-belief, but this, the murder of the Treoraí na hEireann, Doyle would not compromise in this, nor would he give up until he was satisfied with the outcome.

Doyle summoned his calm and opened the door.

"Ah," he said, "thank you for waiting."

***

Siobhán felt acute embarrassment when Inspector Doyle entered the room. The wistful nonentity of Cullen had allowed her to shed her first tears of mourning. They had been tentative and then plentiful, but she choked them back into her chest in a painful gasp that felt like an oversized piece of food was struggling down her throat, so tangible was her grief.

"Ah," said Doyle, "thank you for waiting." He took turns, first initiating a reluctant handshake from Cullen, and then kissing her on the cheek. Siobhán felt he had a fatherly air that reminded her of happy days spent in Walter's instruction. How he loved to discuss his complete theory of politic, and invite her arguments in the hope that they would prove his theory and even strengthen it. So unique were his ideas of icon and government separation that there was talk of it being published worldwide. But Walter had always declined; saying that the greatest test was yet to come, and some day the world would be able to see the mastery behind his complete political philosophy.

"Miss Sloane?" said Doyle with a look of real concern. "Are you alright?" Siobhán blinked.

"Yes, Inspector, I'm fine. What have you found out?" She was straight to the point, because she wanted to find out who did this terrible thing to her life. And, if she could spend enough time trying to work it out, then maybe there would be less opportunity for her to stand at the edge of the precipice, looking down on a life without Walter Thisgo, and what that would mean to the country, her career, or if she was honest, her broken heart.

"Well," said Doyle, "I want you both to go through the last couple of weeks in your mind. Who had the Treoraí been in contact with that he might not have been before? Politically, had he made any public statements that may have upset certain people, government policy decisions that would have meant disaster for anyone?"

"Upset people," Siobhán laughed, "oh, he upset people all the time. But there was nothing very different about the last couple of weeks."

"Policies? Laws?" Doyle asked.

"We've been pushing job actualisation recently, but it hasn't met with any real opposition at all. Because it's just a really good idea." Doyle turned to Cullen.

"Mr Cullen?" The security man looked down from the window and raised an eyebrow.

"Mr Cullen," Doyle tried again. "Is there anything you can tell me about the last couple of weeks, even days, that was out of the ordinary?"

Cullen looked at Doyle, his face blank and pasty from lack of sleep. Siobhán could see that the man had been drinking heavily, but she couldn't blame him for that. Cullen gave a sigh before he spoke. It turned into a shudder as the words came out, and a whine as he lost control of himself once more.

"The system was faulty-" said Cullen and Doyle put a reassuring hand on the broken man's shoulder. "Yes, I know that. But what else? There has to have been something else? Anything."

"His dinner with the Regressives!" said Siobhán with a start. She couldn't believe that she hadn't though of it before. "Walter- The Treoraí had dinner with the Regressive leaders the night before he died."

"Really?" said Doyle, keeping blank. "Why?"

"It was his idea, he said that there needed to be some-ordering of dissonance- is what he called it -amongst all of the people's representatives."

"But the Progressive party have a huge majority."

"Yes, but Walt- the Treoraí did not believe in the

Progressive Party."

"It was a movement," Cullen butted in.

Good, thought Doyle, *at least they were both talking.*

"That's right," said Siobhán, "Walter didn't want Ireland to be divided into parties, he was merely using the system that was already in place to free the country from that sort of politics."

Doyle Probed further, "So he went to the opposition to talk them into his ways?"

"Ha!" said Cullen. "Those bastards would never change their ways."

"But the Treoraí must have felt some good would come from the meal?" This question paused both Siobhán and Cullen.

"Em…" Siobhán tried to think why Walter had gone to the dinner. 'It'll be a waste of time,' he'd told her the afternoon before going, and she'd just laughed. But now she realised her error. When had Walter Thisgo EVER taken part in something that was a waste of time? The Treoraí had had no time for such inefficiency.

"So why did he go?" Doyle asked again. Neither Siobhán nor Cullen answered. The inspector didn't like their silence and changed his questioning-

"So how did it go, the meeting? Was it a success?" Doyle looked to Siobhán first.

"He made a joke and said that there was only a faint hint of ludicrosity. But later on, he told me that they had been rude and obnoxious: They said he'd better watch himself, because his stupid ideas were going do him more harm than good." And Siobhán grew angry. *How dare they say such a thing to the Treoraí?*

"Really?" asked Doyle, "Can you supply me with the names of those who attended?" Siobhán nodded, she was sure Walter had given her one the next day, he'd written it down too, which was odd. He needn't have bothered; they were not using the event for any press coverage.

"It was them, wasn't it?" Cullen demanded.

"Now, Mr Cullen, it is far too early in the investigation for us to assume any such thing." Doyle was wondering himself whether this obvious avenue was far to obvious.

"Don't, now Mr Cullen me! Tell me who did this? I know there was a tape. The system was faulty, but there was one tape. Show it to me!"

Doyle tried to calm Cullen,"Yes, yes, there is a tape," he said, "but only a few second of footage, and even then all it shows are three kids in the grounds of the Áras."

"I don't care," Cullen demanded, leaning forward and using his bulk to intimidate Doyle, "I want to see the ones who did it."

Doyle did not shrink away, however. "You think that this sort of behaviour will get you somewhere with me, boy?" The inspector stood and stuck his finger into Cullen's chest. "I am a Garda Síochána, and you are spitting your gums at me in Gardaí Headquarters. This place is not usually used as a holding area, but there are cells in the basement, ones that you could spend a couple of weeks in, if you want? Would you like that?" Doyle turned his back to both of them and began to pace the room.

"Now," he said, as he walked, "I also want to find the murderer as soon as possible. But there is no way of knowing that these mere children are capable of such a thing. I will concentrate on them, however. The only thing that is clear right now is that there were three young people in the grounds last night: One young man; tall with black hair and a pale complexion. One girl with dark hair of medium height, and another young man, blonde with spiked hair. All three were wearing casual clothes and were spotted on CCTV at the rear of the building at approximately the time of death. If these three were not involved, then they must at least have seen something, so I will be concentrating our efforts on finding them."

Doyle noticed whilst he was speaking that Siobhán began to fidget; she took a pen from her pocket and clicked it on and off before putting it back.

"Now, before you go. Is there anything that you can tell me that you may not have mentioned already?" Doyle looked first at Cullen, who merely looked back, still chastened from his earlier reprimand. Then the inspector turned to Siobhán, whom he knew had something to say. She didn't speak. Doyle raised an eyebrow [really?] as a signal to her that she should go ahead.

"What are we supposed to do now?" Siobhán asked, not

wanting to speak out just then.

"Ok," said Doyle, disappointed that he had gotten little out of the two people that were closest to Walter Thisgo in the lead up to his murder, but there was nothing he could do about that. "I've been ordered to release pictures of the three on the news. Not my choice, but the decision is out of my hands." Doyle gave them both a measured sigh, to let them know that this troubled him. "After that, there will be hundreds of leads for my people to waste their time on, but at least we will know who these youths are, and why they were in the grounds of the Áras that night. So, what I need you to do, both of you, is try to remember everything that you can about the last two or three days. If anything out of the ordinary comes to mind, anything, then you should contact me immediately." He gave them both a card and continued, "Even if you just want to call and tell me about a strange comment the Treoraí made, or if he was late for an appointment, call immediately. Ok?" Siobhán nodded and Doyle turned to Cullen.

"Is that ok?" he asked the big man. Cullen begrudgingly nodded his head and Doyle smiled. "It isn't easy for either of you. Take heart. I will find out who is responsible."

Cullen looked into Doyle's face and saw an old man but a strong man; a man of experience. Doyle allowed the stare to prove to the former security chief that he meant what he said; that sometimes the best way to convince someone is to say nothing, and let truth show itself. Doyle was open and determined, and it wasn't hard to see that though this was his last fight, he would not stop until he got his man.

***

Siobhán and Cullen left the Gardaí Headquarters together, and both went their separate ways on reaching the car park. Their relationship had ended in Walter Thisgo's own bloody demise. They said, 'See ya,' and got into their cars and drove from their spaces, without any more emotion or ceremony. What was there to say?

Reaching the road, Siobhán turned to the left and headed towards the city, and Cullen took a right heading into the

Phoenix Park towards Áras an Uachtaran, where he would no doubt collect his things and clear out his office, now that his employer had been terminated.

At a practiced distance of one hundred yards, two unmarked Garda cars followed Siobhán and Cullen respectively. They were good cars, a Ford Fiesta and a Volkswagen Golf. Doyle, watching from his office vantage had mixed feelings about deploying them. They were both suspects, of course, but he seriously doubted their involvement. Although Siobhán would probably be fine, Cullen's mental state could prove to be a problem, and if he discovered his tail, he may react stupidly, if he didn't already plan to. Doyle had all of the Regressive leaders under surveillance, and the teams all had Cullen's description.

Doyle turned back to his desk and switched on his TV. All he could do now was watch as his superiors planted those three faces all over the media landscape, and hope that he could get to them before an angry member of the public ripped them to pieces.

The three had now been dubbed the Dark Pupils; due to both the heinous manner in which they committed their crime, and the unfortunate coining of the phrase by the new leader of the Regressives, a TD named Anthony Kilty.

It was going to be, like the murder; ugly. Ugly action, ugly tactics, ugly reaction.

There was much more to all of this than murder. Three youths just waltz into Áras an Uachtaran on a night that there happened to be a fault with the security system, a broken window through which to gain entry, and the head of security's night off? No, there was something else to consider.

Politics.

Ugly Politics.

CHAPTER FOUR
MATERMINAL

*S*iobhán and her unmarked accompaniment reached Rathmines just as rush hour traffic was settling in, and the blabbering DJs began to bombard the overheating car speakers, and spanking the ears of every bumper humping listener on Rathmines road. It took her fifteen minutes to turn into the side road near her apartment, and while she waited, double parked, for a space to open up, Siobhán also turned the dial on her car stereo to the on position and chose a pop channel; she'd had enough news to last her a lifetime. So many questions: Would they ever catch Walter's killers? What was going to happen to her career, money, apartment, and car payments? Was there some sort of assassination recovery pay? There just might be.

Siobhán raised the volume on Radio 6 Licks.

"What a great song!"

"Absolutely, Henry,"

"I can't believe Johnny Cash didn't write that one himself!"

"Really?"

"Totally, Johnny. In fact, I have a bit of trivia to impart about Johnny's Ring of Fire."

"Do you?"

"Yep!"

"Well go on then!"

"Ha, of course I'm gonna go on."

"Well?"

"Just as soon as I can remember...oh yeah! That was it-"

"Was it?"

"Did you know?"

"Go on."

"Ha! That a haemorrhoids cream company offered Johnny Cash's family a multi-million dollar deal to use Ring of Fire in their adverts?"

"No!"

"Yes!"

"Which one?"

"A really big one!"

The joshing of the Radio DJs made Siobhán smile. They were funny guys and always managed to cheer her up after a heavy day. But them the news came.

"Well, Henry, thanks for that bit of fun but now, here is the news- the breaking story of the hour: Three youths are wanted in connection with yesterday's horrific murder of an Treoraí na hEireann. Pictures of the three, two male and one female taken from CCTV footage on the grounds of Áras an Uachtaran last night can be viewed on the Gardaí Síochána's website, www.gardai.ie as of five thirty today. The Gardaí would like to request that anyone matching the descriptions in the photos should not be approached, and anyone who spots the three youths should contact them immediately on 1800 323 323. In other news: in the aftermath of yesterday's events, all league of Ireland fixtures as well as the All Ireland Senior football semi-finals have been cancelled this weekend. A day of mourning has been announced for tomorrow, September 30th. A bank holiday has been announced and all transport services will cease for the day. The deputy leader of the Progressive Party, Mr...-" Siobhán had heard enough. She finished parking her car and paid the meter for the last hour of parking. As she walked to her apartment, she felt her stomach knotting once more and a dizziness break over her. God, was she ever going to feel normal again?

Queasy.

Once she'd locked the front door behind her, Siobhán ran straight for the toilet, and retched over the bowl for as long as it took her to realise that there was nothing coming out, nor was it likely to. The sickness she felt was in her heart and not curable by a quick chuck, or a violent purge. There was a depth to her illness that made Siobhán hope for such a thing, or God's version of it.

There are no remedies for life, she thought and stood to view her paling face in the mirror. She didn't look too bad considering, what? That her boss and mentor, her leader had only recently been torn apart by savages in the night.

"Yeah, you look fantastic," she said and braced for the

impact of leaving the bathroom, entering the sitting room, turning on the television and seeing their faces. The murderers.

The enemy.

***

<u>Pictures, perfect…</u>

Voice Over: - The following is a bulletin on behalf of the Gardaí Síochána.

Siobhán's television showed a still photograph of Áras an Uachtaran.

Voice Over: -At approximately ten o'clock last night, An Treoraí na hEireann was murdered in his bed in Áras an Uachtaran. The following are pictures of three people aged between twenty and twenty-five who were caught on CCTV at the scene of the crime.

The first picture was of a black-haired girl, smiling and looking to the right. *Good,* Siobhán thought, glad that the Gardaí had decided to show the girl first in an attempt to counter some of the immediate anger that the viewers would be feeling against the group; it was a weak attempt, but all that the Gardaí could do. People were going to be incensed and enraged, and anything that could be done to prevent further violence had to be tried.

On her television screen, Siobhán watched the picture change from the girl to a blonde boy, who looked harmless and innocent and from him, to a sullen dark-haired boy. All three were smiling, all obviously happy. Why?

After the bulletin was over, Siobhán ejected the DVD+R and took it to her computer, where she blew up each of the images and printed them out.

She looked at them for a long time, even opened a bottle of wine and smoked a cigarette, things that she usually left for the weekend. Then she studied the faces again; the dark-haired girl, the blonde boy, and the pale boy. What was their story? What…

Her mobile rang.

"Hello?"

"Miss Sloane?" It was a female voice.

"Yes?"

"The one from the TV? The one who announced that he-"

"-Yes," Siobhán cut in. So the media had already gotten her number. "Listen, what paper are you from?"

"No, no, no, you misunderstand, Miss Sloane," the woman sounded angry, or worried. "I've got some information for you, Miss Sloane, about, you know…"

Siobhán waited. She found this a good way to get people to the point quickly. She didn't have to wait very long. The woman on the other end of the line seemed to lose her composure, and Siobhán was sure that she heard crying.

"Miss Sloane," the woman sobbed. "That was my boy up there. Oh my boy, my poor boy!"

"What?" said Siobhán. "What are you talking about?" she demanded, as a loud buzzing began to sound in her head. This was the sound of realisation, the background noise of her mind as it processed information, and came to correct conclusions in quick and ordered fashion.

"Have you seen the Gardaí bulletins?"

"Yes," said Siobhán, quickly scanning the three pictures, "which one is your boy? The dark boy?"

"The blonde boy, Terry," answered the woman.

Siobhán took a moment.

"How do I know you're telling me the truth? How can I be sure?" she asked, and the woman gave a bitter laugh.

"Ha! Do you think I'd be calling and telling you this if he wasn't my son? Don't you think I would like it not to be him? I've loved Walter Thisgo ever since he began his reforms. I…I just can't believe it's my boy. But it is my boy, my Terry! Oh Jesus!"

After these last words, the woman let go completely and followed her guilt and shame across an archipelago of sobbing, taking Siobhán along also as she went from quiet to bellowing, and back to quiet again.

There was desperation in the woman's voice, and to Siobhán it attested to the truth. And, though she tried, Siobhán couldn't help but believe that the caller was indeed genuine. Dear God, the face of that woman's child was all over the news, and the Internet. People all over Ireland, all over the world, were looking at him and thinking about his parents, and what sort of people they must be to have a son as evil as that.

The poor woman.

"Now, I don't know what to do?" the woman moaned, "What should I do?"

"Mrs-?" Siobhán asked.

"It's Miss actually," said the woman sternly, "Terry has no father."

"Sorry, Miss?"

"Giles."

"Miss Giles," said Siobhán, "this is very important. You need to contact the Gardaí immediately, and give them any information that you have about your son and his two friends."

"Those children!" said Miss Giles, her voice growing harsh and cold. "It's their fault. I know it! Them and their stinking Regressive parents!"

"Their what?"

"The two others, Rachel and Peter. Their parents are bloody Regressive fundamentalist scum. I told him to stay away from them, but of course, he did the opposite. Oh Jesus, I drove him to it. It's all my fault!"

So, Siobhán thought. It was looking like the Regressives already. She reached for her bag and scattered its contents across the table.

"Can you help me please?" asked Miss Giles, "I don't know what to do."

Siobhán retrieved Doyle's card from her scattered trappings, and spoke with confidence into the receiver.

"Yes," said Siobhán, "I think I can help you."

***

Across the city, in Clontarf, Dr Rebecca Giles, mother of Terry Giles, hung up her phone and looked at the piece of paper where she'd jotted down Inspector Doyle's name. She didn't know why she bothered; she knew who was handling the case. It was habit, she supposed.

"Nearly there now," said Dr Giles, and smiled as she walked to the kitchen to pick up her keys. It was all going exactly as planned. Could it be that the grand vision would succeed? It warmed her heart to think that it would. She spared only the slightest thought for Terry and his friends. They were finished now anyway. Their part in the plan was over, and she was proud of her son for taking his part.

CHAPTER FIVE
THE ENVIRONMENTALIST

Ranging out west from the cliffs of Glendalough, her dark blue-grey feathers steering and rippling in the morning drafts, the Peregrine falcon screeched to mark both her second sweep of the area, and her frustration. Then, growing bolder despite the presence of the larger creatures, she moved in to capture her prey. There were chicks to feed at home; small and squawking in their newborn plumage, looking like a group of old men wearing white fur coats. This mother was in a hurry, and the two men by the stream were in for a big surprise.

"Listen," said the younger man, "Hear that? That's a falcon!"

Oscar turned his face to the flat blue sky and scanned for the bird. "Really?" he asked, "how do you know?"

"When you've been up here weeks like I - Look! There it is!" Oscar's eyes followed as the younger man pointed upward to the north, and sure enough, there was the falcon. As the seconds passed, it grew closer and closer until Oscar had the insane thought that it was going to attack them.

"It's hunting!" cried the younger man as the bird blurred, so fast was its approach.

In seconds, the Peregrine was upon them, flying only yards over their amazed expressions, and diving into the long grass. There was a brief 'fhlump!' and a tiny squeal before the falcon rose again with huge whoops of its powerful wings. As it cleared the high grass, Oscar could see that in its talons struggled a rabbit, and not a small one either.

"Jesus Mary and Joseph," said Oscar. "What a sight!"

"Yep, yep, yep," said the younger man as the two marvelled at the disappearing hunter, "isn't it? Isn't it? What an amazing creature." The younger man began taking snaps with his camera as the falcon disappeared. Oscar hadn't even noticed that the younger man had a camera around his neck, but there it was.

"You able to see anything with that?" Oscar asked.

"Nope," said the younger man, "not a thing." He let the

camera swing around his neck and turned to Oscar, "Wow! Do you know how fast those things can fly?"

"Well-"

"Two hundred miles an hour!" exclaimed the younger man. Oscar was under the impression that the man's passion for this countryside equated his own presence to a Dictaphone, or even a rock that gave the younger man something to talk at. Oscar had been worried when the man walked up behind him and started to jabber his approval, mentioning 'natural Ph' and other water related terminology, but Oscar was becoming increasingly cowed by the man's manner and his clear priorities towards the surrounding Wicklow hills.

"Well yes. that is fast," said Oscar bending down to pick up the luckily hitherto unused plastic petrol can he was using to carry water back to the others. He held out his hand to the younger man.

"Listen…?"

"Yes?" said the man.

"Your name?" asked Oscar.

"Oh! My name. Oh nobody uses my name."

"Really?"

"Yes, they call me the Environmentalist."

"People call you that?"

"Yes."

"Other people?" said Oscar, raising an eyebrow, not because he doubted that this was what the younger man called himself, but more because he couldn't imagine that the man spoke to anyone at all without the words 'Grant Application' being mentioned.

"Anyway," said Oscar, "it was nice to meet you. I'll have to be getting back to the rest of my friends."

"Oh," said the Environmentalist, only mildly disappointed, "see you around the area then. I hope that your friends get over their food poisoning."

Oscar thanked the Environmentalist for all the advice he'd given him on useful flora and the correct taste of fresh water, and headed back up the hill towards the forest and his waiting companions. He was not happy that someone knew they were in the area, but nothing could be done. It was likely, however, that the Environmentalist would not be going near a town for another day, giving them time enough to decide what to do next. That was the thing. What were they going to do next? So far, he had been concentrating on keeping the group safe, but now that Rachel was awake, and Terry and Peter's fever had just reached breaking point, he had to start thinking of the next step. Or, the fretfully obvious lack of one.

Oscar quickened his pace towards the three murderers - victims. Were they over the drugs now? Would that be the end of their destructive behaviour? Oscar wasn't able to convince himself that it would be. If he was right, and the three had been conditioned to commit the terrible act he'd heard described on the radio, how could he expect such strong brainwashing to just wear off overnight? It could very well be that he too would be in danger at some point, but Oscar shook that one off.

"No," he said. They would just have to take it one disaster at a time. He reached the roadside and quickly darted across and into the forest.

From the field below, the Environmentalist marked the point in the treeline that Oscar entered the forest. He used the massive tree and a fallen section of the stone wall as two points of reference so that he could find it easily, and resolved to pop up there later on and meet the rest of the group. Maybe even have a cup of tea. He could bring the little stove and his new teapot. It was big enough for three or four cups.

"Mmm yes," he said, bending to fill his canteen from the rushing stream, "that'll be very nice." Then the Environmentalist began to sing. It was a strange warbling Ayr that was more suited to a greying gaelgor from the west of Ireland than a man of his few years.

"Did I really put all my faith in you; while you had nothing to give?

Did you lie, or was it I?

And how many stars are there now; if there are any, any more?"

***

Back in the ruined church, Peter was coming to. And while fever still strained his body, his mind was clearing, and he pieced together the unfocused patchwork of broken memory.

After the group had spilled into the Duvlinia exhibition from the St Michan's tunnel, they lay on the floor, blinking their confusion away and appreciating the oddness of their position. Peter knew where they were, he'd been there before. The Duvlinia exhibition lay underneath Christchurch Cathedral. It was a tribute to and reminder of the Viking occupation of Duvlinn, Duv-Linn, meaning black-pool; the dark waters formed by the meeting of three rivers. Peter couldn't believe how far they had come. So it was true, the occupiers of Christchurch-

"Help me here, will you?" called Oscar, "We have to close this door or the whole feckin' river is going to come in after us!"

Shit! Peter thought, the old man was right. He joined Terry and Oscar at the entrance to the tunnel, and added to their strength. Only then, and after a minute or two of real effort, the door ground shut.

"There we are," said Oscar, looking around.

"What are you looking for?" Terry asked.

"Something to cover the broken plaster." Peter looked around automatically and noticed a wall hanging only a yard from the rectangular-ish hole that they had broken through in the the plasterboard.

"Move the hanging a few feet to the left," said Peter, pointing to the mosaic-like depiction designed in dark brown; a Viking at the prow of his ship looking tall and strong. A far cry from the reality of the grossly unhealthy warrior race surrounded by cess-pits and dying younger and younger with each passing decade, until their kings were no more than children who coveted and craved.

"Good idea lad," said Oscar, and the next few minutes were spent removing the wall hanging and retacking it over the broken plaster.

When they reached the foyer of the exhibition, the group were faced with another problem, getting out.

"How do you break out of a place?" asked Rachel. It was a decent question, and one that Peter was at a loss to answer.

"Ok," said Oscar, "where is this car you were talking about?" Peter recalled where he and Rachel had dumped the black Peugeot the morning before. It was just off Meade Street, near a block of flats. Depending on it was a big risk, as there was no guarantee that it would still be there, or if indeed it was, that it wouldn't be clamped and unusable.

"Well," said Terry, "there's only one way to find out."

They would have to break out, and in doing so, set off the alarm. Then they would have to sprint up to a large junction and onto Thomas Street, where they would be out in the open, within shouting distance of the Garda checkpoints on the bridges, all the way up to Meade Street. They would surely be seen. But, as Terry had so succinctly put it, there was only one way to find out.

Terry and Oscar lifted a large bench to the glass front door, and with a swing-heave, smashed the thick glass in one large pane into large dangerous pieces beneath their shoes. For a brief moment, the group were shocked that an alarm had not been raised, but they were too quick to hope for such a thing. The alarm started to ring out like a school bell, splitting the cloak of the night under which they had hoped to remain.

…So they legged it.

The sprint was interjected with doubling over and gasping, followed by dragging, hasty encouragement, and finally, the sound of police sirens. At least two cars had broken away from the roadblocks, and they appeared on Thomas Street just as the group fell around the corner onto Meade. They hid in an alley as the two cars sped past but didn't slow.

…Lucky.

Peter, the one who had been receiving most of the encouragement, found his wind and took them down a side street towards the block of flats. And there it was. A black Peugeot 406, also available in silver, burgundy and tangible relief. As it had been the night before outside *The Inn*, the car was open and unmolested, a strange enough development, but not so much that it bothered the group at the time.

Oscar hopped into the driver's seat muttering something about their needing to duck if the Gardaí went by, and they were off and out of Dublin.

…Easy.

Peter remembered the sound of the car and the sound of Rachel's breathing as she lay on his lap, exhausted. He remembered trying to rouse himself with the memory of what they had done to Walter Thisgo, the horrible truth about themselves that should have reduced Peter to a jittering and frantic, but above all else, wakeful state. Yet he remembered his eyes closing down, and his caring not at all for the troubles of the night.

And now he was awake, but didn't know into what he was waking. He was outside for sure, he could see the sky and he could hear the wind, rushing round about, but he felt warm. Funny that. And, he felt, what was it? Dizzy, yeah, that was it. He was finding it hard to focus, but wasn't interested much either way. He could sleep again, and why not? There were memories waiting to be reviewed, but he let his fuzziness keep them from his mind. Yes, there were definitely things to be remembered. Dead things he was in no hurry to think about.

Go to sleep again, that was his decision. So Peter closed his eyes and began to drift off.

"Peter?" A voice, very close, tempted him to look. But he didn't.

"Peter. Are you awake?" Yes he was. But he didn't want to be, even though now he was feeling warmth towards the voice, despite the inconvenience it was causing him, because it was Rachel's voice. Now, he may open his eyes for her, if she was lucky.

"Peter?"

"Urumm!"

"Peter, it's me, Rachel."

"Yeah, yeah." Peter opened an eye, "If you roll down the window-"

"What?" said Rachel.

"What?" Now Peter was squinting through both lids in an attempt to fight off the bright waking world attached to the pleasant voice. "Oh nothing. Rachel? How are ya?"

"I'm fine," she laughed, "a bit wrecked, but… You look knackered!"

"Mlah!" said Peter decisively as he sat up. "Where are we?"

"Somewhere in the Wicklow Mountains." Rachel was smiling at him, obviously happy he was awake.

"What happened? Why do I feel so - dizzy?"

"You'd better talk to Oscar," said Rachel, "he has a theory."

Peter shook his head, trying to lose some of the lethargy and the fog. So Oscar had a theory. Good, because although Peter had a pain in his head, and a rising sense of guilt he couldn't quash, theories he had none.

"You hungry?" Rachel asked, her face open and filled with concern. Yes he was.

"Let's go outside then, if you can?" she said, "we've got food, some food anyway."

"Em," said Peter, looking up at her. Yeah, he'd go anywhere. Even if his legs were hanging off, he'd go, sure he would and she was plenty worth it. Peter took a chance on his wobbly legs to join Rachel outside. There was no chance of him staying in bed now, so follow her outside he did.

From inside the ruined church, their voices, Peter and Rachel's, could be heard, first tentative, and then rambling beyond adequate volume. Outside, they were finding out that they could replace with their relationship the gaping hole that normality would leave, now that they had forgone any right to it by way of murder.

Inside though. Inside lay Terry Giles, recently roused and alone. He'd been awake long enough to see Peter and Rachel leave, long enough to have to come to his own conclusions about his surroundings, and long enough to feel the hollow resentment of being left alone. Already he was, 'fuck them,' and 'how dare they.' Proof that it wasn't the habit that was hardest to control. It was lack of support and loneliness that were hardest to conquer.

"Fuck them," Terry thought, as the horrible feeling of realisation and chemical infection still coursed through his body. "How dare they."

***

At dinner, Oscar was beginning to dread the conversation that they were due to have; but was impossible to introduce. He knew that he must face it now, or they would simply be left waiting there until the Gardaí arrived, and that was the end of them. There had to be something they could do, aside from hide, but to find out what it was, the group would have to come to a decision, in the face of all the facts, because he was lost.

"Mmmm," said Peter, giving semi-real signs that he'd tasted his food, "this is lovely!"

It wasn't lovely at all, not even to Oscar, who had been forced to eat some pretty rough meals on the streets of Dublin. The fact was that he was lost out there in the country with the beautiful green of the plateau, and the earthy wildness of the forest. How was he supposed to provide for them there, with no idea about hunting or foraging for food? What they were eating could best be described as hot lumps that may or may not be potatoes, accompanied by red berries that may or may not be poisonous. Oscar was sure that if they were left in his hands out here, they wouldn't need to worry about the police. They would surely starve to death.

It was evening, and around the fire sat the four fugitives. It was a good fire, with lots of heat and light, but Oscar wasn't sure that he deserved any awards for that. They were in a forest after all.

Of the three students, Peter and Rachel seemed to be recovering well from the effects of the drugs. Taking strength from each other, it was clear that though they were both still feeling ill, they were finding in each other a reason to put the ordeal behind them, for now anyway.

Terry on the other hand, was - well, Terry. The boy was unpredictable and difficult to talk to. Oscar had tried to make Terry feel comfortable after he woke that morning, but the stubborn little bastard was having none of it. Now, Terry was eyeing Peter and Rachel with an uncontained sneer.

"Terry," said Peter, "how's yours?" Oscar wasn't sure this was a good idea right then.

"Excuse me?" Terry asked and Peter picked up on the tone of his voice.

"I was just asking how-"

"I heard you. It was a rhetorical question."

"Oh," Peter smiled, relieved. Bad idea.

"Oh it's funny is it?" said Terry, standing up and throwing his makeshift plate on the fire. It was made from a piece of bark that Oscar had torn from a nearby tree, and the combination of sap and the sloppy dinner caused the fire to hiss and smoulder, and emit a reeking smoke.

"You think it's funny?" Terry challenged again.

"Eh no, Terry, listen." Peter looked surprised, but couldn't hide a flicker of; was it anger, or fear that crossed his features before he blanked it out?

"Listen?" Terry shouted, "Why? Why would I listen to you?" You're the nightmare that started this!"

"Hey!" said Peter, "that's not fair. I didn't ask for this!"

"Bullshit," said Terry with a scowl, "I was fine until you came along. As soon as I met you, everything went to shite!"

"Oh yeah. You were fine. That's why you told me that you were being driven mad at night. That you were thinking about killing yourself? Ha? Is that fine?"

"Boys! This is stupid-" Oscar tried.

"Shut up," said Terry.

"Stay out of it," said Peter.

"You think you're so fuckin' clever, don't ya? Well I was there. I saw what you did. What we did! I've never done anything so-" here Terry's voice strained with emotion, as the tears tried to break through, but he resisted, "evil!" he shouted.

"And you think that's my fault?" said Peter.

"What else should I think? You just sit there smug with your bitch-"

"Hey!" cried Rachel and Peter together.

"Shut your mouth," Peter threatened.

"Shut my mouth? Come on and shut it for me, please do!" Terry stepped forward, fuelled and bristling, and Peter wasn't slow to confront him.

The two went down after a brief opening round. One punch apiece before their arms got tangled, and the fistfight turned into a wrestling contest. From the outset, Peter had the upper hand, gaining the advantage with a clearer head, and sitting astride Terry, subduing him. But that was where he lost it. Terry had no thoughts of subjugation; he was both intent on winning, and determined not to fail. While Peter tried to keep him under control, Terry took control, and the two rolled on the dry earth until Peter was on the bottom and beset with blows from Terry. Sometimes he hit the target, and often he struck the ground, but it made no difference to the fury of his assault.

All of this happened quickly, and when Oscar and Rachel were finally able to pull Terry away from Peter, the latter had a bloody nose and was headed for a lot more besides. Terry struggled to be free of their grasp, and rose from the ground to face all three of them. There were tears falling down his face and he was panting.

"Fuck you!" he whispered through a break of emotion, and ran out of the clearing into the forest, leaving the rest of the group reeling from the sudden change in their situation.

Oscar helped Peter up, while Rachel examined his face. All three were silent. What was there for them to say, and how could they blame Terry for lashing out. Oscar could see clearly what was happening. Peter and Rachel had each other, and Terry felt he had nobody. Well, Oscar was going to have to make it clear to the boy that he was there for him. But for now, it was probably better that they all left him alone. Terry was vulnerable at that moment, and he needed to come to his own conclusions. He was a good boy and would make the right choices if they left him alone.

Oscar poured some water into the teapot, so that they could clean Peter's scratches. He had planned on going over exactly what happened the previous night, and to tell them what he suspected. It would have to wait for tomorrow now. But how many more tomorrows were there going to be?

The campsite lay inside a pool of light, given off by the fire. While Terry disappeared from the light and headed deep into the forest, a figure stood on the shore of that flickering pool, surprised by what he had just seen, and not yet sure that he should continue into the camp.

The Environmentalist watched as the three remaining members of the group tended, or were tended to, and he made a decision. Perhaps, now wasn't a really good time for a visit? No, definitely not.

The other boy, however, he would need some comfort,

out there in the forest all alone, separated from the others and angry. He might even get lost? In fact, the Environmentalist decided, he most certainly would. So, taking care not to make a sound, the Environmentalist picked his way around the shores of the camp's perception, until he reached the point of Terry's exit.

Terry, he remembered, *I'd better go and have a little chat with Terry.*

CHAPTER SIX
THE PLOT

*W*hen morning arrived, Terry was still livid, though as he took a walk through the forest, he had managed to control his compulsions to confront and attack the other members of the hideous conspiracy. It had been late last night when he'd finally returned to the old church, while the others were sleeping, or pretending to sleep at any rate. The fools thought he wouldn't notice that their lack of movement was more than enough to tell him that they were wide-awake, and fretting for his return. He felt better now. Better for the conversation he'd had with the Environmentalist, and the decision he'd made as a result. He would wait and see what the others wanted to do before committing himself to any more drastic action like that of the night before. They were all against him. That much was obvious, even if it hadn't been pointed out to him. But speaking to the Environmentalist had helped him see it from an exterior point of view. Peter and Rachel had each other. They didn't care about him. And Oscar? Even if he was Terry's father, what sort of father was he? Running off and leaving him alone while his mother worked and worked. To do what? Become a tramp! At least Terry could have tried to understand if there had been another love or a specific hate. No, Oscar was no ally to Terry Giles. At best, he was a crap father. And, at worst, he was a weird homeless guy who'd been following them around whilst they had been out "a-murdering!" This was how Terry felt.

At least, this is what Terry had decided to feel, amongst the drug induced shakes and the uncomfortable sweating that he was experiencing, as well as the bitch slapping his mental state was receiving at the hands of the pure and simple facts of his situation.

"Watch and wait," the Environmentalist had rightly said, "wait for your course to become clear." Also there was something about the medicinal purposes of some barks, as opposed to the poisonous effects of others, but Terry was teetering far too closely to his own personal pit-with-spikes-in to clarify the details.

It was time for him to return to the camp, and make his humble apologies. As he walked, Terry thought about his mother, and how much he missed her. She was such a smart woman, and would certainly know what to do. Or, at least he could find comfort in his presence. Oh, she was a great comforter when he was down, and he wished that she were there.

"Mothers are important," the Environmentalist had said, and Terry knew then, straight away, that the nerd was right.

Terry reached the camp as Oscar was stirring the teapot, and Peter and Rachel were sorting through some berries, picking out the ones that were too rotten to eat. They were going to starve out here if they didn't get some decent food.

"We're going to have to trap something," said Terry, and the others turned their heads in surprise. "If we're going to eat. We're going to have to catch something."

Oscar rose from the fire and came towards Terry, nodding his head.

"Yes," said Oscar, "we should go out and find that Environmentalist fella later, and ask him for some advice on what to catch." The old man looked hopeful. "Me and you could go after breakfast?"

"Sure," said Terry with a smile, "why not." Oscar smiled too and the sun that was creeping up behind them heralded a change in the mood. Terry turned to Peter and looked at his bruises. *Serves him right,* Terry thought.

"Listen, em-" Terry bluffed a shy response. "Sorry about the, eh-"

"Don't worry about it," said Peter, "I understand."

What a prat, thought Terry. "Thanks man," he said.

For breakfast, they had berry and left over, mushy, half-boiled potatoes served with a side salad of happy families. It was at this point that Oscar decided to broach the subject of 'The Plot', whilst Terry held his tongue, and Peter and Rachel nodded their approval as the story went on.

First Oscar spoke about the facts. The drugs they had been tricked into taking. Terry for his anxiety, Peter as vitamins, and Rachel's pill. Even if it was doubtful before, the reaction to their absence was proof enough of the pills' potency. But why had they done what they had done? That still unmentionable deed crushing them from above.

Oscar spoke to them about the reoccurring dreams that all three had suffered in the months leading up to the deed. Even poor Marie, another casualty they had been trying to avoid remembering, had spoken of her nightmares.

Oscar's theory fit the circumstances perfectly. The dreams were connected to the deed. They were conditioning of some sort, driving Terry, Peter, and Rachel into mental unrest, and susceptibility to suggestion. It was even a possibility that Marie was murdered to push them over the edge.

When logical thought like this was applied, even Terry had to admit the truths that were unfolding.

"But who?" Terry asked, "we all saw Thisgo in the bar. You did too."

"It was a hoax Thisgo," said Oscar, "It had to have been. Someone in a good enough disguise to fool three drugged up students in a state of mental disarray."

"Ok," said Terry, "what if it was? We were drugged and trained, by who and why?"

"Unfortunately, the why is obvious," said Peter. "To kill Walter Thisgo."

"Yeah, of course, but who planned it?" said Terry.

"The Regressives?" said Rachel.

"Almost definitely," Oscar nodded his head, "they are the only ones with the motive or the power to pull it off. And…"

"And?" asked Terry.

"And?" repeated Rachel and Peter.

"Well, it's just."

"Spit it out!" said Terry.

"It's your parents," said Oscar, "they must be involved too."

"What!" Rachel cried. She scowled and turned to Peter, "No way." But Peter's expression didn't do much to authenticate her disbelief, and Terry's laugh was just confusing.

"Wait a second," Oscar begged for time. "When I was in

Peter's house, I found a camera behind the sitting room mirror. And somebody must have been making sure that you took your tablets, monitoring your progress, allowing the Regressives access to your homes so that they could - well programme you. Right?" Oscar looked from face to face, all of these were shocked yet they held no disagreement, and not even Terry's cut-eyed craftiness was evident now. But what was Oscar leading up to?

"So your parents were involved," said Oscar.

"No way," Terry came alive, "that's impossible. My Ma loved Walter Thisgo. There's no way that she would do anything to hurt him!"

"Terry," said Oscar, "I know that it's hard-"

"Aw fuck you! Hard. What do you know about hard? What do you know about my Ma? What about their parents, were they Progressives?" Terry turned, and accused the others, straightening a finger at them and sneering.

"Well?" he demanded, "what are your parents; Regressives or Progressives?" Peter and Rachel's hesitation was enough to confirm for Terry what he'd suspected.

"You saw all those things in his house," Terry gestured rudely to Peter, "and it's their parents that are Regressives, not my, my, parent! So accuse them and leave my Ma alone."

"But Terry," Oscar pleaded, "don't you understand?"

"Understand what?"

"Rebec- your mother is an important psychiatrist who holds two patents for developing behaviour modifying medication. And that was years ago. Who knows what she's been doing since?"

Terry couldn't believe what he was hearing. The bastard wasn't just saying that his mother was involved; he was saying that she was directly responsible for the deed.

"You're out of your fuckin mind!" he shouted at Oscar, "She'd never do that!" But in Terry's mind, visions of blurred syringes and the smell of sterile instruments flashed, confused memories, a voice speaking in brash business-like tones. "She would never do that," Terry repeated, "she's never-"

Terry broke off and ran from the camp towards the road,

leaving behind the others, and the revelations that he was incapable of digesting. The wind struck him when he cleared the roadside, and it felt like he was, for a moment, standing in the path of a powerful train, as though he were the elemental one and the rushing air was passing through him, and not he through it.

Sloping away in front of him were the hills and curves of the mountainside. *What was that mountain called*? he wondered. There was one around here called the sugarloaf, just like the mountain that overlooked Rio de Janeiro. He was lost. They all were. There was nothing here for them, in the same way that there was nothing for them back in society. They were cast-outs, unfashionable, and only useful to be put away until a date far in the future. The barren beauty of the area dwarfed him, and he felt truly desperate.

Do? Go? Who? What was he? Where was he? Who could he? Terry's life was burned paper, and the wind had just blown apart the fragments, leaving him- Wait!

What was that moving down in the field? Down by the stream a figure was moving, back and forth from one point to another. It was the Environmentalist, his only friend. Terry began to walk, took to running, and finally, bounded down the hill towards the unsuspecting man. The slope was steep, and there were parts of it that were rocky and other parts that fell away from underfoot where the rains had bogged the earth. Terry stumbled and tripped his way over and into these, but barely kept his balance, coming to a skidding stop finally at the stream's edge, where the Environmentalist knelt, stooped over the river, filling a glass beaker with water.

Terry righted from his crouch and waited to be noticed. He felt foolish now, and the longer he went unnoticed, the harder he found it to justify his appearance. He'd wanted so badly to be by the Environmentalist's side that he'd not thought what he was going to say. The nerdy man helped him out there-

"Hello, Terry, hello," said the Environmentalist, not looking up from his work, "had another fight with your friends?"

"Yes." Terry took to scuffing the earth with the toe of his Reebok like a schoolboy reporting to his headmaster. The man looked up and he stopped what he was doing.

"Please, please, please do tell," instructed the

Environmentalist, walking over to his backpack and retrieving a stopper for the beaker he'd been using. "I hope you don't mind me doing some work while you talk?"

"Eh, no," said Terry. "It's not that bad really." He paused. How much could he tell the Environmentalist?

"It seemed pretty bad last night?" asked the man, rummaging in his bag for something.

"Em, yeah, it is pretty bad. I just-"

"Hungry?" asked the Environmentalist. Terry was starving. They all were. So when the Environmentalist pulled out a set of keys from his bag, Terry was disappointed that it wasn't a bag of crisps or a sandwich.

"I'm going into town to get some provisions," said the man, jiggling his keys, "I have a jeep over there." He pointed over his shoulder where there was nothing in sight but the sloping fields and the rising mountains. "Do you want to come with me? Maybe your friends and you need to get some provisions?"

It was exactly true. Suddenly, all Terry could think about was food.

"Yeah," he said, "that's true. Which town?"

"The lovely Carraigeden," said the Environmentalist, but Terry had never heard of it. "It's really a very small town," he added. "One shop slash post office slash bar, and a chapel across the road, a quiet little place that belongs more to nineteen forty than to modern Ireland." The Environmentalist winked at Terry. "A great place for a bit of peace and quiet, a bit of a break, you know?"

It sounded perfect. So, Terry headed back to the camp and the other left to get his car, and by the time Terry and his friends had decided what they needed, the Environmentalist promised to be waiting at the roadside for him. "See ya later," they said and went their separate ways.

***

Back in the abandoned church, Peter was getting pissed off. He'd already taken a few thumps from Terry, and now the bastard had run off like a little girl. It wasn't fair. They were all in this together and there was no time for this tellytubby bullshit. So what if he and Rachel had found each other? It wasn't their fault. What else could they do, especially now that they would have so little time to enjoy life? Peter was under no illusion that they would all be caught and thrown in jail for what they had done, maybe even hung, if the Regressives got their way and brought back capital punishment. So why shouldn't they try to indulge in something good before everything else went to shit? It made Peter sad to think like that, but he was a logical guy and logic was a prick when hope was out of town.

Then Terry was there, bursting into the camp and speaking quickly.

"Hey guys, I'm just going to get some food in the town. Alright?"

"What?" either Rachel or Oscar said.

"Yeah, the Environmentalist guy is going to town and we need food, right? So I'm going with. It's a small town, one shop, don't worry, I'll make sure that he doesn't call the police or anything."

"What the fuck are you saying?" said Peter coming forward. He'd had just about enough of this. "You can't go into town, you'll be seen!"

"No I won't, it's a one horse town," laughed Terry, "a pony village really."

"Terry," said Oscar, "do you think it's a good idea to go somewhere where they'll have radios and television; our descriptions?" Terry's smile faded for a moment and he looked at his three, whether he liked it or not, cohorts.

"Do you think it would be better if we let him go on his own?"

No one could disagree with him there; Oscar and Peter were silent as they tried to come up with something, then Rachel came forward.

"Ok," she said, "you're going?" Terry nodded.

"Then we need: A pot, tea, milk, meat, pasta, sauce, toothbrushes, paste, soap, a tent, and anything else you can think of." Rachel turned to the other two, who looked shocked.

"Come on," she said, "get your Euros out!"

A car horn sounded from outside the church. They

pooled their money, but it only came to €42.50.

"That's it," said Rachel, "don't waste it."

"Don't worry," Terry assured her, smiling. "I'll only buy one bag of porn."

"Listen, Terry," said Peter, "be careful. Don't let the Environmentalist see a TV or anything, ok?"

"Ok," Terry gave his begrudging agreement. Peter was right, probably. "I'll be careful. Do you want some beer?"

Peter laughed and Terry could see that even this one, with his sulky abstinent attitude could really do with a drink too.

The car horn beeped again, and Terry turned to leave. Oscar echoed Peter's sentiment in his ear, and Rachel gave him a smile. *Perhaps they weren't all that bad a crowd,* thought Terry as he left the church and walked to the Jeep that lay waiting at the side of the road. Even in Terry's mood-shifting state of mind, he registered the satirical value of the vehicle.

"Very environmental," he said, and opened the passenger door.

Back in the ruined church, Oscar, Rachel, and Peter settled in for a long worry. They hoped that Terry was going to be all right, and that the Environmentalist wouldn't see anything that would tip him off as to who they were. But most of all, they hoped that they wouldn't get caught today, as they would have to worry every day until they finally did feel the bony hand of the Gardaí on their shoulders, and a voice saying the words: "You're under arrest, son," or "miss," or "Move along there, old man."

CHAPTER SEVEN
THE INTERNET
AND WIDESPREAD PANIC

"*I* do understand, sir, and believe me, we are doing everything we can to-" The phone went dead in Siobhán's hand.

"Bastard!" said Siobhán, "Joan!" Joan's glasses appeared around the door, and one eyebrow raised itself above the frame.

"Joan, don't put any more crackpots through to me. I've got too much work to do today."

"But that was the leader of the green party," said Joan. Siobhán looked up from the mountain of paper on her desk and gave Joan a look, [exactly].

"Sorry," said Joan, "I'll make sure."

It wasn't going well in the press office. From the second she'd got in that morning, there had been calls from newspapers, television, and radio, all trying to get the latest from her and her team. Politicians were already calling to ensure that they were allotted a prominent place during the coverage of the state funeral. It was imperative, they said, that they were given a chance to say a proper goodbye to "my old friend Walter," or "the revolutionary visionary, commander of his people." The sort of thing that meant - "I want the best coverage." And, " I want to come out of this on top!" It may sound bad to the untrained ear, but to Siobhán, it was proper practice. If it had been a different public figure that was murdered horribly in his bed, she would have advised Walter to do likewise, may even have done it for him, although those calls always went better when the beggar was doing their own begging.

This time it was her boss who had gone to ground, and Siobhán was both emotionally and physically shattered that day, but it hadn't had an adverse effect on her work. She'd even sketched a seating plan for the funeral, with Walter's friends mingled in amongst his Regressive enemies. Not what Walter would have done, no doubt, but Siobhán wasn't going to give the murdering bastards the chance to whisper smug nothings to each other, and belittle Walter's casket. Not on his funeral day; the first day of Ireland's aimless future. For Siobhán believed in the man, but had little faith in the movement beyond him.

Progression onto a different plane of governance had been Walter's fiery-eyed belief; that the Heaven of complete representation could live beyond the existence of its god. Siobhán had always loved the man, but her love was never blind. Walter Thisgo had not quite driven out the demons of the past. They were waiting for their chance. And here it was.

"Siobh," Jane called from the doorway, interrupting Siobhán's clench-fisted daydream.

"What?"

"Open that email I just sent you!"

"Listen, Jane," Siobhán sighed, "I haven't got time for-"

"Yes you do," said Jane, "open it."

Siobhán clicked on her inbox and looked for Jane's name amongst the long list of mails that were impossible to read, but could not be deleted. She found it and opened the most recent. There was no subject, Jane had been in a hurry, and only a link was included. Siobhán clicked on the link and-

"Oh god!" Siobhán whispered as the page opened, "Oh God. Oh no. Oh God."

It was a complete disaster. It was worse than tragic. Even as the little counter below the media file came to the end of its track, Siobhán could not take any relief or solace from its brief playing existence, not when the last frame was merely a still version of the horror that went before. How could this footage exist? The Gardaí had not mentioned any camera in the President's Study, where the Treoraí slept, but here was footage of the night in question. And there they were.

The three "suspects" were stabbing and cracking and ripping the body of the Treoraí apart, crawling all over the mess that was at the present time being reassembled or pieced together by the Lennon's funeral home in Harold's Cross, and continuing in their bloody business long after the last breath of the great man was wrestled from his grasp.

So it was true. They had done it. There was nothing anyone could do now to stop them being strung up. Siobhán tried

to think, had to think, but her mind kept turning back to the scene and replaying the file.

"How long has this been on the net?" she asked, while Jane searched her boss' and friend's face for signs of pain. There were none.

"We heard about it five minutes ago, and started looking," Jane hurried on before Siobhán could interrupt with the obvious questions. "We had to make sure it wasn't just a rumour, and as soon as we downloaded it and saw that it wasn't, I mailed it to you and came in."

"Ok," said Siobhán, "give me a minute to organise myself. But start drafting a release and a brief address for RTÉ and the radio fellas. I'll be out in five."

Jane closed the door, shaking her head at Siobhán's level-headed responses. *Tough bitch,* she thought.

Once the door closed, Siobhán replayed the media file three or four times before saving it, sending it to herself at home and taking down a number of points:

The three figures in the footage matched the descriptions of the three as seen on the exterior footage.

The room matched the décor of the President's study.

No weapons were brought to the scene of the crime. Instead, the murderers used things close at hand.

And, the body was so mangled and torn apart by the time the small film was taken, it was impossible to verify that it was Walter Thisgo's. Only if the viewer had known the great man would they recognise that in the shadows, the outline of Thisgo's hand could be seen, and upon the middle finger of the hand, the victim was wearing a ring. It was a special ring given to Walter by his grandfather when he was a child.

So Siobhán knew that the recording was authentic. And even whilst it broke her heart to view the scene, she had to realise that the perspective she'd automatically begun to work on: The 'it's a hoax!' angle would come to nothing.

This was what she called a transparency situation. The only thing they could do now was respond to public pressure and give out any information they had, leaving them free at least from subterfuge. The only problem was, they had no information.

***

Washed out...

Doyle stopped humming and tried to block out the song that had locked into his short-term memory. He needed to concentrate now. They had been standing right here on the night of the murder, the maybe murderers, hiding from the Gardaí net that caught nothing but a couple of heroin addicts, and a couple of drunken old men.

"I don't want what you want, I don't feel what you feel," the damn song was back, "See I live in a city, but I belong in field."

Managing to avoid the Gardaí roadblocks and the army aid, the murderers had taken refuge in the churchyard at St. Michan's, where Doyle had just parked.

"Inspector," said Phillips, the Garda doing crowd control, "you can't park your car in here. It could effect the evidence."

"Good work, Garda," said Doyle, "I'll be sure to take your advice in future." And he continued to the cordoned off area ahead.

It wasn't much of a crime scene. There were a few feet of trampled grass and the picked lock hanging of a set of large metal double-doors that opened down to the famous remains below. *What had they intended to do?* Doyle asked himself. Hide in the crypt? He'd only just arrived and it was looking like a dead end already. He looked back towards the gate. Anyone standing right here could be seen from the road.

As he descended the stairs with the assistance of the groundskeeper, or crypt-keeper, a name Doyle's subconscious had instantly allocated to the ropey looking corduroy when he/it was first presented to him, Doyle tried to picture the night of the murder.

Ok, they were being chased, probably even came up against a couple of roadblocks before ducking into the churchyard. They must have been in a panic, but had picked the lock quickly and without being seen by the Gardaí when they had done their first sweep, one half an hour after the death. So they had gone underground within half an hour, meaning it may have been planned after all.

At the foot of the stairs, Doyle tried to play the part of one of the culprits. Ok, so he was…Terry, and he had just come down here in the dark. They definitely didn't shine a light because it would have been seen. Terry came down into the crypt, covered in blood, panicking, the Garda right behind him. Why was he here?

To hide? No way, it was a trap of a place, and creepy too.

To clean up? Maybe they had hidden spare clothes here? It wasn't likely.

Or, and this was unlikely; as an escape route. There was something he remembered though, from too many years ago when he was forced down into to crypt by an educational aunt. Doyle had to think. What was here? Wolfe Tone's death mask, a couple of famous corpses? What else? He couldn't remember but there was definitely something else.

"Inspector," said the crypt-keeper, "your men are down there." The man was gesturing in the artificial light down the corridor, where Doyle could see Gardaí picking through the crime scene. When he joined them, he could see immediately that there was blood on the walls, the ultraviolet light showed its presence everywhere.

"Blood?" Doyle asked the nearest man, who looked up and nodded.

"Handprints everywhere, but very dry."

"All from the victim?" said Doyle, looking around at the old caskets, rotting and unspoiled stone alike.

"Yep, I'd say so," the man smiled, "nice place, eh?"

"If you're dead," said Doyle, watching the crime scene fellas do their job. They were going over every bit of ground, looking for anything that they could examine. It wasn't quite CSI Miami, but it was impressive enough. Doyle decided to wait for a few minutes and see what they turned up.

In his mind, Doyle was singing the same song and still picturing Terry, anxious from the chase through the streets, moving his hands along the wall, leaving traces of his victim's blood there to be found. Likely, it was unintentional, but it showed Doyle that not only Terry had been feeling the walls in the dark, there was blood everywhere.

"I don't want what you want, I don't,feel what you feel," Doyle sang under his breath, "I was born in a city, but I belo- Ah!"

That was it. He'd just remembered!

"Hold on a second there, lads," Doyle called, receiving the attention of all the technicians present. He moved through the group and reached the wall where the handprints had been marked and photographed.

"Clear out for a second, while I have a look, yes, yes. Don't worry about that now." Doyle refused a pair of gloves, allowing his bare fingers to search the wall, and in a few moments, he found the same circular holes as had been found one day before. "Here you," said Doyle to the nearest Techie, a woman, "put your finger in there and pull away from me."

"What?"

"The hole, see it?"

"Yeah," said the Techie, a little doubtful that she wasn't just making a fool of herself.

They pulled together. And, despite the obvious weight of the stone and the size of the handholds, the wall swung apart, grinding on powdered masonry. This substantiated Doyle's original summation. There was indeed a tunnel like the tour guides said; an escape route for priests in a lawless time when a back door was an essential utility for survival.

"Amazing," said Doyle, squinting into the black hole. He turned to the Techie, who was gawping into the tunnel. "See that? Do you know what that is?" She shook her head in wonder [no].

"That's an escape route."

~*~

In the churchyard, Garda Phillips could hear a noise coming from the interior of Inspector Doyle's car. Phillips was annoyed that Doyle had ignored his earlier request to move his car, and seriously thought about leaving the phone unanswered. Like, who did Doyle think he was? Phillips was trying to do his job, and Doyle had belittled him. But the phone had rung out three or four times already, so it was obviously important.

Phillips reached for the passenger door.

~*~

Below in the crypt, Doyle was taking his first steps into the mysterious tunnel. Well, not as much mysterious as it was disconcerting. The difference between standing and looking into the gloom, and actually stepping across the threshold was a mere matter of thousands of tons of water. And, if you knew the River Liffey, a fair few bikes, shopping trolleys, cars, and maybe the odd full-sized male folded into a suitcase. *No, actually,* thought Doyle, *that bloke was found in the Grand Canal, not the Liffey.* Doyle entertained the vision of his own autopsy, where it was discovered that he hadn't been drowned or crushed by the river, but actually run over by a rusting Ford fiesta as it was swept past him. Charming. Still, there probably wasn't much difference between standing in the crypt and going in there now, not with the entrance open, he'd have no chance of survival.

So Doyle ordered the Techies above ground and entered the tunnel. It was pretty easy going at first, and he'd even started to hum along to the familiar tune.

"I don't feel better when I'm fuckin' around, and I don't write better when I'm stuck in the ground, so don't-" which he resolved to ask the youngest of the Techies to identify as soon as he was finished having a look around.

Doyle walked about halfway under the river, imagine that, halfway under the Liffey? He was impressed at the masonry work that-

"Inspector Doyle?" a voice shouted from the direction of the crypt. Doyle winced. He was almost sure he'd heard the tunnel creak under the reverberations of a sure sharp sound.

"Inspector Doyle?" said the voice, louder this time, destroying the darkness and the peaceful repose of the ancient stones. "Your phone went off. It's a woman called Siobhán! She says it's an emergency!"

"Shhh," whispered Doyle, "you'll bring the feckin roof down on us!"

"What?" came the firm and voluble response, and Doyle was sure this time that he heard a grinding noise from above his head. The tunnel was getting moody.

"Shhh, for fuck's sake, chap," you're going to trash the place." Doyle moved back towards the entrance, but stopped when his foot struck something that wasn't a stone or part of the floor. He bent down to investigate it.

"Inspector Doyle!" shouted the Garda again. "Can you hear me?"

This caused a chain reaction in the stonework, and suddenly there arrived the sound of spray jetting from the walls. Doyle broke into a run.

"Get the hell out of here, boy, now!" he shouted as he neared the Garda. "The river's coming after us." And, although the Garda in question was obviously slow on the uptake, his survival instincts were top notch. Doyle reached the crypt and ran to the stairs, his tormentor leaving only a trail of dodgy aftershave in his wake.

There was rumble from behind him, and Doyle felt himself being lifted up the steps as the water acted like an airtight pump, thrusting forward in a single solid unit. When he cleared the crypt doors, Doyle scrambled forward, unable to gain his feet, being too interested in escape.

Behind him, a jet of water shot upwards from the crypt and it seemed that the entire churchyard would be flooded, but as the surge returned to the ground, so too did the water recede to its normal level, some metres below, and moving westward towards the sea.

Doyle watched the water leave, sitting on the sodden ground and feeling generally relieved and thankful.

"Jesus," he heard a voice behind him say, and turned to cast an eye upon the Garda who had so nearly killed him. The Garda was still sitting in the mud when Doyle approached, clutching the Inspector's mobile phone in one hand. Doyle reached down, and the Garda mistakenly thought that he was offering his hand to help him up. Doyle slapped the man's hand away.

"The phone," said Doyle, snatching the phone from the Garda and looking solemnly at it. On the screen was the word,

'Call' so he put the phone to his ear.

"Hello?"

"Hello?"

"Hi."

"What was all that noise?"

"The tunnel collapsed. Who's this?"

"It's Siobhán. I have some bad news. What tunnel?"

"Hi Siobhán! It doesn't matter. What's the bad news."

"There's footage all over the internet."

"Of the three kids?"

"Kind of. Footage of the actual murder."

"What?"

"There must have been a camera in the room."

"Are you sure it's-"

"Yeah, it's real. The… em victim is wearing Walter's watch."

"Oh."

"Well, what are we going to do?"

Doyle said nothing, instead, he just looked around the churchyard. This was going to make a haimes of everything.

"Inspector?" said Siobhán.

"You're right," said Doyle, "that's not good news."

"I know," said Siobhán, "and there is something else I haven't told you."

"You mean, Terry's mother?"

"What? How did you know about her?"

"It is standard practice to put a tail on any suspects."

"What, I'm a suspect!"

"Come on now, of course you are," said Doyle in a friendly manner but with more authority; a stern father. Siobhán paused.

"I suppose," She conceded, "when do you want to speak to her?"

"We've pulled her in already," said Doyle, "but I'll give you a call when we've spoken to her."

"Ok."

"Good. I'll talk to you then," said Doyle, who then added- "And Miss Sloane?"

"Yes?"

"No more secrets, ok." It was a statement.

"Yes, Inspector."

"Bye."

Doyle put his phone in his pocket and pursed his lips.

"So don't teach me lessons that I've, already learned," he hummed.

***

Siobhán put the phone down, staring at the frozen image on her computer screen.

***

If it was possible to have exactly the same thought as someone else, at least a mile away, Doyle and Siobhán wondered in unison.

"How could this mess have possibly gotten worse?"

But it had. And, they didn't know now that it was going to get even worse.

CHAPTER EIGHT
WHERE WERE YOU?

Carraigeden was a quiet sunny village on the slope of the mountain. There wasn't much there, but what there was had been there for a very long time. The post office slash bar slash grocers slash pretty much everything else had always had a Murphy in it. And when Terry and the Environmentalist walked into the shop and met her, it seemed to them that it had always been the same Murphy.

Mrs Murphy was a smiling old woman whose wrinkles were more like crevices, and her hair was balding in patches. The hair that Mrs Murphy had was jet black and her teeth, like her husband's, were nowhere to be found. She was the kind of woman that you warmed to almost immediately, and she always seemed to have a bandage on her ankle beneath her hardwearing tights, and in need of a change no doubt.

It was the smile that Terry and the Environmentalist first encountered when they entered Murphy's general store. The locals called it that, but there was no name on the door. Mrs Murphy looked up and gave her two new customers a smile devoid of ivory and ill humour. It soon became apparent, however, that Mrs Murphy was not in a happy mood at all, and that her smile was an involuntary indicator to her general good nature.

After their initial receipt into the shop, Mrs Doyle's attention was redirected to the radio, and it had a grave effect upon her.

"The suspects," stated the radio, "are still at large and the Gardaí urge anyone who has not seen the photographs to switch on their televisions or log onto www.gardai.ie to view the culprits and aid the Guards with their enquiries." And this caused a tumultuous reaction in the lady grocer's disposition. First, she tutted then sucked her toothless gums and then she raised her hand above her head in exasperation.

"Good Lord bless us and save to a man," she cried at the radio, which was missing some essential equipment itself, "Holy

God in heaven above. What sort of a world are we living in? Sure it was always headed that way, right?"

The Environmentalist looked startled to realise that she had turned and was addressing him.

"Isn't that right?" said Mrs Murphy.

"Eh-"

"Sure them young lads would walk over ya as soon as look at ya, if ye stopped em again in the street!"

"Eh-"

"That's right. Sure it's no wonder that the poor man is dead."

"Who's dead?" asked the Environmentalist.

"So we need milk and bread anyway," began Terry, turning to face the back of the shop where the fridges were waiting, humming in expectation. Terry had a couple of words for God himself, but more in the way of being thankful for the old woman not having a television on the counter.

"Do ya not know what's happened?" said Mrs Murphy.

"No," said the Environmentalist, "I've been up in the mountains for the last week."

"Oh Jesus, wait there now till I tell ya," exclaimed Mrs Murphy, seeing her opportunity to wag. "Sure wasn't the Treoraí himself killed beyond in Dublin."

"No!" the Environmentalist exclaimed.

"Yes!" answered Mrs Murphy. "Killed in his own bed no less. By a few school kids. Well, I say school kids, but they were going to that, you know, DTY place."

"The DTI?"

"That's it!" she cried, turning her attention back to the radio, "but I expect them to catch the bastards before long. Especially with the entire country after them, believe you me."

"That's shocking!" said the Environmentalist, shocked.

"Oh, it is to be sure," said Mrs Murphy, "a worser thing you couldn't imagine. Oh, but he was a lovely fella though, Walter." She clutched her heart and looked to the ceiling, and back to the Environmentalist.

"When did this happen?" asked the Environmentalist.

"Did you know that he was from around here?" asked Mrs Murphy, sucking her empty gums and ahumming in self-agreement. The Environmentalist tried again.

"When was this?"

"Two nights ago," Mrs Murphy responded, "his father's brother was married to one of the Hackett's from below in Avoca. And he was up here many a time on walks, traipsing up and down them hills, you'd think that they were never going home."

"Murdered?" said the Environmentalist, scratching his beard in shock while the radio sang out its bulletin song again.

"Breaking news in Treoraí's brutal murder-" the newscaster said while the music was fading out. "Police have made contact with the mother of one of the suspects. Dr Rebecca Giles, mother of Terry Giles, was interviewed this morning at Gardaí headquarters, and had this to say as she left, under police protection: 'I am heartbroken to realise that my son, Terry, was involved in this terrible event (sniff-pause). Oh Terry, please! Wherever you are, go to the police and turn yourself in. I love you, son and I promise that the Gardaí will listen to what happened the night before last. Please, Terry (sniff-pause). Please!'

"Sad words there from Dr Rebecca Giles, mother of one Terry Giles a suspect in the Treoraí's murder. In other news, the Irish world cup squad are preparing for their qualifier against Serbia and Montenegro tomorrow night in Croke Park-"

Terry stood at the back of the shop, looking through the dirty glass of the fridge but seeing nothing but the face of his mother looking back at him. In his mind, she spoke the words that came from the radio, and he could see the tears running down her face as she did so.

"Oh, Terry, please, please!" he heard her say again and again, until his own face was wet. It was time again for him to feel the pain of what he had done. The everlasting damnation he would surely receive from his actions. What a freaking nightmare.

Alright, he said to himself, *concentrate man.* What did they need? He opened the fridge and took out a litre of milk, butter, sausages, and bacon, closed the fridge again and began to wander around the little shop looking for everything else. He found a pan, bread, jam, and a ground sheet but no tent, some soap, toothpaste and one towel.

That was all he could think of, so it would have to do. Anyway, thinking about the mundane necessities he'd been charged with bringing back was allowing Terry to ignore the words he'd just heard. The words his mother had just spoken.

Terry gathered everything he'd collected and brought them to the counter, where he caught the Environmentalist staring agog into the Irish Times newspaper. Terry did not find this immediately suspicious, and it was only when the Environmentalist noticed his return and shut the paper in a crumpled hurry that the correct notion presented itself.

"Hey," Terry smiled, "something weird in the paper?"

"Oh nononononono," said the Environmentalist, flustered. "I mean, yes! Of course, the tragic death of the Treoraí. What a terrible shame." The man gave Terry a nervous smile. "Did you know," he added, "that he was from around here?"

Terry gave the Environmentalist a look [oh really] and then smiled back.

"Seriously?"

"Yes, the good Mrs Murphy here was just telling me."

"Wow, that is a strange coincidence."

"Ah yes," Mrs Murphy joined, "a fine fella he was too. Now young man-" Mrs Murphy sucked her gums and made a wet clomping noise with her tongue, as she named the items and used a pencil to total their value, whilst placing all but the groundsheet in a big thick plastic bag.

"Bread –Clump!- Jam –Clump!- Ground sheet –Clump!-" It was really quite disgusting. Terry winced from the sounds and was almost driven to cry out, 'Stop please, urgh!' when the woman finished.

"That'll be twenty-three euros please?"

"Eh?" said Terry, "Are you sure?" It seemed a little too cheap to him.

"Oh yeah," said Mrs Murphy, looking at her calculations, a little leaning tower of figures on the back of an envelope. "Why, are ya a bit short?"

It was at this point that the Environmentalist left the shop, and Terry became anxious to keep an eye on him. He looked back to the old shopkeeper and began to explain that his purchases were closer to fifty pounds than twenty.

"No, no, it's the opposite actually. I think it should be- Tell you what, don't worry about it. Here you go: Twenty and one, two three. Thanks very much."

Terry walked to the door only to hear her call him back.

"Wait, wait, young man," Mrs Murphy called. Terry turned back to her.

"Yeah?"

"Here," she said, "your friend left his paper. He already paid for it." Mrs Murphy held up the paper and Terry could see, as clear as spring air, his picture on the front page. He paused and looked at the old woman. She didn't react. Could it be that she hadn't made the connection, or hadn't seen the picture yet?

"Would you like a world cup pen?" she asked.

"What!" Terry didn't understand.

"I have a load of pens from the last world cup, you know, with different flags and all?" Mrs Murphy produced one of the pens and Terry stepped forward, mystified.

"Ok," he said and took the newspaper and pen, "thanks."

Terry left the shop and walked to the jeep. Inside, the Environmentalist sat at the wheel and nodded as he approached. There was something different about the Environmentalist, and not what Terry would have expected. He thought that the Environmentalist would have looked fearful or perhaps angry, but the man was looking through the windscreen at Terry, and looking annoyed. Not at all like a man who just found out that he was sharing his car with a murderer, but more like a man who had missed the bus and would have to wait twenty minutes.

This upset Terry, and he felt unable to understand the Environmentalist's expression. Why wasn't the man rushing to the police, why was he sitting calmly in his jeep, waiting pinch faced, seeming more concerned with losing his place in traffic or some such minor distress.

Terry felt robbed of his power: Hadn't he just killed a man? He felt outraged that fear, the one side effect from his nefarious position as a murderer had been denied him, and he felt like shouting in the Environmentalist's face. But Terry knew that doing that was the worst thing he could do, and he had to keep his nerve around such an odd character as this.

He opened the Jeep door, threw his bags onto the back seat and smiled at the Environmentalist.

"Hey man," said Terry, throwing the Irish Times onto the driver's lap, "you forgot your paper." The Environmentalist picked the paper up and handed it back to Terry, without rush or expression.

"You're all right," said the Environmentalist, starting the engine and pulling away from Murphy's shop. "I've already read it. It's your turn now."

***

The background crackled, but Doyle turned all his powers of observation to the choppy signal and it started to make sense.

"Finally, some bloody progress!" said Doyle into his phone as the crime desk relayed him the new information. "You're sure the group were definitely seen getting into a black Peugeot 406? Where? - I said where? Meade Street. What time? Did anyone check the time the alarm went off in the Exhibition- Good! So it was at the same time. Ok, what? Ok, give me a call if you get some footage of the licence plate? What? Sure, talk to ya."

Doyle put the phone back into his suit jacket and looked across the river from his vantage point. He was standing in the archway that was built over the road to join the two buildings of Christchurch Cathedral. From here, he could see St Michan's, where he had only narrowly avoided drowning in a tunnel, which he was now tracing with an imaginary line under the River Liffey. He followed it to the point where it hit the bank, to where it ended, below him, in the Duvlinia exhibition.

It was a great escape route, perfect almost. The type of planning that made it impossible for him to prove that the three students did not set up the entire getaway. But that was what he found himself doing, more and more, until his stomach ached. He wanted to prove them innocent, but why? He had no connection to them, no discernable options other than their definite guilt. Yet he didn't believe it, not even when he listed the pros and cons and came out with a guilty verdict. None of it convinced him, least of all, Terry's mother.

Dr Giles...

"Inspector?" Dr Rebecca Giles asked, as she was let into the interview room where Doyle had been waiting for twenty minutes.

"Yes, Mrs Giles, please have a seat." This wrinkled the woman and she responded.

"Miss Giles, actually," said Terry's mother, "or you can call me Dr Giles."

"Dr then," said Doyle, impressed by the woman's composure.

The reason he was using the interview room was to hurry things along. The room had the power to intimidate, which in turn made them nervous and prone to blurting out much needed information. Right then, with Dr Rebecca Giles sitting across from him with her smugness glowing forth, Doyle was feeling the urge to blab himself. Well, not exactly, but her confidence allowed him to make the observation.

"Now, I'm sure that you are aware of the enormity of this matter?" She nodded. "So I'll be quick and to the point."

"Good," said Dr Giles in an even voice, and without any hint that she'd considered the enormity at all.

"Emmm, anyway. I want to know everything you know about what your son has been up to in the past couple of weeks, even months, but the more recent the information, the easier it is to act on. I want to know where he's been hanging out? Who with. What's his schoolwork like at the moment? Everything he said to you in the last couple of weeks. And, I want to hear about your life too. Ok?

"On my side, I will attempt to fill you in on any developments with regard to your son, and act on the information you give me in as discreet a manner as possible."

Dr Giles looked across the table at Inspector Doyle. To the inspector, she seemed to be in no hurry to speak her part, but when it came, it came in a well-rehearsed bundle of words designed to answer his question implicitly.

"Right," said Dr Giles, "As you know, I'm a doctor; a

psychologist in fact. The reason that I mention it is simple. I should have noticed. [Sigh]

"I should have talked to him when he said he was losing sleep and having vivid daydreams. I should have listened. Oh it's all my fault, it's all my fault!" At this point, Dr Giles covered her eyes with a handkerchief and sobbed loudly. Doyle found that the sound of her sobbing made him angry. Strange that, when everything she was saying was so reasonable. But the inspector in him was shouting 'Liar' at her from the pit of his stomach.

"Please continue, Mrs Giles- I mean Dr Giles," said Doyle. Terry's mother sniffed and lowered the handkerchief.

"Certainly," she said in a meek tone. "As soon as he started hanging round with those other two, I knew that something was up. He wasn't eating; he wasn't talking to me, and worst of all, it seemed that his personality had changed completely. Naturally, in the beginning I assumed that it was merely a matter of a phase he was going though, but oh, my Terry!" She set off blubbing again and Doyle was forced to hold his Easter Island expression to hide the curl that was bound for his bottom lip, only stopping for a retort along its hurried way.

"If only," Dr Giles returned to the story, "if only I had thought at the time that even my own son, raised in a stable home could turn to drugs and crime, and on such a grand scale? Do you know what I think?"

"Go on," said Doyle, positive that he would find out immediately.

"I think that it was those other kids that turned my Terry from the path of normality, of Progression, like the one our great leader Walter was so determined to pave for us-"

Jesus, thought Doyle, *it's a party political broadcast.*

"And do you know what?" said Terry's mother, whispering and leaning forward.

I may as well, thought Doyle.

"Their parents were behind it."

She left it there for him and Doyle made a note on his pad by way of acknowledgement. He fussed about the wording and kept his attention from her. It was a way of keeping his calm. He dotted Is and Js and underlined a word he didn't remember writing before raising his head to face Dr Giles once more. Even then, in preference to speaking, Doyle raised an eyebrow, [go on] it said.

"Oh, I'm positive," she said, "and I have their names too, if you want them. Regressive bastards all!"

"What?" said Doyle, letting his mouth do the talking this time.

"I said, they're all Regress-"

"What?" Doyle raised his voice. "You come in here with your little speech and you don't tell me straight away that you know who the other two children are; exactly, who they are. Their parents' names and all?"

"But-"

"Ok, Mrs Giles,"

"It's Dr-"

"Fine. Just write down the names of the other students and their parents as quickly as you can so that I may use this information to solve a murder crime."

It was here that Doyle got worried. He'd expected her to be incensed, to be pissed off; even shout at him for being so rude to her, but this would not have worried him. Dr Giles' expression changed, and she became another being entirely.

"Excuse me, Inspector Doyle," she asked, forgetting the slur, "Would I be right in thinking that you do not feel you have found the perpetrators?"

"Dr Giles," said Inspector Doyle, avoiding her eyes and internally berating himself for misjudging the woman, "I am investigating a murder. And I must follow every lead until it is exhausted." He rose from the table and gestured to the paper in front of him. "Now, please, Dr Giles, the names?"

Behind them the door to the interview room was tapped politely, and opened enough to allow the head of a bespectacled Garda with ruddy cheeks and a thick country accent.

"Eh, Inspector."

"Yes?"

"You said if they had any more news on the car, to give you a shout."

That was good news. Doyle had forgotten about the car, but he didn't want Rebecca Giles to know anything more than she already did.

"Oh, it's fixed is it? Tell me-" said Doyle, walking to the door and leaving with the Garda, "did they say how much it was going to-"

Doyle shut the door.

"What?" said the Garda, mystified.

"Oh nothing. Tell me about the car."

"Oh right yeah. Anyway, we got the reg. from a traffic camera off Thomas Street and gave out a description around the country."

"And?"

"And it was seen at a petrol station in Roundwood on the night."

"What sort of station. Esso? Shell?"

"Statoil?"

The inspector winced, then asked, "Cameras?"

"One, beside the twenty-four-hour hatch. We've sent a couple of lads to get the tape."

"Grand," said Doyle, trying not to get his hopes up, which was useless, they were headed for the sun. "Keep me informed. I want to see that tape."

"Sir."

"Garda."

They gave each other a quick nod and Doyle was back in the interview room.

"Dr Giles," said Doyle.

"Inspector?" asked Rebecca Giles.

"I think we're finished here."

"Good," said Dr Giles, standing and making a fuss about her purse and its contents. Doyle looked at the pad and could see that she had jotted down names and other information on it.

"If I need any more help, I'll-"

"You give me a call," she said, and headed for the open door. Rebecca Giles turned in the doorway and smiled at Inspector Doyle. "Now," she said, "I have a statement to make."

After Dr Giles' departure, Doyle went straight to the sergeant on duty and enquired about the black Peugeot 406. The petrol station cameras had caught the license number, and the search was on. Much to his embarrassment, Doyle was also forced to ask the sergeant where he could find the lab, his retirement having moved a great many offices to different locations. He delivered the blue pills to the lab ten minutes later, and left express instructions to be contacted as soon as a conclusion could be reached as to their composition.

"We'll call you," said a blonde man with an easy smile, "as soon as we know anything."

And that was that. The blonde man handed Doyle a receipt for the bottle of pills and looked suggestively towards the door.

"I'll just go then," said Doyle, "you're probably busy."

"Extremely," said the blonde man, smiling, "see ya."

Not for the first time that day, Doyle was left with the impression that he had little control over his own investigation. Well, so what? He was a traditionally trained venerable Garda Inspector, trying to unearth those responsible for the assassination of the Treoraí na hEireann. What did he expect?

This wasn't just a matter of political manoeuvring. There were real signs of conspiracy here, and Doyle was going to have to come up with some new tricks if he was going to catch up with the ones who were predicting his moves. The only problem was; he had no clues as to whom the architects could be. Not one clue. Not even a sniff. He was sniff-less. Blind. Ignorant and in the dark. Unconscious, oblivious, naïve, and thick as two short planks.

As an experienced inspector, Doyle knew that his investigation was screwed.

But why then was Doyle smiling? Because he had something better than a clue or a lead, or even a vague admission.

Doyle had a feeling. Inspector Doyle had a feeling. And every time he got that feeling, the inspector caught his man.

Every
  Single
   Time.

The thought made Doyle smile as he headed for his office. Maybe they didn't know that simple fact, the ones who chose him to either fail or follow the well-lit path. Well, that was their tough shit, wasn't it?

CHAPTER NINE
LOVE AND BETRAYAL

A grey-blue hare stopped at the base of the abandoned church wall. He scuffed the ground with his front paws and twitched his nose at what he found. More dried wood, not very good. From inside the ruin came the sounds of heated conversation, which drove the hare deeper into the forest. There was nothing for him there either, just dried wood and leaves, but the hare knew this, and continued through quickly and without pause, until he reached the furrow that lay between the forest and the long grass. He wanted to continue on, his senses alerting him to the presence of new fresh green.

"Shhh," said Rachel from amongst the tall grass, "I think I hear someone." Peter reached up and parted the wall of green that waved between them and the wood, and peeked through. There on the dried-out ditch stood the hare, looking in their direction with a curious expression.

"It's a rabbit, look!" said Peter, and Rachel also raised her head to see.

"Oh yeah, but wait. That's a hare. See its long legs?"

"No," said Peter, his voice muffled, "but I can see its boobs." Rachel laughed out loud.

"Stop it. Get your hands off!" she cried through fits of laughter.

"I can't," said Peter his mouth full, "themmffummmff!"

"Ahaha stoppit," Rachel laughed as the autumn breeze parted the waving grass so they could be glimpsed for a moment from the hare's perspective at the edge of the wood.

For the last hour, Rachel and Peter had been rolling around and laughing; playing in the tall grass. They had soon discovered that when they sat down, the grass towered above them, and their first thought had been that of every new adoring couple, to take advantage of the situation.

There was something magical about lying in a circle of flattened grass and staring up into the sky. All at once, you are both ensconced in solitary comfort, and free in the open air and beneath nothing but the blue sky. To a child, it becomes an impenetrable castle that can serve as a venue for numerous games, but for the young couple, it served as a place for only one thing; it was a great place for a ride.

As they shed their clothes under the dying sun, the paleness of their skin began to turn a glowing orange. And when they looked at each other, the sight was attractive enough to extinguish any more doubts about their situation or location. They had each other and wanted nothing else. In such a moment, it was possible to view the world in throes of indifference to its many twists and uncertainties. With every movement, first slow and careful, then strong and impassioned, Peter and Rachel moved closer into each other, both physically and otherwise; until the two were brow-to-brow and heart-to-heart, and settled into a rhythm that built a force inside them. And then this force was released in one shuddering movement, the stress of the last months gone, and the nightmare of the last days dissipated for a time, as they held each other in the scarlet end to the evening.

They had each other, and that was enough for now.

***

Oscar was aware of what Rachel and Peter were doing. It didn't bother him greatly, apart from some healthy jealousy, he thought that it was a good thing that the two were able to find some comfort in their romance. If only Terry had something to distract him from the murder and their flight. But Terry was immersed in guilt, and his sanity was suffering greatly from the amount of inward reflection he was subjecting himself to.

Oscar knew all too well how such thoughts could feast on a man's fears, and trample his hopes. Sure, hadn't he done the same to himself, many times, since leaving his wife and child to walk the streets of Dublin? And he was doing it again now. He had thought that his self-exile as a tramp was all the better for everyone, himself, his son and his wife, but now it was obvious that he'd made a giant mistake, and placed his son in the hands of a political scheme so deranged that it made Oscar's head swim to even think about.

Oscar began to make a fire. It came easily to him and in a

few minutes, he had a small cooking flame ready for action. Of course, he was assuming Terry would come back with the provisions they needed; assuming he came back at all. Oscar tried not to think about Terry down in the town with the Environmentalist, being recognised by the police. Would the Gardaí already have pictures of them? Of course they would, from somewhere. They had murdered the Treoraí na hEireann for God's sake, the police would know by now, exactly who they were dealing with.

Oscar had to confess to himself a certain cowardly thought. Did the police know who he was, or even if he was involved? Maybe they didn't, and if so, could he sneak away and save himself? The answer was definitely yes, but Oscar knew that he wouldn't do something like that. He was as responsible as they, at least when it came to Rebecca's involvement.

"Bitch!" said Oscar, and rose from the fire, walking from the church to the road. Why had she gotten herself involved with this scheme? She worshipped Walter Thisgo more than anything, but was involved in his murder. How could that be?

For a long time, Oscar looked down into the valley towards the stream. What a beautiful place this was, especially now with the sun dropping to the horizon, and red-yellow streaks colouring its departure. It was the kind of place you would always come back to, even if only in your mind. In a time when Oscar and the three students were at their most vulnerable, it was a safe refuge by virtue of, not only the walls of the ruined church, but its simple beauty and solitude.

"What bad things could happen here?" said Oscar. And as he spoke, the Jeep belonging to the Environmentalist rose over a hump in the road and bore down on the hideaway. Behind it in the fading sunset, the dark clouds were forming and it seemed to Oscar that the large vehicle was towing them towards him. He dreaded its arrival and what that could mean to the respite they had found amongst the Wicklow hills.

"What bad things could happen here," he said again, and turned back towards the church to wait.

***

At dinner, the air was full of questions. After he'd returned, Terry brought the Environmentalist with him to the camp, something which set the others on high alert, and although Rachel and Peter didn't let it get to them too much, it was clear that their earlier mood was fading in the face of certain uncertainties.

What news from the town? Were they in the news? Did the Environmentalist know? Had Terry been spotted? Questions that they were afraid to ask of him in fear of giving the Environmentalist too many clues as to who they were. After all, would he be there and walking amongst them, helping with the cooking, and the baking of potatoes in coals if he did know? Surely not.

"Em eh," said the Environmentalist to Oscar, "you'd better get everyone ready to eat. These spuds are ready." The man was kneeling beside the fire where the potatoes lay amongst the coals, with a little knife that he periodically jabbed into them whilst muttering under his breath.

"Oh good," said Oscar. "Hey, dinner's ready, everyone."

Peter and Rachel were already nearby and came to take the sausages that were spitting fat into the flames, and Terry, who was slouched in the front seat of the black Peugeot where it was parked behind the church, was drawn into the church despite his growing distrust of all within.

"So," said the Environmentalist as the group ate in silence, "did yez here the news then? Did ya tell em, Ter?" As a unit, Peter, Rachel, and Oscar turned to Terry.

Don't worry, he thought, *it's nothing serious.*

"Oh yeah," said Terry, trying to look amazed, "you won't believed what's happened since we left Dublin?"

"What?" said Peter, catching on and playing along, "Wexford didn't win the All Ireland, did they?"

"That's next week," said Oscar.

"Oh yeah."

"Anyway," Terry continued, hoping all the way that the group would react correctly, "the Treoraí's been assassinated!"

"What!" Oscar, Peter, and Rachel said as one; they had been expecting the revelation.

"Seriously," said Terry, "it's in all the papers and on the news."

"A terrible thing, a terrible thing," said the Environmentalist, who stood from where he was eating and looked around him, taking in each face and visibly expressing his fervent disgust. As he spoke, actually snarled, the Environmentalist paced up and down and clasped his hands in anger.

"That man was a treasure to this country; a treasure. A visionary. A leader. A king! And to read that he was literally pulled apart by a group of disgusting, despicable thugs, thugs, well that has broken my simple heart. And it has left me furious, furious, furious. I'm appalled, appalled, so appalled."

As Terry listened, the Environmentalist's words clawed at his weakened chest and grasped his heart; crushing his pride in their tight fingered sentences. Dear God, what had they done? How many times was he going to feel like this before it went away? The words were stealing his soul away, and Terry felt like curling up in a ball and crying.

Peter, Rachel, and Oscar, however, reacted in a completely different manner. To them, the words were filled with blame and knowledge. The Environmentalist knew what had happened, and was castigating them for what they had done. He was the first, outside their group, who had looked them in the eye and shown them the anger that the entire country, even the world, was likely to assail them.

Peter, Rachel, and Oscar had one unified idea; the Environmentalist knew and he must not be allowed to tell. So they closed in on him, even as Terry was stepping away.

"What's the matter?" asked the Environmentalist, his face changing from the red hue of breathless utterance to the paleness of fear and doubt. He backed away from the advancing three, but was foiled by the ruined church wall.

"Please," he said, "don't yez look at me like that! I, I, I, I." The Environmentalist shook as he beheld the resolve and quiet determination of Rachel and Peter.

"Grab him," said Peter.

"Tie him up," said Rachel.

"Hold on, hold on," said the Environmentalist,

"Hold on to him," growled Peter, as he grabbed for the

Environmentalist's hands.

"Wait a second," said Oscar.

"Wait there now, please," cried their captive.

"Shut up!" screamed Rachel, and slapped the Environmentalist across the face.

"Ok, jaysus," said Oscar, stepping in to help them subdue the shocked ex-dinner guest, "just don't hurt him."

It was over in a couple of seconds. The Environmentalist was tied up, and placed in the back of his own jeep, and the group was safe once again from the threat of the outside world. They were safe and free.

Free to bicker.

"What the hell do you think you're doing?" Terry screamed at Peter, Oscar, and to a lesser extent, Rachel. He'd never had the stomach to shout at girls.

"Didn't you hear him?" said Peter, making no effort to hide his irritation and growing disinterest in Terry's opinion. "He knew! Tell me that he didn't know. Go on?"

Terry was at a loss for words. He could remember seeing the Environmentalist looking at the paper, in which their faces were prominent. It was unlikely that the man didn't know. But could they actually tie him up.

"But we can't just take him prisoner!" said Terry.

"What do you suggest we do," said Rachel, the excitement of the confrontation still giving her face a flustered hue.

"I don't know, but I know that this is wrong." Terry spoke strongly to her.

"Listen, Terry," said Peter, "for once in your fucking life. Why don't you just shut the fuck up and leave us alone?"

Terry lost his temper and swung for Peter, who narrowly avoided the blow. They grappled, and swiped at each other, trying to get the upper hand, but never quite managing it.

They fell to the ground and tussled there, rolling back and forth, even coming close to the fire at one point, until Oscar managed to pry them apart. The old tramp pulled Terry away from on top of Peter, who was presently beneath his enemy/friend, not because Terry was winning, but the rolling had brought them to that position.

"Let go of me!" Terry shouted, breathless, struggling from Oscar's weakening grip. "This isn't right, you know it isn't."

"What are we supposed to do?" Peter cried back, also panting, and being pushed back by Rachel.

"Listen, boy," said Oscar, holding out his hand in a gesture of pacification, "just relax, ok?"

"Shut up! Don't tell me to relax. Have you all lost it completely? Can't you see that we're losing it again?" Terry turned and walked from the ruin, into the trees and away.

Peter and Rachel turned to each other and knew that he was right. Was this behaviour a further result of the drugs they had been taking? After all, hadn't they been taking them for months, according to Oscar's theory?

Rachel looked into Peter's pale face and saw only sadness there. In such a short time, the two of them had realised that they were deeply in love, but what good was it? They would never be free. Even with brainwashing theories and displacement of blame, they had, all three, murdered a man, and in the most grotesque manner. There was no escaping the fact. They were going to hell. Rachel looked around at the forbidding darkness of the autumn evening, and remembered the beauty of the earlier sunset that she and Peter had shared.

Lies were those moments of peace, because beneath it all there had only been guilt and impending calamity. Maybe they were already in hell?

***

Terry sat back in the trees and watched Oscar, Peter, and Rachel as they went through the motions of cleaning and tidying after dinner and a fight, without speaking to each other of either.

Ha! It made him smile. So this was human nature keeping them afloat in yet another time of crisis. What a load a shit it was. There was only one thing left to do now.

Face up. That was it. It was time to face up to what they had done. Otherwise they would have to stay here, in this hellish half existence. Silencing any strangers that came by, and ultimately condemning them to a life they didn't deserve.

Terry waited in the trees until the lights had been extinguished, and even an hour beyond that. Then, when he was sure that the others were asleep, he crept down to the little side road where the Jeep and the Peugeot stood. He went to the boot of the Jeep and opened it as quietly as he could, and was shocked for a second to see that it was empty.

"Psst!"

Terry looked around. It sounded as though the noise had come from the front of the Jeep.

"Who's there?" he asked in a whisper, moving around to the front of the Jeep and peering into the darkness. Then the darkness of the night was shattered by the sharp intervention of the Jeep's headlights.

"Jesus," Terry exclaimed.

"Shhh!" said the voice. It was the Environmentalist. Terry moved to the passenger door of the jeep, rubbing his light assaulted eyes, and climbed aboard. The Environmentalist turned the headlights off again and they were left in darkness. For a while, Terry didn't turn towards the other man, he simply sat and stared into the night and breathed slowly.

"Terry?" said the Environmentalist.

"Yeah?" asked Terry, still facing forward into the blackness.

"Terry?" Terry turned slowly to face the man in the driving seat. "Are you ready?" asked the Environmentalist.

"Yes," said Terry, "I am ready."

The environmentalist took off the handbrake and allowed the Jeep to roll down the path and onto the road before turning on the engine and speeding quickly away.

From the trees, Oscar watched them drive away. What could be done now? The running had been only a temporary solution. Now, the three would have to return and prove their innocence. And what could he do to help, well, nothing from behind bars. He was going to have to get to her and get some proof.

Oscar crossed the road and climbed up on the ditch,

facing out into the fields of the valley that he couldn't see through the black of night. It was going to be a long walk. Before he left, Oscar spared a backward glance towards the abandoned church to where Rachel and Peter lay sleeping in each other's arms. *It was a pity,* he thought, *they would have been happy together, in any other circumstances.*

The night breeze moved his beard and raised his long grey hair from his shoulders, and Oscar felt invigorated. Even at night, this place was beautiful and bracing, and it gave him strength for the difficult journey ahead.

For the walk and what lay beyond it; what may be beyond him.

These were terrible times, and someone would pay for what had been done. Oscar hoped it was the right someone, because without that hope, the future seemed a dark and dangerous place.

CHAPTER TEN

THE COLD GREY MORNING

Doyle looked up into the early morning sky and traced the flight of the falcon as it swooped over the valley. The weather was changing and there was a redness on the horizon that did nothing to brighten the grey clouds above him.

Lowering his gaze, the inspector could just make out the outline of the Garda van and the other vehicle that lay in wait down around a bend in the road that swooped eastward, and gave the viewer the impression that the vehicles were parked in the middle of a field and far from the road.

They were still a bit too close for Doyle's liking, but he understood that his men, as well as the local Garda were very excited that they were on the verge of taking into custody the suspected murderers of the Treoraí na hEireann.

Overhead, the hawk screeched what he felt was a warning to his prey. "Run!" she screeched, "They're coming!"

"Paranoid." Doyle shook his head and turned to the line of trees, beyond which he expected to find the old church that the boy Terry had described to him only a half hour ago. No, not "the boy" Terry, no. The young man whom Doyle had just interviewed was no boy. Around his eyes had been the wrinkles of age, not brought about by time, but through concern, worry, and guilt. It was clear that he felt a lot of guilt, but when he spoke, he was certain and firm.

"Help us," Terry had asked, "we didn't know what was happening."

Doyle stepped across the road and walked westward until he came to a wide path into the forest, with recent tyre tracks on it. He walked up the path and came across the black Peugeot; the escape car. Before moving on, Doyle took the time to release the air from the front right tyre, an old trick to guarantee that should the suspects get away, they would have trouble exceeding thirty miles an hour. As he walked into the old church, Doyle noticed the layout of the campsite. There was a blanket on a pile of leaves in the back corner, and a fire pit, in which a fire had recently been lit, was dug into the middle with a pot of water boiling in the flames. To his left, below an old church window, a figure was huddled in sleep. One of them was out.

Doyle walked to the cooking gear that was piled nearby and found a small teapot, and after a brief rummage he found teabags to go with it. He scooped out a pot full of water and added the teabags, placing the teapot beside the fire. Bloody kids, didn't know how to make a cup of tea.

Behind him, there was a sharp intake of breath and Doyle turned to see Rachel halfway through a crumbled section of wall, with a role of toilet paper in her hand. She was frozen.

"Hi," said Doyle, "I've put on some tea for ya."

Rachel didn't move.

"You know," continued Doyle, "if you put the tea in with the water and let it draw, it ends up much stronger and tastier."

Rachel looked from Doyle to the fire, and then over to the huddled form sleeping below the window, then finally returning to Doyle. Her eyes began to fill with tears, and Doyle felt his heart moving for her predicament.

"Come on, Rachel," he said, "don't cry. Sit down now and have a cup of tea before we go."

Rachel stepped into the church and moved to the fire, the grey morning was cold and she reached her hands out above it to warm them. Doyle said nothing but found a cup and splashed some milk into it. He handed it to her and she took it easily enough whilst he took a towel and lifted the teapot. Doyle filled her cup and she murmured an automatic thanks.

"There you go," said Doyle, sitting down on a heap of stones with both of them in sight.

"What's going to happen to us?" said Rachel, her eyes growing larger as they filled with tears. "We didn't know-"

Rachel stopped speaking as Peter moved himself awake and sat up squinting.

"Wha?" he said. "What's-" It was then he noticed Doyle. "Who?"

"Doyle," said Doyle. "Peter, isn't it?"

Peter looked for a moment that he might deny it.

"Yeah," said Peter, "you the Guards?"

"Yeah," said Doyle, "I am."

Peter looked at Rachel and a palpable umbilical of sentiment passed between them. Then he turned back to Doyle, his eyes sharper and his sleep forgotten.

"What's going to happen to us?" said Peter. "We didn't-"

"I know," Doyle reassured them both. "Something is happening here," he gestured around, "everywhere. Something beyond you three."

"Terry!" said Rachel.

"Yes," said Doyle, "we have him."

"He turned us in?" asked Peter, but his tone strayed towards a statement. Doyle paused.

"Yes," said the inspector, "he did."

"He wanted it to end," said Rachel, nodding. Neither Peter nor Rachel looked annoyed.

"Are we going to be on TV?" said Rachel.

"Only if you want to be," said Doyle.

"Good," Peter and Rachel both agreed, "let's stay inside."

Doyle poured a cup of tea for Peter and all three sat in silence for another few minutes.

"Why are you being so nice?" asked Peter.

"I'm not," said Doyle. "The longer it takes me; the better I look."

"Really?" asked Rachel.

"I don't know," said Doyle, "but I'm dreading bringing you back."

"Why,"

"Because you killed the Treoraí."

"Yeah," said Peter.

"Yeah," said Rachel.

They drank their tea. And in the grey morning, the feeling was confused. There were large doses of responsibility to be soaked up, and side sauces to be taken that would be bitter indeed, and painful. But at this last breakfast in the Wicklow mountains, there was mostly relief. Peter and Rachel need not run. Where would they go? Being the same age and having passed through the same syllabus in school, both were familiar with and reminded of Julius Caesar.

"Oh conspiracy," Brutus had said, "shamest thou to show

thy dangerous brow when evils are most free? Oh then by day, how wilt thou find a cavern dark enough to hide thy monstrous visage?"

The truth was, never. They could never hide from their own guilt, and the old adage was true in its sentiment. So that even the sword can feel the guilt of the victim's passing, as the trap can weep for the freedom of its tortured prey.

Doyle led the couple out of the church and onto the road. Before he radioed to the paddy wagon, he allowed Peter and Rachel to share a kiss. It was an embrace that they may never share again. But as they lingered upon each other's lips, they heard the shriek of the Peregrine falcon as it dropped from the sky between the three and the Gardaí vehicles. Down into the long grass it plunged, and then rose, forcing the air beneath its mighty wings as it headed for the grey clouds again. And, grasped in its talons struggled a rabbit, no a hare, its long legs visible against the blank background of the worsening weather.

A capture, beyond all, the struggle of life attempted and then forfeit. Humbled by the height at which it would travel, the prey was alone and at the mercy of the falcon. Only fortune could save the creature now.

Only fortune. Only bravery. Only love.

PART ONE:

THE DEED

CHAPTER ONE:
ALONE & AVERAGE

*E*verything was dark and cold, and his emotions merged, running loneliness and expectant dread together into a grey seam.

Peter stepped out onto the landing amongst the shadows and the lines of the open Venetian blinds. The gaps let in the divided light of a streetlamp from the road outside, and shapes were visible in its glow. Yet there were no sounds.

Peter walked into his sister's room to have a look, hoping to see the reassuring mound of her little body outlined there under the duvet. The duvet cover was white, and it had a tiny picture upon it, repeated over and over again with stamped uniformity. Peter shied from it, not wanting to recognise it.

"Oni?" he said to nothing. There was no response, and he left the room.

He headed for his parents' room. It was not a place that would usually have brought him comfort, but in this horrid silence, with the fear creeping up behind him, and his sense of uneasiness already overloaded, Peter was willing even to undergo his father's usual scornful disappointment if it meant that he was not alone in the house. His parents' bedroom was also empty, and on the bedside locker was the statue of a man; the same man that was printed into the duvet cover in his sister's room. Peter ran from it.

Peter jumped down the stairs in two moves. One leap landed him on the half landing, and the other brought him into the open wooden sitting room that took over much of the bottom floor of the house. His bounding would usually cause a resonant boom from the wooden boards of the stairs and sitting room, but not tonight. Tonight, all was quilted and smothered by the overbearing silence of Peter's soul.

"Hello," he tried, and again, "hello?"

He ran to the phone and began to call. He rang his parents' mobiles, and he called the Gardaí. He even tried the speaking clock, but he shouldn't have bothered. There was no one there, nobody to listen to him, not another soul anywhere in the world. He knew it to be true. Nobody would ever witness him living, nor mark the time with him as he faded away. The world was empty, and there could be nothing more horrible. He turned on the light to try and chase away the colossal monster of isolation. It only made things worse.

With the room alight, Peter was able to see that a huge picture frame was hanging above the fireplace where the oversized mirror of his mother's choosing was supposed to be.

It was a painting of a man, the same man as before. The image he had been trying to avoid, but could evade no more.

The figure was on his knees in the darkness. His face pulled apart in a desperate howl. His eyes were drowning in tears of misery, as he screeched and pleaded out into the nothingness around him.

Abandoning all plans and lapsing into desperate panic, Peter began to run around the house, screaming and throwing open the doors.

"Hello! Where did everyone go?" he screamed, "Please come back." He burst out of the back door into the garden. Even Ralf was missing in the one moment when the hateful and vicious dog would have been a welcome sight. Peter barrelled through the side gate and ran out onto the street. There would usually be noises from the motorway, cars whizzing by, dogs howling at the moon or lack of it. There was nothing. Peter was alone.

As he ran up the road crying out for somebody, anybody, to show him that they existed, or at least, had once, Peter's steps became staggered and less determined.

It was pointless. Everything was useless now, so there was no point in running. He was merely moving from one point in the void to another. It was over.

"Where did you go!" he cried, his screams mixed with sobs as he slumped to the ground. All around him the lights began to blink out. *Good,* he thought, *at least I won't need to see how alone I have become.* The streetlights winked out and the stars ceased to shine, but Peter wasn't left in complete darkness.

There was one light left, and it came from inside of him. And as long as it still shone, he would always be able to see how alone he really was. The light of his soul exposed him. It was his last torture.

Peter began to scream and bawl again. He was on his knees in the darkness. His face pulled apart in a desperate howl. His eyes were drowning in tears of misery, as he screeched and pleaded out into the nothingness around him.

***

Radio…

"Well there you go, Henry…"

"I stand corrected, Johnny…"

"The sounds of the Velvet Underground played on the pan pipes…"

"It still amazes me, Johnny."

"Well not me, Henry, because nothing surprises Henry Hutchins when it comes to music. That's why I'm always right here, invading your morning, showing you…"

"His trousers!"

"Very funny, why don't you get us updated on the latest from the Administrators of our fair land, Johnny?"

"Not a problem, Henry, good morning everybody, and welcome back to Dublin's only Radio station; Radio 6, hope the musical choices of Henry Hutchins didn't wake you too abruptly this morning. I'm Johnny Deansworth, and it's eight o'clock. And, as always, it's time for the news and weather. In a bold move, the Progressive Party announced today its newest plans to reform the health system…"

Whack! Peter slammed on the snooze button and whimpered. *Every night,* he thought. *Every fuckin night!* Peter rolled out of bed and headed for the bathroom, annoyed at being roused. As a matter of fact, he was pretending but to whom, he didn't know. He was glad that it was morning, he knew that much. Every night since the summer began, and his parents had gone to the Progressive caucus, he'd been having that same dream. Night by night, it became clearer and clearer, until last night's most recent and vivid episode. Entering the bathroom, Peter stopped in front of the mirror and took in his appearance.

His eyes were puffed up, from where he'd been crying. The first time he could remember having the dream; it had left him only with a vaguely uneasy feeling. Now, he was crying in his sleep again. Things were getting out of hand. Could it be that he missed his parents so much, that his dream was some sort of longing for their return?

In the mirror, Peter's pale and red-eyed face grimaced a firm, no. That was definitely not it. He took his vitamin pills, picked up the comb, and tried to untangle his hair, but it told him not to bother, and stayed in its usual tangled mass of jet-black curls. Peter had the type of hair that you could only like if you didn't have it, and would surely hate if you did. Why are people always so sure that everyone else has it made?

Peter walked back into his bedroom and sat on the bare mattress of his bed, the sheet of which lay balled up on the floor. His thoughts returned once more to his restless sleep, but only briefly this time, as he struck a shallow vein. He was going back to University today, and he was going through the most childish of all emotional states; fear of acceptance.

Today, Peter was going back to the bustle of the Dublin Technological Institute (DTI), where the normality of routine and student life could only help his current condition.

He was cracking up.

"You are not cracking up," he said aloud. He just couldn't allow it to happen. He was having dreams and that was all. They were all consuming, and sometimes they overwhelmed him, but was that not the condition of the teenage mind? Even though he didn't have a sister, such dreams were the manifestation of his fear of acceptance, and the obvious logic of this statement made him feel especially normal. And the inclusion of a non-existent kin, was proof that it was all an average dream.

"Congratulations," he told himself, "you are discerningly average."

Peter prepared for his normal day in a manner that was both emotionless and determined. He ate his food without seeing it, packed his books automatically, and studied his timetable with little interest. On purpose, he avoided the truth of his dreams, and the hollow nature of his explanation.

The simple fact was that this supposed reality was

beginning to feel less substantial than the dream. His life was becoming dreamlike. So the real question was: Which one was real?

He didn't want to know, just in case it was the other.

CHAPTER TWO:
TEACHING THE MIND

Back and forth, the old man paced and muttered. At odd times, he would stop and just mutter, and sometimes he would stop muttering and just pace. But rarely did a moment pass that he did not do one or the other.

Pacing could mean a lot of different things, and as such, it did little to describe the mind of the man, but the muttering when heard was enough to do the job of both. It prescribed to him a certain haunted personality, in which only a professional with a degree likely preceded by a Psy- should take an interest.

"Then he speaks," muttered the old man, paused for now in his pacing, "when he speaks, I speak what he speaks. Then, and only then, he speaks again." The man held up his hands as if awaiting instructions. Then he mumbled on, his voice rising in volume and echo as he proceeded.

"Then he speaks an action and I do the action. If he says 'shout', then I shout aloud what he speaks. If he says 'strike', then I strike where he says I should strike." The old man followed this last sentence with a downward stroke, a practiced motion that was fast and controlled. All of this was followed by the first real absence of sound or movement, and five long audible breaths.

One- two- five seconds passed and the old man again began to pace and mutter in much the same way as before.

"Then he speaks," says the old man, "when he speaks, I speak what he speaks." He continued in that manner.

He continued in that manner.

He continued in that manner.

***

Half a mile away, another student from the DTI was also preparing for his first day back. And, even with the reoccurrence of Peter's horrific nightmare taken into account, it is a fact that this young man, Terry Giles, was losing his mind.

The pills weren't working, and Terry was a wreck. He

was sitting at his kitchen table with a rolled up cigarette in his mouth, staring at the wall. Terry hadn't slept at all, well maybe for about ten minutes early the night before. But as soon as he'd seen *her* coming, he'd gotten out of that dream sharpish. Terry had devised a method to rouse himself from sleep; he called it scream waking. As soon as his dreams began to head in the wrong direction, more often now than not, he would begin to scream and roar. Then he would yell, holler and bellow in his dream, until the volume of his night terrors woke his physical self. It had been working pretty well so far, but it was a solution only to a side effect, and did nothing to either identify or remedy his root problem. Terry Giles was losing his bananas.

Terry stared into his coffee mug. No, no bananas in there. The mug was empty, and much-ringed; at least six of which were darker and stood out from the others. He recognised these as the points during the night where he had zonked out, but not slept.

During these periods, thankfully, Terry hadn't dreamt. It was closer to zombiism than anything else. Anyone that has experienced a continued period of insomnia will know how it feels, and those who haven't shouldn't worry that they're missing something grand or terrific. Terry once surmised, in a thoughtful mood, that if the brain was deprived of sleep for long enough, the grey matter moulded itself into the shape of a surly school caretaker, climbed out of the head through the ear, the left one, and went off somewhere for a smoke break, and maybe a cup of tea.

The moral to this seeming to be, "If you've not got any work for me to do, mate, I'll be over at Mary's. Give us a shout when you need me." The thoughts are frozen, like an old computer pretending to think when it has really just crashed indefinitely. And, according to the rings on Terry's coffee mug, this had happened at least six times during the student's long wait for the saviour of dawn.

Terry found it amazing to experience what had been going on in his mind when the caretaker finally came back from his long lunch. During once such zombiefied phase, Terry had actually managed to climb into one of the kitchen cupboards, which was disturbing enough to the recently roused Terry, sitting high above the sink, looking out into the kitchen from the cupboard. But when he found that he had thoughtfully emptied the cupboards for that specific purpose and grouped the contents on the kitchen table in colour order? Well, Terry had realised then how seriously mad he was becoming. The real prize was that though these actions were bizarre enough, the fact that he could remember doing them but not why was far more disturbing.

It was only a blessing to Terry that his mother had chosen to spend her summer in France, and wasn't here to witness his disturbance. She were somewhere near Nantes, where an unfortunate relative, Uncle Joshua, had recently died after finally refurbishing what he had meant to be his retirement home.

Terry always found the humour in it. Poor Uncle Joshua, working himself to death in order to prepare a place that he could live out his remaining years.

"I'm going to die here," Uncle Joshua had stated to Terry, looking proudly out over his land, "remember that." Terry wondered if his uncle could ever have imagined that this statement would be fulfilled so immediately, or whether he would have liked the French farm as much had he known that it would soon become the site of his final clutch-and-fall.

Terry looked at his watch. This had become a most worthwhile habit; to watch the second hand; as it showed him that yes, time was indeed passing, no matter how hard to believe that everyday fact had become. This time though, he focused on the hour and minute hands and actually read the time. It was still too early to be off.

"Damn it!"

Terry slumped onto the table. The DTI was only five minutes away from his house, and it was a quarter past eight; a saunter would get him there for twenty-five past.

God, he was tired, the dream was going to kill him, he was sure of it.

Last night had been the worst one yet, and even right then as he sat wide-awake in his kitchen, relighting a roly, his ten-minute sleep at least eleven hours behind him, the image of *her* was crystal in his mind. He could see her floating towards him, with her arms outstretched, drawing him into her, welcoming him. And he'd nearly gone to her too. Even in those few rare minutes of sleep, it was obvious that he could not resist her for much longer. It wouldn't be long before he accepted that embrace.

He had to sleep sometime.

With his parents away, and most of his friends either gone down the country, or in the States for summer, Terry had done nothing but spend his time in various attempts to pass it. The most successful of these attempts was his taking up smoking again after two years without a pang.

The loneliness and the waiting were wearing him out, and destroying his nerves. His mind was cracking open. Soon, it would bare all, and his fantasies would be in full control. He felt that his senses were beginning to play tricks on him; Terry hoped that was all they were, tricks. It would be a comfort to discover that all of this was a phase, which would end some day soon. With a drunken night of snoring maybe, or a stoned comatose, both of which he'd tried. The former making him sick and helpless, and the latter leaving him so paranoid that he'd contemplated wearing a long silk tie to ward off his nightmares. The details of how this was supposed to help him seemed sketchy to the now-sober Terry, although it was definitely something to do with the idea that witches and demons were afraid of salesmen. Again, he was unsure how this could possibly be the case.

Terry took a breath, and built himself upwards into a standing position. He would take the long way to the DTI; the very long way. Second year engineering was a welcome prospect when compared to the weirdness of his summer. It would be best to go now and forget his rut for a while.

"Now that's sad," Terry said aloud, commenting on his eagerness to return to university. He picked up his bag, packed since last Tuesday, and left the house.

The door slammed behind him, and his relief to be outside set him strutting off down the street towards the river.

Upstairs in the Giles house, Terry's room was a tip; a mass of clothes and rubbish, with paper in all its different forms covering every near horizontal surface. There was the rolled-up, ripped apart, and the scrapped type, as well as the laid-out-and-kept variety. If the images on both were compared, it would seem that the contents had little effect on the treatment of each drawing.

There were pictures of cloisters and letters of script. Many of the sheets were notes written to no one, but signed, Terry Giles. The most common image Terry had sketched on the papers was the form of a female; a dark figure wearing clothes of a religion, but unrecognisable. She was a nun of sorts, or a priest maybe, it was obvious that Terry didn't know.

Again and again, Terry had attempted to draw her face correctly, but each time he'd either failed to illustrate more than a line or two, or completed an unsatisfactory whole; a hint of a nose- dismissed; the beginning of a mouth - disregarded. Or the woman's face had been scribbled out so entirely that he had torn the paper in his hurry to destroy it.

Every night for the last two months, Terry had dreamt of this woman. She was always walking towards him; her face blurred, and her footsteps inaudible as she glided ever nearer. With each dream, she slid closer to Terry, and recently he'd noticed that she had something in her hands, but he'd always been too terrified to look closer and find out what.

There was no doubt in Terry Giles' mind that soon he would be powerless to escape her grasp. Once, maybe twice more he could survive his nightmare, but in a day or two, she would be upon him for sure. And when she caught him; what would happen then?

When *she* reached out her cold white hands and touched him, what would happen then?

TEXT MESSAGE…

> Exercise one.
> Observe and
> only intervene
> when necessary.

CHAPTER THREE
PUT DOWN ON WATER

At the edge of the fountain in the centre of the DTI courtyard sat Peter Price. He was writing in his diary. Peter thought that once he had a pen in his hand, and a scrap of paper to write on, he could take on any confusing incident or emotion, break it down, and explain what it meant to him, and why he felt the way he did.

Yet Peter wasn't stupid. He knew what his writing really did for him. It alienated him. And rather than lead him to recognise that confusion was a frame of mind and an emotion shared by everyone his age, Peter chose to ignore this truth. He was more comfortable with life that way. It was easier for him to do nothing that would force him to make a connection with another person, simpler than trying and looking like a fool.

Under September 28th – Thursday, Peter wrote:

I'm finding it increasingly difficult to concentrate these days. The dream is beginning to have an effect on my daily life. I'm afraid of talking to anyone, and I get angry when I look at the news on the TV. Why? It never bothered me before? Why is this happening to me? What can I do to stop it? Are all these question marks in a row really necessary?

Peter laughed as he wrote this. Well, maybe he did have a sense of humour, or it could be that he was just one of those lunatics who laugh at things that aren't there? The dreams were becoming realities of the night, but he felt as though he had a purpose.

At least he was back in University for the moment. He could sit there and write. He liked it by the fountain. The DTI had such a beautiful campus, and he was there, right in the middle, where it could be seen at its best. He took a deep breath and froze; he could feel her watching him again.

Peter stopped writing, but resisted the urge to look up. Rachel was watching him from the gate; he knew that she was there. One day last year, the girl had actually walked up to him while he was writing, but her shyness had got the better of her and she had, like always, retreated back to her loud-mouthed friend, blushing and being taunted in retreat.

Peter wished that she would speak to him some day, because he knew that he could never talk to other people like that. He could probably write her a note, but knew that would be useless, and a bit sad.

He just wasn't a part of her world, and he would never be able to communicate with her at the correct colloquial level that would be required for such an encounter to succeed. And with such an unwieldy vocabulary, it was obvious that his book-loving nature would bog down any actual attempt to speak.

He was a coward. Mr Spineless had come to town for the good weather, and was staying for the company.

Through his eyelashes, Peter watched Rachel Impey gaze at him through an embarrassed flush, and he pretended to resume writing in his book. He couldn't imagine what she was thinking as she watched him. Could she actually be attracted to his pallor? Maybe she though he was mysterious? It was a possibility, seeing as Peter found himself mostly inexplicable these days too.

"Come on, will ya?" called Rachel's best friend, Marie, from the steps of the Arts Building, "Either go over there and ask him to go out with ya, or come on inside!" Rachel turned red and sprinted after Marie, letting her long black hair fall over her face as she did, trying to hide her shame.

"Shut up, you cow," she said to Marie, who was, as always, enjoying the tormented embarrassment that her loudness caused Rachel. They finished climbing the steps and entered the building, with only Marie bold enough to look back and catch Peter's eye.

Peter, who had risked a glance when he thought it safe, was treated to a wide smile from the brazen Marie, and he quickly looked back down to his diary with a grin. Marie laughed at him and gave him a little wave.

"Bye, little guinea pig," she said as she turned away into the Arts building.

Peter's smile became half and sadly drawn. He found this

last comment of Marie's difficult to tolerate. Lately, he had begun to feel sub-human and it was as if the girl knew what he was going through, his hangover from life.

How could it be? It had been a month since he'd had a pint, let alone gotten pissed, or taken drugs, or anything. Yet he was feeling queasy even now in the morning, when a sober body should be feeling fresher than at any other time.

Peter looked down into the pond below the fountain. There were waves of emotion that gradually took him over, and spasms of blackness, like little tastes of his dream presenting themselves in the daylight, confounding him with their continued existence.

Below him in the fountain, autumn leaves were spinning, and Peter felt that his head was also rotating with sickening consistency; directionless and completely under the power of the water's current.

"You're asleep," he told the leaves, his eyes closing, "I wish I was like you and couldn't see the flow of the water."

With that, Peter Price lost consciousness and slumped into the fountain pool. It happened slowly, and without grace, until his head entered and became immersed in the water. He began to drown.

***

By then, Terry was ten minutes late. How the hell had he managed to be late? Some people are just late all the time, no matter how hard they try. There were six ways to the university from his house, and picking the longest should have only added a few minutes to his journey time. Terry blamed his ability to zonk-out and stare into space at nothing. Out beyond the faces, he could gaze mindlessly, over their heads into the pixels at the edges of the painting. He could gawk at nothing until the colours of light changed into evening reds too quickly. Until they became so dark, they formed a hand on his shoulder, or a disembodied head shaking its disappointment to him, telling him that night was fast returning and the dreams of a few moments before were about to spread from memory to becoming the horrible present.

"Bhla!" There it was again, another... how long? Five minutes gone! Now Terry was fifteen minutes late. Aw, what was the point in going into that first lecture as it neared its halfway point? Boredom, that's what. A few minutes in his "Reintroduction to Modern Engineering" lecture were sure to feel like forever. That was exactly what Terry wanted, an eternity between now and later; a stay of delusion before the inevitable struggle against sleep.

Another few minutes wasted.

As Terry fussed impotently on the steps, trying to decide whether he should go and learn something today, he felt a peculiar strain on his mind. As peculiar strains did not often populate any part of Terry's person, he certainly noticed the feeling, and it caused him to turn around and face the source of it.

It wasn't an, "Oven left on at home" feeling, but more like a, "Hairdryer left in the bath" sort of thing. And, unlike shivers and creeping nags, the feeling moved around with him, until he felt it in the muscles of his face. It was like being drowned in icy water, and having a radiant light shone in gloom-accustomed eyes at the same time. The world around him was a sharp trail of blurred colour that tunnelled towards the fountain in front of the Arts building, where a form was slumped and drowning.

"Shit!" he shouted, and ran down the main steps and sprinted to the aid of the black-clad boy with his head in the shallow water. In Terry's mind, the thoughts raced around and came to possible conclusions. Was the guy drinking from the fountain? No. Was it some sort of prank? Nah.

Terry reached the boy's side and leaned down to grab his shoulders. Was it on purpose? Maybe? Terry shook his head. Addled though he may be, crazy he certainly was becoming, but there was no way that he was gong to let some guy die in right front of him, suicide or no. Ooh, there was that word. The one he'd been avoiding.

"Ah fuck!" Terry shook himself out, grabbed a hold of

Peter's collar, and pulled the drowning boy out and away from the water. "Yes!" Terry cried, "There you go, ok, ok..." Terry watched Peter lie unmoving for almost too long before he reacted again. "Come on." He urged the cold body at his feet, "Dude, I'm not kissing you."

Terry looked around then. *Damn it,* he thought, *I could punch him in the chest.*

So he got down on his knees, strained hard and thumped heavily on the victim's chest.

"Come on," thump, "come on," thump, the blows came down. Until Terry felt a devil of enjoyment sitting on his shoulder, and he stopped.

Everything went quiet again, and Terry stared at Peter's face, while the other looked blankly at the sky, his eyes growing darker as his body began to shut down.

"Ok," Terry told the body, "That's alright." He leaned closer to Peter's cold face, rubbed the dead boy's cheek with his hand, and pictured her, the woman from his dreams. Though Terry had no idea where she had come from, he was positive of where she waited, maybe for everyone. "You shouldn't die," he said, "for whatever reason." He pressed his lips to blue ones and blew hard into his liquid-filled lungs.

It worked, but not like Terry had hoped.

In the time it had taken for Terry to reach his side, Peter's body had done a wonderfully thorough job of sucking in as much water as it could in order to kill the young man as quickly as possible. It was ever-efficient biology, taking no sides, just working in the way that it works.

The water began to kill Peter. It starved the lungs of oxygen until the heart's supply was stifled, and his blood began to darken. Then the black blood began to slowly invade Peter's body, and headed for his brain. During all of this, Peter's heart was only kept moving by the thumping it received when Terry had first attempted to revive him.

Once Terry began to force bursts of air into Peter's waterlogged lungs, there began an instant reaction.

Phumpfh!

Out the water shot in a geyser muscle spasm, straight out of Peter, and into Terry's open mouth.

Terry fell on to his back and barked loudly, spitting the second-hand water from his mouth. The two of them coughed in unison, it echoed round the yard. It was possible that someone was watching them from a window, a bored student, a pensive lecturer, or a tramp across the road, peering through the gates; but no one came to help them up, so it was difficult to tell.

Terry was the first to recover, and he helped the recently revived Peter to his feet, still reeling and gasping for air. Though his senses had been shocked, as much by his energetic revival as his drowning, Peter's head was still a blur of dead brain cells and thickened veins. Yet the rush he felt at being alive was akin to being out of it at four in the morning, when the only possible way was down.

"Oh god," he groaned, "haw, what the..." Peter staggered in a circle around Terry, shaking his head.

"Hey! Hey!" Terry straightened Peter up and shook him. "You alright?" Peter steadied some, but not much.

"Yeah, yeah, thanks. Jesus, what the hell happened?"

"You don't know?" Terry asked, and Peter looked at him, puzzled.

"No, I was just sitting there and - I don't know really. I fainted or something?" Peter looked to Terry for help.

"You were just lying in the pool when I came along."

"Yeah?"

"Yep," Terry assured him, "You look cold, are ya cold?" Peter nodded, shivering and Terry turned him around and faced him towards the canteen. Peter's rescuer was eager to be away from the site of his recent boy-on-boy action.

"Let's go get a coffee," Terry said, leading the way across the autumn courtyard; Peter shook his head as he followed.

"I don't drink coffee," he said and Terry laughed.

"You're so fuckin awkward, aren't ya? First you're all – 'I'm dying in the fountain' and then you spit water all over me. And now!" Terry slapped Peter on the back as he spoke. "Now you don't even drink coffee. Well, you're in luck, because that's all I do. So you can watch me drink, and maybe you can get some warm milk or something?"

Peter laughed out loud at this.

"Actually, I hate milk too," he said, and Terry joined in his laughter.

"Fuckin awkward," Terry repeated as the two of them headed for the canteen. It was typical, Terry thought, that when he was at his lowest, something crazy like this could happen and he could meet someone that was already, without any need for further qualification, at least as fucked up as he was. Life was beautiful all right.

***

Peter was at least as surprised, if not a little more worried about the outcome of his morning. So, he was bad enough now to collapse and nearly drown himself, like an old man, or a State-Care projectee? But that wasn't what really worried him, though. As soon as he saw Terry's face, he knew. There was something that connected them beyond this incident, but the reason was much too far away from him to see yet, and it frightened Peter to realise the building force of destiny.

Stop looking so deeply into everything, he told himself, and joined Terry on his way to the canteen.

Across the road, there was someone watching; someone who'd been watching for a while.

CHAPTER FOUR
RECOGNITION

It was much colder today; that was for sure. Not as cold as this day last year, Oscar felt, but definitely far colder than yesterday. The winter was ready to set into the grey stone of Dublin, and the steps below him would soon be impossible to warm, irrespective of how much prolonged arse cheek contact they were subjected to. Soon, it would be time to take refuge in the Gaps beneath the city, and sleep through the worst part of the winter.

Ah well, at least he had his health, the wet part of it anyway, the part that was intermittently friendly with the fresh whiskey bottle that was in his coat pocket. Yes, he had that, and a couple of quid that he'd scabbed off a student that morning outside the university, where Oscar often went to watch.

Students; god love them. Beautiful and bright, the robots of tomorrow, marching into the shredder with their eyes wide open, and their hopes higher than that junky cougher fella that hung around on Pearse Street in the mornings. Oscar went there frequently too, to watch the robots lead each other off the DART, and file slowly towards work.

Every day with their brains dying and flattening out, the robots went to work, all of them trying to better each other at being more the same than anyone else. The new government, of course, claimed that all of that was about to change.

"We are reawakening the Ireland that died over a thousand years ago," they cheered on television. But Oscar was sceptical about anything that came out of a mouth with a suit attached.

Yet he still wore his own, as punishment, beneath his now tattered Cromby. Like a fully uniformed Nazi Soldier, walking through the town in plain view, inviting hatred and revulsion upon his person; Oscar traipsed through Dublin with his head held high. Yes, he too had been a robot, years ago now. Until one day. D-day.

Marching with the others, Oscar had been walking beside the Liffey towards the forecourts, on his way to a series of meetings outside the courtrooms. It was there that he and the other solicitors scurried back and forth with counter offers, and promises of steadfast representation. But on that day fifteen years ago, something had happened that made Oscar stop dead in the street. In fact, he stopped so suddenly that a sleepy fellow with a paddy-cap on ran straight into his broad back and cursed him for a bastard.

"What are you doing?" the man had cried, all angry and repressed. But Oscar had only been able to look at the man's face, grey it had become to him, and he shook his head.

"I don't know," he told the man with the grey face, "do you?"

"I- I-," the man had been confused and, failing to find the words, continued on, shaking his head in a sad fashion; unsure of his purpose.

At that moment, Oscar was sure; sure that something had happened to fix him, sure him of suppression right then and there. He had seen the city lit dimly with grey dead bodies, walking and talking, but too faint to be real; shadows of which he was one, being vague and timely.

Now, it was the young ones he noticed, as he roamed the streets. They had brightness and power in them. Such potential. Maybe this new government was going to rekindle the county's once great history, and give these young ones a chance to be free?

Oscar shivered. Yes, it would be time to hit the Gaps soon. To burrow down into the tunnels under the city for the winter, and to drink, and sleep in the darkness; that was all he had in his near future.

But not just yet, he felt. Something was happening with the boy. He had to watch the boy.

Oscar had a family from before. Oh yes, a wife and a child. He missed the child and was painfully aware that he had abandoned him. Did he miss his wife, the doctor? Well, they had had their good times, which were hard to remember now amongst the disagreements. It was amazing how many little details he could recall from their arguments, of actual examples used, and points made. It was astonishing really, but it was pointless to dwell on it now that he'd left them high and dry.

Oscar was sure that they would understand if they had seen, through his eyes, the grey bodies that clogged the city streets. If they looked out from within him and took in the enormity and uselessness of it all, they would have to comprehend, wouldn't they?

Especially when he had looked down at his own hands and seen the dreaded lack of colour there too. A grey man like the rest he had become, with nothing to live for, and no hope of a real future.

That was the day Oscar had stopped walking to work, or to anywhere in fact. From then on, he had looked around with new eyes at the world he had been tricked into, that he'd been trying so hard to fit into. That was the day he sat down on the steps of the nearest building and began to wait, to watch, and to look.

What was he looking for? Well, if he knew that, then he would have seen it by now. What did he know? Whatever it was, it was the students that held the key. The young were always the ones that make the big changes. There was one that he had been watching in particular. One future robot that Oscar felt drawn to, who passed by him every day, and never took any notice or looked sideways at an old tramp.

This youth was different from the rest, but lately, even he had been acting in an unusual manner.

Across the world, a jaded example, the chaos butterfly was lying dead in a pool of wax. Things weren't being caused by tiny wings any more. This was a time for human endeavour, and their actions were going to cause enough harm by themselves. The thought made Oscar uneasy, because he felt that it was true, that everything was on the verge, and all that he could do was watch.

***

Café Hola...

In the university canteen, Peter was trying coffee. Now, it wasn't as though he hadn't tried it before. *Hasn't everybody?* he asked himself. Even people like Peter, with severe allergic reactions to caffeine, have been tempted into, nay, forced into trying it. For some reason, coffee was cool, Peter didn't know why; it just was. There was never a way around it.

Peter smelled the brew on the table before him and thought about drugs. Among the diminishing number of pleasures left to the average human that was detrimental to the common health, coffee was the last to retain its coolness. Some things, of course, would never be cool.

Heroin wasn't cool, and Peter didn't care what anyone said about Iggy Pop or Lou Reed. It was just too dirty and unseemly. Hash/Marijuana, however, was cool, whether some people wanted to admit it or not; it was really cool.

These were illegal, or what Peter called NO drugs, of which there are more than two, but to list them all and to NO or YES them all would have been pointless, although Peter was prone to pointless listing.

For example: Legal, or YES drugs, like sugar, nicotine, alcohol, Prozac, diet pills (speed) and orange juice had all lost their coolness factor, or so Peter felt, although alcohol still managed to remain both cool and massively uncool at the same time. It depended on the time of day, in his book.

The big 'N' in cigarettes had been the coolest of the YES drugs until recently, but it was growing unpopular, now that people wanted to live longer and be happier; bless them.

So what could you do, Peter wondered. All the YES drugs were bad for you and all the NO drugs, some of which weren't so bad for you, were - well, illegal-ish. So what was left?

Coffee? Probably not, but it would have to do until the government found a way to put ecstasy into alcohol pops. So, regardless of its inherent dangers, Peter was stuck with it always being shoved in his face, and offered ad nauseam.

So there he was, again, trimethylxanthine intolerant with a mug of coffee in his hand, and he was actually considering having a sip. In normal terms, Peter was a bit of a freak, because unlike nearly everybody else in the whole world, he could not do caffeine. Even a sip could stop his heart. It was amazing really, but Peter felt rather, that it was just plain annoying.

"Come on, man, drink up," said Terry, "it'll get cold!"

Peter stared into his mug and considered again. *Don't be an idiot,* he told himself.

"I prefer it cold," he told Terry, who had gone back to staring at the girl behind the counter.

"Yep," said Terry, "They make great coffee here." He gave the blonde-haired girl a cheeky smile and, to Peter's surprise, she smiled back openly.

"So," Peter began, "What are you stu-"

"Studying? Ooh, bad question, you don't get out a lot, do ya? It's all right. See that girl?" Peter didn't need to guess who Terry was talking about.

"Yeah."

"Well," Terry whispered, "We used to go out last year." Terry nodded and pointed as though Peter still hadn't guessed the subject of the conversation.

"What happened?" Peter asked, getting the idea that he was only filling in the lines so that Terry could run off his mouth.

"Summer," said Terry, "She's from Galway - Went home - Relationship over." After he said this, Terry turned back in his seat to face Peter properly. "I suppose some things don't mean anything. But there was this other girl in my course last year, man, she had the biggest jabs you've ever seen. Did you ever see her, I mean wow! And she was skinny too, so they weren't fat knockers, ya know. What was her name again? Oh, it doesn't matter, you'd remember if you saw her, man."

Peter got a sad feeling from Terry then, as the talkative one continued on about some girl's lips and another girl's arse. It was a feeling he recognised in himself. It was there behind the other boy's eyes. Not betrayed by a glint, but worse, it was marked by a dullness. And lack of shine. Terry was also worn out. In the core of Peter's brain he had a dark patch, and he recognised the same in Terry. It was scary, like he'd known the other boy all his life. What could it be that connected them? The hint of madness in Terry's voice; the matching dark rings under their eyes? Yes, that was it, or if not, it was a common symptom of-

"Do you sleep?" Peter interrupted, and Terry shut his yammering immediately.

***

What the fuck? Terry thought. He was suddenly unsettled and his stomach had gone off. Too much coffee probably, he thought but he still finished his cup. How was it that he felt like he knew this Peter guy? What was going on in his head? So, Peter had noticed that he was suffering from lack of sleep. So what, it wasn't as if Terry had hidden it very well? But if Peter knew for another reason, then he had to find out. These last weeks and months couldn't be regained, but if someone else were going through it too, then at least that would be something.

"Yeah, I sleep a bit – sometimes," Terry said, guarding his expression, unsure of what to say next. "You?"

"No," said Peter simply, "None." Terry grew nervous and picked up Peter's coffee and sipped at it.

"Urah! Man, it's frozen! I'll get you a new one." Before Peter could stop him, Terry was off to the counter to get him a hot sup.

"Hey there... Mama!" Terry said to the blonde-haired girl, trying to look ever so cool.

"Gonads," she told him.

"What?"

"Gonads," she said again, "they're playing tonight at eight." Terry looked down to his trousers.

"Really, how did you know?" The blonde-haired girl smiled.

"Very funny, Terry," she said, pointing to a poster that was drooping on the wall, its blue tack stolen by an irrepressible yet decidedly nerdy vandal. "The Gonads, they're going to be the band of the year." Terry looked over both the picture and the blonde-haired girl.

"You want to go?" he asked, as brusque as he could, though his back was now sweating.

"Em..." the blonde-haired girl looked up to the left with mock indecision, "Oh, all right, I'll go." Terry smiled.

"Yes! I mean, cool yeah, whatever. Meet you outside your place at eight-ish then."

"You still can't ring the doorbell?"

"I don't do doorbells, baby," said Terry spinning around and failing to strut down the length of the canteen to the table where Peter was waiting. He sat down.

***

"You forgot my coffee," Peter couldn't help but smile through his sombre nature. Terry was a likable character.

"Well," said Terry grimacing, "there is no way I'm going to go back up there after that bit of skill. You have to know when to make yourself scarce. You'll just have to give up."

"Done," Peter assured him. He became serious then, "Now enough messing around." Peter had been given time to go over his options while Terry was arranging his date. "We have to talk about things."

"Things?" Terry asked.

"Yeah, things," Peter agreed. Honesty was the best way forward. "Like what's been happening to you this summer."

Terry raised an eyebrow. "And, what's been happening to me this summer?" Terry looked like he was considering disagreement and denial that anything had happened to him at all. Peter could see that it was in Terry's nature to make light of things, and he was more likely to say that everything was great, happy days, breezing through, and other words to that effect. But he stopped himself.

"Ok," Terry said, dropping his initial pretence, "but you go first."

Peter took a deep breath and searched for the beginning. He couldn't find the exact moment that he'd begun to feel off world, but he did know one thing.

"It's like this," Peter said, "I've been having these dreams."

***

Robot Dance…

"What sort of dreams?" Rachel asked Marie, feeling a shiver run around her neck, causing her to hunch her shoulders, "you're having dreams, too? I mean, are they? Like, what sort of dreams?" Marie looked uncomfortable and lowered her eyes to the table and her cup of tea. The two girls were sitting in Rachel's kitchen having their lunch, and though the heating was on, it seemed to Rachel at least that it had gotten perceptibly colder and less habitable since the subject of sleep, or more accurately, lack of sleep had been broached.

"You know," said Marie, "kinda disturbing dreams, ya know? The ones that seem to be really real like, and you could swear they were definitely real, even after you wake up and find yourself in your own bed." Marie scowled at her own vagueness. "It sounds stupid I know,' she said, "but, it's hard to describe."

"It's not stupid at all, Marie," Rachel interrupted. "Maybe you've been having too much caffeine or…" Rachel trailed off. She'd been having weird dreams too, and she'd asked herself the same questions. "Or, you might be stressed out?"

"No really… wait a second. You said too, didn't you?"

"No."

"Yes!"

"Wha… Well yeah, yeah I have. Well, only one dream really. Again and again, the same one, over and over, it's sooooo fucking freaky."

"Well?" asked Marie, "go on, tell me?'

"You tell me?" Rachel retorted, not wanting to go into it just yet. It was far too vivid.

"Ok, let's leave it then," said Marie, "and talk about something else."

"Like?"

"Well, maybe we need to get out and get laid or something?"

"Oh yeah, has it been long for you?"

"Bitch," Marie laughed, "ok, so it hasn't been that long for me, but when was the last time you got a good poke?" Rachel laughed and said, "Aw!" as Marie made a fist and gave the air an uppercut with it.

"A poke? That's disgusting! You're such a tramp, Marie."

"Well," said Marie, "don't worry about that, let's just get you out there and see what happens, haw?" She rummaged in her bag and brought out a blue halterneck top. "I bet you'd look great in this."

Rachel hissed at Marie. "Yeah, bloody right I'd look great in that; it's my top, you bitch!" Rachel squealed in high-pitched disbelief.

"What, no it's not. Well alright," Marie tutted, "you loaned it to me when we went out for our exam piss up in May, remember?" Rachel seriously doubted that she had, in fact, she was almost positive that her blue top, a favourite, had only gone missing a month or so ago.

"Give that to me," she said. "I can't believe you just took it? You cow."

"Oh, shut up," Marie chuckled, "let's just worry about what you're going to wear with it, shall we? You're not going out with me wearing those crappy jeans." Rachel looked down at her jeans. They were a bit crappy. She supposed that she could wear her blue skirt; no, it would make it look like she was wearing a uniform, maybe she could wear that brown belt and...

"Wait, where do you think we're going?" Rachel asked.

"To the gig, where else?" Marie tried to act coolly. Rachel's phone started ring and she knew exactly who it was.

"Eric's Gig? Greasy Eric?" Rachel asked.

"Phone's ringing," Marie interjected, as Rachel's Samsung picture phone with built in mp3 player and mega-pixel camera rang loudly again.

"The same Eric who you called a useless cu-"

"Your phone is ringing!" Marie repeated. Rachel sighed and shook her head. What was the point? She answered. There was no name on the screen. It just said CALL.

"Hello?" Rachel answered the phone and rolled her eyes, "What? What? Oh, it's you?" She handed the phone to Marie. "It's the stupid cu-"

"All right, all right!" Marie was all, yeah, yeah, and yeah as she took the phone. "Hi honey," she preened into Rachel's receiver.

"Get your own phone," Rachel muttered as Marie blabbered in the background.

Rachel turned her attention to the window, not wanting to hear Marie talking rubbish to greasy Eric. Outside, she could see the garden, with its tall grass and overgrown bushes. How long ago was it since her dad had tended it? It must have been ages; so long that she couldn't remember.

Actually, now that she thought about it, Rachel couldn't remember how long ago it was since she'd seen her father. He was at another party conference, the Regressives were hard at work these days, and her father was working to get high up in the party. Rachel didn't know why, it was obvious that it would be ages before they were back in power. Since the Progressive Party had taken over, Ireland had become a well functioning democratic state, not a model of the same.

Now Ireland worked; it thrived and prospered under the power of the people, and the watchful eye of Walter Thisgo. Rachel felt a hot flush run over her when she thought of the country's most successful leader. Probably the weather, she thought. Since the fallout in West Britain, Ireland's coastal seas had become wilder, and the capital was often treated to chills out of season, all part of life now that Sellafield was a spent threat.

Rachel wanted to know what the wonderful Thisgo was doing about that. Where were his innovative and oriental style techniques when it came to the nuclear world pact?

Rachel brought these thoughts to a halt. What was she like? Why did she give a shit about any of that political stuff. She shook it off. Her parents' ideas were obviously leaking into her again. She'd never even seen Walter Thisgo, wasn't that weird? The old UK was the least of her worries.

It was Peter she thought of much more than anything else. Sad but true, she was in love with an-

"Rachel, hello?" Marie chimed.

- an antisocial oddball, she'd never even said two words to, and when the whole island went K and big time boom, she would probably still be wondering what he liked to eat? What sort of music did he like? Was he a good kisser? Could he ever be as wonderful as she dreamed he must be?

"Rachel, hello?" Marie tried again. "You're not in his bed again, are you?"

"What? Oh, not yet no!" Rachel laughed. And wanting to deflect attention from the familiar flush she felt was rising, she said, "Well, where is it on, this gig?"

"Oohh, she's getting embarrassed now. You mean, you want to go? I was expecting a bit more of a struggle, Impey. You know, more: 'Oh please,' on my part. And a lot more: 'Uh, I haven't got any money and I won't know anyone,' out of you. This is great!"

"Yeah, yeah, where is it?" Rachel smiled. *Why not?* she thought, she needed a night out, at least most of Greasy Eric's greasy friends would actually be on the stage where they wouldn't be able to annoy her.

"It's on in *The Inn*," said Marie. "Eric is mad excited. They're going to open with a Pink Floyd number that'll blow your mind."

"Really, which one?" Rachel asked.

"I don't know. Number forty? Whatever. Who cares? I've never even heard them," said Marie, and Rachel laughed again as she looked out the window at the washing line; there were clothes on it that seemed to have been there forever. Why could she not remember how long her parents had been away? She didn't know, but she just couldn't recall. Her mind lazed over the inquiry; it was like she wasn't bothered about remembering.

"Anyhow," she said aloud to Marie, "do you have a belt I could borrow?"

"Yeah," said Marie, "a green one with a blue dolphin pattern."

"You total bitch," Rachel exclaimed, "that's mine too!"

CHAPTER FIVE
EXPANSION OF THE ONEIRIC POTENTIAL

*A*mongst paint cans, broken amps, and old promotional beer boxes that never quite took off, Eric was pacing and fussing in a fussy and paceful way. They weren't coming, that was that. It was obvious; they had all decided to play some sick joke on him and embarrass him in front of all the girls he'd invited.

Parking his rear on a case of Clausthauler Extra dry, the beer that the Danes were quite willing to export, Eric contemplated the realities of music, i.e. women. He was a lead singer in a band. A new band at that, and it was his first chance to get the real snotty bitches to take notice of him. Girls like Lisa Smeddly and Marie were going to be there. The type of chicks that were all ,"Oh sure, real cool," and "What a sap!" to all the guys in Uni, and all it did was make them more popular. That type of girl was only interested in a guy they could brag about, Eric felt. Not too good-looking though, they were still supposed to be the pretty ones. Well, that was all right with Eric. He was crazy about those snobs, and the only reason he was in a band at all was so he could score one of them, and treat her like shit. Eric didn't just want to be with one of those girls, he wanted to own one.

Now everything was ruined. No music, no cool indifferent attitude, or minor, if slightly unattractive celebrity status. No snobbish women. And, without a bass player, guitarist, and drummer: no band.

Eric stared around the room, and bassists there were none. He'd called but the drummer was a no show either. That left his brother, Al. And where was he? Well, Eric didn't know, but he wasn't anywhere he'd looked, and he'd looked almost everywhere.

"Bastards!" Eric shouted, and then, "Fuckers!" he screamed. He really wanted those women. He had a thought then, a sprig of sage into his disaster casserole. He could go out there and play on his own. Then he returned to Braintown. Yeah sure, and play what songs, on which instrument? The Gazoo?

Oh, there would be females aplenty then.

"Bastards," he muttered, sitting back on a box of promotional Green Hill Cider hats, the ones with the foam front and the stylish plastic netting. The box buckled and Eric ended up absolutely in it. He didn't even try to get out. Maybe he could get inside and live there until those caps came back in fashion?

"Fuckers," he muttered. He really wanted those chicks. Extremely badly, in fact; if he'd known where his giblets were, he would have been feeling a little down in them.

There are people everywhere who are all sorts, this Eric knew. Every type of person possible existed under the sun, or around the back of it waiting in daylight, and as such, they weren't a bad bunch, really. Eric's sort was a loud and obvious breed. They wanted what they wanted, and they got all uptight and freaked out if they didn't get it. 'A decent sort, but prone to fits of impudence,' would be a good description of himself.

It was partly because of Eric's being the former of these, but most especially due to the latter that at that very moment, the rest of 'The Gonads' were waiting outside in the hall, tittering and enjoying snickers, as all good-natured practical jokers are prone to do.

And, with the good sense of timing of a decent rock and roll quartet, which 'The Gonads' were, they picked exactly the right moment to burst into the tiny backstage room, and begin to slag off their troubled front man.

"Aha, ya fucker," roared Stevie the bassist, or as he liked to be known, 'The one loan from a real band.' "Al, did ya see his face?" Al, Eric's brother and slipper of many a Mickey, laughed and slapped his little brother on the back when he saw how far their singer had sunken into despair.

"Come on, Er, it's all right, we're here."

"We might be here," said Dean the drummer. "But it's not alright!" he added. He said this because drummers are 'funny' as in, not very much. Actually, the better the drummer, the 'funnier' they are, it's a made up fact.

Meanwhile, Eric's relief was large and reprieving.

"You bastards, I swear to god, phew! Here, Tony," Eric called, seeing what was in the guitar player's hand, "give me some of your snickers."
***

Below the backstage room, the old man had stopped his pacing and was looking up at the ceiling. He could faintly hear the voices of the band in the room above, but he could not make out what they were saying, or even if they were real. A lot of things were not real. He couldn't remember a time when anything was, and when he did remember things, they seemed far too fantastic to be believed, and so he forced them away lest they open his mind to another period of pain and torture. Better to keep thinking about the words, he thought; concentrate on the words. They never hurt him. They never changed. They were words.

"He speaks," said the old man, "when he speaks, I speak what he speaks."

***

A Grey Tramp…

Outside *The Inn*, the streets were awash with thin stream; the skies had opened up and the rain had driven down hard and fast. Peter cursed this entrance of *The Inn*'s lack of a porch, and stood as close to the wall as he could, but he was nevertheless soaked through and feeling fairly pathetic. He wondered why he'd bothered to come, weighing the reasons and the circumstances in his very calculating and over analysing way. What did he stand to gain? He didn't know, but he was sure that he needed to be there.

As he thought this, Peter noticed a peculiar man walking in his direction on the other side of the road. The man was old, with a long grey beard, and was dressed in the manner of a tramp; he even had a ripped pocket in full view, and battered old hat on his head. The old tramp didn't walk like a vagrant though, no. His homelessness seemed like a disguise; he could have been an actor taking a break from shooting his part as a wino in one of those awful American-Irish movies where all the actors are Yanks.

The appearance of the grey tramp confused Peter greatly,

for as much as he seemed to walk too upright for a man of his standing, he fit into the surrounding street like he was at home, and he moved with a comfortable swagger. Peter couldn't decide whether he was watching a hobo, or just a man who had recently been mugged and was in need of assistance.

The grey tramp got closer, and Peter began to hear the drunken mumbling. *Oh,* Peter thought, *a wino.* So it was definitely a tramp then.

Peter watched as the grey beard came to a stop across the road from *The Inn* and flumped down on the steps of an old Georgian building, where he continued to speak to himself in gibbertalk, and drink from a bottle that appeared from his tatty Cromby.

Peter continued to watch the bum, only half convinced of his authenticity and validity, or indeed any other words of that sort.

"Hey, Peter," came a call from his now-soaked left. He turned to see who it could be. There was one second during which he had no idea why anyone would be calling his name, and then he was relieved to see that Terry was approaching from up the street, with a girl on his arm. It was the girl from the cafeteria. Had it been so long since he'd had a friend or heard a friendly voice?

"Hi," Peter said, as the couple reached him, "ah, how are things?" Terry and the girl from the cafeteria looked at each other.

"To be honest," Terry laughed, "We're a little wet, aren't we, Sam?" Sam laughed.

"Bloody right we are. Hi, I'm Samantha. I hear you and Terry are great friends?"

"Erm," said Peter, or something like it.

"Well," said Terry, "it's good that we've all met and that, but can we get inside? I'm dying for a pint."

"Yeah, let's," said Sam, squinting through the downpour. Peter opened the door to *The Inn,* quite happy to let everyone precede him into the lounge. That way, anyone in the bar that might look towards the door would see Terry and Samantha coming in and he could just creep in behind. It was the type of thing that he was beginning to do more often these days. It was antisocial, he knew, but for now it was better than being at home.

"Hey dude," Terry said, still standing in the street and putting his hand on the door, "Go on ahead." Terry held the door back and motioned for Peter to go inside. Peter shivered slightly and entered the bar.

"Cheers," said Terry, "I prefer to go in last."

As he entered *The Inn* behind Peter, Terry caught sight of a figure across the street. There was an old man sitting on the steps of a building watching him. Their eyes may have met then, but it was too rainy for either of them to see the whites, and confirm the contact. They did, however, share a definite moment, Terry was sure of it. So, not knowing how to break through it, he waved across the showery street. And after a moment, the old man waved back. Terry felt free then to enter the bar, and he did so, with a shiver of his own and a second glance across the street.

"Odd," he said.

***

Oscar felt a twinge of guilt as he watched the boy disappear into *The Inn*, but there was no point in it. He simply put his empty bottle back into the inside pocket of his Cromby, and settled to waiting.

A bit of drunken mumbling, thought Oscar; *that was all it took.* As soon as someone looked at him in a funny way, like the pale boy had, all Oscar needed to do was take out his empty shoulder of whiskey and take an imaginary swig.

No, of course the old tramp wasn't watching me, they would always quite evidently decide. Oscar the drunken bum was beyond disdain, below suspicion; he was a smell, not an actual person. A lot of times, it hurt him to see the wash of pitying dismissal and shame cross their faces, but when he really was looking, he was glad of it.

Tonight was one of those times, as he was there to watch. The boy was here with that pale chap, and Oscar had seen those two girls approaching *The Inn* earlier. It could be a coincidence, but then again, it couldn't be.

They had come to his attention five or six months ago,

four students going to the same university, with no connection to each other. Sleepwalkers all four, with the same spaced look, lost as they walked the streets. Oscar didn't know why they stood out amongst the crowds of students that piled in and out of the university every day, as he sat and watched from the park across the way, sometimes drinking from his make-believe whiskey bottle to distract attention. No alcohol tonight, he was busy.

He had thought until recently that his brain had just chosen these four to save him from losing his mind. He had thought that maybe he had already lost his mind and he was seeing things that weren't really there. He had thought that, until recently.

But now they were meeting each other, first becoming two pairs of friends; the newest of which having been formed that very day in very odd circumstances, Oscar had seen it happen. And tonight, all four were under the same roof, within yards of each other, it felt wrong somehow, unnatural even.

In fifteen years, Oscar had seen nothing like it. He intended on watching them round the clock from now on, until he satisfied himself that it was all just serendipity, and that perhaps he was experiencing fractures in what remained of his creaking brain bones.

Oscar sat there in the shitty weather, getter wetter and more sodden, tuning out his discomfort with a set of practised mental exercises.

Using his favourite, he drifted off into an armchair by the fire in his mind and settled down to wait for as long as it took.

But it didn't take long.

Chapter Six

Breathe

Breathe...

Peter, Terry, and Sam hovered at the bar of *The Inn,* which was three-deep, and smelling. All around them there were empty seats, but the obvious opportunities for finding somewhere to sit for the gig were deceptive, due to the smokers all being corralled into the beer garden that was basically, but not legally indoors, if the canvas covering was taken into account. This was the way in every Dublin bar since back in 2004, when the government got sense and decided to try and drench the addiction out of the Irish. Good call at the time, but the numbers never went below twenty percent, and extra mild were replaced by extra tar, a very Celtic, 'If you're not going to stop, go for it full on,' attitude seeming to ensue from the liberal correctness. So, trying to sit down had become a series of, "Is this seat taken?" and the inevitable, "Yeah, they're out having a smoke."

The smokers were being punished for their habit, and their healthy opposite numbers were seated alone, fending off the advances of the newly arrived, yet it actually worked quite well.

"Hey, isn't that your man?" Marie asked Rachel as she pointed towards Peter. Rachel didn't follow Marie's gesture, she knew very well who was standing by the bar looking pale and uneasy.

"What are you talking about?" Rachel lied, "I don't have a man." Marie looked at Rachel with a dubious and fed up expression on her freckled face.

"Oh yeah, like you didn't notice. I saw ya start preening yourself as soon as he walked in. If you don't talk to him tonight, you're a complete loser. Or...?" and Marie said it with an evil grin, "I could go back over to Rat-face and tell him you are interested?"

"Urgh!" Rachel cringed, "Did you see the state of him? What a loser!"

But what a funny loser he had been.

Rat-face was a friend of Eric's, who hid his awkwardness when left alone with girls that he didn't know and felt horribly self-conscious around, by being a complete arsehole. Though Rachel had to say one thing for him, but not to his face, of course; the boy had balls.

Twice so far, the obnoxious belligerent had grabbed one of Rachel's boobs without missing a beat in his sleazy rhetoric. Greg saw himself - that was his name, Greg, - as a man with ideas. Admittedly, a lot of these ideas were slurred sounding, and involved Rachel's breasts in some way, but he did have other definite views on life, women, and how both should be treated.

Women wanted to be controlled, he felt. They wanted a man who was not afraid to tell them what he wanted. They wanted a man like him, even if they didn't know it yet. Rat-face was a real man, a ladies' man, and coincidentally, he was a single man.

Although Rachel found him repulsive and quite literally, laughable, she managed in her weakness to allot Rat-face some minor respect. When a guy manages to look you in the eye, and, taking himself completely seriously, say: "Can I suck on your titties?" Rachel couldn't help but applaud the confidence that it took, misguided though it may have been, to come out with something so unbelievably stupid.

Who could get away with that? Brad Pitt, that guy from East Enders? And, even then, Rachel doubted that it would have sounded cool.

Amid insurmountable adversity, Rat-face was carrying on in the face of, and including, a loud slap in his own face. *What a man,* Rachel thought. A man's man if ever there was one.

Then, while Rachel was refusing Rat-face's generous offer of a look at his cock, Peter had walked in. This was her chance to do something, to talk to him. Now she could show him that she wasn't just some weirdo that stared at him while he wrote in his diary. She was an intelligent girl with a lot to say for herself, and she found herself drawn to him. So all she had to do was to tell him that, which she would do, in a minute.

Just as soon as she'd had a couple more drinks.

Just for courage.

She didn't want to seem desperate, even though she wanted him desperately.

As Rachel came to this conclusion, Rat-face decided to clamp onto one of her boobs again, but this time Marie was ready.

"Fuck off," she shouted, grabbing him by the hair and holding her cigarette up to his eye, "you stupid little freak!"

And fuck off he did. Problem solved. "Hey, isn't that your man?" Marie asked Rachel as she pointed towards Peter.

***

"Want a drink?" asked Terry, and Peter shook his head.

"I don't drink," Peter told him. Terry and Sam laughed loudly at this. Peter didn't know what to say.

"Don't drink?" Terry exclaimed, "Yeah right." Peter nodded. "Well," said Terry. "It may have sounded like you said - you don't drink, but what I heard was – 'Mine's a beer, Terry, cheers!'" Terry turned to the barman, who had just grudgingly turned up to serve them. "Three of those, what's the promotion?" he pointed to the poster that said three for a fiver.

"Clausthauler Extra dry," the barman smiled at him, an action that included two rows of teeth touching each other, and not much else, "It's the next big thing." Terry doubted very much whether it was, but continued to order.

"Three of those then, mate." He turned back to Peter. "You're not allergic, are you?" he asked, serious for a moment. Peter made the rooky mistake of telling Terry that, no, although he seemed to be allergic to a lot of things, alcohol wasn't one of them. The reason he didn't drink alcohol was that he found that it dulled the senses, and with all that was going on with him at the moment, the last thing he needed was to have an unclear perspective on events.

Terry only heard the first part.

"Great," said Terry, "then I won't feel guilty getting you pissed then. Make it six," he called.

Peter was about to refuse when he noticed a girl pointing at him from across the room. It was that girl Marie, the mouthy one with the really nice- And there *she* was too. Oh God, Rachel was here too. Peter didn't know what to do with himself as their eyes met across the room. Then she turned quickly away in embarrassment, breaking the connection. *Thank you, God,* he thought; he'd nearly had a heart attack.

"Come on, man," Terry prompted as Sam signalled to them that she'd negotiated the grudging release of a table. There was another bloke sitting in the four-seater, but his friends had just left and he was leaving, so he didn't mind that they sat down.

"So go on, tell us?" Sam asked. "Who's the girl?" Terry looked at her and oohed.

"Ooh, yeah. I saw that too; the girl over there with the nice boobs."

"Hey!" Sam exclaimed and Terry laughed as she slapped him.

"I was just saying. You know, on first impressions from the other side of the room. All I could judge about her was her appearance. You can't fault that, can you?" Terry turned to Peter, while Sam jokingly gave him the evil eye. "Come on, Peter, back me up here. That's all I can see of her. She's probably really nice, isn't she?"

Peter shrugged. "I don't know," he admitted. "I've only ever seen her around."

"No way," said Terry, "but it looked like she was into you."

"Yeah," Sam agreed, "you have to go and chat her up. She's definitely into ya."

"Eh, anyway." Peter avoided the subject and stuck his bottle of Clausthauler into his mouth. But Terry and Sam weren't the kind of people to be put off by something as simple as silence, no. Terry and Sam were the type of people who were quite happy with Peter's silence, because it allowed them to fill it themselves in any manner they wished.

"So," said Terry, "you just go up to her and say… What should he say, Sam?" Terry looked at his girl with a grin, letting her in.

"Well…" Sam thought, for the briefest moment and was about to tell Peter exactly what he should say to his potential love but was interrupted..

***

"All right, all right, all right!" Eric plagiarised from the stage, hoping he sounding like Jim Morrison. "We're gonna start you off with some Pink Floyd. So hold onto your hats. This is called Breathe."

And with that, the lights were lowered and there was shushing, followed by an expected silence, broken only by a drunken Marie saying, "Look at him, he thinks he's fuckin' great, doesn't he!" in a slurred and very audible voice. The room sniggered and almost ruined Eric's manufactured mood, but he was mostly disappointed when the members of his band joined in the laughter. But there was no time for that, Dean had already switched on the metronome, and they were off. This was the opening number. If they fucked this up, the gig would surely suck ass.

The song began to build.

~ As the hum from the bass became more pronounced, Peter felt a cold chill run through him, and he almost dropped his beer. He looked around for help, and then he saw her.

Rachel, he thought, he had to go to her. He felt so strange and disorientated, and when he brought his hands up to eye level, they were damp. Also there was a strange taste in his mouth. What was happening?

~ *It tastes like iron,* Terry thought, he was sure it was iron, or some metal. Perhaps it was just the beer, but he was beginning to feel like he did when he sat at his bright and lonely kitchen table. He was detaching from his ID. He tried to look at Sam, but she was watching the stage and he didn't want to look at her anyway. He wanted to find Peter, and he looked around for him, but Peter was moving away.

~ *He's coming towards me,* Rachel realised as the pale boy she had so often watched came closer to her. She wanted him to, needed it actually. She didn't know why, but at this moment, Rachel felt that she had to be beside him, something had been triggered inside her, something that made her feel an ache in her stomach. She'd felt that ache before. It was throbbing fear, and it was attacking her core; it made her want to curl up around it and protect herself from…

She felt her face was soaked in sweat, but when she wiped her brow with the back of her hand, she found it dry and tepid. Rachel felt sick, and a strange taste was in her mouth. She didn't know what to do, but she didn't panic. At least he was coming to her, his need for her evident in his eyes, as clearly as her need must have been in hers.

The song continued to build. It was nearing its crescendo. In a few seconds, it would reach its loudest point and like a volcano or an atom bomb, it would explode outwards before the waves of noise would even out and become flat.

~ For Terry, it seemed like catching Peter would be impossible; the pale boy seemed so far away. But Terry knew that he had to reach him. His heart was racing and he shook with nerves as he struggled through the crowd. To his relief, he saw that Peter was nearer now, since he'd stopped in front of a girl: the girl they had seen earlier. Over her shoulder, Terry saw another girl, a red-head. She was looking directly at him.

~ Marie watched as Terry approached from behind Peter. This was it. It was happening now. She felt a moment of terrible dread before she cornered her resolve and stepped forward, reaching for Rachel's shoulder.

The song hit its peak as Rachel, Peter, Terry, and Marie came together. It was the beginning of the universe; the sound of the loudest notes ranging out, while the melody beneath found its form. It was a breathtaking moment, but like all moments, it was gone before it could be counted.

And it wasn't just the moment that was gone, disappeared, departed. There were other things that used to be, but now were not; things like everything, or to be accurate, everyone.

It was all gone. The music was gone, along with all the sounds. The smells were missing too; the bar was odourless, the stink of beer had been wiped away. Yet there were much more important things missing from the room, depending on outlook of course.

All around the bar, there were empty seats and tables. The stage was nothing but an empty space, and the bar was clear and unused, as if it had always been so.

All had vanished, except - in the middle of the now empty bar of *The Inn* stood its only four inhabitants: Peter, Terry, Rachel, and Marie. They faced each other, but were more aware of the room about them than each other's sweaty and surprised faces, as each of them realised that everyone had disappeared.

Everyone except for those four had gone, and the room was still. For too many slow seconds, one, two... seventeen... twenty-six, they continued to look through each other into the room beyond. It was punishing, but none of them wanted to be the first one to say; "What the hell!" or call out for help. Instead, they waited for as long as they could, as long as anyone could have been expected to wait, before beginning to panic.

In a circle, and almost as a perfect unit, it began; the silent terror of their situation tore them apart.

"Oh my god, what the fuck, what the fuck!" Marie was the first to form the words, her freckled skin luminous, and her face drawn with what could easily have been mock dread. She grabbed Rachel and attempted with little success to draw her friend's attention. "Where are they?" she tried, but Rachel just shook her black curls slowly from side to side.

"They're all gone," Rachel said, turning slowly to Peter, who was ashen and terrified, but not as shocked as the rest. "Where have they gone?" she asked him.

Oh, Peter knew this feeling. The taste in his mouth and the company was a new one on him, but that sinking desperate feeling, the super-loneliness as he'd often called it, was overtaking him. And from what he saw on the faces of the other three, it seemed that it was catching up with them too.

The powerful emotion from his dreams was a hulking shadow that became more and more solid as every second passed. And the beast was in no hurry; why should it be? It recognised Peter easily, and he was going nowhere. This was a new version of horror for Peter; it was no dream, not with the others there too. It couldn't be. All he could do was try and steel his resolve so that he didn't crumble to his knees, as he had so often done in his fantasy. It must go differently now that he had companions. Maybe they could help him?

Peter looked at the other three, and then around the room. It was real, oh Jesus, it was definitely real. He turned to Rachel.

"This is mine," he told her. "There's nobody here. This is my dream."

"Dream?" she looked at him, dazed.

"What's happening? What's going on?" Terry asked and Peter, Marie, and Rachel all shook heads to answer. "What's happening? What's going on?" he asked again, his voice straining, with a quiver not far way.

"What's happening?" Terry cried again, in mounting tearful anger as the weeks of sleepless horrible nights took over him.

"Oh no," said Peter, "Terry?"

"Tell me what's happening?" Terry screamed, and cast about him in a maniacal rage. "Where is everyone?" Peter stepped to his side and found that he needed help to subdue the frantic Terry. The three of them managed to do it, but it was a tentative restraint at best.

"It's ok Terry," said Peter, trying his best to sound soothing, "It's alright, man."

Marie joined in. "Yeah. Terry is it? It's cool, don't worry about it, it's nothing." Terry looked in turn at all three gathered around him, attempting to console him. He could see that they needed to comfort him as desperately as he needed to give into hopeless abandon.

"Yeah sure," he whispered calmly, his words making Rachel smile with relief. She hadn't been sure that she could take it if Terry started to freak out, not when everything had just turned crazy.

Marie was obviously relieved, as was Peter, and they all relaxed their grip.

"Yeah," Terry said again, free from their grasp, "Yeah, sure, really! It's fuckin grand, isn't it?" he exploded as he broke free from them and ran towards the bar. "This is it? Everybody just disappears? That's grand, that's fine; that is just perfect!" Terry hopped over the bar and grabbed at a bottle of whiskey from where it hung on its optic. He pulled it down and it splashed everywhere, but he saved most of it with his mouth as he drank hungrily, gulping and eating the alcohol into his belly.

"It's fine, it's fine, it's fine, fine, fine, fine, fine, fine, fine, fine!" And another bottle came down.

"Peter," Rachel shouted, pleading, "stop him." But what could Peter do? The fact that she knew his name was enough to delay his reactions. But even so, what could he do? Terry was no physical marvel, but he was broad enough and displaying enough mad energy that Peter felt, and rightly too, that he should be running away from the guy and not towards him.

It was Marie who did react, but all she could do was cry out.

"Stop it, stop it!" she shouted. "Stop... It!" But Terry didn't stop, nor was he stopped. With his third bottle in hand, he hopped across the counter again and made for the door.

"They're outside, they're outside!" he screamed as he barrelled through the opening. Then he was gone, and all the others could hear was his screaming and yelping as he ran down the street.

"Where is everybody? What happened?" they heard him scream. The three stood face to face in the empty bar, and attempted to read each other's expressions. It was hopeless. None of them could explain what was happening. Terry had just freaked out in a truly disturbing manner, but was he overreacting?

All around them was empty space, and for all they knew, all over the city there was silence. What was happening? Why had they been left alone?

CHAPTER SEVEN
THERE'S NOBODY THERE BUT ME

On the street, Oscar's heart was pounding. He'd just watched as Terry erupted from *The Inn* with a bottle of whiskey in one hand and the other in the air.

"Where is everybody? What happened?" Terry's voice was a desperate squeal of a thing, with fear so audible that it transmitted the feeling to Oscar, and now he was also deathly afraid as he trotted down the road in Terry's echoing aftermath. The old man's only thought was to save the boy, and he tried not to concede to the voice in his mind that asked for the cause of Terry's agony.

On and on, Oscar ran, always too far behind to see Terry's face, but easily close enough to hear that horrible yelling.

"Jesus boy, what's the matter with ya?" Oscar asked aloud, as he turned off Capel Street and onto an empty cobbled road. Up until now, Oscar had managed to keep Terry in sight. Now there was nothing in the street but the wet shutters of the fruit companies, and the beer cans emptied earlier by the young, or the tramps like him. Where had the boy disappeared too? Oscar listened to the night and heard nothing.

There were all sorts of sounds going on around him, the cars, the snatches of music from bars, the sound of the rain, all of it drowning out any chance Oscar might have of hearing Terry's now quiet progress and direction.

"Come on, Come on." There had to be some sign, Oscar knew it. There was always something to see if you looked.

Then he saw the cat. It stood at the entrance to a narrow alley close by, and over to his right. It interested him. A cat out in the rain; he'd rarely seen that before. Felines didn't usually allow themselves to get wet unless it was absolutely necessary. This was odd to Oscar because he shared the streets of Dublin with dogs and cats, and far too many rats. Cats were very clever and would usually be huddled in a dry nook or doorway until the downpour stopped, and even then they would vigorously shake off any drops that fell on them in the aftermath.

So why was this cat standing in the rain? Something or someone had disturbed it from its comfortable situation.

"The boy," Oscar nodded, and approached the cat's alley, nervous about Terry's state of mind. The boy had become suddenly unstable that was for sure, and something had happened tonight to set him off. That was obvious, but what would his reaction be when faced with Oscar, would he strike out? Oscar wasn't worried about his own safety, he was plenty strong enough, but the thought of having an altercation with the boy was not a welcome one. Well, he decided, there was only one way to find out.

Oscar walked slowly into the alley, ready for anything.

***

In *The Inn,* Marie was also getting nervous. How long was this going to last, and what were they going to do? Peter seemed to be taking it with a sort of sulky determination, but Rachel, her poor friend Rachel was becoming frantic.

"Let's get out of here," Marie suggested, "this place is giving me the creeps."

Both Peter and Rachel looked at her; they were lost. It took a moment or two for them to register what she had said, but when they did, they could only agree.

"Yeah," said Peter, "we can go to mine, my parents are away."

"So are mine," Rachel said, unnerved that her voice didn't carry as it should have done in the quiet of the empty bar.

"Well, let's go somewhere," said Marie, "as long as it's out of here." She made for the door, hoping that the others were following her and then breathed a sigh of relief when she heard that they were.

Having exited *The Inn* without incident, the three stared around them.

"Still no one," Peter reported, more to fill the silence than anything else. "How can this be really happening?"

Marie felt a wave of disgust flow through her and she lashed out at him, slapping him hard across the face. The loud smack shocked Peter almost as much as the force behind it. The sound reverberated into the dead empty night, proving that they were indeed completely alone.

"Marie!" Rachel reacted.

"There," shouted Marie, "do you think you're dreaming now?"

"I…" Peter was far beyond an answer. "Sorry?" he tried.

"Marie," Rachel cut between the two, "There's no need for that. This is fucked up enough as it is without anyone else losing it," Rachel regretted saying the words even as they left her mouth. Now all their thoughts were of Terry, and his screaming panicked flight.

"I hope he's alright," said Peter, who took to examining the wet pavement with the toe of his shoe. Rachel also became very interested in his excavations, and Marie knew she had to do something.

"Ok," said Marie, "Peter, let's go to yours, yeah?" But Peter just stared at her as though she were paving too, only vertical. She grew impatient. "Listen, I'm sorry that I hit you, alright? Can we just go?"

"Yeah I suppose," Peter said, looking around. "But how do we get there? No buses, no taxis, it's a long walk." He looked at Marie, and she smiled.

"Well," we could always take a car?"

"What car?" Rachel asked, not understanding Marie's meaning right away.

"Any car. That car," said Marie, pointing at a black Peugeot across the street that looked fairly nifty. "That looks fairly nifty," she said.

"No, we can't, can we?" Peter said, hanging another question out above them. Could they really do whatever they wanted? Why not, if they were the only people on Earth? Or whatever planet this was?

"Look," said Marie, "this is happening now. It may all turn out to be a crazy trip, and we'll wake up any minute. But if it isn't and we're the only ones to have survived whatever it was that- disappeared everybody else, then what's the point in us walking around for hours?"

The logic was there, perfect and clean. And, if a copper did show up and nab them for joyriding, then at least they would have a real problem, and a real person would be arresting them.

"Ok," said Rachel, and then turned to Peter, and said, "I think we should take the car. Don't you?" Peter looked at her and realised who she was. She was, well, *her*! The amazing stranger that stared at him sometimes, beautiful and soft, looking into his eyes and hoping he would agree.

"Yes," he said. "Of course. I think that we should take the car."

And so they did.

***

"Ohgod, ohgod, ohgod, ohgod, ohgod," Terry whispered, with his eyes firmly shut against the night. He held himself and pushed his body as far back into the wall as he could, trying to disappear completely behind the wheelie bin with the word 'Noble' printed on it. He shivered and attempted to block out the sound of the approaching steps as they came closer and closer to him.

It was obvious what had happened tonight. Firstly, he had been torn from the world, or the world was torn from him, in order for her to hunt him through the phantom streets, and finally take him. That was why he'd stopped screaming, and why he had hidden in this alleyway. The only thing that didn't fit was the inclusion of the other three in his torment. But it hardly mattered now. The woman from his nightmare was almost upon him. He was finally going to see her face. The horror of the thought brought a kind of relief, and the encounter was almost welcome.

Night after night, he had seen her walk towards him, in no hurry but relentless and unyielding. Terry had been dreading the day that she drew close enough for him to discern from the mental blur the actual features of her elusive face. He desperately wanted to see whether she had a familiar face or not. If she did, it was surely just a dream and he had simply given her a face from his memory. If he didn't recognise her, if her face was new to him, then he would know that she was an outside force, acting upon him in his sleep. So, this was it.

"Ohshit, ohshit, oshit, oshit." Terry shivered, his eyes

still firmly shut. There was a sound directly above him, he could hear her breathe, all he had to do now was open his eyes and take her in. He was caught and that was that. He was doomed. "Oh please, I can't do it," he said quietly. "Don't make me look at you, please." Terry started suddenly as he felt a hand pat him on the head gently. She was coaxing him to look up and he knew that he should.

"Boy," said a voice.

"No, no please, don't make me look," Terry said, and he started to wail and ball, the tears falling on his horror-stricken face. "I can't. I can't. I can't," he screamed, but he knew that he must.

Terry raised his head and wiped the tears away from his eyes, so that when he opened them, he would see her clearly. His heart was a-humming, it was pounding so swiftly the moment he raised his lids. There was an ache all through him from the wet and cold. But it would all be over soon, he felt, and his eyes came fully open.

All around her was a blinding bright and radiant halo. It took Terry a few seconds before he could discern her features from its piercing light. His eyes adjusted, his vision cleared, and the face above came into view so he could behold it in perfect clarity. It was not the woman of his nightmares that looked down upon him. It was an old man with a shaggy beard.

"Who the hell are you?" said Terry to Oscar, before he fainted dead away.

TEXT

Successful trigger. SAGE...
Peter is to be the
leader.
Concentrate on
him.

CHAPTER EIGHT
MEET WALTER THISGO

Walter Thisgo paced in the hallway as he waited for his car to be brought around. The Áras was becoming a pain to live in these days, the security alone managing to stifle his enjoyment of the wonderful mansion that housed Ireland's leaders. The Regressives were becoming openly physical in their resistance to his party's changes. It troubled him deeply that this would be so, as it was counter-productive to the entire Progressive ethos. The changes being made were not supposed to cause the country harm. They were meant to free the country from an over-bureaucratic shadow of the antiquated British system of government.

"That was an unwieldy sentence," he berated himself. This was why he needed his PR people. It wasn't that Walter Thisgo didn't have a very clear view of what he wanted and how it was to be attained. In fact, the opposite was the case. He knew precisely what was best for Ireland, and had minutely detailed plans laid out ahead to ensure his success. It was the five hundred words or less part that gave him trouble.

Walter sighed. If only he could cogitate and sift down his ideas into manageable bite-sized chunks, in the manner his PR people could do...

But what of it? Walter was a realist. If the simplification of ideas for general consumption was not one of his strong points, then he would concentrate on the things that were. Leading and improving, which he saw as being one and the same, and making quick decisions depending on the constantly changing tide of national and international politics, which as Walter often imparted to his only child, was simply a matter of having a very good memory.

Progress had to be made. As a child, Walter had watched his father fall victim - correction, permit himself to fall victim of the old steamroller of party politics. Often, Walter had beseeched his stricken parent to resist, to pit himself against the status quo, and at least gain self-respect, instead of weight and self-pity. It had been a very difficult period for young Walter to see his father fail in such a manner, and it was still a terrible burden on him.

Well, not this Thisgo. When the offspring of Walter Thisgo looked back along the branches of the family tree, they would see their father as a man who had tried to change things for the better. And were his future plans to succeed, which he was sure that they would, Walter's children would see a successful man who sacrificed a great deal for the good of his country and for their future. Not a filthy drunken...

"Sir?" it was Cullen, Walter's bodyguard.

"Em... Yes, yes, my man. How is it?" Walter smiled.

"Your car, Mr Thisgo, it's ready."

"Great, thank you," answered Walter, and took his cue through the main door and down the steps to where his car and his assistant sat waiting.

"Good morning, sir," Siobhán greeted him as he stepped in, and Cullen closed the door after him, "how was dinner last night?" She was referring of course to the 'friendly' dinner with some of the Regressive leaders Walter had been forced to tolerate on the previous evening.

"Oh yes," Walter chuckled. "It was a magical evening with only a faint hint of the ludicrous, and hardly any spitting."

Siobhán laughed at this, "Here is your speech for this morning," she said, handing him his Palm computer, "I think they've explained you quite well, sir."

"Indeed," Walter answered, as he read the script for the official introduction of the national Job Actualisation Scheme. After a few seconds of speed reading, Walter could only agree with Siobhán, and he set about memorising the sentence layout and the structural pauses.

This was another talent that Walter was proud of, yet modest about. Although he may have needed help in reducing his one-hour speech into the correct ten-minute format, Walter was a whiz at taking the evenly weighted words and making them his own, in the manner of the true and charismatic politician that he really was.

By the time his car pulled up outside the Dáil, Walter was in full control of the speech, and chatting to Siobhán about another meeting taking place later that day. He stepped out of the car, and with controlled strides, he walked to his position on the pavement outside the gates, not inside, behind bars. Walter stood outside with his people, where he listened as his Minister for Internal Operations read out the main body of the proposal.

As usual, Walter felt a thrill building in him as he prepared to address his people, but today there was also something else that he felt building. Anxiety; he was extremely nervous. His dinner with the opposition leaders on the previous night had troubled him terribly. They had been smug and overly confident. Not the type of behaviour he would have expected for high-ranking members of a disintegrating political party.

This was it. They were making their move against him. All the plans he had made were at the mercy of human nature now. Well, that was the way it should be. That was the way he wanted the country to operate. The people were supposed to be in charge. And, very soon, they would have their chance.

The Minister for Internal Operations finished his segment and introduced his leader. Walter took a deep breath into his wiry frame, pushed his glasses back on his nose, and ran his hand through his uniform grey hair. It was a move designed to define him before he began to speak. Walter stepped up, congratulated his subordinate on his good words, and turned to address the cameras.

"People of Ireland," he began, "I am very excited..."

***

Waking up...

In Peter's house, the three students were woken by the sound of the television. After a unanimous decision not to separate, they had decided the night before that they would all sleep in the large sitting room. Before finally drifting off to sleep, the three had discussed all manner of reasons for their singular situation, ranging from a Gypsy curse to the Twilight Zone. They had exhausted all, but validated none, in favour of lights out and hours of blind nameless panic in the darkness until sleep finally overtook them.

Peter opened his eyes and looked at the television screen for a moment, before he realised what was happening there. The news, but that wasn't what caught his attention. Something was on, it didn't matter what. He looked around the room and took on board the fact that Rachel and Marie were still there, before looking back at the screen. Some politician was speaking about something that Peter had no interest in, and it was great. It was a sign of humanity and that was all that mattered.

"They're back," he said, and rose from the floor where he'd been lying. He stood and stepped towards the television as the politician introduced another, older man. This smaller, grey-haired man smiled at Peter from outside the Dáil.

"People of Ireland," said the old man, "I am very excited."

The face insulted Peter somehow, and without any control over his reflexes, the youth growled and kicked out at the television, knocking it from its stand. Stunned, he watched as the set thumped to the wooden floor, and the screen went dead. Behind him, both Marie and Rachel were roused by the noise, and sat up on the two couches where they had spent the night.

"What the hell happened?" Marie shouted, and Peter turned to look at their inquisitive faces.

"Eh... I'm not sure but." Peter moved across the room and pulled open the curtains. Outside on the street stood the Peugeot they had used the night before. Peter noticed that it was more dark blue than black like he'd previously thought.

"What's happening? Is everything still, gone?" Rachel asked with fear in her voice.

"Shh! a second." Peter held a hand up to them both as he watched the road for a few moments until it finally happened.

A car passed, and then another. The girls joined him at the window, and after a brief pause, a young woman pushing a pram walked down the road on the opposite side. They watched her, enthralled as she passed unawares, left to right. It seemed to take an eternity. Then she was gone and they turned back to the room, with its three makeshift beds and its upturned television. Peter walked to the stricken set and heaved it back onto the stand. It didn't work, which was just as well, he thought.

"They're back," he said into the air, not wanting to see their faces, trying to hide his own quivering lip. "They've all come back." He slumped on the floor, and Rachel knelt beside him as he covered his face.

"What are we going to do?" she asked, putting a hand on his shoulder. Peter just shook his head and kept quiet, as a couple of tears fell in his silence. *We are really screwed now,* he thought.

Really, really screwed.

***

Gaps…

There were gaps in the city of Dublin. Spaces and cracks that were right there in front of everybody. Some were so vast that it would shock a normal citizen, were he or she to stumble across them, and some so small and seemingly meaningless that even Oscar often missed them as he tramped around the town. On George's Street, there was an old shop, shut down for as long as anyone could remember, and in the doorway when it rained, it was never short of a huddled coughing body, trying to keep out of the cold and the wet. Not even these bodies, these long timers on the street knew what lay so close beside them.

If they had known, there would have been less pitiful huddling and more rubbing of hands together, and happiness at having found refuge from the night and the elements. Because, it was there, beyond that uncomfortably small and sodden doorway, in between the outer and inner wall that the knowledgeable tramp would feel the ground fall away beneath him, as Oscar had once felt more than a year ago.

There, below the abandoned store, lay the first gap that Oscar had ever discovered, though it was to become one of many. In fact, it had become very easy after that to spot the openings and the different spaces in the city, yet this one remained his favourite by far. This was his gap in the city, the one that had saved his life.

One night, a year ago, when the cold had been so severe and Oscar so desperate that he had begun to cry and scream at it to leave him alone, Oscar had been saved.

The cold had begun to reach inside of him, and burn the tendons from his bones. He could still remember the agony of it. That night, when he would have had done anything to end his pain, he'd stumbled into something that changed his life forever.

He'd been standing in the doorway; freezing, and frightened, mere feet from salvation when he saw a rat poke its head out from the crevasse between the wall and the rotten wooden doorframe.

I am a rat too, Oscar thought at the time, his thinking warped by the cold. He was living outside the city machine, feeding off its emissions and its discharge, just like a rat. Why couldn't he go where the rats went? It seemed only fair to him that he would be allowed to.

So he had tried.

It turned out to be a painful manoeuvre and at one stage, he even found himself trapped in a vice of wood and stone, panicking to no avail and wondering if this was how he would come to an end, stuck in a crack; filler for a broken building. But he wasn't the sort to give up, so he shuffled and pulled his way along another couple of feet, until the ground disappeared beneath him and he slid down into a hole until he was up to his waist in earth.

He waited then to ensure that he wasn't going to go any further. Hoping that more of his below didn't become his above. But nothing happened. It actually turned out that his feet were resting on a rough step. And below it, there was another, and another. There were four in total. He was standing on part of an old stairway.

The novelty of it was not lost on Oscar, although it was blurred by his need for warmth, and the end of his wit approaching. Down the four steps he scrambled and slipped, until he fell on his face in the gap below.

For a long time, Oscar just lay there in the darkness. The place exuded eerie warmth that was so welcome; he wanted to let it seep over and into him before he even tried to think again. The feeling soaked into him, and the cold that had not long ago had been anchored into his very marrow was replaced by something that Oscar hadn't felt in a long time. It was Comfort.

When he came round, Oscar could hear scurrying nearby. Ah, the rats were there too. This was their place; probably some cellar or other that had long been forgotten, he thought. It was likely that he would catch lurgy, scurvy, the mange, or something horribly fungal that would rot his skin before he finally died. Or he could be all right. There was only one way to find out.

Oscar lit a match, as it was far too dark to see anything. The match helped, but the circle of light was tiny and clarified nothing for him. He felt his way around until he found a wooden crate, and what turned out to be a ten-year-old newspaper. He set a fire and nursed it in such a way that it was bright, and not built for warmth. Only then was his discovery revealed to him, in full magnitude. He thought of the word magnitude because the room, or wherever the hell it was that he found himself, seemed to have no end that he could easily see. It went on and on out of the firelight, the ground uneven, but the ceiling uniform and flat, like a cave under construction. It was frightening, or would have been, if Oscar hadn't found it so bloody exciting. In all the years since he'd dropped out of society, this was the first sign he'd been given that the decision he'd made to discontinue his robotic life was the right one.

There *was* more to life than what he'd been taught.

This was the first city gap that Oscar had ever seen, but since then, he'd found them all over Dublin. Most were much smaller than the one under South Great George's Street, but a couple were even bigger still. The most impressive of all he had discovered was the underground water tunnel from Vartry to Stillorgan that was four or five kilometres of cool silent darkness, chilling and magnificent. But the most surprising were the sewers that led to and from St Michan's. It had been possible once, he'd been told by another who knew some of the ways, to actually travel under the River Liffey, to the south side and into the grounds of Christchurch Cathedral. But, not being too fond of the idea that the brickwork of a nineteenth century tunnel would be all that stood between him and a river full of filthy, and not to mention, very heavy water, Oscar had passed on the impulse to experience that particular unlikely passageway.

So, it was to the George's Street gap that Oscar always returned; the place was as close to a home as a man like him could have. And it was there that he brought the stricken form of Terry when there was nowhere else that he could think of bringing the boy.

Oscar stirred a pot of tea on a heating fire and waited for his young companion to awaken. He stirred, and he hoped that when the young man woke, he would reveal to Oscar the reason behind the mysterious outburst of the night before. At least that was Oscar's plan.

Oscar watched the tea as it began to simmer. It was the only way to make tea really, to boil it in the water, a little patience always making the best brew.

"What the?" groaned Terry from across the fire. "Where am I? Who the hell are you?" The boy rose quickly and cast around into the darkness and then to Oscar.

"Who are you? How..." Terry stopped as he remembered the night before. "I can see you," he said to the old man in astonishment, "I can see you."

"Yes," Oscar replied. "And without a microscope too. Well done." The grey tramp tutted and poured tea into his cup, which he handed Terry. The boy took the cup automatically whilst counting brain cells and body parts.

"You had a skin full last night, eh?"

Terry winced, it was true he had to agree, but hold on!

"What is it to you?" Terry wrinkled his nose at the cup. "And what the hell is this?"

"It's tea, you ungrateful little fucker!" Oscar chided, hadn't he picked the little bastard out of the gutter?

"This is tea, is it?" Terry grimaced, "When did I ask you for tea? And, how did I get here? Wherever here is."

Oscar growled.

"Watch yourself, boy. I picked you out of the gutter last night when you were stupid drunk and you were screaming and shouting about everybody being gone." Oscar made a pathetic face and said, "Where is everybody? What happened?" he mocked. Terry stifled a smart answer. He remembered now all right. He sat back on the ground and drank his tea. To his surprise, it was perfect.

"Eh... thanks," he said.

"How are you feeling?" Oscar asked him.

"I feel bad. I wonder what happened to Peter and those chicks. I feel bad for running out on them. And..." he stopped.

"And?" Oscar asked, and Terry shook his head.

"I'm afraid to think about what happened. If it really happened?" Terry's eyes widened as he involuntarily recalled his embarrassing panic. Oscar watched him reach into his pocket and bring out a small plastic bottle that rattled in his hand.

"What's that?" Oscar asked. Terry ignored the old man and emptied a small heap of tiny bright blue pills into the palm of his hand. The boy downed them easily, washed them away with a swig of tea and the bottle went back in his jacket. Oscar changed his tack.

"Why don't you tell me what happened last night?" Oscar asked. Terry gave the grey tramp a look up and down.

"Alright," he said, "have you got any more tea?"

"I've loads more," said Oscar, who had no more.

"My name is Terry, by the way," said Terry.

"Oscar," said Oscar smiling, "I'm your dad."

"Yeah sure," said Terry, and they both laughed.

CHAPTER NINE
MARIE-ANNE/MARIE AT THE SCENE OF THE CRIME

TEXT MESSAGE...

> How did it go?
> Terry has
> surfaced ok.
> Don't worry, you
> can continue as
> planned.

The next morning, in the grey and standard drizzle, Marie replaced her phone and stood in the great courtyard of the DTI thinking about the facts.

On the northern shore of the River Liffey, just metres from the famed market streets of Smithfield, an area that had in recent years become a centre of Irish trade, lay the famed centre of Irish learning; the Dublin Technological Institute, or the DTI as it was really known.

FACT: The DTI was originally designed, not for use as a public university, but more as a religious and scholarly place of learning. In centuries past, learned men, devout and intelligent, had been an abundant feature of its corridors and classrooms. Actually, this was true for the entire country.

FACT: The main building was built in 1645 during the confederate war in Ireland. It had been a gift from King George to the Catholics, or what would later be labelled as a bribe, to Archbishop Giovanni Battista Rinuccini, the Papal Nuncio who had come to Ireland at the time, in the hope of driving the Protestants out once and for all.

FACT: The plans were graciously accepted and the College was completed in 1647.

FACT: Archbishop Rinuccini ignored the gesture and continued arming the confederate army.

FACT: Marie-Anne was good with facts. Oh, she knew loads of them. These were just the ones that came to mind when she looked around the courtyard while awaiting the arrival of the other players in her weird little group. Yeah, she was a bloody brain-box, an encyclopaedia futilica, a thessaurian marvel. Her intelligence had become a burden to her. And, even at such a young age, she had grown to hate it.

Ever since she was a child, she'd been able to learn things that none of the other kids were able to learn, and it had made her an outsider. But Marie was smart enough to know how to overcome such a problem. She was a damn fine actor.

A year ago, for a number of reasons, Marie-Anne had invented Marie. Not a huge name change, but enough to associate her new personality to something outside of her real self. This was vital. It wasn't like she was playing a role in a play, this was how she would be spending her life for the foreseeable future, and she'd had to become a separate entity, or lose her real self completely.

So Marie was born. A smart-arse bitch that was popular and not really bothered with learning anything more than the cools guys' phone numbers, and only then so that she could avoid them when they called. But the brain was still there, working things out at an incredible rate. She still had to work at barely passing exams, at looking surprised. She had to try and stop yawning in predictable conversations, had to act interested in the presence of predictable people. It was the same in nearly all events, except, well, last night had been anything but predictable. There were reactions under stress to be calculated, which were incalculable no matter how many mental simulations she had run.

Marie spotted Rachel and Peter walking up the road towards the gate. She could see the match there instantly. The way they smiled in short embarrassed bursts, the way they watched when the other was speaking. Marie was jealous in a certain way. It wasn't that she wanted Peter for herself; it was more that she wanted to have a relationship like that of her own.

Well, good for them; let them enjoy it while it lasted. Rachel was a cool girl, pretty but shy. Marie-Anne was sure that the reason she [Marie] and Rachel got along so well was a simple case of comfort. Marie's rash loudness created a perfect canopy for Rachel to hide beneath. Yeah, Rachel was all right. Marie waved at her friend as she passed through the gate, and received a wave back. It would be a real pity.

Peter and Rachel had driven off in a mildly embarrassed panic earlier that morning in order to find somewhere to ditch the driving offences of the night before. It was amazing how the act of stealing the car had seemed so logical and right at the time, and how now, when it was obvious that 'the disappearance' was not permanent, they had undergone the sudden realisation that they were thieves, who would be arrested and put in jail like any other simple-minded joy-riders caught with a stolen car parked outside the house. Marie-Anne waited until the two had gotten within earshot, and slipped into character once more.

"Well, hey there, guys," Marie laughed at their approaching guilty faces. "Ditch the evidence, did we?"

"Shh!" said Rachel, looking around mortified. The poor girl looked frazzled and embarrassed.

"Oh come on!" Marie goaded. "It's no big deal. Where did you dump it?" Peter shuffled his feet and looked around like the FBI was following him.

"Down near Christchurch," said Peter, "Eh, can we go somewhere else and talk about this?" he said.

"You're joking?" Marie exclaimed, "After last night, you want to go somewhere where there aren't any people? I don't know about you, but I'm not going anywhere that doesn't have at least a million other people in sight at all times." Peter actually smiled a little, he was a strange one, Marie felt, but there was something about him. He was definitely a little sexy.

"Yeah, I know what you mean. Have you seen Terry yet?"

"No, the freak-out artist hasn't shown his face... Oh, there he is, Aha! Cooey!" Marie let out a laugh of surprise and waved to Terry, who was hurrying up the street with his shoulders hunched over like a fugitive. He reddened when he realised that Marie's 'Cooey!' was aimed at him; he saw them and put his head down in embarrassment, but he kept coming.

The three waited for Terry to reach them in a protracted silence that even Marie was unable to break. They were dying to find out what had happened to Terry during the night, and were relieved that he seemed to be unharmed, physically at least. If they were honest with themselves, they would have allowed the word suicide to enter their thoughts, but their nerves were in such a delicate state that its inclusion could have snapped a few important chords that were already frayed enough.

Terry reached the group and started talking immediately. If he was fast as a bullet on a normal day, this was the speed of light in action.

"Hi guys, hey! What's going on ha? How did yez get on last night? Fuck man, that was mad, wasn't it? It really happened, right, yeah? It must have, I mean you're all here together so it must have, yeah? Oh, man, all I can remember is… Peter, hey, how are you feeling, all the people are back, it's mad, isn't it? I don't know what to think. What do you think it was? I mean, it wha-" He stopped for a breath. There was a brief pause and it was Marie who laughed first.

Then the other joined in, Terry too.

"There's a few words for you!" said Marie, and they continued to laugh.

***

Across the road, Oscar watched the students laughing. It hadn't gone so badly, his meeting with Terry, not badly at all, despite the obvious fact that that the boy was losing his marbles. There was something strange happening to Terry, that was really obvious. Oscar sat down in a doorway across from the gate and tried to read the body language of the group. He'd been watching people for a long time now and he was good at it.

That pale boy had a fitful step. He was anxious, that was clear; it was the same with the dark-haired girl. They were together too; Oscar could clearly see they were pairing off. But the redhead, now there was a peculiar stance. She didn't look half as worried as the others.

Why?

Perhaps he was thinking backwards. Why should she be worried? That was the real question.

Oscar decided that there wasn't going to be any wandering the streets that day. He was going to wait right where he was and keep an eye on things. There was something going on all right, and he was going to find out what it was. Once he did, he was going to help Terry any way he could.

...If he could.

***

Welcome to the Internet...

In the library, Peter was sitting in front of a computer with the others huddled round. They were searching, googling, hoping.

Between them, it had proven a difficult task to vocalise the occurrence in *The Inn* into a single phrase that they were all comfortable with, but Marie had made a suggestion, and they had finally come to an agreement: Group delusion.

Peter typed 'group delusions' into a search engine and it came back at them with 1,720,000 possible pages to choose from.

"Great," said Terry, "that narrows it down!" The others gave him wary looks. "Don't worry," Terry smiled, "I'm not going to flip. At least I don't think I am." The rest of the group laughed nervously at the joke, the reality of which was not forgotten.

"Ok, ok." Peter raised his hands. This was his field. Research. "We just have to narrow it down." Peter was feeling unhinged today as it was, without having a group of people leaning over him trying to quantify their problem and decide their fates. They had two options.

1) Everyone had actually disappeared off the planet last night and had returned again sometime this morning.

2) They were all crazy.

Peter didn't care for either option. So they had come to the Internet to find number three. Although, when Peter remembered the resemblance of last night's events to his own reoccurring nightmare, Peter seriously doubted it could be anything besides a clear case of number two.

Something else occurred to him.

"You guys are real, right?" he asked hopefully, waning a smile back over his shoulder. Only Rachel answered.

"Not funny," she said.

"Just narrow your search parameters," Marie suggested in an out of character show of steadiness.

"Ok," said Peter. He thought for a moment and typed: group delusions involving disappearances. There were 62,500 pages.

"Add group," said Terry.

"What?"

"Group disappearances," he added. Peter typed: group delusions involving group disappearances. There was the same number.

"Let's just look at a couple of these?" Rachel asked, "Like, the top five or something." The first one read:

Schizophrenia - Group annexation. Peter clicked on it and was brought to a wordy page outlining 'groups' of studies on schizophrenia, which was obviously not what they were after.

The second choice was about disappearances in Nepal, again, not what they were looking for. This was followed by another paper on schizophrenia, an outline for a Rolemaster character, followed by yet another paper on mental disturbance.

None of them liked where this was headed.

"Try visions instead of delusions. Delusion is a bit negative," said Marie.

"Yeah," Rachel agreed, "you ask a negative question and you'll get a negative answer."

"So what?" Peter asked.

"Group visions... em?"

"Reports of group visions," Marie piped in. They all looked at her. "What?" she asked.

Peter typed: reports of group visions. It took only a second before they all saw that these were indeed the correct key words. There were hundreds of thousands of pages too, except this time, it seemed every one of them held an account or accounts of events that were, if not identical, at least vaguely similar to what had happened the night before.

"Shit," Peter exclaimed at the screen, "this is going to take a while." Marie pulled her seat up beside his and took control of the mouse.

"Ok," she said, "I've got it. Go and get a coffee or something."

"I…" Peter began but stopped. He looked up at Rachel. She looked like she could do with a coffee, "Ok? Do you want anything?"

"Two sugars, no milk, cheers," Marie answered, never taking her eyes off the screen.

"What about you?" Peter asked Terry, "you coming?" He hoped for a no. Terry looked at Marie, and she gave him a haughty sniff.

"I'll follow you guys after I narrow this down. I'll meet you in the canteen," Marie said. Peter saw Terry decide very quickly that he would prefer their company to that of Marie, and judging by the look on his face, there were also wild animals with whom he would have preferred to hang. It was obvious that Terry was spooked, well, weren't they all? It would probably be better to keep an eye on Terry himself, just in case there was a repeat of the night before.

"Well, come on then," Rachel called from the door, and the two boys followed her out.

     *

When she was sure that they had gone, Marie stopped scrolling through the choices on the screen and opened her email. She chose from her inbox a mail with the subject: 'reports of group visions', she then pressed print and waited impatiently for the dialogue box to open on her screen. She checked her watch; she had to be going soon.

***

From where he sat, across from the DTI gates, Oscar had an excellent view of the courtyard. He'd been sitting there for an hour when the group came out of the library and headed across the yard, but there was one missing, the redhead.

In the brief moment that he noticed this, Oscar found that he was staring at Terry, who was looking back at him with a worried expression. Oscar though about waving but decided not to, in favour of a nod; Terry just clenched his jaw and turned away to follow the pale boy and the dark girl into the canteen building, without looking back again.

"Well, you might turn away, boy, as well you might." Oscar spoke softly as he looked back towards the library for the redhead. There was no sign of her.

The mid-morning was grey and quiet, and Oscar wasn't expecting any more movement for the next half an hour at least, when the door of the library opened again, but only about a foot or so this time. *What is this?* he thought.

A few seconds later, the library door opened fully and out trotted the redheaded girl. She was empty-handed and her bag was absent from her shoulder as she hurried along, not to the canteen but towards the University gates. As the redhead came towards him, Oscar noticed her looking back at the canteen doors a couple of times. It was obvious that she didn't want the others to see her leaving.

"Why?" Oscar asked the air as she came through the gates and hurried up the street. "Where are you going in such a hurry?"

This development had him worried. He'd just sworn to himself that he would watch over Terry constantly, and now he was going to do the opposite. But he was sure that there was something in this girl's behaviour that demanded his attention. And what if it was nothing? If she was just late for an appointment? There could be a hundred valid explanations for the redhead's behaviour. He had to decide quickly, she was moving fairly quickly up the street, and would be gone from his sight in a matter of moments. Stay or go, stay or go, stay or go?

"Go!" he said, and rose from his step. "Definitely go." So Oscar shuffled off after her in his usual manner; not attracting any attention to his progress, but moving quickly all the same. He was good at following. All he had to do was stay the right distance away and she would never spot him. This was his talent. And, it was miles better than freezing your ass off waiting for something to happen. Easily.

***

In the canteen, Peter was shocked. The place was packed full of people! It was supposed to be the middle of a lecture, but there were more students in there than he'd ever seen, even at lunchtime.

"What the hell's going on?" Peter asked the other two.

"What do ya mean?" said Terry.

"It's packed in here!" said Rachel, "I don't understand it."

Terry laughed, "What? You mean… aha ha, ha!"

"What's so funny," Peter demanded defensively. He didn't understand it either. Terry jostled a few people down on a lightly populated bench and continued to laugh as Peter and Rachel joined him.

"Ha, I bet you two go to every single lecture in the year, don't ya?" Peter and Rachel looked at each other. Well, yeah, they did.

"Doesn't everybody?" Rachel asked, even as she looked around and saw the answer all around her, chatting and playing cards. It was like a bar without the alcohol.

"This is a university," said Terry, "nobody goes to lectures. I mean," and here he shook his head at them, "lectures are great and all, you know, for learning things and such, but there's no need to go to them all the time. You go when you have to. And, at the vital moments."

"Vital moments?" Peter asked.

"Yeah! Towards the end of the year, the lecturers always get nervous. Oh my god, everyone's going to fail my class and I'm going to get fired. That's the time of year you need to go to lectures, when they starts to 'revise' certain sections of the course. And you just learn those few bits and pieces and, kablammo! You've passed." Terry laughed out loud again. Peter and Rachel were amazed.

Peter gawked around again at the crowded canteen. So this was how normal people got through the year? All those days Peter had spent isolating himself, sitting alone between lectures, writing in his diary, suspecting that he was different from everybody else. And now he'd just found out that he was right. Exactly right.

"Did you know about this?" Peter asked Rachel, who shook her head.

"No, I swear I didn't."

"Hey," said Terry, "you learn something new every day, don't ya?" He smiled at them and then became suddenly bashful. There was something they had all learnt yesterday that was far from having been brushed aside.

"I freaked out last night," Terry said, lowering his eyes to the table, "didn't I?"

"Em, yeah, you did a bit," said Peter, feeling sorry for him. He looked at Rachel.

"Oh, it wasn't that bad," she said, "it was quite funny really, wasn't it, Peter?" Peter smiled at Rachel. She was right. Terry was a good guy.

"Yeah," said Peter, "I mean, what else were you supposed to do in the situation?" This lifted Terry's head and spirits.

"Absolutely. It was crazy, wasn't it?"

"Damn right it was," Peter agreed. "Sure, we ended up stealing a car!"

"Seriously!" said Terry.

"Yeah," Rachel agreed, "that's much worse than legging it."

"Where did you end up anyway?" Peter asked. Terry looked down again. He didn't want to talk about it, that much was clear.

"Don't worry about it," said Rachel, "who wants a coffee?"

"No thanks," said Peter.

"I'll get them," said Terry, who jumped up from his seat at the chance to change the subject. "Oh shit!" he cried and dropped down again so quickly Peter was sure he saw a trail in Terry's wake. "Maybe you should go," Terry said to Rachel, "I think there's someone up there that might slap the face off me if she sees me."

"What?" Rachel turned to Peter, who shrugged.

"Sam," said Terry.

"The girl we were in the pub with last night, before everyone... you know."

"Oh ok," said Rachel, "I'll go. What was it that Marie wanted?"

"The scary chick? Black, two sugars," said Terry.

"Marie's not scary," Rachel smiled, and added, "I wonder how she's getting on?"

"I don't think she's going to have too much luck. Did you see the amount of crap that came up when we searched?" Peter said, shaking his head and searching through his pockets for money. "Get me a 7up," he added. Rachel left his money and went to the counter where Sam was serving. Peter watched her leave.

"Nice view?" Terry asked.

"Eh. Do you think she'll find anything?" Peter avoided the topic.

"Oh yeah," said Terry, "I'm sure they serve 7up here, aha."

"Very funny. I was talking about Marie."

"She better find something. Otherwise..." Terry stopped and let out a sigh.

"Yeah," said Peter, "I know."

Otherwise, there was nothing.

***

Chase scene...

It didn't matter how well a body knew the streets, it was no match for knowing where you're headed. Oscar rounded the corner and the statement was proven once again.

"Damn," he said. Where was she? He cast about him in a hurry. A couple of streets ago, he'd been keeping himself inconspicuous but now there was no need, the reason had disappeared around yet another turn ahead, and could be headed anywhere. Oscar was not about to let that happen again, so he opened his coat and broke into a run, heading in the same general direction as before.

From shop windows and doorways, Oscar could feel the stares pushing him down the street away from them. A tramp they could handle, helpless and drunk in the corner, but if these sorts of people had energy and ran around the place unbidden? What were decent people to do? The bums and winos were supposed to be ill and dying, soon to be no one's problem. People like Oscar couldn't be healthy. It disproved society and every ad on TV.

Oscar knew that these thoughts were his own, but he was willing to bet his health on their accuracy. He was breaking the rules with this show of strength, it would not be a shock should he be arrested.

He reached the corner where Capel Street met the river, and breathed a sigh to find that he had caught up with the redhead again. She was heading north along Ormond Quay, and didn't look like turning off. Before Oscar congratulated himself on his pursuit, he saw that the redhead had slowed dramatically and was barely moving now as she approached a building, a bar...

Oh, that was where she was headed. Oscar felt a fool for not guessing, the girl's pace having delayed his logical thoughts.

She was going back to *The Inn*. He should have known that she was headed to the scene of last night's strange affair.

Oscar watched the girl as her steps slowed so much that it was hard to discern the moment when she'd halted completely. She took a deep breath and let it out. Then she looked around to see if anyone was watching, but it was obviously only an instinct, for if she had really been looking, she would have easily spotted the grey tramp that stood in plain view just down the quay from her. But the redhead didn't notice. Instead, she straightened her body as if to draw strength, and then stepped through the door into *The Inn,* closing it behind her as she went. Oscar took a look around himself before approaching the bar; he felt that the redhead's reticence was still hanging in the air around him, and he was dreading reaching the building too, but he continued.

He laid a pox on the glass panel beside the door; it was too stained or too frosted to see through, so he was forced to try the side alley. As he crept along the northern wall, Oscar felt nervous and it irked him. He was Oscar, this was his city, and even if he was caught hanging around by the devil himself, he knew that he would never draw a second glance from the horny bastard. All anyone would see was a grey tramp in an alley, along with the rest of the rubbish. Oscar had nothing to worry about, but he worried all the same.

Towards the back of the alley near the keg-room door, Oscar was able to get a view of sorts in to the main lounge, due to the fortuitous peeling back of a stained glass effect sticker in the corner of a window pane. It was a hole just big enough for a good peek, and he did so through it.

There they were, the players in this part of the mystery; the redhead amongst them. To Oscar, she looked like a little girl as she stood looking at her feet in a broken circle of large men, three or four at least. There was a blonde boy there too. No, it was a smaller man with glasses and white hair. A familiar looking man, but not one Oscar could instantly place.

The small man was doing the talking, and seemed to grow more agitated as the seconds passed. The girl was moving slowly backwards away from him, though she had little room, with the large hand belonging to a large man resting on her shoulder.

The little grey man advanced and struck the girl, felling her easily. Oscar would have let out a yelp if he had been the yelping type. It was lucky for her, he guessed, that he wasn't such a person. The redhead was not in any position to have a stranger interrupting her business or further aggravating the situation. Who knows what would happen? Oscar tried to decide what he should do, as the girl was dragged into a back room by the grey man's hefty help.

Of all the advantages he felt that he had in his free lifestyle, Oscar was hindered always by his standing and appearance. The Garda would not believe him, nor did he feel that their aid would be forthcoming should they do so. Politics may have been changing in Ireland, but there was one thing that Oscar knew to be the truth.

No one would take the word of a tramp over that of the man who stood in *The Inn* at that moment. Oscar had finally placed the face for sure. That was Walter Thisgo in there, Treoraí an Tír, the President/Prime Minister of Ireland, and there wasn't a hope on blue earth that Oscar was going to get any help from the authorities.

TEXT   MESSAGE...

> We're nearly there. Be careful of the old man.

CHAPTER TEN
WATCHING OVER YOU

Rachel and Peter were in heat.

There was a passion growing between them; it raced through their bodies. Their hands were slick with nervous sweat, and hasty self-conscious smiles were being given as answers. There was a buzz forming, linking them with ripples of excitement that were causing giddy outbursts to embarrass each in every faltering sentence.

Terry, of course, was doing his best to ruin it. He couldn't help it, Rachel supposed, but he was definitely getting in the way of her and Peter's humiliating courtship. Terry was right, though; they had no business with romance in their present circumstances.

"Listen, guys," he told the other two, "I know you're getting sweet on each other and everything, but we are in a bit of a crisis situation, you know?"

"Ahem," coughed Peter.

He may be intelligent and mysterious, thought Rachel, *but he is a bit shy.* Although Rachel reckoned that it would be difficult for her to come out with anything more coherent just then. She could feel her face growing hotter. God, was she that embarrassed?

"Well?" Terry asked, without much hope, "Are we going to go and see what's become of Marie?"

"Yeah, absolutely," Rachel answered, "sorry, I just feel a bit disorientated after everything."

"Me too," Peter said to Terry, with an apology unspoken, "probably too much coffee." Terry laughed at this.

"No worries, guys, let's get going, though. I don't want tonight to end up like last night. Ya know?" They were all in agreement.

Rachel followed Peter and Terry out, and felt as she did that they were reaffirming some control over their actions. Sitting in the canteen staring into Peter's eyes, she had felt a strange fondness for Peter, and the emotion, though enjoyable, had seemed too strong to be real. Was this love? Or was she just getting a fever? She wouldn't be surprised if she turned out to have some sort of brain disease the way things were going; she was glad to be out in the cold air again, and her head started to clear as the three walked through the university courtyard.

"Thank God for that," Terry exclaimed, as they walked in file, "It was bloody hot in there."

"Yeah, it was feverish," Peter agreed, and Rachel smiled at the back of his head. So he was feeling it too?

They entered the library and went to the computers at the back. Everything was there where they had left it, except for Marie. They couldn't find the girl anywhere.

"Why not call her on her mobile," Peter asked, "she's probably around somewhere."

"We can't, she uses mine," Rachel answered, at a loss to say anything else. She wasn't too surprised at her friend's disappearance, Marie did as she pleased, but Rachel decided to ask the librarian anyway. It was a waste of time. Maybe in a public library, the librarian would have an idea of who came and went, but in the DTI library, the workers used the place as a hang out, and to get some money off their tuition.

"Any luck," Peter and Terry asked when she returned from the front desk with a bundle of papers. "What are they?" Peter asked.

"Oh, this was left on the printer," said Rachel, who'd forgotten that the sheets had been given to her. "Marie must have printed them out." Rachel looked into Peter's pale and open face. *Concentrate,* she inwardly ordered herself.

She looked down at the printed pages and began to leaf through them. It was definitely Marie's stuff; accounts of group phenomena, visions, and other supernatural crap. She shared them out. "We can read these until she comes back, I suppose," she said, and then began to read what was left.

A half hour later, Peter and Terry were sitting in silence and Rachel was reading aloud.

"During meditation, the Druids used to stand completely still on one leg, with the other foot resting ankle to knee against their standing foot," Rachel read from the printed text, "and there's a picture here." She showed them a sketch of an old man, supposedly a druid, standing on one foot in the manner described. The two boys nodded and handed the sheet back, they didn't have much else to contribute.

"Read it again," said Peter, as though he hadn't heard every word, and every piece of it hadn't rung true to their situation.

"Yeah, just once more," said Terry, "I just need to hear it again, yeah?"

"Ok," said Rachel, "but it's… Ok sure." And so she read the piece again.

The passage was purported to be from a book known as: 'The Myths about the Druids - and how science was mistaken for magic.' And it said:

Amongst the reports in legend and in stories passed down by the Seannachai about the race known as the druids, amidst stories of their ability to control the weather, there are some extraordinary tales about how the Druids punished those who did not believe in their authority, or indeed, that of their King, or High King.

The tales of their ability to control the weather can be easily explained by the druid's knowledge of weather divination, it is easy to call the rain when the rain is due, and there are some other feats that require further scientific examination in an attempt to explain their true nature.

One of the most baffling talents of the Druids was the ability to create large-scale delusions in a victim, or indeed a group of victims, causing them to undergo a complete isolation from the entire human race.

Many reports of group visions (here, the web browser had underlined the key search phrase) have been described in legend when the druids would punish a person in an extremely cruel manner to make an example of them in public.

One account, which is quite vivid in its explanation of the ceremony, was committed to record by a Gaeltacht teacher in

1968 during an Arts Council project in Connemara. The purpose of the project was to record stories that had, up till then, only existed in the memories of the Seannachai to prevent their loss as the discipline died out.

The account tells of a young man accused of betraying the king of Munster. After being found guilty, the youth was sentenced to <u>Daille ó ndruidí</u>, which was new Irish for 'the blindness of the druids'. The offender was then tied with chains to a massive wooden post in the centre of the town, in a ceremony during which the druid involved chanted in a meditative state whilst chewing the meat of a dog. The meat was then fed to the young man, and the people were ordered back to their homes until the following morning.

When the next day dawned, and the people of the village came back, they found that, on the surface, the situation hadn't changed, the young man was still chained to the post and all looked normal.

It was only as the day wore on that the people realised something had happened. The young man could not see or hear the townspeople, and as the morning turned into afternoon, he began to scream and shout to them as though they were still in their houses and had as yet not risen. This went on for the entire day until the offender began to struggle and attempt to tear himself away from the sturdy post, to no avail, thinking that he had been abandoned by the entire town and left to starve.

Always within a couple of days, the victim of this bizarre ritual was reduced to a snivelling wreck, and quite often attempted suicide. At this stage, it was decided by the druids or the king whether the offender had been punished adequately. And, should this be the case, a second ritual was performed where the druid would once again meditate until the tormented individual could see the people around him again, and the curse or 'Mallaítear' would be lifted.

During meditation, the Druids used to stand completely still on one leg, with the other foot resting ankle to knee against their standing foot...

"And that's where it stops," Rachel finished. She leafed through the bunch of papers she had collected from the printer, but there was no carry on page from this one.

"What should we do now?" asked Peter, "I mean, it's a bit on-the-money, isn't it?" And it was; it was bang on, and the three of them knew it.

"We're fuckin cursed!" said Terry, his eyes widening but luckily, not registering the wildness of the night before.

"Relax," said Peter, holding his hands up, "it's just some old Seannachai's story that came up when Marie was doing her search. There are probably still millions of other reasons for the stuff that's been happening to us."

"Yeah," Rachel agreed, "let just find Marie and go somewhere and reason this out. Ok?"

"Cool," said Terry, but he didn't look convinced.

"You sure?" asked Peter, concerned for his new friend's mental health.

"Yeah, yeah! I know I freaked out, but I'm grand, really." Rachel had to admit that Terry did look like he was keeping it together. Or at least that he was trying his best. Rachel was beginning to like Terry and his super-chatty but friendly manner; he was a good guy, she just knew it.

"Well let's go and find Marie then," she said, and they headed out of the library.

***

Security...

To the ignorant newcomer to Áras an Uachtaran, the mansion would seem to be an opulent and welcoming surrounding in which a leader of the highest calibre could easily find the calm and repose needed in order to lead effectively and calmly. Walter Thisgo knew better. He knew the house and its outhouses intimately, in such a singular fashion as would have been impossible for any other tenant of the building. And after all, wasn't that all he was, a tenant?

It had now been three years since Walter Thisgo and his Progressive Party had successfully asked the citizens of Ireland if they would prefer the office of the Taoiseach and the President to be merged in favour of a single driving force. The referendum had been a landslide, and the office of Treoraí an Tír had been born.

Hitler-like, so the Regressives had called his rise to power. But Walter had ensured their silence by leading the Dáil in legislating tighter rules to repair the fractured remains of proportional representation. Soon, maybe, the Party system would die. It was difficult to see it, even though it was his ultimate gain. Each constituency led by a board of 75% of the vote, each candidate voted for on their own, without allegiance?

A journalist would have called it far-fetched, but as Walter had just finished telling such a reporter; "Far-fetched indeed, But as you know, my aim is, as always, to reach far into the future and fetch for this country the objectives of our aspirations." Walter leaned back on his stool and tried to hide his excitement. In a few short hours, he would be realising those aspirations. He thought only briefly of his family. It had been far too long since he had sat with them and had a simple meal, but now was an important time for all of them, and they were not a simple family. Their lives were in politics.

"Treoraí?" asked one young lady, Walter recognised as Sylvia from the 'People' newspaper. She was a good questioner.

"Yes, Sylvia?" he responded, "This is the last question by the way, ladies and gentlemen. I am terribly hungry, and I feel I may fall off my seat in front of you."

"Do you think, Treoraí, that your constant shows of solidarity; the press receptions on the streets, or the stool you sit on now are nothing more than a showman's attempt to cow public opinion?"

This was a very good question, and one that Walter had formulated an answer for, three months, twelve days, and fourteen hours ago.

"Absolutely, Sylvia," Walter responded, "I seek, with every movement I make, and every word that I utter, to guarantee the people of Ireland that I am genuinely in touch with your point of view, and that I will and have always spent every possible moment I can thinking about what you want, and what you need me to do to achieve those wants." As he finished, Walter was sure he heard an excited 'meep!' from Siobhán, his P.A. The girl was young and considered the answer a 'win' for him and the Progressives, which was far from being true. It was the truth and nothing more.

"Thank you, sir," Sylvia responded and stopped her Dictaphone.

"No problem, Sylvia, and let's hope that my formulaic answer serves to finish the subject and allow more time for what is really important, as was my intent?" Walter smiled at the group and they smiled back.

Siobhán stepped forward and spoke to the room.

"Thank you all once more for coming to the Áras to tidy up some of these issues with the Treoraí, since the rain washed us out down at the Dáil. But now he must be off. Thanks again." Walter stood and smiled.

"An glóir na hEireann," he said, and that was the end of that.

Walter walked down the hall towards the President's Study with Siobhán and Cullen in tow, as well as a few of the Progressive thinkers who Walter had been personally training to think in bigger terms.

"It's going well, Walter," said one.

"It's getting bigger than you, sir," said another.

"Yes," Walter agreed, "finally, it is going in the right direction. This country is on the verge of greatness, now everyone; let's keep it going, shall we? Siobhán?"

"Yes?"

"Off you go home, don't worry about me. Everyone else, see you tomorrow." Walter entered the President's Study, a room he had renovated from study to suite six months before, telling everyone that he had little time for stairs. He stepped inside and turned to close the door, the others were already heading down the hall, but his security chief Cullen was ever present, and prevented Walter's privacy.

"Yes?" said Walter.

"I have to have a look around, sir," said Cullen.

"More pigeon trouble?" Thisgo smiled, referring to the offending bird that had smashed one of the lower panes of the many-panelled study window two days before. In fact, the repairmen were slow in arriving and the panel was still only replaced by a fitted piece of wood.

"Just want to check the entrances are secured before the

night fellas get here," Cullen said. "You know the routine. Mr Thisgo."

"Yes, yes. Cullen. Well, on you go." Walter waved his man in and watched as the guard systematically checked every inch of the room. and personally primed the electronic beams that crisscrossed the window, ensuring that the offending pane was covered.

"Thank you. Cullen-" Thisgo smiled as his long-time protector exited- "Enjoy your day off tomorrow, won't you?"

"Absolutely, sir," Cullen smiled.

"A hundred pints?" Walter asked.

"A thousand, sir," said Cullen in a friendly tone, though he did not smile, "see you the day after, sir."

"Indeed," Walter said, and closed the door behind the security chief.

With Cullen finally gone, Walter was left to himself and his plans.

"Security," he said aloud, and he traversed the room doing a stock take of his own. The need to be kept safe was a defeatist blow to his ideas on governance. At present, he sat above the people, protected and watched, given import due to his station, and not his achievements. Soon, that was all going to change. He felt that the ruddy head of a boil was rising out of the skin of the country and its people. And, when it burst, Walter wanted, not to be the one holding the lance, but the man who thought his country to do so for itself.

Urgh! What a distasteful phrase, obviously the invention of a worried mind. It was not like Walter to be so occupied with one train of thought, when he needed to focus his mind on so many things. It was obvious that he should take some rest. Then he would be ready for the challenge ahead.

"Goodnight," he said to the boarded up windowpane, and began to dress for dinner.

***

Watching over you...

"Why can't you call her?" Terry asked again. He had begun to pace half an hour before, and had taken to it in a disturbing way. Rachel was positive that he was describing a pattern in the flowered carpet with his steps, she couldn't yet tell what it was, but she was sure that if she let him, Terry's constant thread would describe itself in missing shag pile.

"I can't call her because she doesn't have a phone. She always uses mine. Besides, I don't think it's a big deal," said Rachel, but she did. "Marie is always wandering off and doing what she pleases. She'll turn up here or at mine later, don't worry about it."

"Are you sure you don't want to stay here?" Peter asked Rachel, his face arranging into unconvincing nonchalance. She wished that she could, but she needed to be on her own for a while to get her head around everything that had happened.

"Yeah I'm sure. I want to be there in case Marie calls in. You'll call me if she comes back here?"

"Absolutely. I could walk you?" said Peter, trying on that cool smile again, but failing again. He was so cute.

"Na," said Rachel, "I think I'd like to have a break from everyone for a..."

"Ha!" Terry laughed from the couch. "Sorry. It's just, you know. After the *break* we got last night?" Rachel laughed too.

"I know, but I think I need some quiet to think." Rachel headed to the door.

"I'll call you if she turns up, you do the same," said Peter, when he opened the door for her.

"I will," said Rachel. She put her hand on his shoulder and darted a quick kiss onto his cheek before he could react either way, "See you tomorrow," she said, and turned away as the redness arrived on her neck.

"Cool yeah," Peter replied and closed the door.

A huge happy smile dawned on Rachel as she looked down Peter's driveway towards the road. She had no right to be so happy amidst this nightmare, but she couldn't contain her pleasure after that spark had travelled between her and Peter just a second before. She wanted to feel it again, or at least know if he'd experienced it too. How could he not? She turned around and looked at the door again. She just wanted to look at him one more time and see if that same smile was on his face.

Rachel shook her head. *Just go home, you lovesick Wally,* she ordered herself, and headed down the drive.

There was a sound behind her and she spun around, her grin immediately reappearing. The front door had opened and Peter was beaming out at her, like an idiot, a beautiful foolish idiot.

"Hi," he said, "I just…you know… See ya tomorrow."

"See ya," Rachel responded, and sent a burst of energy towards him before he closed the door and was gone again.

After that, Rachel really skipped home without a care. It wasn't until she got there and saw the darkness in the place, the abandoned look, that she remembered fully what had been happening to her. That woke her up and she went inside to sleep, and wait for Marie.
***

It was lonely and cold in the cellar below *The Inn*.

Tap, tap, tap! The window above Marie was being worried incessantly. Tap, tap, tap!

"Who is it?" she called in a loud whisper, not wanting anyone but the tapper to hear. The noise stopped, but she heard nothing else. From where she was in the darkness, tied to a chair on the far wall, Marie could neither see a figure, nor hear any movement. Maybe she'd imagined the tapping, or it could even have been a mouse or a loose hinge or… something other than a rescuer. Marie waited. There was a long drawn-out silence, and just when she felt that there would be nothing more, the tapping returned. Except this time, it was different.

The taps were more like raps, and they were succeeded by a: tap, tap, and smash! The glass in one of the little square panes must have been broken.

"Hello?" she tried. Then there was a pause.

"Ah hello, young girl?" she heard a man's voice.

"I'm trapped in here. Help me?"

"There're bars on the windows."

"I know, can you get help?"

"The Gardaí? I can't. That man, he was…"

"Yeah, I know," said Marie, her voice sounding sad, "the Gardaí won't help." There was a long pause before the voice came back again, this time filled with confidence and hope.

"I'll find help, girl. You just hold on there, alright?"

"Ok," said Marie, but there was no further response. The man was already gone. And, what was worse, the wind was now blowing in through the open pane, and its small size was creating a howling whistle. *Damnit it,* she thought. On top of everything else, she was going to freeze to death.

"Hurry," she said into the darkness below *The Inn*, "please hurry."

CHAPTER ELEVEN
THE REVOLVING DOOR

The view was peculiar to Rachel, not by its strangeness, but more down to her position in space. She looked down on the familiar bed from a point in the room that should only have been afforded to a fly, a gecko, or a CCTV camera. Yet she was there, watching from that position in the air, only inches from the ceiling, waiting for the familiar and terrifying future.

Rachel watched her bed, with its flower printed duvet amongst the discarded clothes that she should have cleaned up and washed a fortnight ago.

All hers. All normal.

Even the form that lay beneath the sheets was where it should be; yet her perspective was all wrong.

Rachel was asleep, and she was watching herself asleep, but this was not the most disturbing fact. That was yet to come. On many nights, Rachel's perspective had hung like so above her room, as she watched her slumbering body jerk through the night in its usual restless manner. After all, how could she sleep soundly when she didn't even inhabit her body?

The first time that Rachel had experienced the dream, it had been a shock to recognise her room, but now this was second nature and she treated it as a purgatory, or her pre-nightmare phase where she could take a deep breath and attempt to steel herself for what was to come.

During this process, Rachel waited and watched her outline as she rested in the bed below. It was so odd to see that her nostrils flared as she breathed deeply in sleep, and embarrassing to find that she was a regular hog when it came to snoring. Rachel had considered buying one of those nose things that people wear to stop their unconscious grunting, but thought better of it-

"Do you really want to take the dream to be reality?" she had asked herself. Some things only seemed clear when spoken aloud, and she knew that should she try and cure her snoring, it would mean that she was taking the dream too seriously, so she did nothing. It was a dream and nothing more.

And even now, during the dream, Rachel could believe that. That was until, of course, the man entered. He was small, yet he hunched as he entered the room as though he felt the doorway was low enough to require a stoop. He was an old looking man, or Rachel thought so at least, it was hard to tell in the darkness where grey hair could turn out to be blonde. No, he was definitely old. The way he slid across the floor in a hesitant but so obviously exited way, which he physically expressed by wringing and then rubbing his hands together like a comic-to-movie villain. He was vile.

Her 'real' self mirrored Rachel's discomfort. From where she lay in bed, the body inhaled deeply and shivered as though the man was not a human shape, but more a metaphor for an evil and insidious draught that had suddenly entered the room. The little man walked forward and stood for a long time over her sleeping form, and Rachel felt the skin on her body pimple in reaction to his close proximity. This was the part where he-

-The man leaned down quickly, and the entire scene sped up as it always did at this point. He cupped his hand around her ear and she began to feel the bastard's breath on her neck as he began to speak rapidly. His whisper, the violent repetition of some confused passage, perhaps from some book or a speech, sounded harsh and wet against her ear.

"Gone are the days when the average man can sit and watch the world go by," the man hurried on, "nor can he expect the leaders to lead him for his own good. He must fight and he must involve himself…"

The words meant nothing to Rachel but she feared them still, and wished that he would stop, or that she could stop him from filling her sleeping mind with his words, no matter what they were supposed to mean.

"-He must confront all that he fears, and attempt to understand why the world has decided to run itself without his involvement, why he has been allowed to sleep and let it do so. And, gone are the days when the average man can sit and watch the world go by-"

Rachel flailed her arms in an attempt to push him away,

but they were not the arms on her sleeping body, they were the invisible and useless appendages of her disembodied consciousness.

"-He must fight and he must involve himself," continued the little man in his frantic whisper, and he began to slap himself on the leg as though he were keeping time.

At this point, Rachel usually found that she fainted and came awake in bed, with the feeling that the little creep was still standing over her, and her ear was still warm from his lecherous breath. It always made her jump up and put on the light and pace around like a mental patient, touching all the walls and turning quickly at the bed and the door in turn, attempting to catch these inanimates off guard, doing something that they shouldn't.

But this time was different.

From her suspended view, Rachel let out a scream of frustration and fear like she had never done before, and for the first time since the dream had begun all those months ago, the man stopped whispering. Then he turned around and he looked up with pinpoint accuracy at the place where she hovered. He began to snarl, and in a split, the little man covered the distance between them and grabbed her by the throat, which turned out to be far more substantial than her arms had earlier been.

"Gone are the days when the average man can sit and watch the world go by," the little man screamed at her as he clamped her windpipe shut, "nor can he expect the leaders to lead him for his own good. He must fight and he must involve himself!" he raged on through the passage again. Rachel could feel the strength leaving her and death approaching. In the last few seconds before she blacked out, Rachel found that she was back in her bed but the choking had not ceased, and neither had the sound of the vicious little man's speech. As she came towards her last gasp, Rachel looked towards the spot where she had been, and saw a nightmare vision that would surely live with her beyond her own death.

In the corner of the room, the little man had her pinned against the wall by her throat. He was still chanting his chant, and slapping his thigh as he did it. And, over his shoulder, she came eye to eye with her dying self, they looked at each other as the pain and the lack of air took over, and she slipped down into the blackness between the two.

TEXT MESSAGE...

> What's happening?
> Why haven't you
> answered? Be
> strong, it's nearly
> over.

> I am sorry. I love
> you. Good bye.

<u>The Maelstrom...</u>

Peter and Terry slept in the sitting room that night, much as Peter had done with the two girls the night before, in an attempt to comfort each other by their presence. Though they may as well have not bothered, so much good it did them.

There was little comfort to be found by either in the night, but for very different reasons. Peter felt as though he was floating above the couch, so hopelessly happy was he that the potential relationship with Rachel had turned into something real. His happiness was thrilling, and he felt shivers of emotion running through him that made him want to 'eep!' like a giddy child. He tried and tried to get comfortable, but the perfect position eluded him. He wasn't going to sleep tonight, well that was all right; he wanted to enjoy this feeling forever. Besides, a night without his reoccurring dream was to be enjoyed, even savoured.

~*~

Across the room, Terry was experiencing a different sort of discomfort. He really needed a piss. A couple of times, he decided to get up and go, but when he opened his eyes in the darkness, he began to hear a rushing in his ears and the room began to distort and move around him. It was as though he was drunk or something, and he soon became queasy enough to make him decide to close his eyes once more and try to hold it in.

Shit, that never works, he thought. *Just get up and go to the toilet, you fool.*

"Where's your jax?" Terry spoke across the room to Peter, keeping his eyes shut against the seventies special effects he was sure to experience should he risk a peek.

~*~

"What?" Peter responded, "Oh yeah, the jax, em..." For a second, Peter was sure that he didn't know where the toilet was. "Oh, of course, yeah, right down the long hall, not on the left or right, straight ahead." *It must be Rachel,* Peter thought, there was no other way to explain his cotton wool brain.

~*~

Terry took a quick breath and launched himself off the couch and across the room, stubbing his toe on the step that led up and out of the sitting room area. Shit! He'd forgotten that it was there. He found the corner between the hall and the downstairs corridor, and stamped loudly down towards the toilet. He was bursting now and his need far overcast the feelings of disorientation when he opened his eye to find the light switch.

The bathroom's element-like energy-saving light bulb blazing brilliant into his aqueous humour turned his pupils into pinpricks in his brown eyes. Terry exclaimed and staggered into the bathroom, dropping his boxers as he did. A few seconds later, and he was letting out a long happy sigh of well-deserved relief.

Phew! he thought. It was almost worth the wait. After he shook and pulled up his shorts, he turned to the sink and looked in the mirror while washing his hands. Something different in his appearance shook him from his state of glad reprieve, but what it was, he couldn't tell. Yet there was definitely something different about him. He leaned into the mirror and only then noticed that his eyes had darkened drastically, as though his entire cornea had turned black.

Terry gasped as he realised that someone was standing beside him in the doorway. He was afraid to look, but forced his head to turn to the right where the open door should have framed a clear black canvass. It didn't.

Standing there, arms outstretched and unmoving, was a woman in religious robes. Her face was completely empty of feature, which was a feature in itself.

It was she, the woman from his nightmares. Somehow, she had crossed over into the real world. Terry's face screwed up in reaction to her, and his lips began to tremble as he started to cry. He couldn't help it; it was too much for him and he had no more anger or even fright left inside. All he had was despair, and it made him feel pathetic and tiny.

"No," he said to her through his tears, "please!"

Then, in a sudden shocking instant, the faceless nun moved forward.

~*~

Peter wasn't fast asleep when he heard Terry's scream of terror. No, when it came, and tore through him like a metal fist plunged into his heart, Peter was standing still in the centre of the room, staring up at the picture above the fire.

A few moments before, he'd been lying on the couch, in the greyness that comes when eyes are accustomed to the absence of light. He'd been laying there thinking about Rachel, and generally feeling swell and altogether chuffed. Though his eyes were open, they were not really looking at the room but projecting upon it the face of his newfound love. Then he noticed something.

During a mindless scan of the room, his gaze had come to rest on the painting above the fire. It was dark so he could not make out the details, but - there was a painting above the fire! There shouldn't be a painting above the fire. There was a huge stupid mirror that his mother had insisted was five hundred years old when she bought it. Peter had always suspected that it couldn't have been more than five hundred days old, but that wasn't the point. The mirror was supposed to be there, not a painting of - what was it?

Peter rose slowly from the couch. He was experiencing again the old familiar taste of metal in his mouth, and fear-bile building in the crucible of his stomach. Something was about to happen.

It was then that he heard Terry crying out. It was then that the storm began.

***

The wind was picking up and the rain wasn't far behind when Rachel finally made it to the end of Peter's street. Where had the storm come from? She had no idea, and little time to think it through as she broke into a run. She was wearing dirty jeans that she'd taken from the washroom, and one of those sweaters that always seemed to be lying around but belonged to no one. Both were quickly becoming soaked, and her legs were getting heavier with each sodden step.

As she splashed down the road towards Peter's house, Rachel became aware of loud noises emanating from inside. She ran into the shelter of the carport and shook like a dog, attempting to shed the pounds of cold liquid that had already begun to chill her bones. She knew that she badly needed to dry off, but was prevented from ringing the bell by a loud roar and a thump as something fell heavily on the other side of the door.

She took a step back. What was happening now? She couldn't take much more, she knew. The picture of herself being strangled by the little grey-haired man was still so fresh in her mind that Rachel feared closing her eyes too long, lest she find that the cold rainy streets of that Dublin night were dreamed, and she would be plunged back into the nightmare once more. She paced in the carport, not sure what to do, and started as another loud noise could be heard from inside the house.

Where could she go now? Not inside to whatever was happening to Peter and Terry, and certainly not back home to the vicious little man and his confusing mantra. She had few, so few options, and when coupled with the cold fact that the storm outside was worsening… Wait, what was that?

Rachel turned at the sound of a man running down the street towards her, his booted feet stamping splashes along the waterlogged road. Rachel stared for a moment to make sure that she wasn't hallucinating, but he was there all right, a man with a beard in a tattered old jacket, as real as she was.

When he saw that he'd caught her eye, the man made a grunting noise and waved an angry gesture, a movement that terrified her.

This was a new horror approaching and Rachel did the only thing that she could.

***

Inside the house, Peter was struggling to get to his feet. His assailant was gone now and he found that he could stand up once more without any resistance.

"Peter!" came a shout from outside, accompanied by a banging on the door, "Peter, let me in!" It was Rachel, Peter was sure of it. He quickly scanned the room for his tormentor, but there was nothing to see. The bookcase by door had been pulled down, and the picture above the mantle was once again the gaudy and oversized mirror it should have been. Peter was sure that he was the room's only occupant. *But where is Terry?* he thought briefly, but let it pass as he climbed over the books and shelving to reach the front door.

"Peter, help!" It was Rachel again. "There's a man out here." Peter hesitated and then wrenched the door open, recoiling at the temptation to leave it shut. What sort of person would he be if he left her out there?

"Peter!"

The door opened and Rachel fell on top of him in her panic to be inside, knocking them both back across the shelves and onto the living room floor.

"Rachel?" said Peter, but the girl was up and on her feet again so quickly that he was left addressing the air.

"We have to lock the door," she said, and struggled over the paper pile as a face appeared in the doorway.

"Wait," said the bearded man, who was about to speak again when Rachel pushed hard and the door slammed shut, hitting both the bearded man and the doorframe hard. She stood there for a few seconds, leaning with her back to the door and panting.

Inappropriately, Peter revelled in her beauty. She was tired, soaking wet, and shivering; yet she'd had the presence of mind to shut out whatever inhuman character had been chasing her, before even taking a breath.

"Wow," said Peter, even as the man/thing outside began hammering at the door.

"What?" She smiled at Peter as he helped her into the sitting room.

"Just wow. I mean. Who was that?" Rachel's smile was a ghost and she looked quickly back towards the front door.

"I don't know," she said. "Listen, Peter?"

"Yeah?"

"Something mad just happened to me."

"I know."

"You know?"

"No, not what happened to you. I mean..." He stopped.

"Something happened here too," said Rachel, "I heard it. What?" There was a shout from down the hall.

"Terry." Peter looked over Rachel's shoulder. She span around.

"Is there another door down there?"

"Yeah, the back door. Oh shit, Terry!" The two of them made for the corridor, but were pulled up by the appearance of Terry and the bearded man. Terry was white-faced and trembling, but he didn't seem to mind the presence of the other shaggy character.

"Terry, what's going on?" Peter asked. Terry looked up and shook his head.

"Oscar," he said, "this is Oscar."

"Are you ok?" Rachel asked, as Terry became unfocused and started to look off to one side at nothing.

"Terry?" Peter tried. "Are you alright?"

"He'll be alright, boy, he's had one of his turns," said Oscar. "Listen, something strange is going on with your friend."

"Terry?" Peter asked.

"Marie!" Rachel corrected.

"Yeah the redhead, she's in trouble."

"And who are you?" Rachel asked, looking into the man's eyes. They were grey and hard, but when he looked towards Terry, his brow wrinkled with worry. Rachel had a good instinct about him.

"My name is Oscar," he answered. "I'm nobody."

CHAPTER TWELVE
WHEN THE WHISKEY DROPPED

"*So* what are you saying?" Peter shouted, as he paced the length of the room again. "This Thisgo guy has Marie tied up in a cellar beneath a pub?" Peter didn't know which was more inconceivable; the old tramp's story, or the fact that he believed it. Peter was still freaked by what had happened during the night. There was a shiver running through the length of him that forced him into a constant state of agitation. He'd just shouted for the first time in, well, he wasn't sure how long. Peter looked at Oscar. Who was he? How was he involved, and what had he done to Terry?

"Yes," said Oscar, "that is it, exactly, young man. And no matter what tone of voice you use with me, it remains the truth." Oscar turned to look at Terry. The boy was sitting on the couch with his legs curled up beneath him. His manner was foetal and distressed. It looked as though he was only a moment away from sucking his thumb. This was not the boy he had first noticed walking through Dublin, a person apart from the greyness around him. The old tramp was desperate to find out what was going on with Terry, with all of them. They were flipping out, yammering about all manner of unfeasible hallucinations, and traumatic experiences, all so unbelievable and ridiculous that Oscar was sure that they were mentally disturbed.

But then there was Marie? Wasn't the redhead sitting right there in a dark cellar room below *The Inn*, the captive of the Treoraí and Tír? He'd seen it for himself, and yet he couldn't believe it, so who was he to call the tales of these students ridiculous? He was nobody.

Oscar knew two things then. He would do everything that he could to help these kids figure out what was happening. And, whether he understood it or not, he was sure that it was wrong, and it had to be stopped. Oscar looked to Rachel, as it was her friend that had been taken captive.

"Do you know why he would take her like that?" said

Oscar. Rachel stood up from where she had been sitting, watching the rain from a large red armchair by the window. For a moment, all she could do was shake her head and look at them in turn. She looked to Terry, and Oscar was sure that he could see her lip quivering at the sight of his broken sanity. Rachel turned to Peter, and they looked at each other. At first, it was a sad look, desperate and pleading, but then the two of them shared a second of recognition, and Oscar knew that whatever they were going to do, Peter and Rachel were going to do it together. Rachel broke the contact first.

"Ok," she said, as she turned back to Oscar. "Take us there." Oscar looked at Peter for agreement. The boy shrugged.

"So far," Peter said, "all sorts of weird things have been happening to us. It would be a good idea to do something for once. Maybe find out what's going on."

"And what about him," Oscar asked, drawing their attention back to the shaken form of their most effected party. "Do you want to leave him here?" Terry was sitting up now, his head in his hands.

"No," said Peter, "he's coming with us. We don't split up again." They looked at Terry.

Through his fingers, Terry could see the floor. The brown wood was so simple and necessary. At least something was necessary. He'd been trying to grasp what had happened earlier, but his thoughts kept freezing and losing their way, like a broken computer needing to be debugged. He gathered from the outside that the others were talking about him, and he knew that they were the key to all of this madness. He needed them.

"Damn right I'm coming with you!" Terry exclaimed, coming to his feet, and looking alive for the first time that morning. He walked to the middle of the room and his jaw hardened.

"There's no way you guys are leaving me behind. I don't know what's going on here, really. I wish I could explain it." Terry looked towards Peter. "First, I find you drowning in the fountain," then he faced Rachel, "then we go to a bar and everybody disappears. And ok, I lost it. But then!" He turned to

Oscar, "I wake up in some underground... I don't know what it was, with a homeless guy telling me all sorts of weird crap."

"It's ok, Terry, relax," said Peter, moving towards his new friend, as the boy's lip started to tremble, not wanting Terry to break down again. But Terry had no intention of quietening down.

"No," he said, putting his hand up to stop Peter's advance, "no it's not alright, ok? All of that other stuff was bad enough, and today I was even getting used to the idea. Hey, at least we'd found each other, right? Cos we're obviously all connected, all four of us, for some reason. But it's not alright, because tonight I saw something." And here, Terry's bottom lip was in danger of loosening again, bet he pulled it in with a tightened jaw.

"My worst nightmare," Terry began again, but nearly choked at the memory of her. "I saw my worst nightmare tonight, and she, she was... My heart is a space that's full of her. I'm blackened and hunched over. She's behind me right now." He glanced over his should as if to illustrate the point. And even though he knew she wasn't there, he also knew that she was there. The others were staring at him now.

"You have to understand," he told them, "I'm not going crazy. We're in something now. It's some sick thing that we can't escape from, but we have to finish it, you know what I mean?" He cast a lightning glance to Oscar, and then back to Peter and Rachel. Terry waited and watched as his friends figured out what he was telling them, and nodded their agreement.

"So," Terry looked between his two friends, "we have to stop what's happening to us, yeah? You understand me?"

"You mean the little man, Thisgo?" said Peter, nodding.

"What are we going to do?" Rachel asked, but her face was without expression. She knew.

"Whatever we have to do to stop it!" Peter said. His voice was firm, and then he asked Terry, "Are we all going?"

"Just the three of us," Terry answered and turned towards Oscar. He had a fair idea now that the others knew what he meant.

"Oscar," he said, passing the tramp and walking towards the door, "I think it would be best if..." As he opened the door,

Terry heard a whack, and a reassuring thud as Oscar fell to the floor behind him. Terry turned around and found Rachel standing over the slumped body of the now unconscious tramp, holding a large volume.

"He's not hurt, is he," Terry asked, surprised that he actually felt a tinge of anxiety. Rachel looked as though she'd just put her foot through the Mona Lisa, so it was obvious that she didn't know. Peter kneeled on the floor beside Oscar's stillness, to check the old man's pulse.

"His heart is beating fine," he told the others. "As far as I know, he'll be ok."

"Cool," said Rachel, "let's go then." The three took strength from each other. This was the first proactive move they had made since the beginning of all this madness.

"Let's go," the boys agreed with her, and they left the house together.

***

A couple of minutes later, Oscar rose from the book-laden floor of Peter's front room and rubbed his head, tutting in disappointment. The girl had given him a fair whack, but had only succeeded in giving him a sore head and pissing him off. Yet when he hit the floor, Oscar stayed down.

He didn't understand what was going on, and he needed to find out as quickly as possible. And who would be the best people to ask? Oscar had to find their parents, and tell them what was going on.

He felt that this was a good and rational course of action, even with things being as they were; i.e. Oscar being a tramp, and him not even knowing what to say if he did manage to speak to a group of normal couples, such as he assumed the students' kin would be, he felt that it had to be tried.

Besides, there was no point in attempting to get any sense out of Terry, Peter, and Rachel. They were wired to the moon at the moment, no real idea of what they were doing and no one to stop them from making stupid decisions, like bashing Oscar over the head to begin with. He was the only person outside their little group that had tried to help them, or even acknowledge their existence, but still they had struck him "unconscious" and run off into a dangerous situation with an extremely powerful man. Oscar knew he had to find out some solid facts before quickly getting back to watching over the students, so he tried to figure out what to do next.

It would take them a half hour to get to *The Inn,* and he wasn't able to beat that by much, so all he really had was a few minutes. He set about searching the house properly, taking in every detail.

Front room: Books everywhere, upturned television set, no pictures, huge mirror, and blankets. Oscar judged that there was nothing else of note in the main room, and headed upstairs. He entered the master bedroom. Very cold room, bed made, wardrobes empty, no pictures on the bedside table, no knickknacks. It was odd that everything was cleared out. especially if Peter's parents were away somewhere. They would have left something, a sock even. But no, there was nothing there at all.

Strange…

In another room, a girl's room, there was more decoration, colourful bedspread, and toys all around he floor. Oscar remembered rooms like these. They were the product of good old-fashioned over-parenting, and little regard for the actual child's needs. There was a big mirror in this room too; it was hanging in front of the door so you could see yourself from the hallway if the door was opened. *Nothing strange here,* Oscar thought, and went into Peter's room; it was a real mess, full of all the teenage gadgetry and miscellany that a boy like Peter would be expected to own. There were clothes everywhere, and an old video camera on top of the dresser. A stereo, CDs strewn around, and a musty smell permeating it all.

Oscar began to get frustrated at this. There was nothing strange about this house at all, apart from the parents' room but there could be all sorts of reason for that. He ran downstairs to the kitchen, his head still pounding, and he wondered if he would find any headache tablets.

Oscar stopped at the door of the kitchen. Amazing! He had not been inside the house fifteen minutes and he was already normalising. Headache tablets? When was the last time he had taken anything of the sort? The brain was searched, it took a while, and then the answer came. Ten years. It was ten years since he'd taken such a thing into his body, or had the want to do so. Well no, that wasn't true. He wanted such things all the time, craved and needed, but never succumbed. There were so many comforts denied him that he had taken solace in the blur of their unobtainable distance.

But he was in a house again, a family home. It was filled with warm clothing, pills, and... (!) food, technology and... (!) No! He had to try and not think about the other. There was work to do. He couldn't reduce his choice to avoid the normal life of a robot down to that one bastarding thing!

Now, what had he been doing? Ok, he was thinking about the house, and how it had managed to reduce all his years of independence from the systems of the civil into "outside", so that within minutes, he was looking for Aspirin. He looked at himself in the long mirror that hung in the kitchen.

"Look at yourself," he said, "you don't belong here."

Damn, he needed... (!) No, he didn't. He had to get back to the kids; he'd already spent too long there in that doorway, whilst he should have been looking for clues.

Oscar stumbled into the room and began opening the cupboards. Everything seemed to be where it should, cereal, salt, and salad forks, but then he opened the wrong door.

Whiskey! The cupboard was full of it. In reality, there was only one bottle, and that was shoved into the back of the cupboard behind a large transparent jar of blue pills, but it was all the man could see. It was the (!) hanging in the back of his mind. The one thing he was hoping to avoid was within easy reach, so he grabbed it, quickly and without another thought.

Oscar pulled the bottle towards him, and the large jar of pills came forward too, falling from the shelf and smashing on the tiled kitchen floor. What followed the initial deafening crash was the sound of thousands of little light blue pills bouncing on the floor, like sleet on a glass roof, or old style popcorn coming good in the pot. To Oscar, however, the sound was miniscule, and disturbed him not at all. He had in his hands a rare single malt whiskey, and his reason was lost in its dark amber promise. In a dreadful hurry, the old tramp fumbled with the cap and found that his hands were too wet with sweat to turn the screwed cork. He spun around looking for a tea towel to help him twist the bottle open.

Slip-yelp-thud!

It was pure serendipity that Oscar lost his footing on the pill-covered surface of the kitchen floor. It did more than push the man into a frantic struggle to stay upright. Nor did it simply knock the bottle from his flailing hand, or send his feet out ahead of him and acquaint his arse quite suddenly with the floor. The simple act of falling on his backside triggered in Oscar an essential revelation. It wasn't exactly a 'Eureka moment', followed by naked sprinting thought the streets as the Greek philosopher had done. No, this was a more gradual period of inspiration, seeing as it began with: "Shit," and then "Umpff!" as the sense was knocked out of him.

~*~

After he woke, Oscar lay there on the floor, the escaping whiskey soaking his back, and there were little blue pills digging into him all over. It was like sleeping on gravel, there were so many of the little bastards. Who had this many pills in their home? Little light blue pills, just like the ones that Terry had taken the morning before in Oscar's George's Street hideaway. Was that significant? Both Peter and Terry were acting weird, and that was a certainty. Could it be because of the pills? It was probably a coincidence. Any pills that Terry was taking would come from his mother, and what reason would she have for drugging her son, their son? To drive him mad?

The whiskey seeped into the skin of Oscar's back. In a few moments, he would possibly feel the effect of lying in all this alcohol, or the pills that were right there, dissolving in it. Oscar hurried to his feet. He realised as he did so that he was taking it seriously. Peter and Terry were taking these pills, and didn't know what they were doing. Terry's mother, the doctor, would have to know what the boy was on, so why would Peter's parents be giving the same pills to their son?

It was the same question again, why? There was no reason.

"You're just a crazy old fool," Oscar said, looking into the full-length mirror on the wall. This was a strange house. There were huge mirrors in every room, correction, every room but Peter's. The boy didn't have a mirror in his room. He had clothes everywhere, a TV, a stereo, and a...

"Jesus," said Oscar, "a camera!" He slipped and slid over to the mirror on the kitchen wall, but found that he couldn't get his fingers around it.

"Damn it," he cried, and ran into the sitting room and mounted the stairs, only stopping short of the half landing when a thought struck him. Oscar turned and descended the stairs, not taking his eyes off the huge mirror hanging over the fire. He couldn't believe what he was expecting to find as he pushed the coffee table forward and up to the hearth.

"Ok," said Oscar, and he climbed up, finding his own reflection deeply upsetting. "What are you hiding, Oscar?" he asked the man in the mirror, and reached out to the frame at either side. It really was a huge mirror, but his arm span was just enough and he caught a hold of it leaning forward as he did, his right cheek resting against the glass.

With a heave and a deep breath, the mirror came away from the wall accompanied by a creak as something, maybe just the joists holding the mirror, fell, relinquishing their hold to Oscar. He held it there for a moment,, wondering what to do next, but he soon got over that, turned to his left and let go of the thing. It fell with all its weight on the floor, and Oscar winced, expecting a large smash and brace of bad luck, counted in multiples of seven, but it didn't even crack. This was more proof of what he would see when he turned to the bare wall, but Oscar was still not convinced of the camera's presence until he saw the hole in the wall, and touched the lens with his fingers tips.

He put his hands on the mantle amongst the ornaments, and hung his head for a moment. So, someone was drugging those poor kids and monitoring them. What was worse, it had to be their parents who were doing it. If not Peter's, who may have been cleared out, as their room would suggest, then certainly Terry's mother.

"That fuckin bitch!" Oscar screamed and attacked the camera hole. He couldn't get to it. They could probably see him now. Maybe even she was watching?

"What are you doing, you bitch?" he shouted into the camera, feeling desperate and useless. He just didn't understand what was going on. Why were they doing this to a few students, to Terry? "What are you doing to our boy?" he asked, in a quieter tone this time. This was a pointless exercise, and he knew it.

Oscar climbed down from the coffee table and moved quickly to the door. He might not know what was happening, but Terry, Peter, and Rachel had been heading towards *The Inn* before he was knocked out, and although Oscar could not find a clock, his understanding of the day and his many experiences of being roused from drunken comas by the Gardaí or hostile nightclub goers told him that he had been out for far too long. Oscar had no more time for deliberation, he had to go now and he had as long as the distance to *The Inn* to work it all out, and to prevent the creeping inevitability of events.

CHAPTER THIRTEEN
THE WITNESSING OF MARIE

The Inn was nothing special to look at, at least not from the outside. It was nothing more than a wood-effect front-shell that stood on the long row of redbrick apartments and office buildings. So unremarkable that the face of it looked like it could be easily detached, moved a couple of buildings down, and recreated there, causing no more hassle than a number change in its address.

This is how it looked to passers by, in cars and on foot, but not to the three students that stood across the road with their backs to the river. To them, it was a daunting sight; impenetrable and mysterious. It looked closed and empty, and maybe it was? What, if anything, was going on inside? There was only one way to know for sure. Peter turned to Rachel and Terry. She was wide-eyed and worried, though the fine clenched bones of her jaw made her look fierce, and showed her determination. Man, she was beautiful. Terry, on the other hand, was a blank. Gone were all his jibes and desperate joviality, yet so too was his unstable weakness. Peter knew that what had happened to Terry the night before, probably some horrific vision like his own, whatever it was, had shocked him into this state of passive resolve. Terry was moving forward because it was the only way left to go. As were they all.

"Let's go," said Peter. They nodded and the three of them stepped across the road to the front of *The Inn*.

***

Below them, as the three searched the alley for the spot that Oscar had described, Marie was being warmed by a shaft of sunlight. The beam found its way into her lonely captivity through the same broken pane as the terrible cold had done the night before. It felt good on her face, and she felt the chill in her bones becoming more bearable, though she was still a long way from comfort. This brief moment of relaxation was destroyed, however, when a sound began to carry through from the hallway.

Beyond the wooden door, Marie could hear a voice. It came closer and closer, until it halted just behind the portal's deceptive safety. She dreaded what she knew she would see when the door was unlocked, fearing it because she would be face to face with him again. His warped mind terrified her almost as much as his wretched chanting that had haunted her while she slept. Then, as though he had heard her thoughts, he started the mantra again.

"Then he speaks," said the voice, "when he speaks, I speak what he speaks."

BEEP-BEEP, BEEP-BEEP, Marie heard a phone ringing.

"Then he speaks, then I spe..." There was a pause; he was answering the phone.

"He speaks? Yes. Yes. Yes. Then I speak? Yes. Yes." Marie shivered at the sound of his answers, and what they might mean. She heard keys rattling, and scrambled back as they were inserted in the lock. The door opened, and for a moment Marie couldn't see him where he stood in the gloom. Then the shaft of sunlight that had been lighting her with its contrast to the darkened doorway disappeared, and her pupils adjusted. There he was, Walter Thisgo, coming to get her. He stepped forward into the room, and she saw that he had on an earpiece, and was mumbling under his breath. When he spoke, he spoke slowly and carefully, each sentence unconnected from the last, and the emotion in each manically exaggerated.

"Hell-o Ma-rie. It is ti-me that you came with me. Goo-d. Come on now, let's go." He walked to her and then took a step to one side, admitting two men in suits, who quickly untied her hands before taking an arm each, and rushing her out of the room on her toes. She held in a cry for help as she passed through the door. She was going to have to wait and see what happened, there was nothing more that she could do.

***

Walter stood there for a moment after Marie's departure. It looked like he was going to stand there indefinitely, when finally, he said, "Yes," turned to the door, and left at a slow stiff march.

It was only then that Rachel allowed herself to breath.

"Jesus," she said, turning to Peter. "Marie was just dragged out of there by Walter Thisgo!"

"Are you sure?" Peter asked, "Walter Thisgo, the Treoraí?" He looked at Terry in disbelief. Terry said nothing, swallowed a pill and looked back towards Rachel.

"Can we get in this way," Terry said to Rachel, his voice catching a little as the blue tablet made slow progress down his dry throat.

"If we can get through the window, yes. The door is open."

"We need to smash it," said Terry.

"But they might hear us," said Peter.

"Do you know a quiet way?" Terry asked, and walked over to where an old empty keg sat, covered in scum, its rim full of rainwater. It wasn't like the newer kegs that were extremely light when empty, this one was old-fashioned, pockmarked, and heavy.

"What are you doing?" Rachel asked.

"If we can't do it quietly, then we can do it quickly," Terry told her, holding up the old keg, "This should break the whole window in one go. Then we can hop in." Rachel and Peter looked at him. He was right, they knew, and they could see that he was deathly calm. In fact, it crossed their minds that he had been so since that morning, after their most recent nightmare experiences.

"Ok," said Peter, "let's do it the quick way." He took Rachel's arm and moved back away from the window, not sure how Terry would proceed.

"Take one side and we'll swing it," said Terry, looking at the window. "When it goes through, we do too. Ok?" They nodded and Peter hurried to his side and took the end of the keg by the lip. His grip wasn't great, but he was sure he could hold on long enough.

Terry lifted the empty keg by the handle and they began to swing it back and forward.

"When I say go," said Terry, "let go."

It worked perfectly. The keg was almost exactly the right size for the window, and when they let go, it smashed through the remaining panes easily, and thudded to the floor inside the cellar room below, causing an awful but sudden racket that was hopefully too fast to describe its existence. It was likely that anyone in the bar proper would dismiss it in the absence of any follow up noises. Terry lowered Peter through the window frame first, and then followed. Both of them attempted to help Rachel down, but she flicked away their hands and told them to stand back so that she could drop lightly onto the cellar floor without any more fuss. Peter was impressed.

They listened for a moment. There were no sounds of alarm from above, and no quick steps along the corridor. It seemed that they had entered undetected. Rachel was the first to move, her concern for Marie overpowering any last minute doubts about their actions.

"Let's go," said Rachel, and the three of them left the room as quietly as they could.

In the corridor, they passed another open door that opened into a completely bare room. The only descriptive quality to the room was the presence of a rough circle in the floor that looked like a track, but they didn't dwell there long enough to make any summations about what could possibly made such a distinctive trail around the room.

Further along the hallway, a stairway so steep it was almost a ladder extended upwards into a square of light, and as they got closer the three could hear voices and music coming from the bar above.

When they reached the first step, the group didn't tarry but instead continued upwards, with Peter in the lead and Terry at the rear.

***

RADIO: "Well, Mr Secretary," blabbed the radio, "can Walter Thisgo and his government really expect people to swap their jobs just so they can work closer to their families?"

In the centre of the room, Marie was sitting at a table with Walter Thisgo. On either side of her stood a suited man, each with a hand on her shoulder. Their presence, though nondescript, created an atmosphere of looming and menace in the room that Peter could feel as he raised his head above the bar and took in the scene. Marie and the men had their back to where he, Rachel, and Terry crouched, but they were unable to get a good look at their friend's situation because Walter Thisgo had a full view of the bar, forcing them to stay below and out of sight.

RADIO: "…Well, Johnny, Job actualisation is a very simple idea, and you're forgetting that only participating employers are involved, and only then if they can prove that their staff are favourable towards the plan."

"Which is?"

"Simple, Johnny. Employers that opt for Job Actualisation agree to have their positions in their current organisation audited, allowing their staff the possibility of swapping jobs with similarly skilled individuals working elsewhere. This will then allow fitting candidates to move jobs so they can work closer to their family homes. Giving them more time with their families, and relieving the stress of travel from their lives, and from the life of our capital city."

"Well, Mr. Secretary, it sounds fine but… " The volume of the radio, which was on the table between Thisgo and Marie, was lowered until it clicked into its off position.

"Yes," said Thisgo, who was still wearing the bluetooth earpiece, "Now, young Marie?" Marie didn't move or speak. "Yes, Marie," Thisgo responded. "You have discovered something, yes?"

Behind the bar the three students inhaled together and signed silence with trembling fingers. Was this to be an explanation? Could the months of confusion and torment be explained? They waited silently, dreading what sort of motives could possibly have led them there, in the presence of the Treoraí; desperate and fearfully hoping for some rationality at last.

Walter Thisgo spoke again.

"Yes, you know about the experiment, don't you?" Again, Marie said nothing.

"Answer!" Thisgo barked, his hand snaking across the table to grab hers. She was too slow to escape it, and he pulled her towards him, not close enough to touch her nose to his, but close enough to make her stand up from her chair. She yelped in surprise.

"Yes," said Thisgo standing up, her hand still in his, "You know about the experiment, don't you?"

"Yes," Marie answered. Her voice was small and not at all like that of the girl that Rachel knew so well.

Rachel turned to Peter, and mouthed, [what will we do?] but all Peter could do was shake his head.

[Hey guys,] Terry tapped them both and gestured towards the corner of the room, where the bar took a right angle, [let's go around,] then he pointed to his eye, [we'll be able to see.] Rachel and Peter nodded and followed Terry as he crawled away.

"Who else knows?" Thisgo was demanding of Marie, "Did you tell the others? Tell me!" he shouted.

"No," said Marie, "they don't know about it. I just found out and came here?"

"Why?" Thisgo demanded, his face swollen with rage.

"Because it happened here. This is where everything disappeared."

"But how did you know to come here?"

"The internet,"

"The internet?"

"It was an old legend. The druids used the root of a plant to cause delusions in a victim. They were always tied to a post, kept in one place."

"Yes." Thisgo calmed slightly but didn't let go of Marie's wrist. He shook his head, "Off the internet. Well, isn't that just beautiful?"

Rachel, Terry, and Peter could see the two speakers perfectly now. The three were huddled in the hatch, out of sight of the two suits, but able to view the conversation without fear of being spotted inadvertently.

Thisgo's talk of an experiment had them on edge, and they could have been forgiven for how they reacted to what happened next.

Walter Thisgo and Marie stood together in the middle of the floor. He grabbed her other hand, pulled her close to him and embraced her in a rough and awkward manner.

"My child," he said to her, as she pulled away confused, "you have made a terrible mistake." Marie looked into the old man's eyes and the odd puzzled look was replaced by one of reticence and fear.

"What do you mean?" she asked, and tried to step back.

"Yes, a terrible, terrible mistake, my little Marie." Thisgo looked away from her as one of the suits stepped forward and handed him a gun.

"No," shouted Marie, as the old man brought the gun to her forehead. "You can't!" she cried and Thisgo paused with his finger on the trigger.

"No," he said, shaking his head. He could not kill her. Marie signed in relief, but Thisgo's attitude changed suddenly to the affirmative. "Yes. Yes. YES!" shouted Thisgo into the rafters of *The Inn,* and the gun went off in his hand.

In the brief moment that followed, Marie's body was robbed of life. Her body folded to the floor, without grace or ceremony, a person turned to a corpse in a second.

Rachel began to scream. Peter and Terry also let out cries of shock at the sight of Marie's execution. They only just managed to grab a hold of Rachel as she made a run for Thisgo.

"No," shouted Peter, "come on!" They hauled her back behind the bar, and stumbled for the cellar door. As they reached it, Peter shoved Rachel through and Terry stood to look into the room, wondering at the absence of noise.

The two suits were facing him; their hands were by their sides and they showed no signs of giving chase, but Terry didn't realise that until later on, as it was Thisgo that commandeered his attention. The eyes of man and boy met across the bar, and Terry was sure that he could see a tear slide from the other's eye, and lose itself in a wrinkled furrowed cheek.

Terry was enraged. How dare he show such emotion! That murdering…

"You fucker," Terry growled, but Thisgo just cocked his

head to one side, his eyes not focusing on the boy anymore.

"Yes," said Thisgo to the middle distance, and then he took a deep breath, opened his mouth wide, and screamed. Thisgo's whole face halved as he ejected the scream. "GET THEEEEEEEEEEEEEEEEEEEEEEEEEEEEEEEEEEEEEEEEEE EEM!" he roared, and Terry, shocked from his position, dived after the others as the men in suits came to life and started towards the bar.

The scream lasted as long as it took the three students to tumble down the cellar steps and crash to the hard stone floor below. The pain of impact was quickly forgotten, however, and in moments they were scrambling through the broken window and out into the alley beyond. Outside, Rachel was still struggling, although she wasn't sure what for.

"We have to go back," she said, but Peter held her tight.

"No," he said, "we can't. There's no point, she's…"

"Let's get the fuck out of here!" Terry exclaimed, hearing voices entering the room below. He pushed Rachel and Peter in front of him along the lane, and out onto the pavement. "Come on!" he said, and took Rachel's arm, thinking, and quite rightly too, that this would be the quickest way to get them both to come his way.

They ran down the street, led by Terry's impetus, but they only made it a hundred yards before he stopped abruptly, in front of them, causing an awkward pile up outside a sausage-egg-and-chips café.

"What the!" said Peter, but Terry hushed him quiet.

"Why the hell are we running?" Terry asked, to the others' disbelief.

"But you," Peter stopped and shook his head. Terry gestured to the café doors, [In here]. Peter held open the door for Rachel, who entered without acknowledgment of the deed, or her surroundings. Terry led them to a table by the window. The café was of the kind that always had market lads inside, swapping tips and waiting for breakfast rolls. It was busy now and the three were hardly noticed as they entered.

"They're not coming," Terry said.

"What?" Peter asked, not understanding.

"They haven't followed us out." Peter strained to see

along the street, towards *The Inn*. It looked empty.

"I don't understand." Peter looked at Terry, trying to divine what point the other guy was making. It was just there on the edge, between brain and tongue.

"They expect us to run. He knows that no one will believe us," Terry said, his body shaking in agitation as he rose, then sat, and then rose again to press his face against the glass, trying to get a clear view of *The Inn*.

Yes, that was it, Peter knew now. The Treoraí's men should have been right behind them.

"I can't believe they fuckin shot her!" Terry exclaimed, and Rachel yelped. Some people looked around, but Peter smiled a scary smile at them until they decided that it was better not to get involved with the new arrivals. They were probably all-nighters anyway, in between the early house and a comedown sleep.

"Relax man," Peter said, taking his natural role as level head and mediator. But why should Terry relax? "Actually, you're right, why the fuck should we relax? We're in the middle of some weird experiment that involves the Treoraí. Some sort of crap about druid punishments! Punishment for what? I didn't do anything, did you? Either of you? What the fuck has been happening to us? And for how long? I've been cracking up for... so have you! And then he just kills Marie! And..." Peter paused here as a cold metallic core of purpose rose from the oily confusion inside of him. "Do you know what?"

"What?" Terry looked into Peter's face, feeling the power of this new purpose that now exuded from his friend.

Peter grasped the heart of steel, and held it firmly in his mind. Then he had a quick look around before he whispered, "Do you know what we should do? We should follow that fucker home, and then... Do you know what we should do?"

"Yes," said Rachel, re-entering the group, "I know exactly what we should do."

Both Terry and Peter looked at her, and between the three of them, the understanding crystallised.

For the second time since the ordeal had begun, they chose to take a positive step. They knew, exactly what to do now.

All that was left now was to do it.

CHAPTER FOURTEEN
THE RED MIST & THE DEED

"*B*itch!" Oscar roared, as he stamped along Dame Street, taking Crow Lane and heading trough Temple Bar as the light fading from the sky registered for him the time he had spent unconscious on Peter's kitchen floor. As he hurried on, he left a wake of shaking heads, of people who pitied a drunken down-and-out who cursed and swore as he passed. On another day, Oscar would have been interested to read their faces and discern the thoughts behind them, but he had no time for that today. Today, he was a moron.

"Idiot!" he screamed, the oratory directed inward at his naïve yet understandably ignorant self. How could he have put it together? Even with all the meetings she'd gone to, all the times he'd argued with her about their very different views on what he had always thought about as mere politics. How could he have known that she was heading this way, to this day? How could she use her own son in such a manner, and compromise her all too important ethics, and for what? The assassination of Walter Thisgo. But that made no sense. All those years ago, when Thisgo was gaining popularity and momentum, Deirdre had almost idolised the man!

Oscar continued on in his tirade as he mounted the Ha'penny Bridge, upsetting the rhythm of a busker who played a scratchy section of Handel's water chorus. A part of his mind examined the flaws of modern society that forced a man to get a license to fish, but allowed him to butcher such an influential and as near to perfect piece of music as was now being murdered through the dying autumn evening.

Another part of him wondered at the mind itself for allowing such thoughts to continue whilst it should have been focusing on the main string of thought: His wife had betrayed her family, her own son. The more Oscar tried to understand her duplicity, the more pointers and reasons he conjured to explain her behaviour. Deirdre had always been an avid woman, passionate about what she believed in. Was there ever a sign of such fundamentalism? Yes, plenty of times her zeal had sprung forth in action and conversation. But he had fallen in love with her because of her bright and fervent convictions. He should never have left her when he did. If he had been there, then perhaps she would not have gone so far as to get herself mixed up in a plot as diabolical as this one. No, there was no perhaps about it. He would not have allowed her to drag their son into it, never. It was his fault.

It was his fault.

He was on Lower Ormond Quay now, and if he strained against the failing daylight, he could make out the row of buildings on which stood *The Inn*. He knew now that *The Inn* was the hub of the entire exercise, and that if anywhere, it was there he would find answers, and hopefully, his son Terry. If the boy was still alive to be found.

***

The mob...

"Shh!" Peter cautioned the others as he took cover once more behind the large tree, only a hundred metres or so from the rear entrance to Áras an Uachtaran. He didn't know what sort of tree it was and, for once he didn't care. Peter was full of nervous energy, and the simple details of his surroundings mattered little to him in his state of heightened agitation. He looked at the other two. Terry was shaking in anticipation, and Rachel, beautiful fiery Rachel, was casting glances around her at such speed that Peter thought her head might spin from her shoulders at any moment. He giggled, and the others looked at him in question. He felt so close to them now that he wished he could take them both in his arms and squeeze them hard against him, and so transmit his excitement and love in one simple gesture.

"Fuck it," he said, and did exactly that.

In the shadow of a great elm, Peter, Terry, and Rachel embraced tensely for a brief but emotional moment. Inside of them, the concoction of engineered chemicals raced for that time through one complete and perfect circuit. They were one. A single unit, sharing a common perception and purpose, which broke physically as the moment ended, but mentally, the circuit remained intact. Peter, Terry, and Rachel were ready to advance.

"Group hug!" Rachel smiled and they all began to laugh, letting a wave of comradery envelope them in a surreal cloud of comfort and well being. It was intoxicating.

The entire day had passed like a dream for the three of them. They had found their way to Áras an Uachtaran, taking the longest route possible through the Phoenix Park. Then they had watched and waited for a sign that the time was right.

As the autumn evening dimmed, the light of the sun and outside light had sprung to life inside the gardens. They had recognised the signal immediately, and walked boldly into the grounds to the very spot they now stood.

Then they were ready to begin the final stage.

As a single unit, the three parted from the shadows and began to walk boldly towards the rear of the building, although the back entrance of Áras an Uachtaran did not resemble anything so trivial. The entrance hall to the Áras was located at the back of the building, and the lesser entrance was not lacking in elegance, in fact, aside from the gardens before the main entrance, anyone would be forgiven for assuming that this was indeed the front door to the Treoraí's home.

As they approached the double doors, the group were halted by the sudden existence of a light from a window on their right hand side. The illumination was accompanied by the deep sound of a man's voice that carried only enough to describe it as such, but the voice sent a collective shudder through their bodies, and the group abandoned the double doors, heading instead for the new light and the voice of the one they sought; the voice of Walter Thisgo.

***

After switching the light on, Walter could only see the outline of the students as they approached his vantage point. He feared them; although his eyes defined for him the normal movements of average human shapes, he felt in his heart that they were stalking towards him like hyenas, advancing on their prey. For the first time since the plan's inception, Walter was experiencing actual fear as to its outcome. Of course, being Walter Thisgo, he had factored in the possibility of such doubts, and come up with a simple mantra to solve the problem.

"Walter puts the television on - he puts the DVD player on - he switches the lights off - and he puts himself to bed. Repeat. Walter puts the television on -"

And so Walter continued through his trepidation. He pointed his control to the TV by his side, and switched it on. He then stepped back from his window and pressed play on the remote, bringing the recording to life, and his image to the screen. He turned then and walked to the door, trying not to imagine how close to him the three had now become. Once there, he switched off the light and he was partially relieved by the darkness that hid him and his intentions. In a few moments, they would be coming through the window, hopefully reaching through the broken pane and opening the window outwards, not making enough noise to draw any attention to them before the alarm was set off after its three-minute delay.

There was nothing left for him to do now but repeat the mantra one more time, and finish the list. The TV was on - the DVD player was playing - the light was now off. All that was left was to put himself to bed.

"Come on, Walter," he said blowing out his nerves in a long shivering puff, "it is time to do what needs to be done."

***

Peter, Terry, and Rachel reached the window and were able to see the television clearly. The set was placed at an angle facing into the room from beside a large bed. Its position was such that they could just see the face of Walter Thisgo on the screen, and now that they were closer, could make out what the man was saying.

"Gone are the days," said the recorded face of Thisgo from the high-definition TV screen, "when the average man can sit and watch the world go by. Nor can he expect the leaders to lead him for his own good. He must fight and he must involve himself."

Rachel reacted as though she had been slapped in the

face. She banged her fist on the window and then started to look through the flowerbed for a rock to throw. As she searched, she pictured Marie in *The Inn*, dropping to the floor, her body lifeless, and the figure of Walter Thisgo standing over her.

"Marie!" she cried and she located a large enough stone to smash the window. Spinning around to face it once more, her arm swung the rock as she moved, Rachel was blocked by Peter, who stood in her way and shook his head.

"You're going to stop me?" she asked, confused. He shook his head [no] and gestured to Terry, who was just at that moment pushing at a wooden board that replaced an empty pane low in the window frame. The board gave way easily, and Terry reached inside to release the snip. The window opened inwards, and without hesitation, Rachel stepped up to Terry, who made a step for her with his hands. She entered the room, bathed in eerie green light created by the television set, and the two boys followed her quickly.

As soon as Peter entered the room, he rushed to the television. The hateful face of Walter Thisgo spoke, not in a studio, but with a country field as his backdrop. Peter growled and kicked the set off its stand, and the room fell silent. He turned to where Terry and Rachel stood over the shape of a person in the bed. As he watched, Peter became sure that the figure was Walter Thisgo, and Terry's hand rose above his head.

Terry, having taken the rock from Rachel, had obviously intended on smashing the old man's head open, but with the stone held high above his head, and the blow only a second away, he found that he was unable to complete the assault. The urgency he had felt was gone and his impulses hung over him, like the stone, expectant and delayed. The picture wasn't complete.

Rachel saw Terry freeze, and pried the stone from the boy's hand, holding it up to deliver the killing blow. Peter arrived at the other side of the bed, and caught her gaze before she could strike.

The three of them entered a level of limbo, where they were suspended above the deed. They were ready to attack, but only potential until the fuse was lit.

Walter Thisgo opened his eyes and took in the faces of

his would-be attackers. He had killed their friend, and now they were here to kill him. The guilt of it was too much to tolerate, and he welcomed their arrival.

"I'm sorry," he whimpered in fear and relief. "I'm sorry." And it was these words that brought about his end.

This trigger-match ignited, and the dried powder lay ready in their stricken minds and opened the door to the vicious id that lies waiting inside us all.

Their state of dormancy was now over. The attack began.

With a roar, Peter ripped the cover from the bed whilst Terry grasped Thisgo by the neck, and Rachel brought the rock down on his skull. Her second blow met with the man's face, as it turned blue from Terry's smothering grip.

"Move!" Peter roared, and he climbed onto the bed with a bedside lamp minus its shade, grasped in his hands like a vampire's stake. Terry and Rachel gave way quickly and without hesitation. In a professional manner, they allowed Peter the required space to plunge the lamp through Thisgo's chest, the bulb smashing but the shards being driven deep within the victim's torso.

This display of bloody murder was indeed a gruesome sight, but what followed after could only be described as monstrous. The butchery did not stop there. Peter continued to drive the shaft of the lamp into Thisgo's corpse, stopping only to allow Terry to reach into the bloody gaping holes and rip out pieces of muscle and then bone, cast them over his shoulder, and wait for another opportunity to repeat the gruesome action. Rachel continued to smash the rock down on the old man's head.

Once, twice, three times. Smash, crush, stab and tear. Over and over, and over again, they slashed and tore and damaged, until the body was a wet red stain on the room, chunks on the floor, and spatters on the wall. Until Thisgo's face was a gaping maw of broken white and crimson.

This was not a murder. This was the annihilation of a being, the deconstruction of a body so completely as to obliterate any resemblance to its former self.

The culmination of months of careful mental manipulation had come to pass into reality, but one that far outdid the expectations of all who had a hand in its inception or execution. The three pairs of hands did not stop destroying Walter Thisgo until the pounding of the night watch on the door roused them from their work. Each shoulder charge and shout from the hallway became the alarm that broke the spell and the gust of clarity, dissipating the red mist that had provided the atmosphere for execution.

Now, they crouched, over the remnants of their victim, wet and sticky from the gore of their performance. Slowly, each of them climbed from the bed and cowered from the door. What had happened to them? Had they really just done what they knew they had?

Yes.

Peter, Terry, and Rachel looked to each other for guidance, but found none. Then they looked inwards for answers, but found nothing there either. Only the basest instinct kept them from being found on the same spot, a minute later when the door was finally breached.

"Survive," it screamed at them. "Run and survive."

As a unit once more, they turned to the window.

This time they were running away from purpose, without feelings of togetherness, clarity, or well being.

All they had now was guilt and blood. They were awake now, and God help them, they wished that they were not.

PART THREE:

TRIALS

CHAPTER ONE
FLASHING LIGHTS

Don't walk away now. You can't leave yet. There's something that I want you to do. And don't give me that look, just because you think what you think. I had a perfect vision, yes, one that you don't understand fully yet, but you will I hope, when I tell you the third and final part of the story.

What do you need to know? You think you know everything. But I had a plan. A proper step-by-step plan to succeed where so many others had failed. Where my father, the defeated man, had failed for his entire life.

When I was a young boy, I looked at my father in awe. I saw him making speeches, and explaining to others how he felt the country should be run, on TV, on the podium he was a great man. But in practice, he had no power to change, only to talk.

I changed that. I had the power and the drive necessary to bring the big ideas to the people, and deliver on all of that talk. And then?

The timing was perfect to solidify and perfect these ideas. The moment had arrived to be bold, and I am bold. Let me tell you. I am bold. My death should have ensured my everlasting success and remembrance as a visionary, a radical; as a perfect martyr.

But no, already the misrepresentation and obtuse foolery of the media had tarnished my message. The Regressives. Jesus, how the bloody Regressives were capitalising! How could that be? They were the very ones that I've been fighting against since the beginning of my career. Those that I have endeavoured to thwart and stunt, and gone to the ultimate of lengths.

But no, they weren't wilting under the attack of the populous. They were thriving beneath the slanted halogen beam of the media spotlight.

You look at me like I haven't suffered. But how can you say that? You've been listening to this story, so far unfinished, but told fairly and without bias, and you're wondering why I would want you here? Well, I need you to understand, and it is obvious that you do not, yet.

So I will continue, because, although I know that you want to leave this place, I am doubly sure that part of you is aching to hear the full tale, and hear about your own part in it, because you played a large part, in both the partial success and ultimate failure of my plans.

The two trials…

It began again with flashing lights. A similar arrangement to the instance mentioned before, but different too, in its own way.

Theses flashing lights were operating in the same fashion as before; more hindrance to the peace and calm of the event than was the objects' objective. The lights were calling for attention, but not for a murder this time. On this night, it was more of a celebration.

There were indeed similarities to the to the night of my murder. The location was similar, as these lights too were flashing in the Phoenix Park, if a little further down the road at the Gardaí Headquarters. The main ambition of the spectators was, as is the remit of audiences everywhere, to see blood.

But the overall mood had changed from the dark confusion of the night to the cold anger of the early grey morning. The crowd was so large that the end of it couldn't be seen from the steps of the headquarters, where twenty-eight nervous Gardaí in riot cladding were shuffling and trying not to look anyone in the eye, making it easier to dispense beatings later should they be necessary.

The crowd were silent now. They had gathered more than an hour ago to see the demons of the day, the physical embodiments of disaster. But their breath had become uniform and their heads turned in waves, from the road to the headquarters, and back to the road. And in their hearts, they chanted: "The murderers are coming. The murderers are coming."

The media were there, of course. There were no TV cameras on scaffold though, there having been little time for that. All around on the roofs of cars, and in the trees, the media vultures lay in wait, with their digital Nikons, Minoltas and

Olympus lenses trained on the road and on the headquarters.

Then, in a great ripple of activity, the crowd came to life. Word had spread that down on the Quays, a large white van and a group of other vehicles had pulled in, and the message had immediately reached the yard of Gardaí Headquarters. In the time it took the convoy to reach the yard, the volume of the crowd had changed from a murmur to a horrifying roar, and the officers stationed in two lines to allow their entry to the yard were already beginning to take the strain.

The van's escort consisted of two unmarked cars, one in front and one behind, preceded by two police motorcycles. A hefty accompaniment for any criminal, but one that was dwarfed, drowned in fact, by the huge and ugly rearing crowd.

The convoy pushed its way through the channel lined by fearful Gardaí. As the way grew tighter, the white and blue painted finish on the sides of the crawling vehicles were polished by the rear ends of retreating uniforms. They were wedged in now, and the crowd were only just under control.

The motorcycles and the lead car pulled to either side, and the van was only just allowed to pull up to the large double doors and when it came to a halt, the van's own sliding door stood not ten feet away. The multitude held its breath.

Inside the van, Doyle was eyeing the crowd through the riot-guarded windows. He had the radio on.

"Can you see anything yet, Johnny?"

"Shhh! Not yet, Henry. The multitude is holding its breath here in the Phoenix Park. From where I'm sitting, there doesn't seem to be any activity yet."

"And where's that?"

"Anywhere, Henry,"

"No, no, no, Johnny. Where are you sitting?"

"I'm not sure what type of tree it is, but it has a clear view of the door."

"Describe the tension for us, Johnny?"

"Well, and you'll forgive me for whispering, it's just so quiet here-"

"Forgiven-"

"But the only way I can describe it is…"

"Yes?"

"Well, it's like Willie Wonka!"

"Excuse me?"

"Sorry, but it is. It's like when everyone is waiting outside of the factory. Except-"

"Except?"

"If you take away the happy excitement and substitute it for anger."

"Ohhh!"

"Yes, there's a lot more chance of violence here."

Doyle scanned the tree line and wondered where Johnny Deansworth was seated. There were too many up there for him to be sure, but he did fancy that he could make out the famous reporter in a large cedar overlooking the yard.

It was time now for them to make a run for it into the building. Doyle had thought to try and sneak the three captives in through the back door, or in the back of one of the other cars. But the Superintendent had been very clear.

"Bring em right up to the front door, and make sure that everybody can see 'em," said Doyle, echoing the man's words. But even the normally savvy uber-political Super had not expected such a massive crowd, and Doyle was feeling stupid for allowing this circus to happen. Looking at the faces of the people of Ireland now, Doyle was sure that there was going to be a riot.

"Right," he said, and climbed into the rear of the van to where Terry, Peter, and Rachel sat. They looked frightened, which wasn't being helped by armed guards sitting with them. The squawks on their radios announced that the crowd was ready to pounce, and snatches of talk like: "~we won't be able to hold them back for much longer~" were tightening the nerves of all inside the van to snapping point. Doyle tried a smile and failed. He fashioned a look of determination instead and spoke.

"Let's get this over with then," he said, and addressed the radio. "Ok in there? This is Doyle."

"~Yessir, we're ready for ya~"

"Good. Then on the count of three, we're going to open this door and start walking. When I get to five, you open the door and let us in, ok?"

"~Yessir~"

"You've got that?"

"~Yessir~"

"I don't want to change my stride, you understand. We walk straight through the doors?"

"~Yessir~"

"Ok," said Doyle to the three, "you ready?" It was obvious they weren't. Doyle ushered them to stoop beside him at the door and asked one of the armed officers to open the door on three. Doyle held the radio to his mouth.

"One," he said, and stood out of the way so the three could leave first.

"Two." Doyle raised his eyebrows to the man on the door.

"Three!" shouted Doyle and the doors slid open. He shooed the three captives out and stepped out too.

"Four!" he shouted into the radio as they moved quickly to the doors of the building.

"Five!" They were only a few steps away and the crowd had only just caught up.

"Shit!" said Doyle. They had reached the door just after the count of five. It was a perfectly timed entrance; except there was none. The door was still closed.

"Open the door!" Doyle screamed into his radio as a horrible high-pitched sound began behind him. He couldn't believe his ears and had no choice but to turn around. Keening! They were actually keening!

"AEEEEEEEEEEEEEEEEEEEEEEE."

The sharpness of it assailed his ears and made him wince and try to move away. The volume rose louder and louder until Doyle feared his head would burst.

Oh no, Doyle thought, *we're dead now.* He turned back to where Peter, Terry, and Rachel were cowering at the door. At least he'd expected them to be cowering. What he saw was in the realm of the opposite. The three captives, murderers, victims, were no more cowering than a family of bears would, should they be surprised by a fawn. They stood, upright and shoulder-to-shoulder, facing the horde. And they were keening back.

"AEEEEEEEEEEEEEEEEEEEEEEE!
AEEEEEEEEEEEEEEEEEEEEEEE!"

To Doyle, the sound was fearsome enough, but the expression was much worse. The strained maniacal grin that accompanied the making of that particular type of scream made the three look more like demons than real people. At that moment, Doyle knew that Terry, Peter, and Rachel were doomed. They would never be found innocent and set free. The best they could hope for was not to be killed right then on the doorstep of Gardaí headquarters. He couldn't let that happen.

The inspector managed to tear himself away from the sight and ran to the doors. He began to pound and scream until he felt the sharpness of his ripped throat.

It was useless. The masses were moving in, incensed by the tragedy that had befallen their country, and driven by the taunting sight of those they felt were responsible for that tragedy. The Gardaí were falling back under the pressure, and in a few more seconds they would all be pulled apart just as the Treoraí had been, three days before.

Then the doors finally opened. Doyle almost fell inside, so resigned was he to his impending doom. A group of armed Gardaí moved out from headquarters to shepherd the group into the building, and in a matter of seconds they were inside with the double doors firmly closed. The commanding officer, a sergeant, addressed Doyle.

"Sir?" he said, with a fearful look. "Everything is in order, sir."

Doyle looked around at the armed Gardaí.

"I'll remember that," he told them. "I'll remember your faces. Don't you think that I won't?" After scanning the appearance of the guilty looking men, Doyle turned back to their leader.

"Sergeant? Where's the superintendent?"

"He's not here, sir. Important meeting."

"Really. Sergeant?"

"Yessir."

"Get the Army up here immediately."

"They're on their way, sir."

"Good. Let's hope they don't take their time."

Doyle motioned for the three captives to be led away.

"Bring them to the holding cells, and make sure they get fed."

"Yessir," said the sergeant, and the three were led away.

Doyle watched them leave and then turned to the now bolted door, through which the noise of the crowd could be easily discerned. And though the keening had stopped, it had been replaced by shouting, which was at least twice as loud, and twice as angry. But Doyle didn't mind that. Angry shouts were the soundtrack of any officer's life, and as such could be handled as the beekeeper handles the odd sting here and there, or the mechanic plasters the regular pinched skin and bruised knuckle.

The keening, however, that had been a different thing completely. Doyle actually shivered. That was not a noise that should be heard by anyone, anywhere, for any reason.

This case had begun in the most gruesome and strange manner, and was barrelling ahead in a similar fashion. Could he stop it, and save these kids from the approaching inevitability of a guilty sentence? Doyle didn't answer this question. He would not allow the doubt to creep into his heart again, and would not admit defeat.

Walking back to his office to await news of the Army's arrival, Doyle could only think of two things. The horrible keening he'd just heard, and the little bottle of blue pills he'd found in the tunnel, and he suddenly became very concerned for its welfare. It was his only real lead, and it could mean nothing.

Or it could mean everything.

CHAPTER TWO
EVIDENCE

Siobhán sat at home the next morning with her future on her mind. Not her career, her future. This morning, she had stormed out of the office after TD Kilty's speech outside the gates of the Dáil. But she wasn't worried about the effect that would have on her career, it was her business after all, and being the woman who revealed to the world that Walter Thisgo had been murdered, Siobhán knew that she would never lack for work.

The future...

Without Walter Thisgo, there was no future. At least not one in which she could believe. Her ideals were lost and blurred. Last night, she'd been interviewed on RTÉ and found it difficult to explain the great man's vision for the development of the country, so weak were his ideas without him. Worse than that, the Regressives were managing to gain power, even though Siobhán was sure that they were heavily involved in Walter's murder.

This morning on national television, TD Kilty had praised the former Treoraí and vowed that future leaders, be they Regressive or Progressive, would continue along the enlightened path, paved by Thisgo, a man who was a legend in his own lifetime.

Bullshit! When he was alive, the Regressives constantly questioned both his ethos and his ability to deliver. They always tried to bring up Walter's early career, a time when the great man had problems with self-doubt and alcohol. Walter Thisgo had always been a revolutionary, but as a younger man, he had been unable to muster the necessary drive to fuel his lofty ambitions.

Until ten years ago, that was, when Walter Thisgo had sprung to life and split from the then Democratic Republican Party and struck out on his own. The Progressives were born! In only a few years, their ranks had swollen to bursting, causing those who remained in the DRP to react in the only manner they could. They hounded the new political wave by defending the old ways, and became the Regressive Party.

The political situation in Ireland had become open once more, as it had never been since before the English, before even the Vikings, the Catholics, or even the Druids, had come from northern France. Gone were the high salaries, the Jaguars, the second homes. Politics became work again, and Thisgo had died with even more plans for reform in their infancy. What a waste.

That the Regressives hated him was no secret. Having taken away their life of influence and tailored suits, Thisgo had delivered them all up on a stage for the public to see, and to judge.

Siobhán walked to her kitchen to make herself some tea. Yes, the Regressives had certainly killed Walter. Now they were taking the credit for his great works, and she didn't know how to stop them. She could not disagree with their sentiment, as it would mean going against Walter's memory. She was lost beneath a blanket of good PR. Someone like her was doing a great job in the Regressive camp, and Siobhán was going to have to do her best to help the next Progressive leader to take up the reins, yet candidates there were none.

Soon, everything that Walter Thisgo stood for would be hijacked, and his martyrdom would become a beacon to guide the old ways back into existence.

Siobhán's lament was interrupted by a ringing phone. It was Cullen, and he sounded angry.

"Siobhán," he growled, "they've caught the little bastards' parents."

"Oh," she said, "where are they?"

***

Doyle barrelled out of the interview room and stomped up the hallway to the staircase, on which he descended two storeys to the detention cells.

He burst into the room and passed the Gardaí who were on guard inside the door before they even looked up.

"What the hell is going on!" he shouted into the nearest cell and then spun around to the door.

"Get out!" he barked to the guards. The officers didn't argue. They were out the door before Doyle had a chance to rephrase the request.

Pacing frantically around the room, Doyle ran his fingers through his grey hair and wiped the sweat from his brow. He approached the last cell of the three.

"What the hell is going on?" he asked Terry, who was sat on his bed, wide-eyed.

"Wha-" Terry was shocked, but never had a chance to answer as Doyle had already moved to the second cell.

"Rachel?" he said. Doyle moved along again until he was able to address both Peter and Rachel.

"Peter? Tell me, both of you. What, the fuck is happening?"

Peter recovered his composure to answer first.

"What do you mean?"

"What do I mean?" Doyle stepped back from the bars and laughed. "Ha! What do I mean? I actually believed you, and you were playing me the whole time, weren't you? Oh please, God, tell me you weren't."

It was Rachel's turn to ask, "What do you mean?"

Doyle turned and walked to a chair beside the door, one of two that the startled guards had recently vacated, and he slumped onto it. He was tired. There was a reason that he had recently been a retired inspector. Stress. He had always been susceptible to stress. Especially since the missus had died. Since then, he had no frame of reference upon which he could steady himself, or "someone to blame for everything" as she had always said. Doyle thought about her then, with her little smile and her head nodding as he complained about his superiors, or some failed case. He really needed to see her, to talk to her. But of course, he couldn't, and it broke his heart every day.

"Ok," said Doyle, in a calmer tone, standing once more and approaching the cells. "Guess who I just spoke to?" he said. "Actually, guess what four people I've just interviewed?" He looked at Peter and Rachel and they looked back. Nothing.

"Nothing?" he asked. "No idea?"

Doyle held up a fist and released one finger at a time as he counted, "Laurence, Geraldine, Anthony, and Francis.

Recognise those names?"

Peter stood and came to the bars, as did Rachel. They were smiling and looking towards the door.

"Mum? Dad?"

"Ma? Da?"

"They're here?"

"Can I see them?"

"Did you tell them about the pills?"

"Did you tell them that I didn't-?"

"Stop!" shouted Doyle; he wouldn't listen to them anymore. Those hopeful cries, he was beginning to believe in them again, even after what he had just heard.

"Your parents are upstairs right now, and they're not going anywhere either. They're prisoners too."

"What?"

"Why?"

Doyle looked at his watch. "At eleven o'clock this morning, both your parents, all four, made a statement to me; they confessed. They admitted conspiring to assassinate the Treoraí na hEireann."

"Wha-"

"And! All four assured me; swore to me, that you were in no way, duped, or tricked, or doped, or anything of the sort. In fact, you knew full well what you were doing when you left your homes two nights ago to kill the Treoraí!"

Both Peter and Rachel moved away from the bars in unison; struck by some unseen force. They shook their heads and mouthed [no] over and over again. Doyle cursed inwardly as he watched their reaction. There were no signs of duplicity there, not a whisper. He found that he was beginning to believe in them again. But how could he?

An hour before, with a lot less fuss than the arrival of Peter, Rachel, and Terry, the four parents had been brought into Gardaí Headquarters. Doyle was pleased. The media hadn't been given the chance to broadcast the news, and Doyle would be able to examine this piece of the puzzle in peace, without the possibility of a riot. With confidence, he entered the interview room to find the four parents chatting amongst themselves and smiling as though they were at an extremely pleasant dinner party, and nothing more. But the worst was yet to come.

Each parent in turn, spoke happily of the assassination and their view on its positive outcome on the country. Finally, now Ireland would be able to return to the traditional ways of the Regressives, without the instability that Thisgo and his radical ideas would no doubt cause.

So Doyle proceeded through the questioning.

Had Peter or Rachel been acting strangely lately?

No.

Did either show any signs that they were under stress or having problems sleeping?

Same question, same answer.

Had any of the parents seen any signs that Peter or Rachel were about to commit such a terrible crime?

Of course.

Explain.

They had been planning the assassination for months.

What?

The parents then detailed the plot to Doyle. Over the last four months, a group of Regressives, of which they were honoured to be a part, planned the attack on the Treoraí. Two children were to be picked from the families of those involved to carry out the plan, and oh, how proud they were that "our Rachel" and "our Peter" were the ones chosen. Doyle had felt physically sick to hear it. And in the beginning, he had harboured doubts about the authenticity of not just the story, but also the people themselves. Perhaps there had been some mistake and these crackpots had managed to get picked up instead of Peter and Rachel's real parents. Doyle read through their files, and asked some routine questions and examined their photographs too; there was the same high eyebrow, the same small ear. They were genuine all right.

What about the story? Could it be true? Could he have been taken in so easily? Doyle remembered speaking at length with Terry about what had happened. If they were to be believed, then he could have used coercion as an excuse. But no, although he didn't seem to be on the friendliest terms with Peter and Rachel, he never once blamed them for what had happened. They all had the same story. Wild reoccurring nightmares, growing worse each day until their reality had changed one night and they had witnessed the entire population of the world disappear, followed by the death of their friend. This had driven them to their drug fuelled revenge upon the man they felt was responsible for their torment. After this, they fled and were helped by a tramp that claimed to be Terry's father; the man that led them beneath the Liffey to a waiting car, unregistered.

All three had the same story, and Doyle believed it. Especially after finding the pills, which reminded him, he needed to check how the analysis was going on those pills, as well as the blood screening he had asked for on samples taken from the three.

The big problem was that there were huge holes in the story: The girl, Marie, was apparently on holidays in France; her boyfriend, a singer in a university band, had spoken to her the day before. And there was no sign of this Oscar character. Yet. Doyle was still looking.

These holes allowed the story told by Rachel and Peter's parents to take hold in Doyle's mind. Maybe they were just a couple of weirdo radical children? Either way, the evidence was piling up against the door, and at this rate, the three students would never be free.

So, now Doyle found himself at their detention cells, looking into the eyes of all three and believing them once more. Peter and Rachel looked shattered that their parents had let them down in such a way, and Terry, well, Terry just looked shattered.

"Ok," said Doyle to all three, "do you swear to me that what you've told me is the truth?"

They looked at him and he knew before he heard their answers. They believed it was true, he was positive of that.

"Yes," the three answered.

"Ok," he said, "fair enough."

So what did he have now?
The pills.
The blood samples.
Oscar the tramp, and Marie.

He also had four crazy Regressives upstairs who were now under arrest after admitting their involvement in a plot to kill the Treoraí. In a matter of minutes, the press would have their full details and the witch-hunters would begin anew. Doyle looked at his watch. He wondered how long it would take.

"Sir?" said a hesitant voice from the door.

"Yes?" Doyle answered, without looking around.

"There are some people upstairs to see you. A man called Cullen and a woman, Siobhán Sloane."

"Ok," said Doyle. Time was up already. "I'm coming now."

Doyle made to leave.

"Inspector?" Rachel called from her cell. There were tears brimming in her eyes.

"Yes, Rachel," said Doyle.

"Why would they say that about us?"

Doyle shook his head and left the room. That was exactly what he wanted to know.

***

Doyle took a breath and entered the waiting room.

"Let me see them," Cullen demanded, raising himself to his considerable full height and advancing on Doyle.

"See who?" said Doyle with a smile.

"You know who the fuck I'm talking about. Let me see them." Cullen squared up to Doyle and glowered down into his eyes.

"Yes I do know who the fuck you're talking about. And no, you can't see them. Who do you think you are, coming in here to bully me? You're not the law here. I'm the law here."

"Cullen, come on." Siobhán pulled the huge man away from the inspector. Cullen moved back, but slowly and with a look on his face that told Doyle that his "Law" wasn't the fearful thing it should be.

"Now," said Doyle, picking the correct words, "is there something you wish to tell me, some new information that you have perhaps? What I mean is; is there a reason the two of you are here?"

Siobhán kept her hand on Cullen's arm, as if she could hold him back.

"We want to know what's going on," she said. "You have the parents, we heard on the news. Are they really Regressives? Did *they* plan the whole- thing?"

Doyle walked around them and over to the window. Outside in the road, the protestors had increased in number. They were not nearly the crowd of the day before, but a large enough group to hamper the day-to-day workings of Gardaí Headquarters, and keep them in the news. They were calling for-

"They're calling for the death penalty, you know," said Doyle.

"It serves them right!" said Cullen.

"Does it?" asked Doyle.

"Of course it does."

"Don't you care what happened? Don't you want to know where it all came from?" Doyle turned to Siobhán. "I know that Siobhán wants to know. Don't you, Siobhán?"

"Don't give me your bullshit.," Cullen took a step towards Doyle. "They killed him and they should pay for that. And if their parents are under arrest here too, then they were involved as well. So what's your problem? Let them get their punishment."

"My investigation is still open, and until such time as I close it, there's not going to be any trial, or punishment." Doyle took a step forward of his own. "Your type of punishment is not welcome in a civilised society. And as for you seeing the prisoners? Not a chance. I ask you again, who do you think you are?"

Cullen's response was thunderous.

"Who am I?" he spat as he snarled in Doyle's face, "I'm the man who was supposed to protect Walter Thisgo. I'm the one who's going to get my hands on those responsible at some point, and make them pay for what they did. You see me here and I'm telling you the truth."

Cullen held Doyle's stare for a few more seconds before turning to leave. With a great heave, he nearly tore the door from its hinges as he exited.

Siobhán looked at Doyle and also started to head for the

door.

"Wait," Doyle called after her, "have a seat, Siobhán. We need to talk politics."

.

CHAPTER THREE
THE FAMILY UNIT (E)

The room was not the average interview room. It was much larger than usual, and it contained far too many people. There were windows in the room that a child could open, but that was ok, because for each one, there was a Garda present, and more besides. If a closer look was taken at the clean patches on the carpet and the walls, it was obvious that a coat stand once stood there, and a row of desks used to line up with the windows. This was an office, recently cleared for this purpose.

There were already ten people in the room. There was a Garda by each of the three windows, and on either side of the door. And, in the middle of the room, accompanied by their state appointed lawyer, sat Laurence and Geraldine Price, and Anthony and Francis Impey. They sat on one side of a long collapsible table, the sort you would find beneath a staff party buffet, and they were smiling.

"I can't wait to see them," said Laurence, who wiped sweat from his brow and turned to the other three, from whom he received grinning nodded affirmation before they returned their gaze as one to the door, and the watching of it with interest.

All ten occupants of the room tensed in expectation as they heard a commotion outside the room-

Doyle turned to Rachel and Peter.
"Remember," he said, "you don't have to do this."
"We want to," said Rachel, "I have to see it for myself."
"Yeah," said Peter.
"I understand," said Doyle, "but at any stage, you can ask me and I'll get you out of there."
He opened the door-

The door opened and in came Inspector Doyle, followed by Rachel and Peter.
"There she is!" cried Francis and Anthony Impey.

"Peter," called Geraldine, his mother.

"Congratulations," said Laurence, his father; a man who spoke when his wife prompted and thought almost as much of himself, as he did of single malts.

All four parents rose to greet their children, but Rachel and Peter sat down on the opposite side of the table from them.

"Peter," said Laurence Price, "How are you? How have you been treated?"

"I'm fine. They're treating me fine."

"And you, Rachel?" said Mrs Francis Impey.

"Yeah, I'm fine too."

Both Peter and Rachel took on a sullen temperament, with their heads down and their eyes flicking between parents with great suspicion.

"Aw, would you look at them," said Laurence to his three companions. "They don't look fine, do they?"

"No."

"Come on, Peter," said Geraldine, "I know you've been through a lot-"

"Both been through a lot," added Mrs Impey.

"Yes, yes, absolutely," said Laurence, "but don't worry, either of you. They hardest part is done. We've succeeded!"

"What?" Rachel shouted, disturbing the coddling atmosphere, "What the hell are you talking about."

"Rachel!" said Mrs Impey, "There's no need for that!"

"Oh, it's ok, it's ok," said Laurence. "They've been through a lot since we planned all of this-"

"Shutthefuckup! Shutthefuckup!" cried Peter, sliding back his chair and standing. "I can't believe this is happening. How can you?" he looked at his mother. "Ma, how can you?"

"What?" asked Geraldine Price. "How can I what?"

Peter looked to his father, "Da?"

"Peter?" Laurence Price looked confused, "What is it son?"

But Peter shook his head.

"You're not my parents," he said, and backed away, "you can't be!" Stumbling over his chair as he did, his flushed face reddened from different sources of embarrassment. His voice wavered as he looked to Doyle with an outraged cry, half-filled with tears, the other with anger.

"Get me outta here!" pleaded Peter.

Doyle stepped forward from the wall he'd been standing against.

"Wait, Peter," said Laurence, "it's alright. You don't need to pretend that you're innocent. You didn't do anything wrong!"

"Please," said Peter, turning and grabbing for the door but was blocked by both Gardaí standing there.

He looked to Doyle again, who gave his men the nod and said, "Take him back to the cells."

"Peter?" Geraldine Price was red-faced and spoke to her husband as her son departed. "Laurence, what's wrong with Peter?" Mr Price just shook his head.

Doyle hid a sneer from the four "adults". What was wrong with them? Had they been brainwashed too? He studied their faces when, as one, they turned on Rachel. The area around their eyes was emotionless and unmoving for a moment, before all four expressions changed to care-worn and pleading. So there it was, Doyle realised. They were lying. The fuckers were hanging their own kids.

"Rachel?"

"Poor Rachel."

"Poor dear."

"This must be so hard on you?"

And it was. Rachel, who had gone through so much hardship, even in the small period of time that Doyle had known her, had cracked completely and was weeping into her hands. Bawling would be a more accurate description. The sound of it caused Mrs Impey to swiftly turn to her husband, Anthony, for reassurance.

Got you, thought Doyle. The parents weren't all completely convinced of their success.

But even as he did, Rachel's mother had returned to her decided face, and was attempting to take her child's hand whilst saying, "Rachel, dear. You're not going along with all this rubbish of Peter's are you? Be proud of what you've done. You're going to be remembered for years and years to come."

"Get away from me!" Rachel recoiled from her mother's grasp. She tried to stand, but Doyle had to catch her as her knees weakened beneath her and she stumbled. The inspector helped her up and showed her to the door, where he dispatched another Garda to bring her to her cell.

With both Rachel and Peter gone, Doyle stood looking at the Prices and the Impeys, and they in turn looked at him.

"I don't know what to say to you, Inspector-" began Laurence Price.

"Shhh!" Doyle interrupted the man and continued to stare at them, slowly moving back and forward from eye to eye.

For only a few minutes, this continued and already they began to avoid his gaze and stare at the floor.

"You know," said Doyle, "you're going to hell for what you've done to your children, don't you?" And he turned and left, with an angry ball burning in his gut.

But as he closed the door, he had the satisfaction of hearing Mrs Impey start to cry herself.

***

Outside Gardaí Headquarters, Siobhán Sloane was making her second national/international statement of the week. There was a wild breeze whipping her hair around, yet she managed to keep her focus on the main RTÉ camera and ignore the inconvenience. She looked both strong and beautiful, and there was no doubt to the observer that she was also trustworthy and caring.

Oscar was one such observer, and he could see now that he was going to get his chance. That morning, he'd arrived back in Dublin and taken cover in his favourite Gap under South Great George's Street, to rest after the long journey, and to decide what to do next. He noticed immediately that the city streets he'd gotten to know after all these years had certainly changed in the aftermath of the Treoraí's death.

After a brief snooze, Oscar had taken to the streets again, and spent an hour or two watching the news bulletins in the shop windows, and listening to people talking about what was happening. The murderers were caught and their parents too. Soon there would be a trial. A forgone conclusion, during which would be decided the severity of the punishment. Oscar had heard the death penalty mentioned far too many times. Surely they wouldn't bring that back!

There was no surety to be had on the streets of Dublin. In bus queues, people were shaking their heads, and the smokers outside the bars were saying things like, "Hangin' would be too good for 'em."

And, "I still can't believe it happened. Here. It's just, it's just, unbelievable."

On the corner of Dame and George's Streets, Oscar was once again watching the news unfold, when he witnessed Siobhán Sloane's statement on the night of the Treoraí's death. Immediately, Oscar knew that she was the one he needed to talk to, could talk to about what had happened to the fours students, and about where she could direct the police to find the proof that they would need to set the three survivors free.

The news announcement said that there would be an official statement made later that day with regard to current developments on the case, outside the Gardaí Headquarters by Ms Sloane, who had been appointed the temporary press representative for the investigation.

Oscar checked the time and saw that he had twenty minutes to get to Gardaí Headquarters. He was going to have to leg it.

That had been twenty minutes ago, and Oscar was now watching Ms Sloane begin her statement, with beads of sweat rolling down his face. His heart was still thundering as Siobhán's first words carried above the crowd, and Oscar wondered if the old pump was going to last much longer. He knew he was going to end up in one of the missions soon, looking for medical advice. A woman from the Legion of Mary had told him where he needed to go, and what day he could be seen. That was a good while ago now though, and Oscar had been feeling better lately. It was the waking up at night with his heart spasticating in his chest that had caused him to worry. Though that had stopped happening after he'd begun to watch Terry and see the boy was ok. Somehow, the connection, even from a distance, had helped his poor old pump, but the events of the last few days certainly hadn't.

Now his boy Terry was definitely not ok, and Oscar had exerted a lot of energy trying to help him. He'd been no help so far. The boy was in jail, and was going to stay there for a long time if someone didn't do something quickly.

Right now, Oscar felt, was his best chance, and he began to move through the crowd towards Siobhán as only a tramp can.

"People of Ireland. As you now know, there have been a number of new developments with regard to the murder, and likely assassination of Walter Thisgo, Treoraí na hEireann.

"This morning the remaining parents of the three students currently under investigation have come forward and presented themselves to the Gardaí, and as a result they have been detained to aid further investigation. As you all know, it is more than likely that the Treoraí's death was politically motivated, and the parents of Rachel Impey and Peter Price are members of the Regressive party, it has not yet been confirmed that the Regressive party had any knowledge of the events of three days ago. The investigating inspector would like to ask you again for calm and patience whilst he and the Gardaí Síochána do their job, and grant all of the people of Ireland the justice they deserve.

"Thank you for your time. We will be releasing the names of those being held to the press immediately, and would be grateful if you would once again utilise the free phone number provided to help the Gardaí with any information about the movements of these suspects over the last few months.

"Thank you again and good evening."

Siobhán moved from her makeshift postern and headed directly for the car park, her car keys already appearing in her hand. Along the way, she received only a minimal of jostling as the press remained where they were to receive the names of the detainees from one of Siobhán's subordinates.

Oscar took his chance then and ran headlong into Siobhán, causing her to pull up and exclaim loudly.

"Oh!" said Siobhán.

"Oh, sorry there, young one, are ya all right?"

Siobhán gave Oscar an unconscious up and down.

"No, no," she said, "I'm fine. Thanks."

"Oh, she's giving me that look, ha! Just cos I'm a man of the street."

Siobhán looked embarrassed.

"Oh no, sorry-"

"Ah sure, don't worry about it, a smelly crater like me. Sure you'd better check your pockets, and make sure that everything's still there."

"Aha," she laughed, "of course not. See you then."

Oscar smiled at Siobhán as she headed for her car. In a moment, she wouldn't be able to help herself checking her pockets, and then she would see. But he couldn't afford to still be hanging around when she did; she may come after him there in front of everyone, and he couldn't have that. It was too risky. Oscar pushed his way back and soon he was lost from her view in the crowd.

Siobhán sat in her car. The statement had gone well. The promise of names had quelled the questions, and dropping the Regressives in the soup had been very easy. It was as easy as saying: "The Regressives plotted to assassinate the Treoraí." Siobhán was glad she'd had a chance to talk with Doyle about the matter, and been given the ok to say it. The inspector had also been interested to see what the reaction of his newest prisoners would be, when they heard that the entire party had been fingered.

Yes, it had gone well.

Siobhán sat in her car and resisted. It was just some old tramp that she'd bumped into, but now she was becoming worried about her purse. Why did he have to mention her pockets? She'd have probably forgotten otherwise. Siobhán turned the ignition key and the engine came to life. Siobhán waited. She turned off the engine.

"You're so paranoid!" she exclaimed and began to search through the pockets of her coat and breathed relief when she found that her purse was intact. Actually, there was something extra in her right hand pocket and Siobhán took it out.

In her hand was a matchbox.

OPEN, was penned in bold on either side.

"What the-"

There wasn't much else she could do but open the box, so she did.

Inside was a carefully folded piece of paper that read:

01 86932990 - 7.30pm today - Oscar

And that was all. Siobhán looked back to where she'd bumped into the tramp, but he had disappeared into the crowd. What was she supposed to do? Well, actually that was obvious; she was supposed to ring the number at 7.30pm today, which was in an hour and a half.

Should she just call the number?

Siobhán waited for a minute and then decided on what to do. She got out of the car and began to make her way back into Gardaí Headquarters.

She had to check and see if Doyle had heard that name.

***

In the holding cells, Rachel was inconsolable, though Peter tried very hard.

"Forget about them," he told her. "We'll be alright."

But the shock of having her parents lie and call her a murderer to her face was too much, and on Rachel wept. She lay on her bed that lay against the bars to Peter's cell, and Peter was crouched beside her, his hand stroking her head, his words turning into noises of formless consolation; shhh, umm, and ahh.

It was a long while before either of them realised that Terry was standing beside the bars that joined his and Rachel's cells, watching them in their moment of weakness.

"What do you want?" said Peter with more anger than intent.

Terry looked at the floor and murmured.

"They're saying you did it on purpose. Your parents."

The vocalisation of it revitalised Rachel's miserable tears, which had subsided, with Peter's aid, to a low moaning sound.

"So what?" said Peter, "You think we did?"

"No!" Terry shook his head. "Never. It's really wrong."

He looked at Rachel and grabbed tightly to the bars as he spoke.

"But we killed him, didn't we," said Rachel through her sobs.

The fact was that they had. And the reality once more descended on the three. How many more times it would do so was a matter for the number of instances in a lifetime, because they would never be able to think clearly again.

"Listen," said Terry, drawing strength from the metal in his grasp; the hard alloy giving him the steel he did not posses, "We killed him. and we can't change that. I know that I've dealt with it in a worse way than any of us. And I'm sorry." Here, Terry beseeched his one-time friends. "I'm really sorry. I've been going crazy and I've made it worse on you two, when we should have stuck together. And Oscar too-"

Terry stopped for a moment as he gulped down his emotion and tightened his grip on the bars.

"But we are not responsible! Do you hear me? We are not responsible!" he screamed through clenched teeth as the tears welled up in his eyes.

"What about the woman with no face that I saw, coming closer and closer every night? That was so real! And what about your nightmares? You thought they were real too! And what about the feeling in here," Terry punched hard on his chest, "right in here, that the only way to escape the nightmare was to be rid of him? Even before we watched him kill Marie, we knew. And what about Marie? Does that mean she's still alive? Is this real?"

Terry released his hold on the bars and sank slowly to the floor. There was a long silence and Rachel and Peter also absorbed Terry's emotion. They knew that he was right, though they knew also that it would make no difference to their future happiness.

"We are not responsible," said Peter, nodding his head and stroking Rachel's tousled hair.

"We're not responsible," whispered Rachel in the smallest voice that only Peter and Terry could hear, because they knew that she'd said it too.

They were not responsible.

CHAPTER FOUR
THE GOOD SNAKE

"*D*o you think it's really him, this Oscar fella?" asked Siobhán.

"Yes," said Doyle, "I really do."

"Then?"

"So?"

Doyle leaned back in his chair. There were so few leads in this case. So few that led anywhere other than Peter, Rachel, and Terry: Assassins. It was becoming unreal. There were always leads, mostly useless ones, but that was the nature of police work.

Both the pills and the blood samples had been "mislaid" in the lab, and though this had made Doyle furious, he had pretended at the time that they were only loose ends that he was hoping to tidy up.

The fact was that there were no leads now at all, and this worried Doyle more than he would admit. He was also positive now that all other paths were being swept aside, or covered over, leaving him with only one way forward; a direct route to the conviction of Rachel, Peter, and Terry.

"So?" asked Siobhán again.

"So," said Doyle, "you're going to call him, but we need to make sure of a few things first."

"Like what," Siobhán asked.

"Like, we're not going to tell anyone about this, ok?" Doyle locked eyes with Siobhán.

"Absolutely," she said.

Good, thought Doyle.

"Sit tight," said Doyle, "I'll be back in a minute."

Doyle left his office and went up one floor. He needed to trace the number, but he didn't want to use someone that had been assigned to him. He was going to have to pick someone at random and hope for the best.

***

Paul Carter sat at his desk. This was the most boring Temp job he'd ever had. Entering car registration details into a database, wow, it wasn't worth the seven euros an hour he was getting. People should get more for jobs like these. And there were bloody cops everywhere! At least he was allowed to have the radio on though. The Strokes were playing and he'd just turned it up.

Tab-tab-Surname-tab-First   Name-tab-tab-tab-Reg. Number-tab-Speed Kph-F5-Enter-Tick off the list.

Pg Dn-tab-tab-Surname-tab-First Name-tab-tab-tab-Reg. Number-tab-Speed Kph-F5-Enter-Tick off the list.

Pg   Dn-tab-tab-Surname-tab-First   Name-tab-tab-Reg. Number-tab-Speed Kph-F5-Enter-Tick off the list.

Pg Dn-Shit!

He must have forgotten a tab somewhere and filled in the wrong field. Now the record was gone. Whoops.

Pg Up? No, that didn't work. Paul looked around but there was no one else in the office. It was just after five o'clock and he was due to leave at five thirty.

Fuck it.

Tab-tab-Surname-tab-First   Name-tab-tab-tab-Reg. Number-tab-Speed Kph-F5-Enter-

"Hello?"

Paul turned quickly to the door, unable to avoid looking guilty. There was an old guy there, tall, not in uniform but probably a cop.

"What did you do?" asked Doyle.

"Em," said Paul, "I made a mistake entering in one of the records and I can't get it back." The old guy had on a strange expression.

"Don't know what you're talking about," said Doyle. "Who's that on the radio?"

"Oh sorry," said Paul, "It's too loud, isn't it? I think the fuckin' volume is broke- sorry."

"No, no, no, -I went to the concert, and I fought through the crowd. Who's singing that?"

"Eh, The Strokes," said Paul.

"The Strokes, ok, The Strokes," said Doyle, "listen. Can

you do me a favour? Sorry, my name is Doyle." Doyle held out his hand and Paul shook it.

"Sure. Paul. Hi."

Doyle handed Paul a Post-it note with Oscar's telephone number written on it.

"Paul, hi. I have this phone number and I need to know where it is. Any ideas how I would do that? Maybe call Telecom Eireann and get a trace?"

"Telecom who?" Paul puzzled, "Oh Eircom! Yeah, but you'd probably have to prove that you're the police. Isn't there anyone here that specialises in that sort of thing?"

"Probably," said Doyle, "but there's no one around at the moment."

"Oh," said Paul, "hold on then."

Paul made a call.

"Hello? Hi? Where am I through to? Where am I through to? Nassau Street? Outside Celtic Notes. Thanks, What? No you haven't won a prize, sorry, Bye!"

Paul hung up.

"There you go," he said, writing on the Post-it. "It's for a phone box on Nassau Street, outside Celtic Notes record shop." He handed the Post-it to Doyle, who was looking at him blankly.

"Now," said Doyle, "see that?"

"What?"

"What you did there?"

"Yeah?" Paul was wary.

"That was good solid commonsense, wasn't it?" said Doyle, smiling and clapping Paul on the shoulder. "You're a Temp, aren't you?"

"Yeah."

"Boring, is it?"

"Absolutely."

Doyle took out his wallet and a fifty-euro note from it.

"Thanks," said the Inspector, "it's a pity you don't work here."

"Thank, you," Paul beamed, taking the note.

Doyle stood up and went to leave.

"Oh, Paul," he said, as he opened the door.

"Yeah," said Paul, in a great mood now.

"Don't worry if you make a mistake doing that. So someone doesn't get a speeding fine, eh? See ya."

And the inspector was gone, leaving a happy Temp behind. It wasn't like fifty euros was a load of money to Paul, but as his granddad used to say: sixpence is sixpence.

***

Five minutes later, Doyle and Siobhán were in the inspector's car leaving the Gardaí Headquarters car park, and bound for Nassau Street. As they drove through the entrance, another car pulled out of its space and crept slowly after them. Behind the wheel of this car sat Cullen, Walter Thisgo's ex-chief of security.

Cullen was angry.

Lately, Cullen had been all sorts of angry. He felt shameful self-resentment at his failure to protect Walter Thisgo. He felt universally enraged due to the world's tragic loss of such an important figure. He also felt furious frustration because he couldn't do anything to bring the murderers to justice.

But, right at that moment, Cullen was feeling incensed that Siobhán had betrayed him, and was going about the case with that soft-nosed Inspector Doyle, like she was his little special helper or something. Well, they weren't going to get one up on Cullen. He had plans of his own.

Earlier that day, Cullen had been given the addresses of both the Impeys and the Prices.

He'd received a phone call from a man not wanting to give his name. But he, like Cullen, was disgusted that the ones who'd committed such a terrible crime were being coddled. The investigators were spending too much time trying to prove the murderers innocent, instead of getting them into a trial and onto punishment.

They needed to be sent a message. The people of Ireland wanted justice, not indecision.

Each word had fired a different cylinder in Cullen's already infernal engine, and he had come up with a plan to send that all important message.

Even as he sat in his car, following Siobhán and that

wimp Doyle to wherever they were going, the clock was counting down. At 8 o'clock, the whole world was going to know what the people of Ireland wanted. Cullen would get justice, and satisfaction.

Yet in the meantime, Cullen was still angry with Siobhán going behind his back with the grey inspector. He was even a bit jealous, which made him feel uncomfortable. He'd never had any feelings for Siobhán; he'd hardly noticed her, in fact. But Cullen's anger was all embracing, and he allowed it to wash over him once more, so that he could continue to exist in his new and focused form.

Never in the days succeeding the death of Walter Thisgo did Cullen think as clearly and professionally as would normally have come so naturally to him. If he had, maybe he would have seen what was happening; if he had realised that his fears were being fuelled perfectly by an outside influence, then could Cullen have comprehended that he was being perfectly played, like so many others. He was heading for the flames, with eyes wide open but blinded by the light.

***

Siobhán pulled Doyle's car into a parking space on Nassau Street, with the location in sight. There was no phone box on that part of Nassau, but there was a kiosk, so Doyle had hopped out of the car and asked Siobhán to do a lap around Trinity College and come back while he checked the number. That way, they would know for sure if it was the right phone and Siobhán could try and get a parking space nearby, the latter proving extremely difficult. It took thirty-five minutes for her to find a good space, but the one she was now reversing into was perfect for their needs.

It was now seven o'clock. They had a half hour to wait.

"So," said Doyle, "do you watch the Hurling?"

Siobhán laughed.

"What?" said Doyle smiling. "It's a normal question. We've got half an hour to kill, and I could do with a break from my thoughts."

"I suppose so," said Siobhán, "em, no actually. I don't."

"Good," said Doyle. "Do you like any sport?"

"No, not really," said Siobhán. "I did go to an Irish Rugby game last year, in Lansdowne."

"Oh really? Who were we playing?"

"I can't remember?"

"Oh!"

Siobhán smiled, "There are other things apart from sport, you know."

"Really?" said Doyle, "like?"

"Television."

"What do you watch?"

"The big three," said Siobhán, holding up three fingers.

"Which are?"

"Coronation Street, Eastenders, and Fair City."

Doyle looked out through the window at the kiosk.

"Half an hour is a long time," he said, shaking his head and tutting.

"Shut up, ya bastard!" Siobhán laughed, "Just 'cos I don't watch a load of men running around in shorts hitting each other with sticks?"

"Ah the beautiful game," said Doyle laughing now too. "So all we really have in common is this bloody mess?" Doyle looked at Siobhán and she stopped laughing.

"Are you going to find out who's behind it all?" she asked.

"Yes," said Doyle.

"But?"

Doyle gave her a bitter laugh and drummed on the dashboard in a nervous way.

"But," he said, "it may be too late for them."

"Early," said Siobhán looking at her watch.

"No," said Doyle, "I meant late."

Siobhán shook her head and gestured out the window to where the kiosk stood.

"I mean he's early. What time do you have?" she pointed to the kiosk and a man standing beside it.

"It's seven fifteen. Is that him?"

"Definitely," said Siobhán.

Doyle had good long look at the man by the phone. He was wearing a long Cromby coat that had at least a hundred stains on it, and his entire head was a grey ball of hair. The inspector felt a thrill building in him. This was Oscar, a witness to the events of the last few days. This was someone who knew the truth. And he was someone clever.

"Very smart," said Doyle.

"Why?"

"He's early. If we call him now, he'll know that we're watching."

"Oh," said Siobhán, "so, do we wait?" But Doyle shook his head.

"No way. We have to call now."

"Why?"

Doyle took out his mobile and dialled the number of the kiosk. Then he handed the phone to Siobhán.

"What if he just doesn't know what time it is and leaves?"

Siobhán pressed CALL on the mobile phone, and in a couple of seconds they could hear a faint ringing from the kiosk. Siobhán pressed speakerphone and set the phone down between them.

Oscar looked around and spotted them in the car. He waved and answered the phone.

Phone call...

Oscar:	Hi, how many people are watching me?

Doyle nodded. [Tell him the truth]

Siobhán:	Just the two of us.
Oscar:	Is that the inspector?
Doyle:	Yes.
Oscar:	Hi.
Doyle:	Hi.
Oscar:	They aren't responsible.
Siobhán:	We know.
Oscar:	So why are they getting strung up?
Doyle:	No proof. All we can prove is that they tore the Treoraí apart.

Oscar: They were drugged, brainwashed. You
                should have seen how they were acting.
                They were crazy.
Doyle: They told me. But there still isn't any
                proof.
Oscar: I can get you all the proof you want.
Doyle: Please.
Oscar: Have you been to *The Inn*.
Doyle: We checked it out. No broken window,
                and nothing to corroborate their story.
Oscar: They hid her in the wall.
Doyle: What?
Oscar: When I got there, they'd already gone to
                the Áras. But there were men there who
                put her in a bag and put her behind the
                panelling in the bar.
Doyle: They may have moved it by now.
Oscar: I know. It doesn't matter. If you check
                their houses, there are cameras all over
                the place, behind the mirrors, and those
                blue pills. Even if they've cleaned them
                away, there'd still be holes everywhere.
                Wouldn't there be?

Doyle was smiling now. *Finally they were getting somewhere.*
Doyle: Yes, there would be. I'll get over there
                immediately. But I'll need to meet you
                at *The Inn* after, to show me where they
                put the body.
Oscar: Is it crawling with Gardaí?
Doyle: It won't be. I'll get them to leave the
                back entrance open, so you wont have to
                be standing around, ok?
There was a long pause.
Doyle: Ok?
Oscar: Ok. I'll go there now and wait for you.
Doyle: Thanks. Oh, Oscar?
Oscar: What?

Doyle:	Thanks. Really. This is going to blow the whole thing apart.
Oscar:	Good. See ya.
Doyle:	See ya.

The line went dead and Doyle quickly dialled again. Ahead of them, Oscar pulled his coat around him and headed for Dame Street.

"This is Doyle," he said. "I need to have two, no three, crews dispatched immediately to catalogue some evidence. What? Well find some. What? All right, I want the crew that's available now to go to the home of Laurence and Geraldine Price, and turn the whole place upside down. Right? Yes, cameras, the works. Good, no I'm on my way there now. Oh, and get the officer who's watching *The Inn* to call me. Thanks. Bye."

Doyle hung up and turned to Siobhán. Her eyes were dancing and he was grinning from ear to ear.

"You're loving this, aren't you," said Siobhán, unable to stop his smiling spreading across the car to become her own.

"We're getting there," said Doyle, pointing to the steering wheel. "Well," he said, "come on, let's go!"

Siobhán started the engine and they were off in a flurry of hope and beeping car horns.

***

About fifty yards behind their recent conversation sat Cullen on a wall, trying to act casual, smoking a cigarette. He'd driven around looking for a space, and watched as Siobhán and Doyle just sat there. He was worried that they may have seen him. Unable to find a space nearby, Cullen had abandoned his car near St Stephen's Green, and ran back to Nassau Street where the others were still sitting doing nothing.

Then he witnessed the old tramp waving at them from a phone kiosk down the road, before the tramp took up the phone and began to speak.

"Who are you?" Cullen asked the tramp in the distance, as he waited for further developments. Then the tramp hung up the phone and headed off down the road.

"And where are you going?"

There was something going on with this old tramp; that much was obvious to Cullen. So Cullen crossed the road and followed the old tramp as he shuffled off in the direction of Dame Street.

Cullen had no intention of letting them get anything past him, no way.

No way.

Not today.

CHAPTER FIVE
THE TRIAL/THE FIRE

In the space of five minutes, everything changed. The future was sealed and all options were eliminated, leaving failure and hopelessness once more.

At five minutes to eight, Doyle arrived at the home of Laurence and Geraldine Price, the site of their son Peter's conditioning, his training centre, the murder factory. When Doyle entered the house, he saw a large mirror leaning against the fireplace. And above the fire where he assumed the mirror had been, was a hole. Doyle was amazed that the sight of something so innocuous could rouse in him such strong emotion. He was standing now, only feet away from real tangible proof, and he wasted no time closing the distance to it.

As Oscar had done days before, Doyle stood on the coffee table that was still pulled up to the fire, and looked into the hole. There was a camera there.

"Oh, thank you, Jesus, thank you!" he cried in delight.

"Hey!" said Siobhán, arriving through the front door. "What did you find?"

"Come here," Doyle smiled, "there's a camera. An actual camera!"

"What's that smell?" said Siobhán, wrinkling her noise at him.

The smile froze on Doyle's face as he sniffed the air. Then his joyous appearance was gone completely.

"It's petrol," he said. How could he have missed it?

"Yeah, it is. Do you think someone spilled petrol in here?"

"Get out!" Doyle shouted and ran towards Siobhán. The two of them ran out of the house and into the front garden.

Nothing happened.

Doyle scanned the house for smoke or signs of fire, but there was nothing.

"I don't understand," said Siobhán.

"Maybe we disturbed them," said Doyle.

"Who?"

"Whoever was trying to burn the house down and destroy the evidence."

"What do we do now?" said Siobhán "Is it safe to go back in?"

"I'm not sure," said Doyle, trying to decide what was the safest course of action. "We should probably call the fire brigade to make sure before we go back in. Damn it!"

Doyle reached for his mobile phone to make the call.

It was now eight o'clock.

In the kitchen, the microwave was plugged into a timer plug. The timer was set to eight o'clock. Inside the microwave, Cullen had shoved a rectangular metal petrol can, which could be seen easily, by anyone in the kitchen, because the window of the microwave door was smashed and was itself dripping with petrol.

It was very crude and simple way to set a fire, and Cullen had seen it in a movie once. When the timer reached eight, the microwave came on and began to cook the petrol can for fifteen minutes at a medium heat. Why Cullen had chosen a medium heat was a mystery, but he had turned the dial to fifteen minutes and set the heat to medium. Perhaps he wanted a medium inferno to blaze through the house and paint the walls with medium heated flames?

Unfortunately for Peter, Terry, and Rachel, there was nothing medium about the fire that destroyed their chances of freedom.

After about thirty seconds, the petrol can began to spark, and like some sort of space age infernal game of atomic dominos, the walls of the kitchen simply became fire, as did the hall, the living room, and the wooden staircase.

In seconds, the flames reached the top of the stairs and the weed-killer pump that Cullen had used to spray the house with petrol. The heat reduced the plastic barrel of petrol to goo, and the gallon within was set free adding even more fuel to the blaze.

Out on the front lawn, Doyle was frozen with his phone in the air and his mouth open. Both he and Siobhán had heard the terrific Whoomf! as the fire took hold of the house, and were rooted to the lawn in expectation. They didn't have to wait too long.

Through the open front door, they could see nothing but fire. It wasn't coming from anywhere; it was everywhere. The flames began to lick their way out the door and upwards, covering the roof of the small porch and growing left and right.

"Jesus," whispered Doyle, as he and Siobhán staggered back.

Inside the house, plastic began to melt, and glasses began to shatter. Lenses too began to crack and the plaster of the walls, which should have been fireproof, disintegrated and left the hidden wiring of the house open for attack. Later, the fire brigade would swear that the house had been purposely built to burn. It was a death trap, and the inspector was lucky to have survived.

But Doyle wasn't there to hear them. Nor did he answer his phone when headquarters tried to inform him that another house; the Impey's, had just suffered the same fate.

As the Price house burned down, Doyle left Siobhán to call the fire brigade as he tore across the city to *The Inn*. There, he hoped to save the last piece of evidence that was left; the Dark Pupils' last, last chance: Oscar.

***

When Oscar arrived at *The Inn,* he was reassured to find that there was no Gardaí presence there. So that Doyle fella was for real; good. He took one more look both ways along the quays, and headed around the back, where he found the door open as promised; another good sign.

As Oscar stepped from the back room into the lounge, there was nothing good about the feeling that filled Oscar, and made his tears swell.

When he saw the lounge, he was reminded only of Marie, and the last time he saw her, or her remains.

After watching the Treoraí's men pack her up, and place her behind the panelling, Oscar had entered *The Inn* as they had left. He went in through the smashed basement window, and headed straight into the bar, where he stood for a while in front of the offensive panelling; the resting place of that poor girl Marie.

At the time, Oscar had not known her fate; had no idea that it was the Treoraí who had killed her in cold blood, and that Terry, Rachel, and Peter, were at that moment exacting their revenge. All he knew was that he had promised to find help for the girl, and had failed her. He moved quickly then, and pulled down the panelling, Marie's body falling towards him onto the floor, causing Oscar to recoil and step back from her as one would the presence of a rat.

Oscar sneered at himself [fool], and knelt beside her plastic coffin. He unwrapped her and smoothed the hair from her face, and shed a tear for her, whilst he apologised for his shortcomings as a saviour.

But where were the others? And, if Marie was dead, would they be killed too?

Kneeling on the floor of *The Inn* that night, Oscar had no options. All he knew was that the Treoraí Walter Thisgo was responsible, and he did know where the man could be found. So Oscar had left Marie there, had packed her up, and put her away in favour of the living. Then he had headed for Phoenix Park, where he had encountered Terry, Rachel, and Peter there, covered in blood and panicking.

So was she still there, behind the panelling? Neither a yes nor a no would please Oscar now. Now he knew that the man he saw in *The Inn* could not have been the Treoraí; who must have been a double, disguised to give the three students a target for their vengeance. What could he have done differently?

Oscar was at a loss for answers. Yet she must be found and given recognition. As it stood, Marie had not been mentioned in the media. It was as though she'd never existed, and Oscar was not about to allow that shameful situation to continue. He had held her lifeless body in his arms, he had promised-

"Hallo there," Oscar heard a voice from behind him, and spun around to see a huge man standing by the bar.

"And who are you?" asked the huge man. Oscar was immediately wary. There was menace in the man's stance. His knees were bent, and he had quickly scanned Oscar's hands for weapons. Oscar decided to tell the truth and hope that this man was a friendly.

"My name is Oscar. Inspector Doyle asked me to meet him here-"

" Doyle! That bloody yellow belly. What does he want you to meet him here for?"

[Ok, not friendly] "Proof," said Oscar, "of the conspiracy. Who are you anyway?"

"What do you mean, conspiracy?" Cullen asked, his eyes narrowing.

"The murder of the Treoraí, it was a conspiracy by the Regressives." Oscar watched the man closely as he spoke. There were definite signs of hurt when Oscar had mentioned Walter Thisgo.

Cullen reacted with disdain.

"What! Well done! That's been a bit fuckin' obvious since the beginning!" The security man stepped forward and pointed at Oscar. "You'd better tell me what Doyle is up to."

"I will, I will," said Oscar, in a hurry to appease, but he wasn't sure what the man wanted to hear, and there was menace in the big man. [The truth then] "It's about the students. You know; the ones who supposedly killed the Treoraí?"

"Oh really," said Cullen with a bitter smile, "I think I know who you're talking about. Go on."

"Well," said Oscar, "they were brainwashed."

"Really."

"Yes, they were tormented for months, and then forced to believe that it was the Treoraí that was torturing them."

"Oh were they?" said Cullen. "Forced to kill the Treoraí, really? Oh well, that's terrible." Cullen took another step forward and Oscar knew then that this was not what the huge man wanted to hear.

"And why," asked Cullen, "If you don't mind telling me, does Doyle need you?"

"I was with them."

"What!"

"Not when they did it, afterwards. I helped them escape!"

Cullen moved quickly, and in a second, he had Oscar by the scruff.

"You helped them escape?" Cullen growled.

"And I know about the fourth," said Oscar, desperate to say something to give himself more time to manoeuvre. He knew it was unlikely that the huge man was going to let him away without a hiding, and Oscar couldn't help thinking that if Doyle didn't arrive soon, it could be a lot worse than that.

But Cullen relaxed.

"What fourth?" he asked, loosening his grip.

"Their friend Marie," Oscar hurried, "she was killed, here, murdered by the Treoraí."

Cullen's fist pounded into Oscar's skull with a jarring force that freed him from the huge man's grasp, and sent him sliding backwards across the wooden floor. There, Oscar gasped for air, and held his head, wishing for the pain to stop. It didn't, and Cullen was upon him again, pulling him to his feet and delivering another thunderous blow.

"Wait," gasped Oscar, as he was hoisted up again, "it wasn't the real Thisgo!"

"Shut up!" Cullen ordered, and pounded Oscar to the floor again. "You and Doyle with your bullshit and lies. SO, a fake Walter Thisgo killed this imaginary fourth kid? Ha!"

"Please," Oscar cried, tears of pain in his eyes and blood spilling from his mouth. "It's true, they hid her body here."

Cullen raised the old tramp's face to his.

"Fuck your lies," he said, and struck Oscar down for the last time.

When he hit the ground, Oscar felt his heart spasm, and he knew that he was finished, even if there were no more blows, he was not going to live past the next few minutes. So he began to crawl.

Oscar crawled slowly across the floor towards the panel where Marie had been placed after her death. Deep in his mind, he knew that she had already been taken from there, but he was beyond deep thought. He made painful work of the few yards, and Cullen had time to kick him three or four times before he reached the wall, but he made it.

Cullen knelt and turned the old man over.

"This is the end of it," said Walter Thisgo's bodyguard, as he took Oscar's head in his hand and knelt on his chest, "no more of Doyle's bullshit. They will pay for killing him. They will pay."

Oscar's eyes rolled up as he looked backwards to the panel on the wall, and with the little strength he had left, the old tramp raised a hand to touch the veneered wood.

"Marie," was his last word, as Cullen pulled on Oscar's skull, separating it from his shoulders and breaking his neck.

***

Doyle's car clipped the lamppost as he screeched to a halt on the kerb. He opened the door and fell out of the car as he tangled with his seat belt.

"Fuck!" he cried, as he freed himself and ran to the rear exit. He hoped he had time. *Please god*, he needed time.

When he burst through the door, he was hoping to see Oscar waiting for him there, but his very soul paled at the sight of Cullen sitting on the floor with Oscar's head on his lap.

"What's going on here," said Doyle., "Cullen, what did-"

"It'll be over now," said Cullen, looking up at Doyle and giving him a slanted smile. The big man was running his fingers through Oscar's hair, and it was obvious by the angle of the old tramp's neck that Doyle was too late.

"It'll be over now," said Cullen again, not watching as the inspector crossed the room in silence, and knelt slowly in front of him. Doyle stretched out a hand to Oscar's wrist, just to make sure that the man was indeed dead. He was dead all right.

"I killed him," said Cullen, looking up at Doyle, "I killed him." And the huge man began to cry. "I had to, I had to. So it would be over. It will be over now, won't it?"

Doyle held out a hand to Cullen.

"Yes," he said, his stomach filled with the bitter bile, his face set in resentment, "it's over now."

Cullen allowed Doyle to take his hand and help him to

stand.

"Do I need to cuff you?" Doyle asked, though he didn't have any cuffs on him, but wanted to make sure of Cullen's compliancy. Cullen shook his head [no] there was no need to cuff him. He had nowhere to go now, but prison.

Doyle led Cullen to his car and sat the big man in the passenger seat. The inspector was tired now. All the excitement and near success had taken a lot out of him, and he was left a disappointed husk; a failure to succeed.

As they drove back to headquarters, the SDU Inspector called in the murder of Oscar, the man who was to have been the Dark Pupils' saviour, through the knowledge he possessed.

In Garda Headquarters, there would be a total of eight prisoners, unusual for a place that did not usually deal with them. But these were special people.

Doyle could already hear the commissioner's voice. Eight people to bring to trial, the public would be pleased. The case would be closed now, and Doyle had no means by which to keep it open.

Failure.

Damn, bloody, failure.

CHAPTER SIX
ALL SENTENCING'S EVE

At this point, there was a trial of sorts, none of them good. Doyle received a visit from the Garda Commissioner, who was more than happy with the seemingly polished outcome of the investigation, and the inspector was smiled back into retirement. The solicitors began to do their jobs; none of them hard.

There was a victim.

There were murderers who, although in an outlandish manner, had confessed to the crime.

And there was plenty of physical evidence to corroborate the mainstream view.

This part of the grand scheme worked perfectly, and was carried out with precision by defence and prosecution alike. In fact, the only surprise was the testimony of the SDU Inspector Doyle, which opened up the possibility for a change of scenery for the Dark Pupils, but from prison to mental institute, and nothing more.

"Well," said the people of Ireland, "they must be mad, mustn't they. So long as the parents go to prison, the mental home is all right by us!"

This was the expected sentence. And the Dark Pupils: Peter, Rachel, and Terry were expecting something along those lines as they sat in their cells on 'sentencing eve'. The outlook of all three prisoners was indeed dark that night, their mood not helped when Doyle had visited and informed them, business like, that he had failed to help them, and that he was a pitiful excuse for a Garda, and not worthy of the thanks they offered him. Then Doyle left, they thought forever.

Terry sat on his bed, thinking about his mother. She had never come to see him in the cells, but scowled at him once in court as he gave his account of events. He was sure then that Peter, Rachel, and the absent Oscar were right; she was in on it. She had betrayed him.

It was strange, but her betrayal brought Terry closer to

Peter and Rachel. They were friendlier than ever now, and had even spoken of devising a game they could play, should they be given a pencil and some paper. They had even asked, but received nothing more or less than food and silence from their guards.

Rachel's tears had ceased during the trial, when in its second week, she had been forced to listen again to her own mother's proud words of duplicity.

"Oh, Rachel," her mother had said, smiling openly in court, "you have done your family and your country a great service. We are so proud of you."

Rachel hardened from that point. Her mother was gone and instead there was a supplicant harpy who had sold her soul to the Regressives, and was willing to go down on their grand scheme.

Even Rachel's earlier hopes that her mother had been brainwashed, as had the Dark Pupils, were now dashed.

Peter's emotions had reached a plateau. He no longer cared about the trial or his parents. Even the murder was paling in his mind. At that point, he was comfortable and righteous. He was living and thinking the life and thoughts of a victim. All he had were Terry and Rachel, and what he knew to be true. And that was enough for him.

All three Dark Pupils had become resigned to their predicament. They were even looking forward to the peace that would be afforded them by a prolonged internment, and a constancy of environment. At least now they would be left alone and not have to face the reporters every day, nor would they have to face the questions. They would be alone at last, and would only have to face themselves.

The guards stirred at the sound of their radios squawking. They both stood and one of them picked up his chair and placed it in the middle of the floor, facing the three cells. Then, the guards left the Dark Pupils alone, and wondering. What new development was this?

***

Since the night of my death, I have been waiting for this moment. And, although usually, building to a point can aid the telling of the tell, there is no need for such dramatics. In fact, in this instance, it is the normality of it that proved to be the most effective.

***

Walter Thisgo entered the room. He paused only to close the door, and then he walked to the chair that had been placed at his instruction. He took out a handkerchief and gave the seat a quick wipe, and then he sat down with his legs shoulder width apart, and his hands resting gently on his thighs.

He was seated almost equidistant between the three, and this pleased him. He enjoyed it when things worked out perfectly. Like his plans for glorious immortality, which though they had been going badly for a while, were now returning to the furrow he had ploughed for them.

Walter looked at Rachel, Peter, and Terry: His Dark Pupils.

They stared at him from their beds, but said nothing. That was ok by him. He could wait.

After three minutes, still nothing. They couldn't believe what they were seeing, Walter guessed.

But he couldn't wait too long.

"Well?" he asked, but still they only stared.

"What," said Walter, "no 'you're dead!' Or, 'we killed you!' Eh?"

Peter, Rachel, and Terry looked to each other.

"Can you?" said Rachel. Peter and Terry nodded. They could see Thisgo too.

"It has to be a trick," said Terry, "Or it's a ghost, aha! It's a ghost. Thisgo's a ghost! It's a Thisghost!" The maniac that lay shallow in the pool of Terry's sanity was bobbing to the surface again, and Peter saw it coming.

"Or maybe they're still fucking with us?" said Peter. "The bastards are messing with our heads again. That's it!"

"Oh dear, oh dear, oh dear," said Thisgo, shaking his

head. "I haven't time for this." The dead man stood and walked first to the bars of Peter's cell.

"Peter," he said, "do you not remember all those nights you dreamed that you were alone, with my statue in your parents' room? Night after night, ending with you on your knees weeping under the glow of one remaining light."

Peter looked up at Walter Thisgo, and shook his head, while his face fell [no, please].

"I know exactly how it felt, Peter," said Thisgo. "I watched you closely as you grew into a silent killer."

"No!" shouted Peter. "You're dead!"

"Aha," smiled Walter Thisgo, "that's more like it. Rachel?" Thisgo the man, their victim, moved to Rachel's cell, and looked down into her eyes, large and glassy.

"Dear Rachel, can't you see that it is me?" he blinked, trying to effect the same action in her, so he would feel that she was looking at him, and not right through. "You remember me, eh Rachel? All those nights you watched me come into your room, and look at you while you slept. And you were helpless to stop me, weren't you? You felt weak. You felt that you had been violated. And then you were angry. Oh yes, yours was a very creepy scenario. One that I did not enjoy in the slightest, but was necessary all the same, to prepare you for what lay ahead."

Rachel, though she had no tears left in her, and would never cry again, shuddered under the avid stare of the man she had helped destroy. When she could no longer hold his gaze, she turned away and scrambled along her bed to the back wall of her cell. She buried her head beneath her pillow and began to moan softly.

Walter Thisgo smiled. Well now, this was more like what he'd expected. He had prepared himself for such reactions, but, now that he was there and could see into their poor troubled minds, the great martyr could not stop himself from feeling cruel. But that was ridiculous! He cursed himself for the weakness. All had been done for the freedom of the country, the freedom of the world, in fact. Greater men than he had sacrificed the few to gain such lofty goals. He was Julius Caesar. He was Alexander the Great. He was the mighty Lenin, building towards a grand future and a revolution in the minds of society.

Thisgo smiled. Recently, in fact, he had been comparing himself to Lenin a lot, but now that it was becoming clear that his plan was a success, and the short spurt of Regressive popularity had proven to be exactly that, Walter felt that he had surpassed his hero. He had managed to thwart perversion of his ideal, though he had spent many nights worrying about his own possible perversion. Walter Thisgo had always feared becoming too much like Julius Caesar, and succumbing to pride, and hence arose the need for his removal from the ideal.

Although admittedly, Walter had not lost as much sleep, or even physically suffered to the extent of his Dark Pupils, he was sure that his own mental anguish; his own struggle to serve the bigger structure of his genius was akin to theirs.

"Ah. And now I come to Terry," said Thisgo, coming to the bars of Terry's cell. But the third prisoner would have none of it and jumped forward to grasp Thisgo, only missing the man by a whisper.

"Liar!" shouted Terry.

"Whoa!" said Thisgo. "I see that you are still suffering, my boy. And I am eternally grateful for your efforts."

"Let us out of here," cried Peter. "If you're not dead, then we are innocent!"

"Yeah," said Terry, wide-eyed and grasping at the idea, "yes, we didn't do anything."

"Oh, Terry," Thisgo shook his head. "We pushed you too hard, boy. It was your mother really; she wouldn't go lightly on you, even when you created your own fantasy. A faceless nun? That's not what we wanted. You were all supposed to despise my face."

Thisgo walked back to his chair and sat down, job done, he had their attention now.

"Yet," he said, letting the word stand ambiguously alone, "you did murder Walter Thisgo. That is a fact that you cannot escape from. I saw the tapes too; was there in fact to witness the entire event."

"But you're alive!" shouted Terry. "You can't be alive."

Though Rachel huddled in the corner of her cell, Peter

was now, like Terry, grasping the bars and pressing himself as close to Thisgo as possible. They wanted to get at him and put their hands on him. Even in death, he had been their tormentor. And now he was here.

"How are you alive?" Peter asked. "I don't understand."

Thisgo smiled as he revealed his coupe de grace, his ace; his poison asp.

"The three of you killed Walter Thisgo, and yet I stand before you. You see, my father was-"

"Just tell us, please!" shouted Terry.

"Patience," Thisgo snapped. He would not be robbed of his great revelation. "Now. When I was young, I, Walter Thisgo had a promising career. I planned to be a revolutionary figure, the revolutionary figure in Irish history. I was going to leave Daniel O'Connell and Padráig Pearse falling, standing around back stage while I, Walter Thisgo, really changed the world."

Thisgo Paused for effect.

"What are you talking about?" asked Peter, his face disbelief itself, as his tired mind struggled with the shock of seeing the dreaded Thisgo again.

"You started all of this," Terry growled, "get us out of here."

Thisgo smiled.

"I'm sorry for smiling," he said, "but when you listen to what I have come to say, you will understand. So," Thisgo looked at their faces, Rachel's had only just reappeared, "will you listen?"

Thisgo waited for all three to resign from their protestations and submit to his grand confession. It didn't take long. Then, he settled back into the chair and began to speak.

"Hello," he said, "My name is Walter Thisgo. You killed my father."

And the twisted story began.

Meet Walter Thisgo…

Every since he was a young man, even in the early eighties, Walter Thisgo had believed in honour and, even in the eighties, he held on to these beliefs. In the beginning, his idea of a perfect Ireland and an ideal world were enough to gain him a reputation and the notice of the political bigwigs of the day. But when the man refused to give up those ideals to favour the grand luxury and promise of his brown enveloped, back patting, right-eye-winking peers, Walter Thisgo's political career literally ran out of backing.

Even within his own party, the idealist found that he was being undermined. He was a threat to the status quo and, as such, would not be allowed by anyone to tear down the plush lifestyle of the political elite. It was clear. Walter Thisgo was going nowhere.

Leading up to the tough years that preceded that realisation, Walter Thisgo had a family; a wife, a son and a daughter. The son, Walter Thisgo Junior was raised on the heady aspirations of his father. Once, when the boy was twelve, he went to the principal of the school and convinced the woman to allow him to be in the A class even though his results had been below average for admittance into that level.

"I'm making you a promise," said Walter, "I will be an A student."

So he was allowed in the A class, and Walter Thisgo, then a budding junior TD, was proud of his son. He was so proud, in fact, that at fourteen, Thisgo sent the boy to France where he would school and afterwards study politics, away from the corruption and twisted ideals of his Irish home.

While the boy was away, Walter was being torn apart by his own refusal to buy into the lax ideals of his peers. He lost favour in his constituency, and with it he lost his pride. He began to drink everything. He drank the money that he'd saved through the years. He drank his family into a smaller house. He drank them into a Ford Fiesta. He even drank the mouthwash below the bathroom sink. But it wasn't enough for him. And, eventually, Walter Thisgo drank his son home from university too.

That was a low point for the Thisgo family. Night after night, the drunken father tried to beat into his son the values of his perfect political ideal. Not because the son could not already recite each facet of the ethos, but because the young man looked so similar to his father that the politician could not stand to look at him. By beating his son, and to a lesser extent, his daughter, the old man was punishing himself. Or, so he thought, in his coward's way.

Walter's wife, Anne, already a sickly woman, spent far too much time working in the local pub, carrying plates by day, and her husband home by night; eventually Walter Thisgo drank her into a cheap grave.

It took this to incite the children to revolt.

The rancour and the bile that Walter generated in his daughter and son was such that they were willing to do away with the man. Yet they would not have him locked up, nor would they kill him. They had been forced to listen to their father's once brilliant mind too much for that. Grand ideas spewing from the lathered jaw of drunkenness, interspersed with long pauses that lost the train of thought and changed the subject of the great Walter Thisgo's one-sided oratory.

Walter Junior, a quiet boy, for whom those years of abuse were a shock due to his recent return, grew sick of his father. He detested the all-knowing, do-nothing politician that his father had become. The young man's hatred had been building to the point of desperation, until the death of his mother coupled with the continued ridicule from his father's constituents drove him into action.

Often, as the son walked down the street in the grey evening, he was mocked as though he were his father. In fact, those that saw him in the half light thought that he was indeed Walter Thisgo, their drunken useless representative, walking upright for a change.

On the day they did it, the son and the daughter, the sun was disappearing below the houses of Clontarf. Walter Junior was returning from a job interview, with little hope of success, and dreading facing his dreaded parent, when an old man addressed him.

"Mr Thisgo, sir," said the man from across the street.

The son stopped and prepared his retort. So far that day, he'd already used, "I'm only his son, leave me alone," and, "I don't know who you're talking about!" He found that he was too tired to think of another retort, so simply said, "What?"

"Sir," said the man, "if you don't mind me sayin', Mr

Thisgo?"

"Go on."

"You used to be a great man around here, you know. And you could be again."

"Really?"

"We mock ya," said the man, averting his gaze downward to the road, in the way that one would who found the truth difficult to admit, "but we don't hate ya, Mr Thisgo."

All the way home, the son though of this. He had never even thought that the mockery that his father suffered could come from disappointment, and not hatred. Walter felt that there was something important in that realisation, but couldn't extract the positive from it yet.

He didn't need to wait long.

Two nights later, Walter Thisgo was especially drunk. Sitting by the crackling fire, he spilled port on his shirt and demanded that his daughter go downstairs to the basement to wash it immediately. She went without argument, glad of the respite from her father's foul humour. In a matter of seconds, the drunkard was screaming down the stairs at her to hurry up, making ridiculous and chilling threats.

"Da, give her a chance," said the son, "she just went down!"

"What do you know," slurred his father, "with your French education? You can't even get a job. If your mother was here- Where the hell are you with my shirt?"

Walter Thisgo stumbled down the stairs, shouting all the way, with his son following behind, pleading for him to calm himself. When they reached the basement, Walter Thisgo made a large mistake. He screamed at his daughter and then he struck her to the ground. This was the final push that Walter Thisgo Junior needed, and he struck his old man from behind, sending him directly to the floor and unconsciousness.

"And that was pretty much the end of him," said Walter Thisgo, addressing Peter, Rachel, and Terry.

"It was a long time before the old man was allowed up those steps into the house; only a few weeks ago, in fact."

Thisgo paused in his story and examined his audience. Had they worked it out yet? It was hard to tell. Their faces were blank, their eyes narrowed, and all three were bereft of sympathy or acrimony.

"So," said Thisgo, finally deciding to move on. "You are being sentenced tomorrow. Yet I am standing here. Do you want to know why?"

"Your father," said Peter quietly, like an unsure schoolboy presented with a problem he should be able to solve, "you wanted to take the place of your father?"

"Oh," said Thisgo, "You're not quite there, but you are close. You three-" and here he stood and raised his voice, "*did* kill Walter Thisgo. You killed my father. But not so I could take his place." Thisgo watched as they began to try and assemble the facts.

"I replaced my father a long time ago when he had all but ended his own life. It wasn't hard. A little grey in the hair and I was basically there. All I needed to do then was check into a rehab clinic and come out a reformed man. Then *I* was Walter Thisgo, and I could begin to fight back!"

There was a change then in Thisgo's practiced oratory. Now, he was really getting into it.

"Those bastards drove my father down with their half-way politics! Taking money from sweaty builders, and standing around in hotel bars, gushing and scheming over and against each other. The Irish government were nothing but a bunch of Romans. The Taoiseach was nothing more than an Augustus; the king of the filth. But I had what they didn't have, and I would do what they couldn't do. They were weak and I was strong-"

"Stop!" shouted Rachel. "Please stop." Her face was a miserable mask. "Why are you doing this to us?"

"Why did you make us kill him?" Peter asked.

"You still want to know why?" said Thisgo.

"Yes," said Terry. "Why? We need to know."

"For Ireland," said Thisgo, letting the simple phrase fall dead at their feet. "Everything I did, I did for my love of Eireann. I rebuilt, I renamed, I reordered the government, but not for my sake, for Ireland. We are one of the strongest economies in the world now, not a powerhouse, but definitely a big player, especially since we claimed the oil off the northwest."

"But why?" Peter asked again. "Why did you have to do this to us?"

Walter Thisgo shook his head, [they didn't understand] perhaps they would never understand.

"For all that I was able to do," Thisgo said, with his arms held out in front of him, pleading, "I am only one man. And as such, my effect on the world would not be a lasting one, unless? Unless, it ended in-?" He waited for them say it with him.

"Tragedy! Yes, a terrible lasting tragedy that would stay with the world for decades, even centuries beyond my existence. Walter Thisgo has become the assassinated visionary, the legend, the martyr."

Walter Thisgo smiled. Overall, he felt that his telling of the tale had gone well. "So you see. You three were not only needed to ensure that this happened. You were vital to the cause. You do see, don't you?"

But they didn't see. How could they. What was worth destroying their lives for?

A political ideal?

A plan?

Terry began to laugh.

"Aha!" he cried, falling back onto his cot.

"Why are you laughing?" Walter Thisgo fumed, but Terry ignored him.

"Why are you laughing?" the impostor demanded.

"It was you all along," said Rachel, smiling too. "You're the one who is insane, not us." Peter sat down on his own cot and joined in Terry's laughter.

Walter Thisgo was furious, yet beneath his anger, he realised that there was nothing else the three could do but laugh. So he calmed himself, and smiled back at them.

Then he beamed. After all, they deserved something.

"You have suffered greatly," he said, "And tomorrow you will be punished for a crime I forced upon you."

Their laughter ended quickly.

"I have come here to promise you something."

"Marie!" cried Rachel, her eyes shining in a burst of hope. "Is she still alive too?"

Thisgo spoke slowly.

"I have come here to promise you something," he said, looking away from Rachel's outburst.

"Is she?" Rachel asked again, but Thisgo shook his head.

"Marie died at the hands of my father. Forget her. She is gone."

The pretender turned away from them for a moment before continuing. If they had seen his face, then they may have guessed, but he hid his tears from them. He had always hidden things well.

"I promise you that when the circus dies down, and the country has forgotten you, or at least when the pain in their hearts is not so livid, I will come back." Thisgo turned and spoke to each in turn.

"Peter, Rachel, and Terry, you must believe me when I say that I will return. Tomorrow, you will be sentenced to life in a mental asylum. Thanks to the testimony of your friend Inspector Doyle, you will not be going to prison. I will have to leave the country for a while, so as to let Ireland mourn in peace, and allow the martyrdom of Walter Thisgo to become an integral part of the public faith. But I will come for you, my Dark Pupils. You deserve your freedom."

Walter walked back to his chair and took one more look at his three assassins.

"All you need to do is believe in me," he said, "you can do that, can't you?"

One after the other, they nodded that they would. After all, Walter thought, what else could they do? He was standing right in front of them.

"I will come back and take you with me," he promised, and moved towards the door.

"Wait," said Peter, "Are you real?"

Walter Thisgo smiled at Peter and stepped towards him. He reached through the bars and touched his fingertips to Peter's cheek, and the prisoner shivered at the contact. Thisgo then moved to Rachel, and he took her hand and kissed it.

When Thisgo got to Terry, he was sitting on the floor, with his back to the bars.

"What about my mother?" he asked. "Why hasn't she been to see me?"

Thisgo ran his fingers through the blonde boy's hair, and sighed.

"She betrayed you," he said, and stepped away from them.

And then he was gone from the room. The chair that had been placed for him was picked up by a Garda and taken to the door.

"Did you see him?" Peter asked their guard.

"See who?" said the guard, and went back to his magazine. Peter noticed that it was –'The Phoenix' a spoof political magazine. On the cover, there was a cartoon of a man in a suit nailed to a cross. He strained to read the caption, but he couldn't.

"What does it say?" Peter asked the Garda.

"What?" said the officer, lowering his copy of –'The Phoenix' and raising an eyebrow.

"The caption on the front of the magazine," said Peter, "what does it say?"

"Oh," the man turned the magazine over and read it out, "it says, *Now that you're dead, Walter Thisgo, can you tell us what to do?*" The guard laughed, "Ha, funny."

"Yeah," said Peter, turning and sitting down on his cot, "funny."

CHAPTER SEVEN
THE PROMISE

The radio battled with the silence that emanated from the Dark Pupils, from the back of the Garda van. Once more, Henry Hutchins and Johnny Deansworth were commenting on their lives from somewhere in radio land, their voices unscathed by the many obstacles between them and the van's large aerial.

"Well, Johnny," said Henry, "what's the verdict? Lay it on us."

"Hi, Henry. It has been mad down here at the Four Courts all morning. Thousands of people have showed up to witness the sentencing of the Dark Pupils first-hand, as if by being here they were getting closer to our lost leader and Treoraí, Walter Thisgo."

"But the verdict, Johnny, we can't wait any longer."

"Ok well, at eleven fifteen this morning, the jury returned their verdict to the charges of murder, treason, and other more minor allegations covered under the Offences Against the State Act. The verdict reached for all charges was a definite guilty. Judge Masterson immediately handed down the sentence without hesitation. Obviously, his honour had assumed, as did we all, what the verdict would be."

"And what did he give them?"

"Well, as you know the feeling amongst the press and the public for the last few days was that, though the crime was indeed of the most serious nature, the three Dark Pupils were undoubtedly mentally unstable at the time of the murder. And, as we all expected, the judge reflected this in his sentencing, handing out three Real Life sentences, under the Provisions for Justice Act of last year. Real Life meaning, of course, that they will in fact actually be spending their entire lives in captivity. The one allowance given them was the location of their incarceration. The Dark Pupils will spend the rest of their days in the Via Rosa Criminal Mental Hospital, located in the Wicklow mountains."

"Wow, Real Life, that's the first time they've given out

that one, Johnny."

"Absolutely, Henry. The Act was introduced by Walter Thisgo's government last year under the guidance of the man himself, and it only seems just that this is the first time that the Republic has been forced to use it."

"It does, doesn't it? Well, Johnny, any other comments on the day's biggest event."

"Just one, Henry. The reaction of the Dark Pupils to their sentence should be noted. After it was read out, I could clearly see that they were smiling, as if they were happy to receive Real Life imprisonment. It was very strange indeed."

"Yes, very strange, Johnny. Those poor sick kids. They really are messed up, aren't they?"

"You said it."

"I certainly did. Well thanks, Johnny. I'll see you in the studio. Well folks, it seems hard to believe but the world has kept turning whilst we held our breath, and here is Sean Dempsey with the rest of the news-"

To Terry, the sound of the radio presenters trailed off there. They were on their way to the nuthouse now, and that was all the information that his mind could handle. He looked at Peter and Rachel, huddled together across from him, sharing the comfort of each other's presence, and he was not jealous any more. It was obvious to him now that love would not save them either. The only chance they had was the man who had appeared to them the night before in Gardaí Headquarters, the man who was supposedly Walter Thisgo.

Apart from their two guards and each other, there was little else to see inside the van. Terry was sick of blank walls and cramped spaces. He wanted to see the sky again, and he wondered what sort of view he would have at this Via Dolorosa place. There was a bigger question though.

"Do you think it was real?" he asked Peter and Rachel. They shuddered together, and looked from him to each other for reassurance. It was cute really. They did not answer. But Terry knew that they were the same as him.

They wanted to believe that Walter Thisgo was really alive. Otherwise, they were screwed. For Terry, either option was unbearable, as they were either on their way to the nuthouse for the rest of their lives, or they were going to have to sit there and wait for the man they had killed to come and free them.

Terry watched Rachel and Peter as they hugged each other, and he thought about their future. Would they be allowed to continue a relationship in a mental hospital? Would the three of them be allowed to see each other?

All of these thoughts were difficult to process, but at least they kept him from thinking of- Damn it! There it was again: Oscar, his father? The old tramp that tried to help them when they needed it most was nowhere to be found. Terry had hoped that the man would turn up during the trial to help them, but when he'd asked Doyle, the inspector had grown quiet and counselled Terry to concentrate on the trial at hand.

[Where are you?] Terry mouthed. Yet he had a terrible feeling in his gut that he would never find out where the old man had gone, but he wouldn't believe that the one whom he thought of as Father would abandon him so completely. So what was left? Was Oscar dead too? Before all of this, Terry could only remember one dead thing; a pigeon at the side of the road. Now he had gone so far as to assume that someone was dead without being sure. He had seen murder. He had even killed a person, and days later watched as his victim walked and talked, and turned his world upside down, once again.

So what could he hope for in the future? Peace and quiet, or maybe the chance to see his father one more time? Terry felt that he deserved the chance to apologise to Oscar for his attitude and his harsh words. He knew that it wasn't entirely his fault; his behaviour, according to Thisgo, had been engineered, but now that his mother had abandoned him, he was parentless.

Terry thought about the situation that Peter and Rachel were in, and felt bad for feeling such self-pity. He would take his mother's coldness over their parents' weird behaviour. What a bunch of psychos!

The van came to a halt for a moment, and there was talking in the cab. Then they were moving again but only for a minute. The engine died. They had arrived.

"Shit," said Terry to Rachel, Peter, and himself, "that Junior Thisgo fucker better not have been lying to us."

So what, all three thought to themselves, *what the hell can we do about it if he was?*

CHAPTER EIGHT
SHARED PSYCHOTIC DISORDER

The CMH at Via Dolorosa was not a metal stain on the side of a mountain, as Doyle had expected, but a well crafted sloping building that lent itself to the landscape as much as it benefited from it. So this was where they had ended up? Well, he'd seen much worse over the years. The boys in Mountjoy and Portlaoise would certainly love to spend even a weekend in a place like this.

"It's beautiful," said Siobhán, who had been very quiet during the long drive. Doyle was beginning to have doubts about bringing her here, but when the two of them had met for dinner the previous night, he'd been weakened by her presence. Such a beautiful young woman, her eyes alight due to her obsession with the death of her former boss and mentor. She had said that she still couldn't sleep, that she badly needed to speak to the Dark Pupils; it being the only way she could rid herself of the constant dread she carried around with her. Damn Dark Pupils! He was using that phrase again. Even at his age, ex-Inspector Doyle found that he too was a slave to the media.

"Are you ok?" Siobhán asked, "You're miles away, aren't you?"

"What?" said Doyle, blinking away from his preoccupation, "Oh yeah, I am a bit. Sorry. It is beautiful, isn't it?"

The road curved its way up to Via Dolorosa. And lined with uniform fir trees, it gave the approaching visitor a sense of peace and confidence in the facility's ability to nurture and to cure.

On the outside, the Via Dolorosa joined with the surrounding mountain as though the gods of metal and technology had plunged their hands into the living rock and drawn from it the material used in its construction.

On the outside, the criminal mental facility looked so perfect that it could have been a sculpture sitting on the desk of some ambitious architect.

On the outside, an image was projected that inspired all those who viewed it to think wide-open thoughts of country life and personal well-being.

But that was on the outside.

Those on the inside of the Via Dolorosa did not have the opportunity to draw strength and inspiration from the façade of the building. Most of them were confined to rooms that were bare, and painted a soothing green. They were cells, despite the beauty of the building that housed them.

On the inside, the building looked like all other such places; clinical and impersonal. Each room housed the dangerously ill, the vicious, the demented, and the doers of dark deeds.

On the inside, the Via Dolorosa looked like another circle of hell, reserved only for the insane and the pitiless.

It was here that Peter, Rachel, and Terry would be spending the rest of their lives.

***

Peter and Rachel inside…

It took forty-five minutes for the Care Givers or CGs for short to bring Rachel and Peter to the Encounter Room, and even then it was only after another five minutes of Guideline Training. Doyle and Siobhán studied Peter and Rachel carefully as the attending CG, Ruth, explained why it was impossible for them to speak to Terry. The two just stared at the wall and waited patiently by the door to be seated.

"Here at Via Dolorosa," the female CG spoke with an engineered 'friendly' smile, accompanied by practised limited hand gestures, "we have made the following diagnosis." The woman ignored the fact that Rachel and Peter were in the room, and labelled them by number.

"We believe that the group in question, comprising of Male One, Male Two and Female One, suffer from a rare yet treatable form of <u>Shared</u> <u>Psychotic</u> <u>Disorder</u> – <u>Subtype</u> <u>A</u>." The CG underlined the words by holding her hands out in front of her as she spoke. "Subtype A is termed folie imposée. The delusions of a person with psychosis are transferred to a person, or in this case two persons who were mentally sound. All three persons are intimately associated, and the delusions of the recipient disappear after separation."

Doyle watched Peter and Rachel as the attending CG explained the diagnosis. They were both staring at the wall with drugged expressions, but as he studied them keenly, Rachel's eyes darted up to his and then she quickly returned to her blank state. *So,* Doyle thought, *you're pretending.* That was interesting.

"So what you're saying," Siobhán said, "is that Terry-"

"-Male One," the attending CG interjected.

"Of course. You're saying that Male One is the psychotic, and in time the others will, what? Snap out of it?"

"Yes," said the attending CG, "we are treating all three with anti-psychotic medication, to ensure that the delusions cease, but we are confident that this diagnosis is the correct one."

"Ok," said Doyle, "you can go now. We will be sure to follow all the guidelines with regard to the patients. But unfortunately, this is Garda business."

"Well," said the CG, sniffing at being dismissed but rising to leave, "see that you do follow the guidelines." She left the room.

Siobhán gestured for Peter and Rachel to sit and they slowly complied.

"Jesus," she said, "they're really whacked out of it."

"Mmmm," said Doyle, who stood and began circling the four chairs that stood table-less in the middle of the green room. "Perhaps you're right," he added, in low tones.

"PERHAPS!" Doyle screamed, as loud as he could, causing the other three of the room's occupants to jump out of their skin. All three. He returned to his seat.

"So," he said to Rachel and Peter, who had lost their apathetic expressions, "enough of this bullshit. I don't care why you're acting for the doctors. You're not going to act for me, Ok?"

[OK] they nodded together.

"Now," said Doyle, "tell me about Terry. All this stuff he's been telling the doctors about Thisgo being alive?"

Peter and Rachel looked at each other [you go first].

"Rachel?" Siobhán asked, with her eyes alight and excited. Doyle could see why; she was actually sitting in the same room as two of Thisgo's murderers. "Tell us what he has being saying."

"Who are you?" Rachel asked,

"I'm Siobhán, I used to work for Mr Thisgo." Rachel hung her head at the mention of the name.

"The drugs they give us are pretty strong," said Rachel quietly.

"I heard," said Doyle. "The medicine is called Olanzapine."

"Is it dangerous?" asked Peter.

"Don't worry," said Doyle, "I've checked with some friends, and you would have to take a lot more than you are to be in any danger."

Rachel and Peter turned to each other again. They looked so sad that Doyle felt the same gloomy emotion welling up inside of him.

"Peter?" Doyle tried, and Peter responded.

"Yes?"

"I need to know about Terry. Does he think that Walter Thisgo is alive?" There was a pause.

"Yes," Peter answered, locking eyes with Doyle, defiant.

"Do you?" Doyle asked, being careful to hide any disbelief.

"We killed Walter Thisgo!" Rachel cried, with a pleading look at Doyle. "I'm sorry," she added for Siobhán and dropped her eyes to her lap once more.

Siobhán was beginning to brim with tears, and Doyle didn't know how long it would be before he would join her. Was it this place, or was he just getting soft?

"It's ok," said Siobhán with difficulty, "you didn't know."

"What has Terry been saying?" Doyle tried to divert the flood that threatened both him and Siobhán.

"He's not doing great," said Peter, "you have to get him out of here."

"They told me that he's been saying that Walter Thisgo is alive, and will be returning for the three of you. Is this true?"

Peter studied Doyle, and the inspector was thrown by the

intensity of the young man's stare. Peter had definitely not been taking his pills.

"Why are you here?" Peter asked, "You can't help us. What are you doing, bringing a girl to see the freaks?"

"Peter, no," said Doyle.

"Why then?" Peter asked, taking Rachel's hand. "We won't speak to you any more if you don't tell us."

Doyle believed him. He had asked the question himself. Why was he still obsessed with the conspiracy behind Walter Thisgo's death? Was it because this was the biggest, most public and last case of his career, and he had not uncovered the truth? Or did he just care for these three 'Dark Pupils' he had promised to save? Doyle was not a young man, not accustomed to fooling himself with heroic fancy. And, in time, he had admitted to the real reason behind his passion for this particular murder. It was purely selfish. He did not care about his failure; the plaudits he'd received in the press had actually raised his shallow spirits. He did not even care overly for the three youths. He'd seen the video of what they did to their victim, and even if he almost knew that they were innocent, it was impossible to wipe away the horrific images.

It was therein lay the reason. He did not know. It was as simple and perverse as that. He was dying to know what really happened, to have the whole tale spelled out for him. He was a mystery junky, longing for the final scene when the villain reveals all. Who was really behind all of this? He just had to know.

"I," Doyle began, allowing himself to beg. "I- I just have to know. Please tell me who's responsible for all of this?"

"If you tell me something?" Peter asked.

"Anything," Doyle assured him.

"Tell me what happened to Oscar. Terry is sure that the old man abandoned him." Peter and Rachel exchanged a glance, "We think-" he finished there, unable to end the sentence.

"You're right," said Doyle, "Oscar is dead. He was trying to help the three of you and- a man, who thought that Oscar was involved with Thisgo's murder killed him before he could give me proof."

"He didn't abandon us?"

"The opposite," said Doyle, "you believe me?"

"Yes," said Peter. Rachel's face was drooped in sadness,

"I hoped," she said, "but… I knew."

Doyle allowed Peter and Rachel to digest the information as he thought about Cullen, who was at that moment sitting in prison awaiting trial. The fool had robbed Doyle of a chance to expose the conspiracy.

"You want to know who is behind all of this?" Peter asked, not bothering to wait for an answer. "Walter Thisgo."

"What?" said Siobhán, "You're saying he committed suicide?"

"Ha," said Peter shaking his head. "No. But he planned his own death."

"What are you talking about? Don't talk rubbish!" said Doyle, worried at the direction Peter was taking. Peter started to laugh and Rachel couldn't help but join him.

"Don't you want to hear what he told us?" asked Peter, his laugh turning to a snarl and giving his face a bitter twist.

"What do you mean?" asked Siobhán in disbelief. Doyle could see that she was confused about what was happening. But Doyle had seen it before in interviews and interrogations over the years. The crazy was coming out and Doyle's stomach churned with a sort of grief. Peter and Rachel had lost their minds.

"What do we mean?" said Rachel. "Only that he came to see us, like Terry said, and he's going to come back when all the fuss dies down. Then he'll take us."

"Take us into exile," Peter added, smiling again.

Doyle stood from his chair, and with a grunt he kicked it across the room.

"It that it?" he yelled at Peter and Rachel. "You're crazy? Is that what you're telling me? Let's go, Siobhán, they're not going to be of any help to us."

Peter and Rachel continued to laugh as Doyle and Siobhán walked to the door.

"Oh don't go," said Peter, "why don't you wait here with us? He'll be here soon, then you'll see that we're not lying."

Doyle opened the door and let Siobhán out in front of him.

"Doyle!" shouted Peter, causing the ex-inspector to turn.

Rachel and Peter were watching him with eyes that were wide and deep. There was no laughter on their faces. Nor was there any malice or even sadness. When Rachel spoke, it was as a simple statement of fact, and without questioning or bitterness or regret.

"You came here to help yourself," she said, while Peter nodded, "You could never help us."

Doyle tried to speak. He wanted to tell them that, no, he would still uncover the people behind their tragedy. But he knew that Rachel was right. He never had a chance.

As he walked out of the Via Dolorosa with Siobhán and sat in his car, Doyle allowed himself to think that evil thought; the horrid spirochete that was constantly attempting to burrow into his brain was now feasting hungrily and relishing its success.

"It was them all along," Doyle stated, as he turned the key, "they're just mad, that's all, they're just mad."

Siobhán turned to Doyle and saw the pain sculpted on his ageing face.

"You really believed them, didn't you?" she said, and leaned towards him, kissing him on the cheek. "You tried."

Doyle felt a tear rolling down his cheek. This was what his life's work had amounted to; the meaning he had hoped to find behind a long career of tough cases and less than honourable arrests.

This was the end for him. From that point on, he would truly be retired.

***

General Population…

The administration at the Via Dolorosa hated rooms like this one. It was a black mark on their ethos, and proof for the few that were allowed to see it that their perfect ideal of mental rehabilitation was only that; an ideal.

Every idea has at least one flaw. And every magnificent building, no matter how gently crafted, has its dark corners and its secrets.

This room was one of those dark corners. It was removed

from the rest of the CRs, and walled off from the outside world. Those whose situation was sorry enough to warrant a stay there were permitted neither visitors nor any human contact. The Via Dolorosa hated rooms like this one, because they were needed from time to time, and therefore could not be removed.

The administration at the Via Dolorosa hated Terry not just for this reason, but it would have been enough on its own.

Terry's condition, worsening at a frightening rate, was charismatic in nature. In short, he had become a maniac. And when the mania struck him, he took the others with him. All of those poor souls that the Dolorosa had "repaired" with its drugs and its counselling sessions were swept back years of reconditioning within minutes of their exposure to Terry.

This is why they suspected Terry of masterminding the psychotic episode that led to the death of Walter Thisgo, and why the Via Dolorosa was determined to "fix" him, using methods that they had always publicly scorned.

They hated Terry here, because he was the reason for their darkest rooms, and even darker methods.

Inside that padded example of psychology's past, surrounded by drawings that were crudely drawn onto the tough spongy fabric, sat Terry Giles. This was a time of remission for Terry. It was a point at which his mind had gone full circle. And now, even without the drugs that had originally been used to program him, Terry was back in hell. Despite the large doses of Olanzapine and Aripiprazole, the latter having reached its recommended 25-60 mg PO gd dosage a week ago, Terry was still managing to torture his mind with dreams of the woman without a face. In fact, staying awake, which had been his previous solution to the problem, now only compounded it and manufactured waking dreams that topped any night terrors from before the deed.

Terry sat on the floor and drew his rough pictures of the woman he had drawn before. This time, the images were barely recognizable to anyone but him, the surface being uneven and the paint being of an organic nature. Terry chanted as he drew.

"When they won't let me in the general population," he stated, his voice clear and matter-of-fact, "then the general population is weakened by the absence of correct voice and pre-emptive teaching, training, teaching, training." Terry scrambled over to a far corner, which he had covered with much smaller, more detailed pictures, of a man, with a beard.

"When they don't let me into the general population, he will have no way of finding me. Oh no, he will have no way of finding me." Terry touched one of the bearded faces.

"He'll never find me outside the general population. I am the general, the general of population. Population is the general of me. He is the pop of generalisation. I need to pop into the general population. Aha!"

Terry ran to his door and peered out through the small gap cut into the metal at head height.

"Hello, I'm fine, hello!" he called, anxious to be out of that room, as a new train of thought took hold of him, and spoke of possibilities and brought the feeling of danger into his heart. Danger being, of course, the feeling of hope he was allowing through the heavily constructed netting of his psychosis.

There was a sound from down the hall.

Footsteps.

He strained along the angle of the peephole, but couldn't see more than a yard.

"Hello, I'm fine now," Terry added. "I would like to read the newspaper and have a boiled egg." These, Terry hoped, were the requests of a sane man, and clear signs that he was well enough to be allowed into the general population once more. He turned and took a view of his room, the filth and the drawings.

"Also, I need to put my room in order," he added. "A mop and bucket would be grand, some chewing gum, and some verruca cream too."

Terry strained to see out into the hall again as the footsteps grew closer. All he had to do was keep up a semblance of normality and he could get out of there. The steps were very close now.

"Yes absolutely," said Terry, "good day to get outside for a walk in the gardens-"

Terry choked when he who was coming, but he couldn't look away for anything. He felt like his face was jammed into the slot, and he found it impossible to close his eyes and shut her out. It was like she was sucking him out of the door through the tiny hole, like his body would crack and be reduced to pulp so that it could pass through.

Only once had she ever touched him; the night of the murder. Yet here, now, she was only a step away. In her face, he somehow found expression. Was that a smile growing? That was impossible. And now she was Thisgo, father and son, smiling in at him, the appearance of his face was a shock after the gaping emptiness of her barren likeness.

Then Terry could move again.

"No!" he screamed. "Get away!"

The door opened and three CGs entered, one of them was Ruth, the attending CG that had earlier briefed Doyle and Siobhán on Terry's condition.

"Get him up," said the attending CG, "and get him scrubbed. We're going to try something different."

The CGs moved in and administered a sedative, while Terry kicked and screamed. Ruth, the attending CG, squatted down beside the increasingly subdued Terry and ruffled his hair.

"Electroconvulsive therapy," she said with a grin. "I've never seen it done."

Terry smiled up at her and murmured something softly.

"What?" she asked, and leaned closer to him.

"It's ok," Terry whispered. "You're not him, you're not her, you're not him, you're not her." Terry smiled and closed his eye. "Electroconvulsive mmmmmh," he said, and faded into drug-induced sleep.

CHAPTER NINE
SLIPPING AWAY
(THREE MONTHS LATER)

In a valley amidst the rolling hills, two figures in large warm coats stood in the gardens, and watched a hawk wheel across the December afternoon as it greyed into evening. When they heard the hawk's cry, one of the figures turned to the other and spoke.

"I've met that hawk before," said the patient.

The other figure, a woman, furrowed her brow. Obviously not pleased with the statement, she chose not to answer.

"It's really beautiful here, isn't it?" said the patient to his Care Giver.

"Yes," the CG smiled, happier with this comment than the last, "it is a beautiful spot all year round."

"All year round," the patient copied, "when-" he began and stopped.

"Yes?" the CG encouraged.

"When I came here," the patient said, "it was a different time of year."

"Yes, very good." She smiled at him; he had been through so much that a smile was such a tiny repayment. "It was autumn when you came, and now it's winter."

The patient turned and blinked her into focus.

"It's cold in winter," he said, and rubbed his nose with a gloved hand.

"Yes," the CG agreed, "let's go inside. That's enough for one day."

The two figures walked slowly back across the gardens to the main building of the Via Dolorosa. This was the patient's first view of the outside since he had arrived there three months before. And, for the first time, he was able to appreciate the beauty of the building, and see its elegant sloping roof, even the fire escapes were designed to copy the style of the building;

spiral staircases that climbed and hugged the walls, giving the subconscious impression of turrets.

"It really is beautiful," the patient said again, stopping to take in a last view of the building. The CG turned and smiled once more, nodding in agreement.

"I'm sorry," said the patient to the CG.

"What do you have to be sorry for?" she laughed. "It's perfectly norm-"

Then the patient ran.

It took a few seconds for the CG to comprehend what was going on. Was he just running for fun? Was she going to have to go inside and get the guards?

"Oh shit," said the CG following the line of Terry's flight. She turned and ran for the doors of the hospital.

"Quick!" she screamed. "Help! He's heading for the roof!"

The patient reached the bottom of the closest fire escape and scrambled over the fencing, ripping his hands and tearing his coat before throwing himself over the gate. Something strange happened to him then. When he expected to land on the first step, he found that he was suspended in mid-air, and it took all the will power he had left to convince himself that he was not floating. The hood of his coat was caught in the wiring, and he was hanging on the gate.

The patient opened the coat and fell to the iron steps, the reality of which shocked his joints as the freezing cold weather attached his unprotected arms and waist. But he had no time for hesitation, and he began to ascend the steps, utilising a ragged scrambling motion that somehow brought him to the top before his strength was lost.

He stopped on top of the staircase, and tried to catch his breath, but the cold air pinched his throat and made him gasp for oxygen.

A security man burst out of the internal staircase and advanced on the patient, but he was too late. The patient was close to the edge and reached it quickly.

"I'll jump!" he cried, stepping onto the small safety wall and halting the guard immediately.

"Ok, ok," said the guard, holding his hands up, "it's ok, what do you want?"

The patient looked down the four storeys to the hard ground below, and back to the guard and the CGs that had joined him on the roof.

"I want to see my father," he said. "I want to see him right now, or I'll jump!"

***

Three storeys down, on the opposite side of the building, Peter was lying on his bed, trying to imagine Rachel. Like him, she was in a ward now, with about ten other women, going to sessions during the day and sleeping behind a curtain during the long restless nights.

They saw each other twice a week, for two hours at a time in the gardens, where they were allowed to imagine themselves in private, while dozens of security people and CGs kept a close eye on them from a dozen yards away.

Each time, they sat or lay on the ground and took in the view of the valley below.

They had that to look forward to at the very least. And they were lucky. If the doctors were not so convinced of their Shared Psychotic Disorder diagnosis, Peter and Rachel would surely not be allowed such freedoms.

But the doctors were convinced that Terry was the real culprit, and they allowed Peter and Rachel, still far too dangerous to ever be set free, to spend some time together, so long as they did not touch each other, or incite any jealously in the other inmates.

They was little chance of that though, Peter thought, the other inmates were so doped up that he and Rachel could have stripped off and rode each other in the middle of the gardens, and the only eyebrows raised would have been those of the staff, and a couple patients that were permanently unable to lower theirs. Peter smiled. The day after tomorrow, he would see Rachel again, and he was getting excited and knew that he should be careful not to show it.

There was a commotion in the hallway and one of the attending CGs entered and called his name. Peter was alarmed but he was getting very good at keeping his emotions on the inside.

"Yes," he said, in a dreamy manner.

"Follow me," said the CG, throwing Peter a dressing gown and heading for the door again.

***

Up on the roof, the CGs and guards were playing a dangerous game with the patient. They shuffled forward when his attention was elsewhere, and back when he threatened to throw himself onto the ground below.

"Where's my father?" he shouted at them. "Have you called him?"

"Just relax," said a CG, "why don't you come down and we'll arrange to have him here within the hour."

"You promise?"

"Yes."

"So he's alive then?"

"Oh yes, absolutely!"

The patient looked for the lie in the eyes of the crowd gathered in front of him.

"Ok," said the patient. "I'll wait here for him."

"But it's very cold-"

"Terry!" came a shout from the stairwell, and Peter came into view.

"Peter?" asked the patient then screamed, "Get back!" as the CGs grew closer. "Get away from me, or I'm going over!"

"Step back," said the CG that had just fetched Peter from his ward, "let him speak to his friend." The man said the last part loudly, so the patient could hear. Letting him know that he had a friend right there; someone who would miss him if he was gone.

The CG and the guards stepped back, and allowed Peter through, and when he'd come within two yards, the patient held up his hands.

"That's enough," he told Peter. "I can hear you from here."

"Terry," Peter said, "Are you going to jump?"

"Terry?" asked the patient. "Who's Terry? There's no Terry here. I'm a patient. That's all I am, a good patient, very clean. Look at my hands?" The patient took off his gloves and held out his hands. "See, Peter?"

"Yes," said Peter, looking at Terry's pink scarred hands.

The patient smiled and nodded.

"They're clean, I think."

"Yes," said Peter, "they're clean."

The patient asked, "Are you going to stop me?" Peter shook his head [no].

"Did you hear? They're going to bring Oscar to see me before I go."

Again, Peter shook his head [no].

"That's what they said." But the patient's face grew solemn as he said it. "I don't think it's true. Do you, Peter? Do you think that he's coming?"

"No," said Peter, "he's dead."

The patient nodded and his lips began to quiver.

"I never even-" He choked on his tears and beseeched Peter with wide wet eyes.

"He was trying to save us," said Peter, "that's all I know."

"Do you see him, Peter?" asked the patient, and Peter shook his head.

"Get back!" he screamed at the advancing guards, who were immediately called further back into the stairwell.

"Do I see who?" asked Peter, once they were alone on the roof.

"Him," said the patient, "the one we killed. Do you see him?"

Peter showed the patient his own hands. They were much the same; the physical scrubbing having never cleaned away the mental stain.

"Are they clean?" asked the patient.

Peter shook his head [no], and the patient reached out and touched the side of Peter's face and drew him closer. They were drawn together until the patient's lips, freezing and blue from the cold, were touching Peter's forehead.

"They will be," said the patient, kissing Peter once, and then drawing away.

"Terry-"

"Not Terry," said the patient. "Terry's gone home."

They smiled at each other then, with nothing left to say.

"You're going to jump now," said Peter backing away.

"See ya later," said the patient.

"See ya," said Peter.

The patient looked beyond his friend to the door of the stairwell. They were peeking through, but were far enough away for him to enjoy his freedom. He turned around and stepped from the safety wall, and onto the air that began to rush past him, and even seemed to whistle.

In seconds, the patient's body met with the hard earth and all the soft tissue therein was compacted and shattered, as would be expected.

But Terry never hit the ground. He swooped away into the December evening in the manner of a hawk, borne along on the vision of his father, and the beauty of the mountains all around him.

If it is true that when the Bell of the Soul rings out one last time, it peals of virtue, or of vice, then Terry's resounded through the valley with perfect integrity.

And, on the ground, the evil crimes of the patient were committed to the dull bass of death and finality.

The body that had perpetrated the evil was finished, and Terry was free.

Peter watched his friend disappear over the edge and never sought to look down into the garden where the fall would surely end. A few seconds later, he was jostled aside by the guards and CGs, all too happy to view that gruesome scene.

But Peter preferred to listen to the shriek of the hawk as she called to her young, and he hoped that he would come to know the same peace that he had seen in Terry's countenance when the time came for his life to be over.

The first of the Dark Pupils were dead; he was another victim of Thisgo's treachery.

How many lives does it cost to change the world?

CHAPTER TEN
DARKENED PUPILS
(3 MONTHS LATER)

In towns and cities all over the world, sunny places mostly, a certain midday phenomenon was occurring with frightening regularity. This phenomenon, one that Doyle was fully aware of but powerless to prevent, was a side effect of those terrible events of six months before. When the entire world noticed Ireland, and the Irish awoke from decades of political apathy.

"Ca-va," he said to the girl sitting prim on a stool, reading a French newspaper.

"Ca-va," she answered looking up at his accent.

"Em, Je voudrais, em, jouie L'internet?"

The young woman giggled. She was, as mentioned, girlish, but her little glasses gave her an authority and caused some consternation to the ex-inspector. Doyle had a mind of the type that liked to file people by personality type, and this girl was neither a lass nor a lady.

"Sure," said the unfileable girl, "You can jouie." She pointed to the row of seats. "Take any one you like."

Doyle wrinkled his nose and walked to the end of the row so that he was furthest from the exit, and could see the street without straining his neck. This was done automatically, but not out of mere habit. Doyle was positive that he was being followed. Well, almost positive. He couldn't be sure of anything anymore.

Doyle brushed away his worry and allowed the midday phenomenon to drive him forward, as it did all Irish people and many others besides. Irish politics had become a world addiction. And, once away from it for any length of time, the Irish person was invariably drawn into an internet café to check on developments afoot at home.

Day after day in Ireland, the public were bombarded with media attacks on politicians and various branches of the state.

Though this may have seemed normal, the difference was that the Irish people breathed in every word and absorbed every image. Not long before, they had seen their great leader ripped to shreds; sacrificed for their collective good. The country was now a hotbed of political angst, and yesterday the Irish general election had been held with almost full voter participation.

Doyle still felt guilty for not having voted, and he was eager to find out the results so as to assuage this remorse.

On the eve of the election, the Irish people had looked set to vote in droves for the Progressive Party, and welcome a new era of development and advancement. The tireless efforts of Walter Thisgo, the man who had risen from nothing to become the country's most lamented leader, would finally be realised.

This election, the people were told, would change the world. The radical plans of Mr Thisgo had been unearthed, and called for drastic changes to the way the country was governed. They also called for a complete shift in social awareness, and a new breed of state, left of centre but strong on business.

Surely this was Ireland's destiny. This was the cause for which Walter Thisgo had been martyred.

As for the Regressives, they sang a different tune. It was an old reliable ditty that said, "Hey! Aren't things going good? How about more of the same?"

Doyle had no doubt what the outcome would be, but he needed to see it for himself. So he logged on, placed the earphones on his head and waited for the Radio 6 News Bulletin to load.

"- at the Via Dolorosa after a massive overdose."

"That's chilling news, Johnny."

"Absolutely, Henry. Some would say good riddance, but the feeling I'm getting off the street is one of sadness and hope that now, after this morning's events and the general election, the country will finally be able to put it all behind us."

"Indeed, well, we've been getting a lot of calls in support of the good riddance argument, but nothing that we could read out on air. And as for a feeling of sadness, I have to say, Johnny, that I share those sentiments. Thanks, Johnny, and we'll talk to you again in an hour."

"Thanks, Henry."

"Well, that's the news on the hour, the main stories again: Suicide attempt at the Via Dolorosa, the Republic of Ireland draw nil-nil with Spain. And the recount is on! We'll keep you posted as the second count continues, after a record turnout results in a shock victory for the Regressives in the General Election."

"Sir?"

Doyle must have let out a yelp when he heard the news, because the French girl sounded concerned.

"Are you ok?" she asked.

"Eh yeah, sure," Doyle answered, wiping his face with his hand.

It couldn't be true. He clicked on breaking news and there it was. News of the suicide scrolled across the screen.

"Shit," said Doyle, his stomach folding and the hairs on his neck standing in frightened recognition.

It was peculiar that he could find it shocking, but he did and he was shocked. He had suspected that Terry was bound for suicide within minutes of their first encounter? But now this; shock: the reasonless emotion. Hope had made a fool of him. Yet, as in so many instances, there is little chance of preventing hope until it is too late. Terry had lived, and then he had died; no one cared much either way.

Doyle felt that he had wronged the Dark Pupils somehow. By giving up on them, even after it was obvious that they had lost their minds, Doyle felt he had chosen to be one of the normals. He was an ignorant, a doubter. And though he and the crowd believed in the same outcome; the lack of underlying plot, somehow Doyle felt he should have known better. Especially after having seen what he had seen, and having believed what three students from Dublin had wanted him to believe.

The ex-inspector was paying the price that every copper pays when they fail to resolve a case. He was haunted, and would always be, until he uncovered the truth. The Dark Pupils case was one that he could never fully drop. Wasn't that the reason he was in France?

He told himself that he was merely here to tie up loose ends, to plead for forgiveness from the only ones who could possibly grant such a boon. But Doyle knew that he hadn't come to France just to talk to the family of Walter Thisgo and explain to them why he had never caught their father's killer. Deep down, the old inspector in him was looking for more clues, a lead, anything. Proof that the Dark Pupils were either just crazy and capable of murder, or innocent and telling the truth about Walter Thisgo.

Doyle stood to leave the Internet café and thought, as he paid, about the Regressives winning the election. Now that the news was maturing in his brain, Doyle began to think of the consequences of the result.

The people of Ireland weren't ready to take such huge risks with their futures, or those of their children. Not without their talisman at any rate. The death and martyrdom of Walter Thisgo had only served to rattle the Irish and cause insecurity rather than revolution. They wanted safety.

"Hey! Aren't things going good?" they asked. "How about more of the same?"

After a terrible ordeal, people didn't want uncertainty. They wanted the comfort of the usual.

Doyle stepped out onto Rue Chaudrier and took a left that he hoped would lead towards the sea and his hotel. But in la Rochelle, the sea was in a lot of directions and he was going to have to trust his luck, or God, or whomever it was that was watching him from the black Peugeot parked outside the cathedral.

Doyle didn't mind, since the weather was good. These days, he was glad of a nice walk, a side effect of retirement; better than sitting down. And as for anyone following him, well. One thing Doyle knew from experience. If someone was following you, then a meeting would follow soon enough. All he had to do was wait.

*The day was strange and cold but the sun was shining. Inside their winter coats, sitting on the towels they had brought, Peter and Rachel felt warm, content, and comfortable in their usual spot, lying back and gazing at the sky, never touching, but making love in their minds.

All around them, the CRs of the Via Dolorosa shuffled and even played. On days like this, the place felt more like a holiday haven for individuals, both eccentric and idiosyncratic, and less like a prison for those of loosened intellect.

"Eqriptop dolla assa trizdackime," said a voice above them. Neither Peter nor Rachel looked up. It was Jeffers, a shaggy-haired man who had invented his own language, not a nonsensical language, but one with an extensive vocabulary, which was being studied closely by a particularly interesting CG named Martin.

"Decog," said Peter, using Jeffers' greeting word.

"Decog cosheskia," said Rachel.

"Assa trizdackime?" Jeffers insisted, tapping Rachel on the shoulder. She sat up and turned around.

"I don't know what you mean?"

"Assa," said Jeffers, shaking his head, "trizdackime." Peter rose too and shrugged.

"We don't understand," he said, but Jeffers nodded his dirty curls and repeated the last word again.

"Trizdackime," he said, holding his stomach as though he were in pain. Then he wagged his finger and shook his head; he was disappointed in them. Now they knew what he was trying to say.

"We-" Peter began, but Jeffers was already gone.

Laying down again, Peter and Rachel smiled up into the sky. They were happy despite the chiding of the man who spoke his own language. Only briefly did they wonder how he had known? But it didn't matter. Nothing mattered now, now that they were saved. Because it was on that day, in early March, that Peter and Rachel were finally rescued.

Their time in the garden went slowly, and the two had even risked holding hands for a brief moment when they hoped no one was looking.

The big surprise came when the CGs came to bring them in, or not in fact.

After the two-hour outdoor break, the CGs usually came to gather all of the Care Receivers together, and literally herd them back indoors for their afternoon counselling or treatment sessions. The usual practice being: CRs were given a personal invitation by their own attending CG to come back into the building. And, as this trust building exercise was never ignored, Rachel and Peter lay patiently in the grass, waiting for their turn and generally enjoying every extra second that they could.

But the seconds continued, uninterrupted. Then they turned into minutes, and how wonderful each one felt. They were like children up after bedtime, waiting for the call of their parent but seemingly forgotten about for the moment. Perhaps they would be forgotten for a long time? Indefinitely? No, that was too much to ask, but every minute counted, as they lay their and revelled in each other's company.

Then there was a shrill squeaking noise from below them, down the hill where the great gates of the compound stood. Both Rachel and Peter risked sitting up to see what was happening, and were shocked to see that the gates were opening. What was happening?

They waited for a car to enter, or for one to appear behind them from behind the building where the staff parked, but nothing happened. They looked at each other and laughed. They were sweating, and they could see beads running freely down each other's foreheads.

"The sun is getting stronger," said Rachel.

"Yeah," said Peter, "it's like summer."

They shed their winter coats, standing as they did and dropping them on the newly thawed grass. Wary at first, they looked around for some sign that the CGs were watching them. Perhaps it was a test?

"What should we do?"

"I think we should wait."

"You're right, let's wait."

But nothing happened. No cars appeared from behind the Via Dolorosa, nor did any enter. But more importantly, the gate remained open, the freedom of the Wicklow mountains beckoning.

"Should we go?"

"I don't know either."

"I have this image of mice in a cage, too timid to risk escape and then the cage being closed again with them still inside."

"I had a vision too. Similar, but we were birds."

"What kind of birds?"

"I don't know, colourful ones."

"I like that better."

"So?"

"So, my dear, should we fly away?"

"Yes. Let's go!"

And they walked towards the gates. Still they listened for the sounds of approach from either direction, but the only sound was the beating of their hearts. The concept of sounds belonged to them, and the warm summer breeze that flowed in the same direction. On the threshold, they met the resistance of an invisible barrier, but it was weak. And after taking a deep breath, they stepped through the thin film of opposition and stepped through the gate onto the road outside.

Their hearts grew quieter now. Rachel and Peter were as one unit, hand in hand, walking up the hill away from the memory of the Via Dolorosa. No longer did they fear recapture, nor did they fear the constant recollection of the horrible crime that they had committed. They were moving forward.

When Peter and Rachel crested the hill, a joyful sight greeted them. Below, facing them in the middle of the road stood a white limousine, clean and bright, glinting in what now had become the summer sun.

They had hoped, but had not dared to depend on the limousine. It was in all their dreams of both day and night, allowing them some respite from the terrors they had been trained to experience. But never had they spoken openly about the limousine, and their need for its arrival. It was a symbol of their freedom, a white chariot.

The back door opened and the two remaining Dark

Pupils held their thoughts while they waited for his appearance. Were they supposed to go down to the car and get in? That didn't seem right. Their uncertainty was misplaced, however, as a figure stepped out of the limousine and walked to the front of the car.

He was wearing a white suit and a white shirt with no tie, and his grey hair was much longer than they had ever seen it. The glasses had disappeared, and instead of the small neatness that Walter Thisgo had always displayed, there was a calm commanding air about the man.

For a time, immeasurable, Peter and Rachel faced Walter Thisgo, their torturer and their saviour. They dared not breathe nor blink, for fear that he would melt away from them, and they would once again be alone with the terrible thing that they had done. Then, with a smile on his face that brought joy to their souls, Walter Thisgo raised his hands apart in the gesture of welcome. They ran to him.

It didn't take any time for them to cover the distance. One moment they were running, and the next they were in his arms and he was hugging them and whispering to them.

Through their cries of joy, they could hear that he was speaking, but it wasn't until they calmed a little and looked up into his face- how did he get so big? They were able to make out what he was trying to say to them, and noticed a strange expression on their saviour's face.

"I'm sorry," Walter Thisgo whimpered, in fear and in relief, "I'm sorry." And it was these words that brought about their end.

*

Twice a day, every day, the CRs of the Via Dolorosa received their medication. In an attempt to avoid the old stereotype, the CGs did not ask their charges to line up and take their pills from a dispensary. No, in this new aged Criminal Mental Hospital, they were different. So, each CR was presented with his or her mediation in a small plastic box with a flip lid that could be refilled, not unlike a tic-tac dispenser, but opaque. CRs were encouraged to place their boxes in little recycling bins that were placed around the wards and common areas. This, the CGs maintained, gave the Care Receivers a sense of belonging to their environment. And, as there was no one allowed into the Via Dolorosa to inspect its workings, there wasn't anyone to disagree with them.

Peter and Rachel had dwelled within the walls of the Via Dolorosa for six months, until the day of Walter Thisgo's return, and during that time they had been handed almost 365 little plastic boxes, each.

Inspector Doyle had recognised on his earlier visit that Rachel and Peter were attempting to act as though they were heavily medicated, but since then, both had become proficient at hiding their lucidity, and had saved the majority of their medication. They managed this by burying the little boxes in the spot where they now lay, unconscious, with a half hour left before the CGs came to take them back inside; before their attempt could be discovered.

To be fair, the word *attempt* wasn't very fair. Peter and Rachel had been planning this day for almost the entire six months of their stay at the Via Dolorosa. Even when they knew that they would have two hours to fully succumb to the effect of the pills, they had taken further precautions.

Three days earlier, Peter and Rachel had spent their entire two hours carefully digging up each pill box and stuffing them into the lining of their winter coats. On returning to their respective wards, both had spent each fretful hour emptying the little boxes and hiding this activity from the CGs as they made their rounds and held their group discussions. But Peter and Rachel had always been good CRs, and the Carers were fully aware that with Terry now three months departed, the risk of any reoccurrence of their Shared Psychotic Disorder was nominal.

Then the day had arrived that Peter and Rachel had chosen to finally cure themselves of their tortured lives. They took one more precaution; they didn't eat breakfast. Instead, they returned to their beds and began to wolf down the tablets and capsules, stopping only when each and every one had been downed. Three hours later, Peter and Rachel had been led outside, already struggling to put one foot in front of the other, and keep their eyes open. They made it outside and went to their usual spot and lay down.

Two hours later, they were found deep in the coma of overdose, with little chance of being saved as the CGs frantically rushed them to the treatment room to have their stomachs pumped, as was the procedure. And when all else fails in medicine, procedures are a great comfort.

In their collective mind, Rachel and Peter were already moving away, along the mountain road with Walter Thisgo. They rode in the white limousine, clasping firmly to each other's hands, their souls smiling, contented and at peace. Now they would be joined together forever.

No fear, no dread, no heartbreaking guilt. Love was all that they took with them.

The Darks Pupils were all finished now. All finished now. All finished now.

THE TALE OF THE TENDERFOOT
(POITOU-CHARENTES – LA ROCHELLE)

*U*sed…

The terrible truth is that we use and are used without exception.

The old use the young to prove what they have learnt, and the young, to fight against their future, use the old in defence for their actions.

Use each other. Take, take and be taken. Society welcomes you.

This is where I leave you, I Walter Thisgo, who have used so many, and lost so much. I have failed and that is all. You have seen in great detail, how and why.

You may not understand. You probably disagree with every step that I have taken, but my worst fear is that you do not even care what I have done in my attempt. Yes, I know. Attempt *is* the correct word. You saw what happened to Peter, Terry and Oscar, Rachel, Marie, and my father himself, the cursed Walter Thisgo.

How dramatic, the cursed Walter Thisgo indeed. But I do believe that it is true. That his name, and mine by default, have been cursed, both by his inactivity and my- let's just say, my over-activity.

I am almost beyond grief now. I have not killed myself, but conspired to do so for the greater good. I hope you know that. Do you understand, even a little bit?

Sitting here now, staring out, I am imagining a night when a single boat draws closer to the shore. It moors below and after ascending the stair of le Phare, the travellers are finally delivered onto this very lawn.

For all that I have caused, the state of my utopian state is none the better for my existence. Indeed, it has regressed to a time when my father despaired and resigned himself to a living death.

The fucking Regressives, and I don't just mean the party, I mean the whole bloody lot of them! They stole perfection from their own grasp. They are mules that have taken to flogging themselves to relieve their master's hands from even that small effort. Downtrodden? No one is downtrodden. They have all lain down of their own accord, and I cannot tolerate the sight of it for one minute longer.

I see the passengers of that single boat, walking across the lawn to where I stand in welcome. They are five, but it is the leading pair to which I gravitate.

My father and the second both reach out for me as though they mean to forgive my stupidity, and return to me the love that I have perverted and turned against them. But at the last moment, they snarl and mock me and tear at my chest.

Dear God, I have sinned, but please cushion me from this despair. I know what I need to do, but have not the courage to do it.

In response to my own plea, I must reply that I, Walter Thisgo, remain a lucky man.

There is one man coming for me that can save me from this pain. I have waited months for his arrival, but now he has finally come within my grasp.

My men are following him as I speak to you, and will pick him up from his hotel in La Rochelle soon. Then he will come here, and he will rescue me. Finally, I can count the time in hours and minutes.

Hurry now. Free me from the nightmares. Vanquish these ghosts before they steal my soul.

THE CHAPTER
PRINCE NICHOLAS

"*A*re you listening?" said the man, walking ahead at a brisk pace and gesturing out through the arches to the Atlantic Ocean. "This is a wonderful place, and can only be improved by one thing." The man stopped and span around, causing the group much distress and a lot of polite throat clearing as the three men who had been following their host shuffled away from their embarrassing proximity.

"You two," said the host, addressing his hired men. "Go on about your business now, and leave me alone with this, my new friend." The driver and manservant left quickly and without a word.

"Now," resumed the host, "that's better. Isn't it, Inspector?"

"Oh no, it's just Nicholas Doyle, sir, now. I'm retired for good. And eh," and here Doyle swallowed his initial distaste for his host's over-friendliness, "you can call me Nicholas if you like, sir."

"Nicholas! Nicholas, really? How didn't I know that? That is a very interesting name to have Inspec- ah, Nicholas." The host's eyes lit up at the sound of Doyle's Christian name. "Oh and no, Nicholas, never again call me sir. My name, whether I like it or not is Walter Thisgo Junior, but you can call me Walt."

Walter Thisgo's son held out his hand to Nicholas Doyle, and accompanied the offer with an expectant grin.

"I've been trying it out," said Thisgo. And noticing Doyle's eyebrow he added, "The name Walt. I've been seeing if it fits. Ever since my father was- since he-" Walter Thisgo Junior turned away and moved through the nearest archway and onto the lawn, and Doyle tactfully followed after him. How many times had he done this, interrogated the bereaved; looked for information while trying to remain respectful? Fifty-eight times exactly, was the answer and Doyle could, if pressed, recall the circumstances of each death related interview.

"Sir," Doyle addressed number fifty-nine.

"Ah, ah, ah!" said Walter Junior, wagging a finger in the air but not turning to face Doyle. "It's Walter, please. I've just this minute given up on Walt."

Doyle joined Walter Thisgo on the immaculate lawn, and shared the view. It was amazing. Below them, the garden was tiered and fell away in levels almost to the shore, where it stopped at a cliff where a low stone tower stood.

"That's the Light-tower, *le Phare*, in French," said Walter Thisgo. "Inside there, in the sixteenth century they used to light a beacon for private boats that landed at the Château's own dock on the beach below. Also, there are steps inside that lead from the dock to here. It's amazing really, isn't it?"

"This really is beautiful," said Doyle, in genuine appreciation of that idyllic place, and he yearned to stay there. "A man could live here in peace for ever," he added, hoping to convey the sentiment to his host. But though it was meant as a compliment, Walter Thisgo turned on the shocked Doyle with a snarl.

"Peace?" spat Thisgo. "What would I know of peace?"

"I'm sorry, Mr Thisgo," said Doyle, seeing that he had inadvertently injured Thisgo. "What I meant to say was-"

"Wait!" The little man, so similar in stature to his great father, took a deep breath, and held up his hands. "I'm sorry for snapping at you, Nicholas. I had no right. It's been hard for me for a long time now. Ever since-"

Suddenly, Walter Thisgo perked up. "Anyway, you're right!" he exclaimed. "This is a wonderful place, and why wouldn't someone want to live here in peace forever? You are absolutely correct, Nicholas."

Without warning, Walter Thisgo stepped quickly back towards the Château. Doyle had to skip awkwardly behind him before managing to fall into step with his host, as he resumed his circumnavigation of the building along the cloistered walkway.

"Mr Thisgo?" said Doyle.

"You're not calling me Walter?" said Thisgo.

"Walter," Doyle began again, "I would like to ask you a few questions, if it wouldn't be too much trouble."

"Oh!" exclaimed Walter Thisgo, never slowing his short strides, "So, you've only been here ten minutes and you've begun with the copper questions. Well, ok. If we must play it officially, then I will answer any questions to which you deserve an answer, EX-Inspector." The *ex* was stressed and Doyle heard a bitter warning in the little man's voice. He would have to tread carefully since, as his host had just pointed out, Doyle had no authority here, nor anywhere else for that matter. Not anymore.

"I'm sorry again, eh, Walter. I'm only here out of curiosity, and I'm at the mercy of your good nature."

Thisgo slowed down.

"Walter? Good, good, Nicholas, very good. Well, if you are indeed at the mercy of my good nature, then I would like for you to humour me with a little chitchat. What do you say?"

Thisgo smiled an open smile at Doyle, and the ex-inspector softened to the man. Of course Walter Thisgo's son would be cold and unbalanced at the mention of his father. It was commonsense. The murder had been a terrible thing; gruesome and public.

"I'm in no hurry, Walter," said Doyle, "chat away."

By this time, Walter Thisgo Junior had come to a halt and gestured to Doyle to join him on a bench that was set into an alcove. They sat down and the little man gave Doyle a look that revealed a wealth of pain to him. Then Walter Thisgo smiled.

"That really is great, Nicholas," Thisgo said, nodding his head and beaming with friendly sincerity. "That's really great. Because I need to talk to someone, you know? About all that has happened to me. I feel that I've been dealt a hand sans trumps. It has been so hard on me and my poor family."

"Absolutely," said Doyle. What else could he say? "And your sister? I would like to talk to her if I could too?"

"Ah yes," said Thisgo, "she is here too, in the family home, but unlike me, she is not equipped for strangers. But you never know." Thisgo winked at Doyle in a manner in which the ex-Gardaí found difficult to interpret. "I may be able to persuade her to make an appearance later on. Ok?"

Doyle nodded, unsure of where the question lay in that last sentence.

"Good then," said Thisgo, "we will talk for a while, about

this and that, and I will answer your questions during the evening too. Then after dinner-"

"Oh no, I couldn't-"

"-Bu, bu, bup!" Thisgo re-interrupted. "You will eat here. Sure, it's nearly dinnertime already. Or at least it will be when we've finished. And afterwards, you, my new friend, will do me a small favour. Nothing too strenuous, mind. A trifle really. It's just something that I can't do myself, that's all. We're having wild pig?"

"Em," said Doyle, his uneasiness overcome by Thisgo's most recent jovial outlook. And the promise of wild pork bound him to vow, "Sure. Why not?" Perhaps there would even be apple sauce.

"Perfect! Now, Nicholas, that really is an interesting name. Would you like me to tell you why?"

"Sure," Doyle replied, sensing a lecture but happy that he and his host had reached an agreement that would ensure that his questions would be answered.

"This house," Thisgo's arm swept up and around in an all-encompassing motion, "once belonged to a Nicholas, you see. Prince Nicholas of Montenegro. He was a prince that called himself a king. He was a great innovator of the Free State, but unfortunately, blind to the fact that his own role, as monarch, ensured that his idea would fail. So you see, Nicholas; the idea must be bigger than the man."

Thisgo looked to Doyle for understanding, and all Doyle could do was nod [I see]. But inside, he felt a chill. Something wasn't right, something about Thisgo and the subject on which he spoke.

"When the Austrians invaded his country in 1915, Nicholas was exiled to this part of France. And while the rest of the world fought, Nicholas sat, right here waiting to return home."

"Really?" asked Doyle, unable to avoid being interested. "He lived here, in this Château?"

"Yes, Nicholas, he sat on this same bench, right where we are sitting now, and waited for his chance to go home. But he never did return to Montenegro. A real pity." Thisgo smiled at Doyle, "So, nearly one hundred years later, another Nicholas is sitting here, sharing the same view of the sea in this Château surrounded by forest, a stranger in this land."

"What a coincidence," said Doyle, still trying to place the source of his sudden discomfort.

"Oh, it's more than that," said Thisgo. "It is fate. Its history was the main reason I bought this place. And now you are here, Nicholas. It seems, poetic in a way."

Doyle couldn't think why it would be poetic for the son of a murdered leader to live in the house of an exiled one.

"Was he, Prince Nicholas murdered too?" asked Doyle.

"Why no," answered Thisgo surprised, "why would you ask?"

"No reason," said Doyle. "So, did your father ever live here?" Doyle felt that now it was time to start his enquiries.

"What? Oh," Thisgo said, and looked away towards the sea. "Oh, my father no. We didn't have the money for this in his day-"

"Really, I thought he was quite wealthy when he died. The papers said that he had done well as an honest businessman, and deserved every penny. It was odd, because I didn't remember him being too flashy."

Thisgo looked at Doyle with an expression that the ex-inspector recognised as- was it? Yes, Thisgo was sizing him up; preparing to divulge. Doyle had seen the same expression in the interview room time after time. The face that asked, "Should I tell you?" But the expression was soon gone.

"Indeed, the great man was very rich when he died. And you're right, he wasn't very flashy. Probably in response to all the problems that we had in the early days, when he was drinking, and his politics had died."

"Do you think that the Regressives had something to do with his death?" asked Doyle, taking a risk and bracing for the inevitable retort.

Thisgo simply looked Doyle in the eye and said, "No. I don't believe that they did." Then the smaller man rubbed his hands together and asked, "What do you know about La Rochelle, Nicholas?"

"Nothing really," said Doyle, realising that he'd received his answer. If he was going to get what he wanted, he would have to make sure and ask open questions.

"Well," said Thisgo, warming up once more. "La Rochelle was governed by a council, in a time of feudal lords. The city was the centre of the Huguenot resistance."

Doyle was about to ask about Huguenots but managed to deliver himself from that lecture-filled trap.

"Ah yes, the pearl of the Charente, this wonderfully advanced city state was crushed by Cardinal Richelieu in the 16th century, for the very reason that its people enjoyed more freedom than anywhere in France. Such forward-thinking; if only there was any of the same around now."

Again, Doyle was wrenched by a creepy feeling of familiarity. Though it was obvious why.

"You share many of your father's opinions," said Doyle, "he was a forward-thinking man."

"Yes," said Thisgo, "you are correct again, Nicholas. You could even say that my opinions and those of my late father are identical. Ah!" The little man rose from the bench and clamped his hand over his mouth with one hand and pointed with the other.

"Look!" said Thisgo in a harsh excited whisper. "There!"

Doyle moved quickly to Thisgo's side and saw too that a wild pig had wandered into the garden from the cover of trees that populated the surrounding area.

"Shhh," said Thisgo as the pig stopped sniffing the ground and looked up at them. Doyle was shocked by the size and appearance of the animal. It was massive, with a shaggy brown coat and two large bottom teeth sticking up from its jaw. This was no pig, it was a boar.

"Is it wild?" Doyle whispered, trying not to disturb the animal, but even so, he saw its black hairy ears prick up at the sound. Then the ex-inspector heard a noise coming from Thisgo. It was odd and intermittent. What was it? Could it be? Yes, Thisgo was laughing, chuckling in fact.

"Why are you laughing?" said Doyle, "that bloody thing is huge. What should we do?"

Thisgo stopped tittering only long enough to say in a snickering whisper, "Ha! Is it wild, he wants to know? Does he think it's a pet?"

Despite the very real physical danger they were in, Doyle did see the funny side and smirked with his host.

"Heh, yeah I suppose."

"Shht!" Thisgo froze. "Its hackles are up."

And they were. The wild boar had turned fully towards them now and his head was swaying slowly from left to right. Doyle didn't know if this action was designed to confuse enemies, but he was positive that the sight of the animal's bulk rocking from side to side caused him to raise his shoulders in primeval fear.

"Don't fret," said Thisgo beside him, but Doyle was full of worry. How couldn't he be? "I've got this." Thisgo gestured and Doyle shrank from the sight of a revolver in the small man's hand.

"What are you doing with a gun?" asked Doyle, angry that Thisgo had been sitting with him with a gun in his pocket.

"Shht!" said Thisgo. "It's not what you think. I was out here yesterday, and the thing ran at me. Gaston, the driver, gave me a gun, in case it happens again." Thisgo turned to Doyle and looked him in the eye. "Apparently, it's the season for them."

They didn't have time to argue, as the boar sat back on his haunches, ready to spring.

"Are you going to shoot it?" said Doyle.

"Of course," said Thisgo, pointing the weapon in the general direction of the boar. It was immediately obvious to Doyle that the little man would miss the sky if he was aiming for it, but there was no time. The boar charged them.

"Shoot it!" shouted Doyle, sprinting to one side, hoping Thisgo would do the same. But Thisgo didn't move. Nor did he shoot. He just stood there and shook as the boar bore down on him.

"Shoot it!" cried Doyle again, his eyes closing automatically a yard from impact.

Then he heard the sharp report of a gun being fired, and Doyle could bear to look again. When he did, he saw Thisgo standing with the boar at his feet; the animal was actually touching his shoe. And, for a moment, Doyle thought he had just witnessed the iron will of a truly brave man.

It began as a sniff, followed by a single sob; then Walter

Thisgo Junior began to cry. It wasn't any normal shedding of tears that Doyle witnessed then; it was a display of sniffling and mucus that would put a child to shame.

"Are you all right?" Doyle asked, moving warily towards Thisgo. He couldn't understand why the man was acting in such a pitiful manner. Hadn't he just killed a wild beast? After a few more seconds, Doyle was sure that this was no display of shock or relief. It was fear.

"Jesus," said Doyle, who walked up and gave the man an awkward pat on the back. "You're a bit of a sissy, aren't ya?" he smiled, not sure what to do. After all, he was used to Gardaí who practically dripped with bravado, both men and women. In truth, Doyle was shocked that Thisgo had even managed to shoot the beast. But this was explained quickly as a man that Doyle recognised as the driver moved into sight from the corner of the building.

The man - was it Gaston? - held a rifle in his hand.

"D'accord?" the man called, and Doyle nodded.

"Yeah! Thanks." Doyle gauged the distance and the angle, "Good shot," he mumbled to himself, whilst he led Thisgo back to the bench.

***

The room of secrets…

Inside the chateau, there was a room in which real secrets were kept. The walls were panelled in wood that shined under the electric light, and the air was heavy with the overuse of "pine fresh" products, the presence of which undermined the cleanliness of the room more than added to it.

This room of secrets was full beyond its couch and desk and single leather-backed chair. It was filled above its high ceilings, and muffled its echoing woodwork.

But the plural of secret is a mis-description, because it is all from one secret that the others emanated. Like tadpoles, they skittered in a large pond around the giant hulking form of a toad, so hideous that it would cause respectable eyes to water after a single glimpse.

These insidious, tiny, swimming, barely living relatives

of the larger secret, immersed in the misty waters of disinfectant, journeyed outward from the source. They flowed under the door and meandered in large groups down the hall, and into the dining room, where they were confronted by the smells and wholesome qualities of freshly cooked boar. The battle was easily won by the perfectly cooked meet, whose forces were backed greatly by the introduction of sauces, of both apple and stock into the fray.

Yet the tiny vestiges of the larger secret were not defeated completely, and emissaries were able to sneak through the battle lines to the dinner table, where two men were eating and talking about politics and policing.

"So," said Thisgo after one of the tiny shreds of truth entered his mouth with a forkful of pork, "if there were no Gardaí, their very absence would create a vacuum into which the government could place a different system. Not a police *force*, but a sort of social auditing system. Whereby the people would not see the system as separate from them, but would feel like they were controlling their own society. You see, Nicholas?"

Doyle didn't answer. He just shoved a piece of meat into his mouth; it was the first he'd managed. After the arrival at the table of the roasted boar, Doyle had been feeling positive, and he thought that today was the day he could finally eat something. But when Walter Thisgo Junior, his own excitable nature replenished by a belt of scotch, had begun to speak rapidly about his political ideas and ideals, Doyle began to wonder why he had come at all.

Still he couldn't eat, but why? Doyle was used to his ways when he was on a case. He tried again and again to remember meals, and had managed to force food on himself. But there was no hunger until the case was over.

"You're not eating, Nicholas?" said Thisgo, and Doyle shrugged.

"I have trouble sometimes," said Doyle, "usually when I'm on a big case. I don't know why."

"Oh, but aren't you retired, Nicholas? Surely you've got no big case on now."

"No," said Doyle, "it must be jet lag or something."

"Or," Thisgo said, leaving down his knife and fork and

leaning forward with great conspiracy. He even looked around to make sure that none of his servants were in the doorway. "Maybe, EX-Inspector, you are still on a case, eh?"

"What do you mean?"

"Oh, come on now. Why else are you here?" Thisgo smiled., "Although I am enjoying the Celtic company, we both know that you are here because you're not happy about the outcome of my father's murder case, don't we?"

Doyle could only nod [yes]. "You're right," he said, and stopped pretending to eat his food. "I'm not hungry."

"Well." Walter Thisgo took a deep breath and let out a drawn out and defeated sigh. "Let's get to it then. shall we?" The little man rose from his seat and gestured to the door.

"There are a few things that I would like to show you. Nicholas," he said- "Things that I know you will want to see." He left the dining room and Doyle was left looking after him. He had no choice really. So he followed.

~*~

As the two walked down the hall, Thisgo towards his destiny, and Doyle, unknowingly, towards his; they waded through the stream of mysteries towards the underlying truth. Doyle noticed that Thisgo's stride was shortening as the short walk came to an end. They reached a door, and there was much hesitation on the host's part.

His hand rested on the door handle for far too long, and Thisgo even turned to Doyle as if he were about to speak, but the words seemed lost to him and he gave up.

The door was opened and they entered the study.

~*~

Inside, the mood changed completely. And, as Doyle's nose was assailed by the unmistakable smell of detergent, Walter launched into a tirade that sounded both rushed and rehearsed.

"Well, Nicholas, (have a seat there in the couch, won't you, good man), I feel I should admit something to you. You see, I know everything about this case of yours. Everything! I know all about the blue pills that you found in the churchyard, and I also know about the house fires caused by the security man Cullen, out of vengeance for the killing of his master. I even know that he is due to be on trial next month, not just for these fires, but for the murder of a homeless man named Oscar."

Thisgo took a breath.

"So?" asked Doyle, noticing the carvings on the walls for the first time. "Everybody in Ireland knows that."

"That's true, that's true," Thisgo raced on- "And the Dark Pupils claimed that they were subject to mind control, something which made them a laughing stock-"

"-Again," Doyle interrupted, examining one particular carving of a man standing on one leg with his eyes closed, "these are all things that anyone could have read in the paper."

Thisgo seemed annoyed.

"Yes, yes, yes. No interruptions please! I'm getting to my point." Thisgo walked around the desk and opened a drawer and took out a leather satchel. "I also have in here," he dropped the satchel on the desk top, "some information that the papers either didn't release, or maybe didn't even have."

Doyle waited, but it became obvious that Thisgo was pausing for effect. The man was so measured; so like his father that- Doyle froze and struggled to control his expression. He became aware of Thisgo watching him; waiting.

"Like what?" Doyle managed to ask.

"I know about the druids," said Thisgo with a sly smile.

"What?" said Doyle, growing colder as the seconds passed. That's what the pictures were. They were like the druids described by Peter, Rachel, and Terry during one of their long interviews.

"I know that those poor kids even thought that the blue pills were the same as a drug the druids used in ritual punishments, and that when they first came together, the entire population of the world disappeared around them, and they were alone. They even read about it, didn't they? On the day before they committed the deed."

"How did you know that?"

"They told you that they were driven to murder when their friend Marie was killed by my father in front of their eyes, and it was that which pushed them over the edge." Thisgo's shoulders hunched and his head stooped forwards so as to get closer to Doyle's own.

"And you believed them, Nicholas, didn't you? Every word. You tried and tried to prove them right, but you couldn't, could you? Why? Was it because there was no proof to be found? Or was it because you were stopped at every turn?"

By now, Doyle was grinding his teeth in anger, but the sneering words that flowed from Walter Thisgo were drowning him in rage to such an extent that he could hardly move.

"Oh!" exclaimed Thisgo, in full flood now. "And that last opportunity, when you arrived at *The Inn*, the site of so much mystery, and you found the old man dead? What did you do then, eh Nicholas? Answer me one question, Nicholas, before we are finished here today?" Thisgo took two careful steps forward and leaned into Doyle so that their faces almost met.

"Did you ever look behind the panelling, Nicholas? Did you?"

Doyle shuddered with fury.

Thisgo asked, "Did you find her there?"

It was this spiteful little whisper that finally set Doyle free, and he pushed Thisgo away from him with such force, the little man slid when he hit the ground and struck the solid front of the desk.

"Get away from me!" screamed Doyle, rising as he cried out. "It's you! It's you!"

"Yes," Thisgo shouted back at him, struggling to sit up against the desk.

"You're alive." Doyle advanced on Thisgo, reaching the prone man quickly, and grabbing him by the front of his shirt. "You were the one who killed them, all of them! They're dead. Did you know that? Four kids and one old man, dead. You killed your own father, you- you- sick bastard!"

Doyle shook Thisgo in angry frustration, striking the man's head on the wooden desk.

"Yes," whispered the little man, "yes, go on!"

"What?" shouted Doyle shaking Thisgo with more ferocity, "What are you saying you- you- Ahhhhhhhhh!"

"Yes," said Thisgo, louder this time. "I did it, you fool, I did it!"

Then Doyle felt a pressure against his neck.

"What the-" It was the handgun that Thisgo had failed to fire earlier that day. "You won't shoot me, you little bitch!" cried Doyle, tearing the gun from the little man's grasp.

"You couldn't even shoot a pig," said Doyle, spitting hatred at Thisgo, and pushing the gun into the tormentor's eye socket. "But I could shoot you- you- coward."

"Y-Yes," Thisgo stammered, "you can. Go on. Please." His eyes were wide open and he was nodding despite the gun. Doyle hesitated.

"There's something else," Thisgo rasped, and Doyle was sickened by the man's pallor and the sweat that was oozing from his slimy face.

"What?" Doyle growled, "What else could there be?"

Thisgo's only visible eye looked away over Doyle's shoulder. "Do you want to meet my sister now?" he said.

Doyle spun quickly, expecting to be struck from behind, but there was nothing else in the room; nothing else, except for the smell of detergent, and the wooden panelling.

"The wooden panel-" Doyle turned around and glared at Thisgo. "Your own sister," he whispered. "Your own sister!" he roared. Doyle's temper was beyond control. He was boiling with frustration and wrath. The gun was returned to Thisgo's eye.

"I *will* kill you," Doyle assured the devil that sat in his grasp. Then in a burst of emotion, Doyle cocked the revolver. "Tell me why?"

"Why?" gasped Thisgo.

"Why?" roared Doyle.

"Why? To save the world, of course," said Thisgo, "but it's not worth saving."

Doyle leaned forward to pull the trigger and end Thisgo's life, but something stopped him.

"You want to die," Doyle lowered the gun. "You want me to kill you. You bleeding coward! All of this, you can't live with it. And you're too much of a coward to do it yourself."

Doyle un-cocked the gun and sat back, causing Thisgo to

cry out in disbelief.

"No," he pleaded, "you have to!"

"You coward! You- Tenderfoot!"

"Please!"

"Save the world. You can't even save yourself." Doyle threw out a bitter laugh. "You wanted to martyr yourself for some stupid cause? The great sacrifice! But you couldn't even do that properly. You had to use others. Three innocent kids, and an old man, people like Siobhán and Cullen who loved you, or what they thought you were; and your own sister too?"

Doyle struggled to his feet. He was feeling light-headed and tried to shake it off. He was shocked beyond- no, he was devastated. He felt like he was floating, and found it hard to step across the room. He stumbled and had to steady himself against the wall. Behind him, he could hear that the snivelling filth-bag had begun to weep like a girl. It made Doyle physically sick to comprehend all that he had just learnt, so he took it one thing at a time.

It didn't take him long to find the panel that had been removed, and Doyle pulled it free to reveal the plastic-wrapped remains of Marie Thisgo; ill-fated co–conspirator, who hadn't known how personal her involvement would be in her brother's plan.

Doyle hoisted the body over his shoulder and retrieved the leather satchel from the desk, ignoring Thisgo as he dripped his pitiful mucus on the floor.

"Wait," begged the great leader. "Help me."

But Doyle just dropped the gun in front of him.

"Do it yourself," he said, "for once."

Doyle left the Château of Prince Nicholas and Walter Thisgo through the front door, and walked down the driveway. He did it with Marie Thisgo and a leather satchel over his shoulder, and without any resistance from the staff of that place.

Both of Thisgo's men watched Doyle, grim of face, as he passed them and continued on; they made no attempt to stop him. And, as he walked down the long winding driveway, Doyle listened for a sound behind him; not the sound of pursuit. He listened for the sound of a gunshot to disturb the quiet Poitou-

Charentes evening.

But there was nothing but deathly silence, and the absence of disturbance.

This was the sound of failure; it was the sound of bitterness.

It was the insignificant sound of cowardice.

THE BEGINNING / THE END

At the nurses' station, the radio was set to Radio 6.

"- Doyle of the independent commission to investigate the Dark Pupils conspiracy?"

"That's right, Henry. In a few minutes, Ex-Gardaí Inspector Nicholas Doyle will be walking through these very doors on the first day of the commission, and we're all waiting to hear, officially, the names and the details of this; well, it's just horrific, Henry, isn't it?"

"Absolutely, Johnny. I can still hardly believe the stories that have been coming out over the last few days. The whole terrible affair has set my head spinning. I'm sure that everyone listening will agree with me when I say that. It's just too difficult to imagine how we've all been duped, Johnny."

"It really is, Henry. If even half the reports that have been leaked are true, then there are literally dozens of top medical personnel, both from Ireland and abroad, who were involved in the conspiracy. Including Rebecca Giles, the mother of the deceased Terry Giles, God rest his soul. It really is turning out to be a very disturbing period in Irish history, Henry."

"Yes, Johnny, from mind-control to assassination, it's awful what those poor kids went through, and we didn't believe a word of it, before. We owe them a lot. Well, we'll trust you to keep us updated on events as they unfold, Johnny?"

"Will do, Henry," said Johnny Deansworth, news correspondent.

A female doctor walked to the nurse's station and picked up a chart. It said: Rachel Impey – overdose.

The doctor turned and walked across the hall and into a private room with an observation window. Through the window, the nurses watched as she performed routine checks on Rachel, who had lain in a coma since the day that she and Peter attempted suicide in the gardens of the Via Dolorosa.

When she returned from the check up, the doctor handed the chart to a nurse, who asked, "How is she, Dr Giles?"

"No change," she replied shaking her head, "exactly the

same as yesterday. They could go either way."

The radio blared.

"Johnny Deansworth here, outside the Four Courts. So, there really isn't much more to say on the matter until the rest of the facts come out. I'm sure all of you listening are as anxious as I am to finally find out the truth behind all of the events of the past six months. All we can do now is wait and hope. Hope that Peter Price and Rachel Impey survive their attempted suicide, so that they can receive their pardon, and in fact, the public apology that they deserve. We will, of course, have regular reports from Beaumont Hospital where they are in the care of Dr Rebecca Giles, mother of the deceased Terry Giles and their condition remains critical. Our thoughts and prayers are with them now as they struggle for life."

Pause.

"Well, that's the end of the show for today, folks. I'll see you all same time tomorrow. But before I go, I'd just like to say one thing.

"Let's learn a lesson from all of this, yeah? Let's never forget our Dark Pupils."

***

Outside the hospital, spring had overcome the city of Dublin. It was still quite cold but the sun was out and people, being Irish, were already pretending it was summer. Striped clothes were being worn, students were braving the beer gardens, and those special people; the ones who had seen fit to buy convertible cars in a country where it rains for nine months a year, were having their eyeballs frozen as they attempted to unravel the latest version of the Dublin one-way system.

South and westwards going out of the city, past the herds of houses that were corralled by the Dublin Mountains. Following the Wicklow hills upwards and in between the peaks; there was a certain valley, surrounded by woodland and containing a long sloping field that was cut across by a stream.

In this valley, there was an old ruined church, back from the road and overgrown with vines, and bushed and carpeted with grass, and every day the place received all manner of visitors.

Squirrels, both red and the invading grey, the Irish hare, the pine martin, and even the odd badger made an appearance from time to time, sniffing through the old ruins, causing the hedgehog to curl up in fright.

And from the sky, the falcon keeps watch as chaffinch, warbler and jay, flutter through the woods and hop from fallen stone to fallen stone.

The place is teaming with every sort of life, both wild and free. And, if memories could live, then they reside there also, because there are souls in that place that cannot exist in hospital beds, or in the ground.

They live in the light, where no darkness can be found.

ÉND

AN EGG-MANIAC'S GUIDE – TO SUICIDE

"Oh, by the way, if you are starting to get bored, I am about to tell you the story of how I planned my suicide. So, do not worry about all the family history stuff. It's just that this isn't the sort of tale that I can get you to understand, and I need you to understand it, without some clues as to my reasons.
"Excuses," this is my mother again, "there are no such things as reasons, only excuses." And, maybe she was right, I'm not sure, but there must be something in it. These two bits of oratorical genius were the only things that my mother said that ever made any sense to me. Nineteen years of maternal experiences condensed down to two phrases. I am not joking.
So, maybe she was right that there are no such things as reasons, only excuses. So fine, there you have my first excuse, and there will be plenty more to come. Because, if you ever commit such acts or deeds as I have very recently, then you will need plenty of excuses too, to make people understand.
Because, if you remember I said that I need you to understand."

For more information on this author:
Visit:

WWW.EANNA.EU

UPCOMING TITLES:

THIS SPACE LEFT INTENTIONALLY BLANK

"Ouch! The music overpowers you and forces you into a corner. You can't catch hold of it, before the handle only misses you by an inch. It drives a hole into the dry-wall. It will no miss again."

For more information on this author:
Visit:

WWW.EANNA.EU

www.ingramcontent.com/pod-product-compliance
Lightning Source LLC
Chambersburg PA
CBHW051530250626
47156CB00001B/304